Rosings Park

Also by Diane H. Morris

Cousin Anne

Read the author's blog at
www.moorgatebooks.com for information
about medicine, childbirth, inheritance,
and the lives of women
during the Regency period:

There's a Leech for That!
Mr. Darcy Was a Second-Class Citizen
Warm Caudle: A Potion for Regency Women in Childbed
Linseed Tea: Popular in Jane Austen's Day and Today
Why Isn't Mr. Darcy a Lord?
It Is A Truth Universally Acknowledged
Jane Austen and the Ginger Rogers Syndrome

Rosings Park

A Novel

—ɯ—

Diane H. Morris

Moorgate Books
Knoxville, Tennessee

MOORGATE BOOKS

Manufactured in the United States of America
10 9 8 7 6 5 4 3 2

www.moorgatebooks.com

Cover design by CreateSpace
Printed by CreateSpace

Library of Congress Control Number: 2016901219

ISBN 978-1-941033-03-6

For St. Peter
and
my ever-lovin' brothers, Scott and Steve

Volume I

Chapter 1

A liveried coach lumbered toward the west Kent village of Hunsford, its two passengers each contemplating their arrival at Rosings Park. The elder traveler, Mrs. Jenkinson, was unremarkable in appearance and indulgent in character. Her chief flaw was an abundance of confidence, the fault arising from her years spent as a governess and companion to the heiress of Rosings. Even now, when she might be expected to withhold her opinions, she bewailed the rutted roads, the March weather with its blustery wind, and their late departure from Tunbridge Wells. Turning in the twilight, she said, "You know, my dear, I wish we had not stopped at the Crown and Crow. Such a meagre dinner. I feel quite bilious."

The younger passenger, Miss Anne de Bourgh, offered a tepid smile and took up her own thoughts. At six and twenty years of age, she was still unmarried and had, of late, been contemplating her future. If she hoped to realize her potential through matrimony, she might claim two qualities in her favor: large hazel eyes (so like her dear Papa's) and a handsome annual income. In the ledger's other column, however, she counted several defects, among them being a dislike of officious interference. This last shortcoming accounted for her present antipathy toward Mrs. Jenkinson. Finally! Her companion had worn herself out talking and now rocked sleepily against the squabs as the coach lurched in the dark.

Anne welcomed the quietude, for time was needed to prepare for a homecoming that might manifest rather more trepidation than tranquility. There would be a reckoning with her mother, Lady Catherine, over Dr. Vaccari's treatment, which Anne believed had never held much hope of success. There would be disputes about Tilly's delivery and, worse, persistent haranguing over her cousins' anticipated visit. "I shall speak with Darcy about your marriage when he arrives," Lady Catherine had warned, "for it is time the two of you married." Any discussion of marriage could not please, for Anne dreaded the prospect of being bound to Darcy. As her coach marked the miles, she stared into the night and pondered how best to seize control of her life and lay a fresh course. If she did not find the unexpected spark, the brightest blaze of joy, her very soul would shrivel.

Before long the glowing windows of the Hare in Hand came into view, followed by Hunsford's high street, sitting quiet and tidy in the moonlight. After passing the church and parsonage, both dark as tombs, a noisy spray of gravel signaled their turn onto the drive, and the house with its tall windows and modern façade came into view. Anne felt a prick of pride. This was her home and the seat of her estate, bequeathed to her in the year seven on the death of her father, Sir Lewis de Bourgh. Since his demise, her homecoming often proved bittersweet, and so it was likely to be this evening. She expected no warm embrace, no tender maternal smile, no harried mother rising from her fireside chair, exclaiming, "Oh, you are arrived safely. I have been worrying." Lady Catherine had probably gone to bed.

When a footman opened the coach door and let down the step, all morose thoughts, worldly cares, and imagined vexations vanished.

"Welcome home, Miss," said Hobbs. "You are looking well."

Anne raised an eyebrow at the butler's ridiculous statement. "Is all good here?"

"Aye, ma'am. Her ladyship did not wait up, but Cook made your favorite soup and Shaw is warming bricks for your bed. We shall make you comfortable."

"You do me a great kindness. Please help Mrs. Jenkinson, who found the travel tiring."

"Of course, ma'am," Hobbs said, suppressing a smile.

Anne gave him a speaking glance and passed into the Great Hall, where the housekeeper, Mrs. Faber, greeted her warmly and the parlor maid Nichol bobbed a curtsy. Receiving their smiles with gratitude, she mounted the stairs to bed.

The reckoning began after breakfast. Lady Catherine sat at her writing table in the drawing room. When Anne appeared, stiff-backed and wearing a grimace, a quizzing gleam rose in her ladyship's eye. "You look as ghastly this morning as when you left two weeks ago. Did the leeches defeat you?" Ignoring Anne's withering look, she added, "What was your purpose in traveling all that way only to return looking sickly? You will never get well if you resist Dr. Vaccari's physicking."

"I went to Tunbridge Wells at your insistence," Anne reminded her mother as she eased herself onto a tufted sofa. "Every demand was met. I walked the promenade before breakfast. I drank the waters and submitted to leeches. I endured fomentations with mustard and plasters of pitch. I did all that was asked of me. If I am not recovered from this rheumatic affection, it is not from want of trying."

The memory of the writhing leeches made her sickly and cross. Fifteen of the nasty creatures had been plucked from jars, laid on her belly, and allowed to slip about until each wriggler determined the best spot for feasting on her tender flesh. The nurse was generous with the allotted time, allowing the ravenous tormentors their pleasure until fully engorged, at which point they released their victim. Two days had passed since her treatment, and the leeches' sucking wounds, though covered by a pad, were still inflamed, making a misery of every chafe.

"Then it is good you returned to Rosings," said Lady Catherine as she inked her quill-pen and bent to her letter. "There can be few demands on you here." In profile, her ladyship's face was marked by a prominent nose and resolute chin. She was a woman of noble parts, being confident in her opinions, intolerant of ignorance, enamored of rank, and proud to be an aristocrat. Educated as befitted the daughter of an earl, she would never be thought stupid, but she could sometimes, as now, be irritatingly obtuse.

"I must meet Roger Tench today or tomorrow," Anne said, thinking of several urgent duties related to running the estate, "and you forget: I shall serve as a gossip to Tilly."

Lady Catherine rounded on her daughter. "Don't use that word. It is vulgar. There is no need to sit with her."

"Tilly invited me to attend her delivery and so I shall do."

Her ladyship's lips twitched. "You know my opinion. Such action is unseemly, especially for a maiden such as yourself, and it would tax your health at a critical time. Darcy and Colonel Fitzwilliam are expected soon. Your being in good health for your cousins' arrival is more important than sitting with Mrs. Sparke. Her sister can attend her."

"My mind is quite made up, Mama." Knowing her mother would worry to death the issue of Tilly's delivery, Anne pulled a piece of white cotton muslin from her tapestry-bag, threaded a needle, and began embroidering.

"Why are you so stubborn? What can you offer—you, who have never birthed a child?"

"I offer affection as Tilly's dearest friend. My agreeing to her request should not surprise you, for we have been friends for twenty years or more, since long before she married Mr. Sparke."

"You are too soft-hearted by half, always befriending those beneath our station, which does you no good." Her ladyship shook her head. "I had not thought Mrs. Sparke so old-fashioned as to demand the assistance of a midwife. She would do better to travel to London where she can secure the services of an accoucheur."

"Tilly cannot hire a man-midwife, unless, of course, you are prepared to accompany her to Town." Anne caught a look of scorn crossing her mother's face. It was as she thought: Lady Catherine would never stoop to such familiar behavior. "As there are no accoucheurs in the district, Tilly must rely on a midwife; and since her mother is no longer living, it is natural she should seek the comfort of her sister and friends during the delivery."

Each time the topic had been broached, Lady Catherine objected.

"Sitting with a pregnant friend during her delivery suits the lower classes, but it is abominable behavior for polite society. And a maiden should not serve as a gossip. It is highly irregular."

Anne resisted her mother's argument and silently posed a question: Does not every woman who attends a sister or brother's wife or friend during a child's birth serve as a gossip? Rank had nothing to do with it, and in this case she had every right to attend, for Tilly was a sister to her. Indeed, some ladies of the first water favored the practice, so her neighbor said. When approached about the particulars, Lady Metcalfe spent ten minutes describing her own childbirths and the sometimes overexcitable state of her gossips: "When William was born, the nurse entertained me, my aunt, a sister, and a neighbor with bawdy ballads. She stirred such mirth among us that the midwife threatened to banish her. Dear Aunt Arabella was so amused she drank too much caudle, grew faint, and had to be carried from the room. And when I sat with my cousin Lady Langford during her second delivery, I had to fight for a chair, her bedchamber was that full of friends and sisters. Of course, many years have passed since then and the custom is changing. As for hiring an accoucheur to direct the delivery, I cannot support it. The idea of a man-midwife is unnatural to me."

Anne learned much from Lady Metcalfe—such a kind lady, so affable, so free with her affection and opinions—and pondered the mystery of her being so comfortable speaking with her neighbor on any topic. Why could she not approach her own mother so easily?

Hobbs drew near the sofa. "Your phaeton is ready, Miss."

"I shall be there directly." She fingered the tiny garment laid across her lap—the long dress, the puffed sleeves, the pin-tucked bodice. It was a gift for Tilly's firstborn. Would she ever sew a baptismal gown for her own child? Would Providence be kind to her? Sighing at the absence of answers, she placed the dress in her tapestry-bag. "I shall deliver food to the Browns, since Mrs. Brown has begun her confinement."

"I don't approve of such charity," said Lady Catherine. "A broken leg or deadly cancer are reasons for visiting tenants. There is no call for coddling a pregnant woman."

Anne refrained from throwing a challenge, but said lightly, "If you have no errands you wish me to undertake for you, I shall go directly from the Brown's farm to Tilly's house. Her delivery will begin soon and I wish to see for myself how she fares."

Not bothering to look up from her task, Lady Catherine commanded, "Do not overtax yourself. You must be well for Darcy's visit."

Anne acknowledged the obligation and retrieved her coat and bonnet. On the pebbled drive, Young Kitson handed her into the phaeton. She snapped the reins and called to the ponies. The phaeton pulled away from the house and passed the barely budding trees and low bushes bordering the drive. A break in the hedgerow gave a pretty view of the lawn dotted with spreading yew trees. When the wind lifted her bonnet, she all but laughed to be out of doors and free of the house. She was eager to see her friend.

—⁓—

"Welcome, Miss. You are a sight for sore eyes," said Tilly's housekeeper. "Did the waters do you good?"

"Good morning, Mrs. Cadman. There was little time to rest, but I enjoyed the change of scene. How is Mrs. Sparke?" Anne shed her pelisse and bonnet.

"Tired, ma'am, very tired, being ready for the child's birth and worried about the young midwife. She is anxious to see you."

"I shall go up then, if you don't mind." Anne climbed the stairs, one hand on the railing. Pausing on the landing, she inhaled deeply to quiet her pounding heart. When her breathing eased she knocked on the first door and entered.

"Anne, you have returned." Tilly rested in a chair near the window, her legs splayed for comfort. One hand caressed the top of her swollen belly; the other stretched in welcome.

"Look at you!" cried Anne as she clasped Tilly's hand and took the chair nearby. "I believe the child may arrive before luncheon."

"Don't tease me, for I have lost all perspective. Each day brings a new discomfort."

"You look as lovely as ever."

This was mostly true, for Tilly, born Matilda Sullen, the younger daughter of Hunsford's much-loved former rector and now the wife of Mr. John Sparke, was quite the prettiest lady in the district. Most everyone said her crowning glory was her hair—thick, wavy tresses the color of roasted chestnuts—but Anne found greater beauty in her violet eyes and dark eyelashes. This morning, however, her complexion was pale and her curls lay damp against her face.

"How do you and John do?"

"I am restless and grumpy. He is mostly excited, although he grows anxious for my safety. I insisted he return to the shop this morning, where he can stay busy waiting on customers. I needed a few minutes of peace in the house. But your arrival is a great pleasure. Does Lady Catherine know you are here?"

"She does. I am determined to annoy her whenever I have the opportunity."

"Anne! You should not say such things."

"Perhaps not, but I speak the truth, if only to amuse you."

Tilly returned a grin. "She objects to your sitting as one of my gossips, I suppose."

"She continues to advance every impediment to the idea."

"I am glad you believe otherwise, for I shall soon need your steady presence." Tilly shifted in her chair. "How were the waters? You seem improved."

"I survived Dr. Vaccari's ministrations, but Mrs. Jenkinson drove me mad with her babble."

"Nothing new there. Your companion shall forever be a pebble in your boot. Was all well on your return?"

"Mama is much the same, but the Tench brothers' rivalry is worse than ever, I hear. I shall speak with Darcy on the matter when he arrives. It is a delicate situation, requiring some diplomacy." When Tilly apologized for distressing her, Anne exclaimed, "Oh no, you never distress me. I am merely overthrown by Tench's death. I suppose I thought he would live forever. He served the estate for three and twenty years, after all, and was more friend than steward to Papa. Tench has been my counselor and trusted servant. I have relied on his guidance more than any other since inheriting Rosings, as you know." With Tench's death she felt the full force of her responsibilities. "I miss him and wonder how to fulfill his dying wish. He implored me to appoint Roger to the office, which I have done for the time being, and now George Martin is in high dudgeon. Neither brother is happy with my plan to name a new steward by the end of April. My only goal in delaying the decision was to seek Darcy's guidance."

"That is a wise decision. Darcy has uncommon good sense, and his advice will be readily seconded by your mother."

"True. She receives any of Darcy's views with something akin to complete acceptance. Would that I could achieve the same power over her."

Tilly smiled at the familiar lament. "Darcy is her favorite nephew, possibly her favorite person in all the world, and therefore perfect. What course does her ladyship hold to?"

"She is mindful of precedent and tradition and believes George Martin has every right to succeed to his father's office."

"Whereas you think Tench's younger son, Roger, is the better choice, and therein lies the problem."

"Precisely."

Tilly caught her breath. "The child is restless. Place your hand here."

Anne laid one hand on Tilly's belly and sensed the child's stirring. A foot pushed forward? A head turning? "You look tired today. Are you not resting well?"

"I am ready for this act in the play to end."

"Soon you will cradle your child," said Anne, giving Tilly her most reassuring smile. "What can I do for you?"

"Would you help me to bed?" asked Tilly as she pushed herself up from the chair.

Anne was happy to be useful and spent a pleasant half hour describing her recent adventure. She spoke of Tunbridge Wells; of Dr. Vaccari's soft hands and dark looks, of his menacing glare when he did not comprehend her complaint; of Nurse Greenbury's perpetual frown and gloomy conversation; of listening to Mrs. Jenkinson's prattle as they browsed the toy shops or strolled the Upper Walk, their feet growing achy from treading the unyielding Purbeck stone; and this morning, of driving to Smockden and smelling newly-turned earth as farmers took to their fields. At one passing farm she spied two men trying to rope an ornery bull, which put her in mind of Old Red, the Rosings bull that had killed Tench.

"Will you consult Darcy about Old Red as well?" Tilly asked.

"I think not. I cannot threaten Darcy with all my problems, else he will never marry me."

Tilly eyed her friend closely. "Are you looking forward to your cousins' visit?"

"About as much as I ever do."

"Ah, then not much at all. Perhaps their visit will prove different this year. You have sometimes enjoyed their company."

"I do not care to speak of my cousins. What I most look forward to is the birth of the Sparke family's first child." Anne saw a shadow cross Tilly's face. "What troubles you, dearest?"

"Should I feel uneasy about my present situation?" Tilly gripped Anne's arm with surprising vehemence. "Mrs. Roberts has left the district and I worry how her daughter will do. Of course, Mrs. White is one of the sweetest girls in the parish, but she is young to midwife. If the delivery should go wrong, can I rely on you to assist John if—if I should—?"

Although Tilly's woeful look begged for reassurance, Anne fought to hide her own concern.

Mrs. Roberts was a skilled midwife who had served the women of Hunsford and its surrounding farms for two decades. The previous year she began training her youngest daughter, Mrs. White. The daughter was said to possess great potential, but by virtue of her youth, she lacked the wisdom that comes from years of experience. Some pregnant women, on hearing the news that Mrs. Roberts would attend her niece's delivery in Dorset in March, arranged to stay with family elsewhere for their childbirths, even if it meant traveling by coach to the next county. Such an arduous journey was itself a danger to a woman with child. Tilly would not leave her husband or travel as near as Surrey to stay with her sister, Margaret, for her confinement.

As for supporting Mr. Sparke in the event of the worst possible outcome, it tempted Fate to agree to Tilly's tacit request. Anne's words were meant to reassure her friend as well as herself. "Mrs. White is young, but she birthed her own child last autumn and exhibits much good sense."

Tilly's smile was brave but it did not light her eyes. "I suppose I must rely on Mrs. White's skill and the competence of Dr. Bailey, should a physician be needed. I have a great foreboding, Anne, that I cannot lift."

"You are tired and your mind is excited by unnatural misgivings. Don't forget, Margaret and Mrs. Beath will sit as gossips. Both women have children of their own and can comfort you. When is Margaret expected to arrive?"

"She comes tomorrow."

"Good. She will lift your spirits. Meanwhile, kind Providence will keep you safe."

—⁂—

Downstairs, Anne spoke with Mrs. Cadman. "Send a chitty to Hobbs when the delivery begins. It matters not the hour."

"Aye, ma'am. I have not forgotten my pledge. Well I know how close the two of you are—like sisters. It shall be done."

"Thank you. Your assurance is a great comfort."

There came a ring at the door. "Who would impose on us now, with the Missus confined to her bedchamber?" asked the housekeeper as she prepared to battle interfering neighbors.

"Good morning, Mrs. Cadman," said Mr. William Collins, who advanced into the hall, never doubting his welcome. "Ah, Miss de Bourgh. I had not thought to see you here. You are looking well." He bowed, his hat pressed to his chest.

Anne merely smiled, knowing the rector to be a great confabulator and only mildly interested in her welfare. He proved her true by continuing his little speech: "I will visit Rosings later today, for I begin to write my Easter Sunday sermon. I seek Lady Catherine's guidance in penning those words that will inspire my flock to walk the path of redemption." Forgetting his manners, he added, "Her ladyship is well, I hope."

"Her ladyship is well and will be glad of your company," Anne told him. "May I be of use to you?"

"I nearly forgot my purpose in my pleasure at seeing you. I brought a copy of Reverend Bospidnick's essays for Mrs. Sparke." He flashed a book not a hand's span in width. "The good Reverend provides excellent advice to young married women on their duty to their husbands, on fortitude and the importance of sobriety, on virtue and piety, on—(his face turned an unflattering scarlet)—on many moral and practical issues of importance to mothers."

"You are very good." Anne took the book and turned to Mrs. Cadman. "Be so kind as to present Mr. Collins's gift to Mrs. Sparke and inform her of his thoughtful concern. We shall leave you now." She and the housekeeper traded a knowing look in which their understanding was united: the book would be hidden where Tilly was not likely to find it.

"When does Mrs. Collins expect her guests to arrive?" Anne asked the rector as they walked toward the road.

"Mrs. Collins's father, Sir William Lucas, her sister Miss Maria Lucas, and her friend Miss Elizabeth Bennet are expected tomorrow."

"Please give Mrs. Collins my regards and tell her I happily anticipate meeting her family and friend."

"You are most gracious," said Mr. Collins, bowing again.

Anne accepted his eager compliment and was assisted into her phaeton. For all that he meant well, Mr. Collins was exceedingly tiresome.

On the short ride to Rosings she pondered the many unknowns in this endeavor. Mrs. White's midwifery skills could not compare with her mother's, for Mrs. Roberts had delivered several hundred children over the course of her practice. It could only be hoped Mrs. White had learned all that was necessary to bring Tilly and her child through the delivery. And Dr. Bailey was an added complication. Only Divine Providence could preserve his sobriety in the coming days when his skills might be needed. Even if Dr. Bailey were sober, was he sufficiently skilled in midwifery to make an informed decision should Mrs. White need his assistance? If he had used instruments to deliver a child, what was his success?

Terrifying images gleaned from the medical books in uncle Darcy's library leapt to mind: the crotchet with its curved, elegant handle and mangling hook; the crooked, long-handled bistory; the blunt hooks, so simple in design, so deadly in use. With Tilly's delivery at hand, Anne regretted ever seeing drawings of extraction instruments, for their purpose was truly awful. And what of Tilly's request to offer John solace in the event of the worst possible outcome? Of course, she would do her duty as a friend, but God help her, she could not think of Tilly being dead and buried. The grief would be unspeakable, almost as wrenching as when her dear Papa died. How could she bear to think of her truest, dearest friend lying stone cold in her grave? How could she attend church services with Tilly's grave marker standing erect in the graveyard nearby, its weathering stone a testament to her short life? How could she attempt anything after so much loss?

She must guard against these unnerving thoughts. It did no good to allow Tilly's anxiety to infect her. Yet even as the resolution to calm herself formed, she pictured the sombre Mr. Collins leading the order for the burial of the dead; she heard his dense voice intoning the words first heard when her father died and now received in sorrow for Tilly and her child: *I know that my redeemer liveth, and that he shall stand at the latter day upon the earth. And though after my skin, worms destroy this body; yet in my flesh shall I see God.*

She shivered as the phaeton approached the house.

Chapter 2

"Do you receive word from Mrs. Sparke?" asked Mrs. Jenkinson, who sat opposite, buttering a bun. Weak sunlight fell on her lacy cap as she bent to her breakfast.

"Yes. It appears her delivery has begun, although her pains are few." Anne watched her companion tear the bun with her teeth. How did the woman remained so spare? To look at her, one would never know she relished her food above all other pleasures, for her thin frame belied the force of her appetite. The kitchen staff likely lamented her deeds of gormandizing, for extra portions must be added to every platter to satisfy her. "Vaughn," she said, looking from Mrs. Jenkinson to the servant standing next to the sideboard, "tell Mrs. Faber I wish to carry a basket of food for Mrs. Sparke's household."

"Do you go to her?" asked Mrs. Jenkinson.

"Not at present. Mrs. Sparke or the midwife will write to let me know when I may attend her."

Mrs. Jenkinson nodded sagely as she speared a sausage.

With the delivery drawing nigh, Anne's feelings swayed from excitement at the prospect of a god-child to annoyance at the midwife's orders. Discipline would be needed to submit to Mrs. White's instructions, for the midwife ruled the household when the delivery began. Even the lowliest midwife held dominion over a woman with child, be she a duchess or the wife of a button-maker. Anxious thoughts of how the next few days might unfold prompted action. She called for a coat and shambled toward the stables and carriage house, where she sought the comfort of animals: the snuffling of horses, the calm gaze of the old nanny-goat, the wary watchfulness of barn cats. As she rounded the gentle curve of the drive, shouts and grunts echoed down the road. A ring of stable boys and laborers stood in a rough circle as two men—the Tench brothers!—grunted and rolled in the straw.

Hardly thinking what she did, she broke through the circle and marched on the brothers as they climbed to their feet and fixed to throw more punches. She shouted, "Would you knock me down, George Martin? And you, Roger? Cease fighting this minute."

At her command the brothers swayed with fatigue. George Martin relaxed his clinched fist. Roger wiped blood off his lip with the back of his hand. Anne looked around at the circle of men and boys. "Have you no work to do?" As the onlookers drifted away toward the barn or the fields, she rounded on the brothers. "I am ashamed of you. What would your father say to see you scuffed and bloodied, fighting like school boys in the Rosings stable yard? I am glad he is not alive to see this day."

She turned back toward the house, catching sight of Young Kitson standing near the mounting block, goggle-eyed by her actions.

Her blood was up. Her heart raced. Her bites itched.

"Miss de Bourgh!" cried George Martin.

She turned around, her eyes ablaze. "I don't care to hear explanations, for I promised to make a decision by the end of April."

"We have a right to speak our views."

"You forget yourself. You speak at my pleasure." She gave him a haughty look and stalked toward the house. By the time she gained her bedchamber, her blood had cooled, but her heart still pounded in her ears. She pulled the bell-rope, took the chair at her desk, and hurriedly scribbled a message. She waited impatiently for Shaw to heed her summons.

"Where is the girl?" Anne uttered the question aloud as she sat hunched over the desk, her thoughts centered on Tench. The memory of her last private conversation with the steward moved her almost to tears. She recalled his unyielding grasp, his breath coming in great gulps. "Do what is right for Rosings above all things," Tench had panted. "I have faith in you." She could hardly bear to look on his woe-worn face, knowing he deserved a better fate. How many times had he supervised the handling of Old Red? He took precautions and would risk no injury to a farmhand. Then to be kicked himself beggared all belief in life's fairness. Old Red's nasty blow had caught him on the leg, bruising the muscle and fracturing the long bone. The wound became inflamed and none of the apothecary's physicking could prevent the inevitable.

How angered Tench would be by his sons' stable-yard kerfuffle. If one of the brothers had thrown another punch, would she have turned them out? Yes, she would, no matter how trying the effort to replace her steward.

"Finally!" exclaimed Anne when Shaw arrived.

"Excuse me, ma'am, I did not know you had returned."

"I only just arrived. Give this message to Hobbs. Tell him to ask the boy to wait for the apothecary's reply. I need more salve for these leech bites." Seeing Shaw turn away, Anne recalled her. "Before you go, do fix my hair. It has fallen loose."

"Yes, ma'am." Shaw slipped the note into her pocket and moved to assist her lady. She prided herself on being the soul of perception when it came to reading her mistress. When the wind blew foul, she held her tongue and acted a proper lady's maid; in fair weather she indulged her mistress with gossip from the village. Like as not, she was apt to misread the wind and clouds, as happened now, her being excited by the prospect of news not heard.

"How do you suppose Mrs. Sparke goes? Emily says she feels some birth pains, but her waters are dribbling. Have you ever heard of such a thing? It seems mighty peculiar to us, but it may account for Mrs. White exercising the poor lady half to death. Mayhap she hopes to cause the great rushing of waters as usually happens when the delivery begins."

"Since you and your sister and I are not midwives, I think none of us experts in the area," Anne argued. She struggled to recall the meaning of "dribbling waters," knowing the topic had been addressed in one of Dr. Smellie's books. His three-volume collection of midwifery cases had been a great favorite when she was a girl and found herself alone in uncle Darcy's London library. The term must refer to the womb waters in which the child lay, but more than that she could not say.

"Emily finds Mrs. Beath strange, too, an' wonders how Mrs. Sparke came to know her. Mrs. Sparke is not the same sort of lady as you, but she is a gentlewoman, being the daughter of Mr. Sullen, God rest his soul. It is odd she should know her. Do you not think so? I always give Mrs. Beath a wide berth when I see her in the village."

"Mrs. Beath has lived in these parts for many years, Shaw. I believe she helped nurse Mr. Sullen before his death, which explains how Mrs. Sparke knows her."

"Maybe so, but she looks a witch."

Mrs. Beath was Hunsford's most peculiar resident. Some claimed she was a Gypsy Traveller by birth, her girlhood spent roving the Kent countryside in her family's rustic cart, stopping as need be to work the hops fields and orchards during season, their bender tents hidden in the woods nearby. Rumor had it her husband had been hanged by angry farmers for stealing sheep. Many in Hunsford were prepared to believe such a tale. Dr. Bailey lost all patience with such tattle: "She is a poor woman whose husband and children ran off, leaving her to raise her idiot son, Neddy, without help. She keeps to herself, it is true, but that is no reason to besmirch her reputation. The woman knows more about plant leaves, roots, and flowers than some apothecaries. Frankly, I would rather endure her physicking than my own."

"Will that suit, ma'am?" asked Shaw as she stood back to appreciate her handiwork.

Anne touched her hair. "It will, thank you." She stared at her wan reflection in the looking glass: *What is to be done if no one within twenty miles knows the cure for dribbling waters?*

Chapter 3

"The wind is sharp today," said Mrs. Jenkinson as she steered the carriage toward the village.

Anne cared not a whit about the weather. The previous day's long, fruitless wait for news of Tilly's delivery had been exhausting in its way, and she had not slept well. Simply stepping down from the carriage and advancing to Tilly's front door were agreeable actions.

Mrs. Cadman welcomed her. "Good morning, Miss. Will Mrs. Jenkinson not come in?" From the doorway she watched Anne's companion turn the phaeton toward the village.

"Not today. She has errands in the village and shall return for me shortly, but she asked me to give you her warm regards." Anne proffered a wicker basket. "I thought your household might have need of additional food."

"We appreciate it, and thank you for the lilies. Kitson brought them yesterday."

"You are very welcome. Tell me, does the delivery go well?"

Mrs. Cadman lowered her voice. "I cannot say. Mrs. White keeps her thoughts to herself." She cast a furtive glance up the stairs. "Allow me to apologize for the lilies being moved down here. Mrs. White won't have them upstairs. Their smell is too overpowering for the lying-in chamber, she told me. I must say, she has us servants at sixes and sevens with her orders for moving furniture and oiling hinges. This morning I was told to change the drapery!"

"The flowers are of no consequence. Mrs. White is only doing her duty to ensure a safe delivery. Is Mrs. Sparke dressed for visitors?"

Not being one to cringe at a gracious rebuke and, in any case, making allowances for Miss de Bourgh, who appeared unwell, Mrs. Cadman smiled. "She will be glad of your company."

The bedchamber had been transformed since Anne's last visit. The rug had been removed, leaving a clean, bare floor. Three hall chairs stood along one wall. A fire burned with vigor. Its heat made the room overly warm; its flame lit corners darkened by the window's heavy drapes. An assortment of items lay arranged on a small table near the bed: a knife, several sponges, two goose quills, a length of tobacco pipe, and a pile of folded linens. Dark bottles of healing oils and cordial waters stood on the mantel. All were the accoutrements of the midwife's profession.

Tilly paced the room, her gauzy shift damp from perspiration. Mrs. White curtsied and left the friends to visit. Mrs. Beath was no where to be seen.

"Will you not rest a minute?" asked Anne.

"Mrs. White's instructions were to exert myself, and so I am doing."

"Is it helping? You seem distressed."

"The pains are weak and come infrequently. I am unaccustomed to parading around in my nightclothes. Mrs. White wants me to sweat, which is no trouble in this stuffy room, but I have thrown over her idea by removing my wrapper. She is not happy with me at the moment."

"May I fetch something for your relief? I will do anything to help."

Tilly shot her a look of rank determination. "If you can move forward the hands of time, I would be most grateful. Mrs. White advises patience. She believes the pains will quicken when the child is ready to be birthed."

Anne had never felt so useless. Casting about for an innocuous topic, she inquired after Margaret.

"I expect her soon, and my friend Mrs. Purkess arrived last evening. She is staying at the White Horse Inn. You will enjoy her company."

Anne said all that was kind and agreeable about Margaret and Mrs. Purkess and excused herself, leaving Tilly to pace the room, her arms cradling her massive belly. On descending to meet Mrs. Jenkinson, she caught the midwife on the stairs. "Are you satisfied with how the delivery progresses?"

Mrs. White paused in her climb. "It is best to let Nature take her course," she said in a girlish voice. "We watch and wait."

Anne could not countenance her reserve. "Please," she pleaded, only refraining at the last moment from grasping the midwife's arm. "I am concerned for my friend. She is the dearest person in the world to me."

"It goes tolerably well." Mrs. White offered no other reassurance, not even a flimsy smile, but gathered her skirts and proceeded up the stairs.

How young she is, Anne realized. How young to shoulder such responsibility. A snatch of text read long ago came to mind: a midwife ought to be a decent, sensible woman of a middle age. Middle-aged. Mature. Experienced. Confident in the art of examining the pregnant woman, in reading the bones of the pelvis, in knowing when true labor begins. Anne stared at the midwife's retreating figure. She looked a mere girl with her slim figure and simple dress.

Anne felt faint, for she was not immune to Tilly's fears. Every woman in Hunsford had heard the story. When Tilly was four years old and Margaret six, the family lived in the parish of Fritwell Cross, where Mr. Sullen was rector. Mrs. Sullen, being at the beginning of her ninth month of pregnancy, was near paralyzed with grief at the death of her only sister. A week after the burial, she was seized with flooding and weak contractions. The midwife, having struggled a day to staunch the flow of reddened waters, sought assistance from a local surgeon against Mrs. Sullen's wishes: "I submit to the will of God in this, as in all things," she had said feebly. The surgeon, annoyed at being called away from a card table where he was winning against a drunken squire, arrived several hours later, examined Mrs. Sullen, and declared the child dead. He proceeded to deliver the child with a crotchet, the extraction of the brain and body being protracted and bloody. He later admitted to being unacquainted with the instrument. The unhappy outcome was a dead child, a boy; a dead mother; a grieving husband left to comfort his two daughters; and an angry midwife who scorned the surgeon for his arrogance and carelessness.

No one could blame Tilly for feeling nervous about her prospects.

When Anne climbed into the carriage, Mrs. Jenkinson was all cheer after accomplishing her errands. "Does it go well?"

"I don't know. My ignorance prevents me from possessing a rational outlook."

"What says Mrs. White?"

"Very little."

"She is young and inexperienced. I am not surprised there should be trouble. Like as not, she would prefer fewer attendants during Mrs. Sparke's delivery." Mrs. Jenkinson took no heed of her charge's disdainful frown. "Her ladyship charged us with stopping by the parsonage to invite the Collinses and their guests to dine at Rosings tomorrow."

Anne's first thought was in no way flattering: How like Mama to invite the Collinses and anybody else to dinner without so much as mentioning the idea. After all these years, she continues to thwart my plans and peace. "Then let us go now," she said, knowing she had no choice but to submit to her mother's whims.

—⁂—

As Mrs. Jenkinson threaded the carriage through the village, Anne considered whether her mother's decision to host a dinner party was a punishment for her sitting as a gossip with Tilly. It would not be the first time she had been disciplined for pursuing her own path against her mother's wishes. Truly, she most wanted the solitude of her bedchamber, where she might rest, regain a positive perspective on Tilly's delivery, and calm her whirling emotions. A slather of salve on her leech bites would be very welcome. But her filial duty could not be ignored.

The parsonage came into view. Situated adjacent to the church at the north end of the village, the parsonage lay only half a mile from Rosings if one walked directly across the Park. Anne knew every hearth stone, every knobby rafter, every defect and beauty in this small house. A lifetime of memories arose whenever she beheld its plain façade. Since the Collinses had moved into the house, however, she felt little pleasure sitting in the parlor, partaking of tea and small talk.

When the phaeton stopped before the gate, she was reminded of how all had changed. Instead of Tilly and Margaret and Mr. Sullen, here came Mr. and Mrs. Collins, bounding down the gravel walk. Poor Mrs. Collins was nearly trampled by her excitable husband in his quest to reach the gate first.

"Good morning, Miss de Bourgh, Mrs. Jenkinson," said the breathless rector. "You are both well, I hope. And my lady patroness? She is well?" Mr. Collins had been ordained the previous Easter and offered the parish living on the commendation of Lady Catherine, whose appeal to the Bishop of Rochester for help identifying a suitable candidate had been answered with alacrity. For his part, the Bishop considered it a stroke of luck that he had become acquainted with the peculiar, self-conceited Mr. Collins at about the time he received Lady Catherine's letter. The Bishop believed this tall, ponderous man of five and twenty years would prove to be a sensible, malleable clergyman who would happily serve her ladyship's wishes and feel all the honor of her condescension.

Like the villagers, Anne had no say in the choice of parish clergy and continued to mourn the passing of Mr. Sullen. She saw in Mr. Collins a perfect reflection of her mother's superior character. To Mrs. Collins she said: "I trust your family and friend arrived safely."

The rector's wife smiled as if she hid a secret under her cap and said, "They arrived a short while ago and look forward to exploring the beauties of Kent."

"Then they must travel to Tunbridge Wells, for it is very interesting country," Mrs. Jenkinson interjected. "Miss de Bourgh was treated there by Dr. Vaccari, a tall, handsome man. I personally cannot care for a man with a mustache, but I make an exception in his case, for his beard is nicely trimmed. He has something of the Italian in his look …"

Anne scowled at her companion's gleeful interference. Merciful heaven, can the woman not refrain from expressing her opinions to everybody?

While enduring Mrs. Jenkinson's description of the manly doctor, Anne was diverted by the actions of a guest—presumably Mrs. Collins's father, Sir William Lucas—standing in the parsonage doorway, looking very puffed up with the scene unfolding before him, much like a farmer gratified to hear his neighbors admire the suckling piglets in his sty. Whenever she turned away from the sun's brilliance, the gentleman bowed to her. On testing this discovery, a twitched window curtain caught her eye. Was the scene being secretly observed? She glowered to think she might be the object of surreptitious scrutiny. How unfortunate if Mrs. Collins's guests proved to be country bumpkins.

At last, the dinner invitation having been tendered and accepted, Mrs. Jenkinson motioned the carriage toward Rosings. "I like Mrs. Collins exceedingly well," she declared as she teased the horses with the leather whip. "She is a calm, genteel sort of person and nothing like her husband. I wonder at the success of their marriage."

"They have not been married above a year and, in time, will likely adjust to one another."

"Only if she claims the patience of Job," said Mrs. Jenkinson with a flick of the whip.

Chapter 4

"What were the Tench brothers fighting about?" asked Shaw as she pulled a linen shift over her mistress's head. "I heard they fought for their father's office, 'though Cooper believes a woman was more likely the spark. I think she said that to annoy me, for she likes to tease, her believing I am partial to George Martin when, as you know, Young Kitson is more to my liking." Shaw continued in this vein for several minutes, praising Young Kitson's manners and belittling the older Tench brother, who needed only a tail to trot like a fox. "How does Mrs. White do? She is young to manage Mrs. Sparke's delivery. T'is a terrible duty." She took a breath only to adjust her lady's gown of blue spotted muslin. "Perhaps Dr. Bailey will be called to help her. Ma spoke with his landlord this morning. He claimed to see the doctor heading past the market stalls on his horse. 'Dr. Bailey be over at the Three Bells in Little Wouldham, mark my words,' Ma said. You know what my mother thinks of spiritous liquor: she cannot abide it."

Anne's ears pricked at the mention of Dr. Bailey's being seen leaving the village, but she felt no obligation to answer any question or respond to every comment, for Shaw never noticed her reticence. Did some aspect of her person draw out this behavior from her maids? Shaw's inquisitive bent was as strong as dear Dobbie's had been. Like Dobbie, Anne's childhood maid, Shaw felt comfortable to chatter and speculate and query without fear of remonstrance. How did Leticia Le Dispenser (whom everyone called Letty) get on with Lady Catherine? The young maid was probably cowed by her ladyship's demands and complaints and would be as likely to query her ladyship or express her own opinion as to balloon over the Kent downs. As for Dawson, Lady Catherine's upper-maid, she was cowed by nothing and no one. She had married the estate's head coachman, served her ladyship for five and thirty years, and felt all the strength of her seniority.

By the time Anne dressed for dinner, she was in no mood for company. A headache had formed and her mood was distempered by Shaw's chatter and the lack of information about Dr. Bailey's whereabouts. She recalled Tilly's crypt-like bedchamber that morning: the fetid air, the dismal silence, the grim advance of worry. The midwife's futile examinations wearied everybody. So distressing was the situation that Anne had argued with her, had actually pulled the midwife into the parlor, barred the door, and demanded information about Tilly's lack of progress. Mrs. White's indignant words still rang in her ears: "No one has a right to treat me so, not even a lady of quality, not even one who owns half the district. Why, you're no different from Lady Catherine! It would be just like her ladyship to poke her nose into my business." Anne recoiled at being so grossly compared with her mother but was not deterred: "I only wish to be prepared for whatever may happen. I must be strong for Mrs. Sparke and her husband. Do you understand?" Her words reverberated about the small room and provoked Mrs. White's temper: "*My* wish is to deliver the child without killing the mother."

The ensuing exchange bled the heat from their disagreement and, after a short lull, culminated in a reasonably civil discourse on the problem—the midwife could not determine the position of the child in the womb—and their options, the best being to seek Dr. Bailey's opinion. Frankly, Anne was not sure he would have one.

She wished to accost the doctor herself, but the privilege must wait, for here came Mr. Collins, all smiles and servility, with Sir William Lucas and the ladies trailing behind.

Lady Catherine greeted her guests with great condescension. She wore a green crape dress and a pearl necklace; her hair was ensnared by an odd turban topped by an ostrich feather, worn with all the confidence of a queen. She did not so much converse as hold forth all through dinner, demanding Mrs. Collins's attention and delighting in the ignorance of their guests regarding the French fare (even though she herself preferred good English beef and potatoes).

While Mr. Collins and Sir William tarried over a bottle of port after dinner, the ladies settled in the drawing room, where Lady Catherine continued to expound without restraint on one topic after another until the servants laid the coffee table. Coffee cup in hand, she interrogated Mrs. Collins, asking questions of a personal nature about her domestic arrangements and parish duties and offering advice on the care of her cows and poultry.

Anne hid her embarrassment. Surely Mrs. Collins had every right to manage her house to suit herself and her husband and no one else. And how could Lady Catherine presume to offer suggestions on animal husbandry? So far as Anne knew, her mother had never met with Tench while he lived, nor had she deigned to inspect the dairy or learn of the estate's sheep breeding program. The soles of her ladyship's shoes seldom tread on grass or clay, far less dirt or muck.

Eventually Lady Catherine turned her eye on Miss Bennet, asking intimate questions about her sisters and their ages and education, and inquiring about the type of carriage her family kept. "What is your mother's maiden name?"

"Harrison, ma'am."

"Is she related to Isabella Seymour, wife of Lord Seymour? She was a Harrison before her marriage."

"Not that I am aware, your ladyship." Miss Bennet was polite and composed during this inquisition.

Next, Lady Catherine observed, "Your father's estate is entailed on Mr. Collins, I think. For your sake," turning to Mrs. Collins, "I am glad of it; but otherwise I see no occasion for entailing estates from the female line.—It was not thought necessary in Sir Lewis de Bourgh's family.—Do you play and sing, Miss Bennet?"

"A little."

Lady Catherine next interrogated Miss Bennet about her upbringing, eventually asking, "Has your governess left you?"

"We never had any governess."

"No governess! How was that possible? Five daughters brought up at home without a governess!—I never heard of such a thing. Your mother must have been quite a slave to your education." Her ladyship's shocked look aimed to inform Miss Bennet of her belief in the impertinence of such folly, as if all society felt the insult.

Anne shrank at her mother's insolence, but Miss Bennet smiled and explained that any of her sisters who wished to learn had always the means to do so, while those who chose to be idle, certainly might.

"Aye, no doubt," responded Lady Catherine on hearing of such parental laxity, "but that is what a governess will prevent, and if I had known your mother, I should have advised her most strenuously to engage one. I always say that nothing is to be done in education without steady and regular instruction, and nobody but a governess can give it." Lady Catherine continued in this vein, mentioning her role in finding positions for four of Mrs. Jenkinson's nieces, and claiming credit for securing a good position for Miss Pope. Turning to the rector's wife, she said, "Mrs. Collins, did I tell you of Lady Metcalfe's calling yesterday to thank me? She finds Miss Pope a treasure. 'Lady Catherine,' said she, 'you have given me a treasure.'"

While Miss Bennet held her own against the meddling onslaught, Anne studied her person. Flawless skin, expressive eyes, and a comely form were Miss Bennet's most handsome physical features, her appearance bringing to mind an image of the fetching Miss Derrythorpe, whose kittenish looks had excited Darcy's regard many years ago. And she was a rarity at Rosings, for she seemed immune to intimidation. Once or twice her irreverent look suggested she relished Lady Catherine's challenges.

Under other circumstances Miss Bennet's liveliness would be a welcome diversion, but Anne cared not whether she was rude to her fair guest, for Tilly was uppermost in her thoughts: there had been no spark in her friend's violet eyes, no bite to her observations, no joke on her lips. During the morning's futile examinations, the midwife's face hovered over Tilly's bulging belly. A clammy fear had gripped Anne as she read uncertainty in Mrs. White's furrowed brow. The prospect of a sad outcome smothered her with worry and made a mockery of polite conversation.

When the gentlemen returned the group settled to cards. More accurately, Anne shuffled and led as required, but spent the time being annoyed with Mrs. Jenkinson for fretting over her comfort and deeply anxious to hear from the midwife. *Surely Mrs. White will not punish me for trapping her in Tilly's parlor or fail to inform me when Dr. Bailey is found. God rot these leech bites; they itch.*

Finally their guests accepted Lady Catherine's offer of a coach to take them home. As the carriage disappeared down the drive, Anne noted her mother's vigorous mounting of the stairs. Hobbs stood to one side, a look of nervous consternation on his face.

"Hobbs, you look distressed. What is the matter?"

"I had no choice, I never meant—" the butler stammered.

"What is it? Explain your concern."

"A chitty came for you before dinner. Her ladyship—she asked for it, ma'am. I was obliged to give it to her."

"Wait here," she commanded. "I may have need of you."

"Yes, ma'am." He stood his ground, not sure of his safety.

Anne charged up the stairs, thinking no French spy on English soil was as cunning as her mother. When she reached her ladyship's bedchamber, she rapped on the door twice and entered, not waiting for permission. "Mama, I have been told that a chitty was delivered earlier this evening. You have no right to confiscate my letters."

Lady Catherine was a little surprised at her daughter's dramatic entrance but otherwise unperturbed. "I was only thinking of you, my dear, since you don't look well. This business with Mrs. Sparke weighs on you. It is making you ill." She sat at her dressing table, her face reflected in the looking glass. "As your mother, I have a right to take actions that protect your welfare."

"You must think me a fool," said Anne. "You have little concern for my well-being. If I were Darcy, your precious nephew, you might make a genuine effort, for he is the only person you truly adore. We both know he is the son you so desperately long for and never had. Yet I wonder: As much as you admire him, do you intercept his letters? I think not. Perhaps I shall warn him when he arrives. 'Be on your guard,' I shall say, 'for my mother is a thief. She steals letters and who knows what else.'"

Lady Catherine's lips quivered. "Mind your tongue, for you don't know of what you speak." She reached into the pocket of her wrapper. "Take your chitty. It contains no new information. Dr. Bailey is dead drunk—again. We all, but you, knew to expect it."

Anne snatched it from her.

"Tilly's life is at risk and you withhold vital information? If she dies, I shall blame *you*."

"If Mrs. Sparke or her child is lost, Dr. Bailey deserves the blame. He has deserted her. I am not surprised to learn of it. He would do well to hide."

"Whatever do you mean?"

"It is none of your concern. But hear this: you will not call on Mrs. Sparke tonight. The hour is late and you appear ever more sickly with each passing day. I will not have you looking a ghost when Darcy arrives. Do you hear me?"

"In this matter I shall do as I please," Anne rejoined before fleeing to her bedchamber where she read the chitty. Mrs. White wrote in an uneven hand: *I received word from Dr. Bailey's housekeeper. Mrs. Killick writes that the doctor has been found but is indisposed. Mrs. Sparke asks for you. Please come.*

The time was going on half past six o'clock and the sky had darkened. A maid was lighting the fire.

"Cooper, the carriage taking our guests to the parsonage must be on its return. Ask Hobbs to hold it for me. I shall be down directly."

"Yes, ma'am."

"And Cooper, take care Lady Catherine does not see you."

Cooper pulled the door closed behind her, pleased to be charged with a novel task.

—⁂—

"Anne, I am glad you are come."

"I was worried about you." Since no good would come of commenting on Tilly's obvious distress, especially with Mrs. White eyeing the tableau at her patient's bedside, Anne said, "I had thought Margaret would be here."

"I received a letter," replied Tilly with some effort. "Albany has the measles, which is no surprise, for she feeds him too many raw fruits. The child's fever prevented her from traveling."

"Margaret's letter was short," added Mr. Sparke, "because the surgeon needed help restraining the boy for bloodletting. She expects to make the journey next week."

"Poor little Albany," said Anne, withholding any comment about Margaret's mercurial nature. It was anybody's guess whether Albany was, in fact, ill, for Margaret had been known to invent stories for her own convenience. It was exasperating that Tilly's only sibling could not attend her. There being no point in belaboring the issue, she asked: "Where has Dr. Bailey been?"

"He hid himself at the Bear and Bugle in Ashton, drinking pale ale," explained Mr. Sparke. "It took four men to heave him onto his horse and two boys to lead him home. I am going to his house now."

"I shall come with you," said Anne.

"We should not be seen alone together on the road. It is not proper." He started down the stairs.

Anne gave Tilly a determined look and caught the midwife's arched eyebrow as she turned to follow him. "Mr. Sparke, as Tilly is a sister to me, you are like a brother. I care not a whit what anyone might think. Those who know us will not criticize. Those who think poorly of us—well, the devil take them. I am coming with you."

He shrugged into his coat and gave her a long, hard stare. On seeing Mrs. Cadman's earnest concern over time lost, he relented. They made haste without further comment, so frantic were they to secure Dr. Bailey's assistance. On entering the doctor's residence, however, their plan for rational discourse was given up, for Mrs. Killick was wrestling the man upstairs to bed.

"Unhand me, you beasts," snarled Dr. Bailey as he threw punches and bumbled about.

Mr. Sparke's perseverance, with the women pushing from behind, got the intoxicated doctor as far as a bench on the landing at the top of the stairs, where he sank down in a sottish heap. The three captors, somewhat out of breath, gathered around him and considered the best treatment.

"We might force tea down his throat," said Mrs. Killick, hands on hips. "Tea and a little clove. Mayhap a good dose of Hepar sulphur would help."

Mr. Sparke took a different view. "Nay. Let us try hair of the dog. We must be bold."

A pint of warm beer proved restorative, for Dr. Bailey woke to his predicament. With much slurring of words and smacking of lips, his wit was sufficiently restored to thwart any plea for help. He claimed a delicate but persistent indisposition that prevented his interference. "I canna' do it, I canna' do it," he mumbled over and over.

His handlers refrained from pointing out the obvious and, after much patient coercion, at last obtained a proposal to write the doctor's nephew, who was visiting family in Chatham, a distance of some twenty miles.

"The lad's a surgeon an' London trained, for whatever tha's worth," said Dr. Bailey thickly, a fat grin on his stubbled face.

The sister's direction was obtained, the letter signed by Mr. Sparke, and the missive dispatched. The courier was paid to ride there and return with an answer: Would he come—yea or nay?

When Anne crept to her bedchamber it was past nine o'clock. She worried their planning would come to nothing: God help us all if the surgeon cannot or will not come.

Chapter 5

"Am I a sight?" Tilly lay limp against the bed pillows, her hair a straggled mess, her forehead dotted with perspiration.

"I have seen you look better," replied Anne.

Tilly's smile rose and faded. "I am uneasy about John. Men are not made to withstand the rigors of childbirth."

"Which is odd, seeing how prepared they are for war." Anne listened to the house sounds and worried. Dr. Bailey, the wretch, was sure to be indisposed most of the day. What if he disappeared again? What if Mr. Sparke's letter never reached Chatham? What would Mrs. White do if new troubles arose during the delivery?

Not until nearly noon did they learn their fate. The London surgeon planned to arrive by five o'clock.

The long wait gave way to odd moments. Mrs. Beath sneaked into the bedchamber while Tilly dozed. Anne moved her feet when the nurse stirred the fire to life with a poker. Mrs. Beath whispered, "How do ye leech bites do? I hear they be very tender. If ye please, I shall mix an ointment to 'asten their healin'."

Anne looked up at her brown, lined face. "Why, that is most generous of you." The look of satisfaction on Mrs. Beath's face was a wonderment.

Later, after luncheon, Anne found herself in the parlor with Mrs. Purkess. Tilly had explained that her friend was given to rebellious headaches: "The poor woman suffers dreadfully."

Anne was pleased to see Mrs. Purkess feeling better and said so.

"Thank you. These headaches often lay me low in times of great distress, as now, when I worry for my friend."

"I believe you met Mrs. Sparke when she traveled to Gosport to visit her aunt many years ago."

"Yes, her aunt lives near the parsonage and is a favorite among our closest companions. Indeed, Mr. Purkess is very partial to her gooseberry pie."

Their conversation ranged widely. Mrs. Purkess offered advice on treating rheumatism; Anne suggested an application of leeches to the temples for the relief of nervous headaches. When her parish duties allowed time for pleasure, Mrs. Purkess enjoyed painting landscapes with overarching skies and hazy vistas of sheep and cows; Anne preferred the intimate study of fruit and flowers, the fine portrait of a leaf or pear distilled to its simplest essence. When Anne grumbled at the long wait for the surgeon's arrival, Mrs. Purkess quoted Milton— "They also serve who only stand and wait," which mention led to a discussion of poets and novelists, of heroes and miscreants, of kind and despicable characters. Within half an hour, their friendship was fixed, each finding kinship where none was expected.

When Mr. Sparke arrived, Mrs. Purkess excused herself to attend Tilly upstairs.

"I spent the morning fetching spice packets and tins of tea for customers, but every request pained me," he told Anne as he collapsed on the parlor sofa.

Anne felt tears rise. Such a good man he was, a kind man and hard-working. He was big, like a bear, with blue eyes set beneath coppery eyebrows. Broad shoulders made him look built for manual labor—ploughing or smithing or coopering—instead of stocking imported goods and delicacies shipped from his brother's London warehouse.

"What will I do if—if—I cannot bear to think of it." He covered his face with his hands and stifled a sob.

Anne placed a hand on his arm. "We have received good news. The surgeon is expected this evening."

"He cannot come too soon," said Mr. Sparke, jumping to his feet and taking the stairs two at a time until he reached Tilly's bedchamber. Eventually he came downstairs in search of tea. Anne offered to sit with Tilly, which is where she found herself at half past four o'clock. The door-bell chimed. Then came Dr. Bailey's raspy voice, sounding stronger than it had in the night. Other voices she did not recognize.

Footsteps on the stairs signaled the arrival of the London surgeon. Mr. Sparke led the cohort. Next came Dr. Bailey, looking pale and sheepish; then, two other men, both a little dusty from travel but otherwise elegant in their dress; and finally Mrs. White, whose face wore an eager expression. The men gathered solemnly at the foot of the bed.

"Dearest," Mr. Sparke began, his voice full of emotion, "Miss de Bourgh, Mrs. Purkess, Mrs. Beath, allow me to introduce Dr. Bailey's nephew, Mr. Cole, and his friend Dr. Granville."

Two more different companions could not be imagined. Mr. Cole was tall with wavy, black hair. His blue eyes scoured the room like a warden searching for felons, first observing Tilly's dark tresses lying tangled across the pillow, then noting the wrinkled mass of bedcovers bereft of order, and finally discerning Anne's own weary person, her hair hanging loose, her eyes lacking brilliance. He locked his hands behind his back and frowned, a summary judgment. Standing close to his surgeon friend, Dr. Granville seemed almost placid. A more average person in form and appearance could not be imagined. His build was stocky, but not overly muscular. His brown hair fell in layers from the crown of his head, providing a feathery frame for his dark eyes and sensual mouth. Reddish hairs flecked his long side-whiskers.

Of the two men, Mr. Cole was undoubtedly the more handsome in his bearing and dress, but Dr. Granville possessed a natural ease that was very attractive. So interested was Anne in his person that she startled when Dr. Bailey cleared his throat and began speaking: "Mrs. Sparke is five and twenty years of age, a primipara. She has been in a lingering labor for three days and reports no fever, fainting, hemorrhaging, or vomiting; no erratic pain, cramps, or numbness; no diarrhea or convulsions." His crisp recital was followed by silence, excepting only the crackle of the low fire. Anne could not resist sneaking looks at Dr. Granville. Whenever he glanced in her direction, she shifted her gaze, seeking safety in the familiar faces of Dr. Bailey and Mr. Sparke.

"I shall examine the patient now," said Dr. Granville. "Mrs. White." He gave a nod to the midwife to indicate his wish that she assist him. "Cole, escort the other ladies and Dr. Bailey downstairs. Mr. Sparke, may I speak with you privately?"

Anne did not wish to leave Tilly. She thought to persuade the doctor to allow her to remain, but one look at Dr. Granville's face quelled her resistance. Where she had thought to see defiance, a fortress against any challenge to his wishes, she instead saw sympathy, concern for her welfare, and recognition of the service she did her friend. She whispered words of encouragement to Tilly and pulled her shawl over her shoulders. She felt Dr. Granville's scrutiny as she left the room. It was as well she did not spy Mrs. White's triumphant smile.

When Mr. Sparke came downstairs, Mr. Cole declared his desire for fresh air. Mr. Sparke balked at quitting the house, but the surgeon slapped him heartily on the back, saying, "Come, man. We do no good waiting here. Let Granville work his magic, for he is very skilled. Now, a turn through the village and a stop to sample the local brew would be most welcome."

"Capital idea!" exclaimed Dr. Bailey.

The men strong-armed Mr. Sparke through the front door. He had never looked so defenseless.

—⁓—

Mrs. Purkess soon returned to Tilly's bedchamber, leaving Anne to sit alone in the parlor, waiting for Mrs. Cadman to bring tea and biscuits. She heard Dr. Granville, Mrs. White, and Mrs. Beath come down the stairs and stop outside the parlor door.

Dr. Granville said, "Mrs. Beath, alert me when the plaster is ready."—"Yes, sir," came the faint reply—and then: "Mrs. White, you must not …"

Anne strained to catch his words. Their conversation was unintelligible, and yet she felt at ease simply listening to his voice. Judging by the tone of Mrs. White's replies, he instructed rather than lectured, for the midwife did not sound resentful or wary or indignant, and well she might have been any of these, considering a strange doctor had been called to help her. It seemed she made no defense against criticism because he rendered no reproof.

When Mrs. Cadman brought the tea tray into the parlor, Anne heard Mrs. White's step on the stairs. Dr. Granville then appeared in the doorway.

"You are so kind, Mrs. Cadman," said Anne as the housekeeper departed. "Will you join me for tea, Dr. Granville?"

"It would be my pleasure. I was hoping to speak with you."

While Anne prepared their cups and waited for the tea to steep, he settled himself in a chair. "I understand you have long been a friend to Mrs. Sparke. Will you tell me something of her usual temper? She seems unduly anxious, almost to the point of nervous exhaustion, which emotion might arise from this being her first child and from the fatigue of labor over the past three days." He meditated on the teapot before speaking again. "Once or twice, I felt her eyes on me with something very like fear, as if she believed I were a menace. Please enlighten me if you can."

His beseeching brown eyes, so luminous, so kind in their cast, made Anne nervous. She dare not pour the tea for fear her trembling would be noticed. "The information you ask me to divulge greatly pains my friend," she said as she fiddled with a tea towel. "May I trust in your discretion?"

"Of course. I wish to know only such information as will allow me to serve her." His calm gaze was reassuring.

"I believe Mrs. Sparke's anxiety arises from the memory of her mother's death during childbirth. Please understand, I cannot speak with confidence of the story's veracity, but it seems an arrogant surgeon could not be troubled to quit his card table to attend Mrs. Sullen's delivery. After a lapse of several hours the surgeon arrived, declared the child dead, and proceeded to extract the boy with a crotchet. The midwife believed the surgeon's ignorance killed the mother and her child." She drew a deep breath and poured tea without incident. "Mrs. Sparke and I seldom speak of her mother's death, even as close as we are, but I know she is much affected by it. She is not naturally suspicious. Indeed, of the two of us, she possesses the more trusting disposition."

Ignoring his teacup, Dr. Granville stood abruptly and strode to the fireplace. He stared down into the ashes, his rigid stance revealing his displeasure.

His reaction alarmed her. Had she offended him by speaking ill of the surgeon? Was he shocked at her blunt description of the event or disgusted by her apparent willingness to rely on hearsay? More likely, he was appalled at her crude manner of speaking, his being from London where ladies were more genteel.

The man-midwife turned to her. His cheeks were still flushed, but he seemed more in control of himself. "How is it that you know what a crotchet is?"

Anne felt her color rise. If she had the sense God gave a goose, she would have been more circumspect in her speech. What little knowledge she possessed of physicking was bound to cause trouble one day, and, finally, that day had arrived. Dr. Granville would scorn her; he would label her a Blue Stocking. It was too late to claim ignorance. It was too late to do anything other than speak the truth. "I read Dr. Smellie's volumes on midwifery."

"You read William Smellie's volumes on midwifery," he parroted.

"Yes. I am also familiar with Dr. Hunter's anatomy book on the gravid uterus."

He gave her an odd look.

"When I was a girl," she explained, "my parents took me to London once or twice a year where we often visited my uncle Darcy's house. His excellent library was a source of great joy to me, and his liberality allowed me the freedom of reading mostly whatever I desired. My own father was equally indulgent, I must say."

Dr. Granville walked to the window, where he stood looking out across the yard. After two or three minutes, during which time Anne feared she had ruined her chance of finding a friend in the agreeable doctor, he returned to his chair.

"I must beg your pardon for my rude response to Mrs. Sparke's story. I am easily disturbed by such accounts, knowing only too well the harm an untrained surgeon or physician can do. The circumstances surrounding the death of Mrs. Sparke's mother will remain forever a mystery, but I am relieved to have such knowledge as is available. Fortunately, the science of midwifery has progressed since Dr. Smellie published his tomes." His eyes flickered merrily but then turned grave. He took a draught of tepid tea and set his cup on the tray. "There is an issue I must raise with you."

Anne's hand flew to her throat. Was he about to warn her to expect the worst possible outcome?

"Don't be alarmed. I mean only to prepare you: I may need to use forceps to deliver Mrs. Sparke's child. You are familiar with the forceps?" He spoke to her as if she were a serious student and not some hare-brained country lass who ought to stick to her sewing.

"I have never seen the instrument," she replied, "although I recall Dr. Smellie was not much impressed with it."

"It would be correct to say he was not impressed with its original form and so worked to improve it. And remember: Dr. Smellie practiced fifty years ago, when the forceps were fairly new in general practice and few practitioners were trained in their proper use. The situation is different today."

"Do you advise me to say nothing of the matter to Mrs. Sparke?"

"Hmm. I must ask your opinion on a related topic, for I am considering a course of action that has proved successful in a few other cases." He leaned forward. "Women are frightened half to death by obstetrical instruments. Fair enough, I say, for they are deadly-looking, unnatural tools, even when used for benign purposes. Because the sight of them makes most women nervous, practitioners usually hide their instruments in a pocket or a wooden case so as not to cause alarm." He patted the right-hand pocket of his frock-coat. "In recent years, some accoucheurs have tried a novel method: relieve the patient and her friends of terror by demonstrating their use. Since Mrs. Sparke's delivery may require the use of forceps, I shall show her the instrument this evening and thus hope to relieve her fears. Is it your opinion that Mrs. Sparke will view this method favorably?"

His tender, earnest look eased any concern Anne might have felt at risking his censure. He would not punish her for reading such medical books as interested her. He was surprised, but not offended, by her daring to improve her mind, knowing she risked being scorned by society. She felt quite giddy on realizing the extent of his tolerance. What an extraordinary man!

"I cannot be sure of her reaction," she said, "but isn't it better to know what to expect?"

Mrs. Cadman appeared at the parlor door. "Excuse me, sir. Mrs. Beath has prepared the loaf-bread."

"Thank you. Let us go upstairs." He came to his feet and offered Anne his hand.

Anne looked up at him. It took every ounce of self-control to keep from giggling like a schoolgirl as she placed her hand in his.

—⁂—

"Mrs. Sparke," said Dr. Granville, "would you be more comfortable with the window open?"

Tilly was weak but had no doubt of her preference. "Yes, a little fresh air might revive me."

The doctor readily complied with her request, surprising everyone by so bold an action. Mrs. White could not have been more shocked had he set the drapes on fire, for such things were not done in the district. It must be a London custom.

He tied a drape on one side, saying, "I shall apply the poultice Mrs. Beath prepared. Help Mrs. Sparke shift toward the edge of the bed." All hands assisted Tilly into position. Mrs. White took her place at the doctor's elbow, her head cocked to hear his dulcet tones: "The opening to Mrs. Sparke's womb is swollen, which makes it difficult to determine the child's position. The poultice will decrease the swelling." He dipped his hand into the bowl and lifted a small mass.

Tilly felt sufficiently revived to ask a question: "What is the nature of the poultice? I am become curious after many years spent in friendship with Miss de Bourgh."

Dr. Granville flicked a smile in Anne's direction. "It is composed of softened loaf-bread mixed with milk and hog's lard."

Anne and Mrs. Purkess stared at each other. Surely this recipe had been known for a hundred years.

"I see what you are thinking. You are wondering at my old-fashioned ways. In truth, my friends often tease me for adhering to my grandfather's precepts. My grandfather attended many tedious and preternatural births. The poultice was one he favored in some circumstances. Even though it is not a modern treatment, it often does the trick." His calmness of temper put everybody at ease and made the delicacy of the situation more bearable, especially for Tilly, who felt embarrassed on exposing her privities to a strange man in her own house.

"I am finished." Dr. Granville wiped his hands on a cloth pulled from his coat pocket. "Let us move Mrs. Sparke to a more comfortable position and prepare her for bed." To Mrs. White he said, "I have prepared an anodyne mixture of Aqua Fontana containing three ounces of Tincture Thebaic sweetened with sugar. Give her two spoonfuls every half hour for the next two or three hours. The laudanum will hasten her sleep. And withhold the caudle; it may make her restless and counter the actions of the tincture."

"Will she be bled, sir?" asked the midwife.

"I think not, at least not this evening, but fix an emollient clyster, for she is quite costive." To the attendants he said: "Carry on while I speak with Mrs. Sparke about our expectations for tomorrow."

Mrs. Beath removed the crock and headed downstairs. Mrs. Purkess followed close behind, carrying soiled sheets and one of Tilly's nightgowns. Mrs. White departed to prepare the clyster. Anne hesitated, not certain whether to stay or go.

Dr. Granville, alert to her confusion, said, "Miss de Bourgh, you will find this interesting." He extended a hand to indicate she might stay close to her friend.

"Mrs. Sparke," said the doctor as he positioned a chair next to the bed, "let me ease your mind about tomorrow. Your health will be improved after a good night's sleep, for your body will be rested and sweated. The dribbling waters are nothing to worry over and I expect the birth pains to resume shortly after you wake. When the poultice is removed, I can determine the child's position in the womb. Forceps may be needed for the delivery. Don't be distressed by the idea. If you please, I shall show you the instrument." Tilly's eyes grew wide when he pulled it from his pocket. "You will observe its small size: a mere twelve inches long. Forceps can be made from silver or wood, but these are tempered iron." He showed her the wooden handles, the thin leather covering, and the curved loops designed to grasp the child's head alongside the ears. "If I must use them, I shall first heat them gently in warm water so they will be less of a shock to your feminine parts. I may have no need of them. Do not worry but rest well." He patted the bedcovers and stood.

Anne plumped the pillows behind Tilly's head and said in a low voice, "I shall come as soon as you wake in the morning. Mrs. Cadman will send for me. All will be well, dearest." She kissed Tilly's cheek and squeezed her arm.

Tilly caught her hand and pulled her close to whisper, "He looks too young to know anything about delivering children, but he has fine eyes. Do you not think so?"

A blush crept up Anne's cheeks. Had Dr. Granville not been watching them, she might have pinched Tilly for her teasing ways.

When they stepped out into the corridor the doctor pulled the door closed, saying: "What was my success?"

"Mrs. Sparke says you appear quite knowledgeable about midwifery," Anne replied before hurriedly descending the stairs.

Chapter 6

Anne woke to the sound of rain. No sooner had she slipped on her wrapper than Shaw entered, carrying a tray. "I bring hot chocolate, ma'am, and a chitty from Mrs. Cadman."

Anne grabbed the letter and read:

Dear Miss de Bourgh,

Dr. Granville came at half past four this morning when Mrs. Sparke awoke. Mrs. White gave her a good washing under his guidance and found the swelling much reduced. After my mistress's waters broke proper like, he waited going on two hours for her pains to increase, but the process is slow. He has gone to the inn for breakfast and is expected to return by eight o'clock. Will you come? My Missus is asking for you.

Your obedient servant, Mrs. Cadman

"I must dress. The Sparkes shall welcome their first child today."

At Tilly's Anne handed her wet coat and umbrella to a maid before climbing the stairs. Their wait for Dr. Granville was not long. On entering the bedchamber he smiled and said: "Are you prepared to take a pain, Mrs. Sparke?"

Anne was bewildered by the bustling that erupted around her. The other women understood his meaning, for they laid Tilly across the bed, turned her on her left side, and instructed her to pull her legs up toward her belly. Mrs. White placed a large pillow between Tilly's knees for comfort when Dr. Granville touched her.

Anne stood with Mrs. Beath on the opposite side of the bed, her scrutiny trained on the doctor's every move: his turning to whisper to Mrs. White, the gentle placement of his hand on Tilly's hip, the imperceptible twitch of an eyebrow while he concentrated. His style was tender and respectful, his intimate deliberations conducted with delicacy and consideration for his patient's privacy. When finished, he said: "The child has descended and the pains are regular. We must wait." He checked his watch.

The gossips placed three folded sheets underneath Tilly to keep the bed clean and dry. Mrs. White moved her stack of folded linens closer to the bed. A morning gloom descended upon them while hail rattled the windows in short bursts. Anne sat in a cane-bottomed chair near the head of the bed, the better to offer the comfort of a familiar face and a strong handhold. Tilly grimaced and panted in the firelight as the pains strengthened. She squeezed Anne's hand suddenly and barked a sharp cry. The stink of feces filled the room.

Mrs. White approached the bedside with clean linen. "Loose stools are perfectly natural during childbirth, I assure you."

"I am making a mess of the bedchamber." Tilly gasped as another pain descended.

Anne teased her friend: "We could move you to the stables, where you might rest on a bed of straw and bugs."

Tilly half-laughed, half-cried as another grinding pain took hold. When it passed, Anne blotted her friend's sweaty forehead and arms with a vinegar-soaked cloth.

Coming quickly on the last, a fierce pain caused Tilly to groan. "Oh, oh—oh, God."

"Try not to push," enjoined Dr. Granville. "Allow the child to emerge at his own pace."

Tilly's look was one of pure evil.

The pains now coming with an earnest purpose and being only minutes apart, Dr. Granville touched Tilly again during a powerful pang. His brow knitted with concentration. After six or eight strong pains, he said: "Bring her to her feet. Mrs. Beath, would you allow Mrs. Sparke to sit on your lap?"

Mrs. Beath waited while the gossips helped Tilly out of bed, the process being delayed by a powerful pain. Tilly doubled over, her sharp cries and animal grunts filling the room and carrying down the stairs. Mrs. Beath took Anne's chair alongside the bed, steadied Tilly on her lap, and positioned her legs to allow Dr. Granville to deliver the child.

"Ah—ah, oh," cried Tilly. She thrust against Mrs. Beath's ample bosom to catch her breath and gripped her attendants' hands as the next pain descended.

"Mrs. Sparke, I must feel the child's head, which will create a pressure inside your womb. Steady—steady." Dr. Granville waited patiently on his knees for the pain to pass. For several minutes, he concentrated on some mysterious activity, while Tilly moaned and panted. Anne's eyes flitted from his face, so calmly determined in its aspect, to Mrs. White's, which was a study in befuddled worry. Not until she saw the muscles along the doctor's jaw relax could she breathe easily. Some crisis had passed.

"Stay calm," said Dr. Granville. "Let the shoulders come down. Good."

Tilly loosed a piercing yawl and grasped Anne's hand with such strength Anne feared her fingers might be bruised. All was quiet for many seconds, until a soft hiccup, followed by a gusty wail, was heard.

"You have a daughter, Mrs. Sparke." The child's rugged cry stirred everyone to laughter, except Tilly, who sobbed with relief and joy.

"Mrs. White, kindly hold the child, just so. We must allow as much air as possible to reach her. Before tying off the navel-string, observe first its pulsations. When the pulsation ceases and the navel-string is flabby, it is a sign the life force, the blood, has circulated until it inhabits the body of the child. You may stroke the navel-string to stir the blood passage." He gently demonstrated the desired action. "By delaying the tying off, there is no loss of blood, thus allowing the child's natural breathing to become perfected. In my opinion, the navel-string should not be tied until the pulsation has ceased."

While the child mewled and spluttered, Tilly collapsed against Mrs. Beath, quite exhausted. The attendants waited for the navel-string to grow flaccid, giving Anne time to study the child. How reddened was her skin, how active her tiny arms and legs. She caught Tilly's eye and said, "Your daughter is beautiful."

As the midwife gently cleaned the child's skin, Tilly reached across the bed sheet and touched her daughter's hand. The tiny fingers clung tightly to her finger. "She is strong for such a little creature," she said, surprised by her daughter's tenacity.

"Aye, ma'am. She is strong an' has dark hair like yours," said Mrs. Beath.

"We shall name her Marianne, to honor my dear mother and also my true friend."

Anne's eyes shone. To see such tenderness, such love, caused her chin to quiver. She shed tears of delight and relief for Tilly and John, tears of regret for herself. Would she ever experience such joy? Would she ever know the affection of a dear husband who waited in the parlor during her trial? Was she not deserving of love?

"Miss de Bourgh, are you well?" asked Dr. Granville.

She dabbed a cheek. "I have never been happier."

Chapter 7

An idle brain is the devil's workhouse. So goes the proverb mouthed by every scolding parent to every lazy child. If it be true, Anne knew the devil had no truck with her this day, for her brain was busy. Her body, on the other hand, hardly stirred, being an odd mixture of parts: exhausted after witnessing Tilly's struggle, contented on recalling Mr. Sparke's joy, and calmed by the memory of Dr. Granville's cheerfulness.

She had awakened late to the sound of rain. Stirred to look out the window, she saw scudding clouds, rain-swept grounds, and tousled trees. Happiness welled up at her prospect. Here was a morning best spent indoors resting. The day began with a leisurely breakfast, followed by retreat to her private parlor.

Located off the main entrance hall, her parlor's three sash windows overlooked the front drive and, beyond it, an evergreen mass of rhododendrons. Sir Lewis had used the room to welcome his friends and conduct business with Tench. After her father's death, Anne claimed it for her own, despite her mother's disapproval. "Why, it faces full west," her ladyship had said, "and will be miserable in summer. You will find the house staff underfoot in that part of the house." It had taken determination to ignore her mother's criticism.

The small room was decorated in her own style. Where her mother preferred *le style rocaille*—its overabundance of exuberant scrolls, leaves, shells, and arabesques embellished every public room—Anne sought simplicity. The room's heart was anchored by her father's desk, where she toiled daily, believing she fulfilled every duty under his guiding hand. A pretty, delicate settee covered in a simple floral pattern gave the room an airy look. A japanned cabinet served as storage. Even during the gloom of winter, the room was bright and inviting, for the walls were painted yellow above the dado rail; below, a rich red wallpaper complemented the carpet. She was seldom happier anywhere but here.

The first duty of the day was to meet with Roger Tench. His mood was sullen; his recitation, brief: there had been poaching in the north woods and the dairy barn roof had sprung a leak.

"Did you bring the Rolls? I wish to check the rent posts."

"No, ma'am," mumbled Tench.

"Bring them tomorrow. What of Mr. Baker? Is he recovered from his fall?"

"I do not know, ma'am."

"You do not know? Go now. Today. I wish to know whether he is still abed or, worse, dead. His sons are too young to handle the ploughing on their own." Before he moved away, she asked, "What were you and George Martin fighting about?"

"He expects to succeed to Pa's office, but his opinions don't signify. He knows nothing of farming and managing tenants." Roger Tench glared at her before stamping out the door.

After Tench's departure she stifled any worry over appointing a new steward by writing letters: the first to Tilly, merely to send her love and ask whether she might visit the following day to admire her god-daughter; another to her dressmaker, who was pressed to choose a pretty summer shawl—a gift for Tilly in honor of her labor; and one to Edmeads & Co. in Maidstone for sheafs of artist's white cartridge paper, a gift for Mrs. Purkess. Next she began a letter to Margaret, in which she congratulated her on the birth of her niece and expressed the hope that Albany had recovered from the measles.

Cooper entered. "Ma'am, do you need more fagots for the fire?"

"I do. Also, tell Hobbs I would speak with him." This interview would be awkward, but it must be done. A few minutes later she heard an "ahem." Hobbs stood in the doorway, looking like a man waiting to take a ride to Tyburn.

"Ah, Hobbs. Come in and close the door, if you please."

"You wished to see me, ma'am?" He looked tentative, having rarely been invited into her parlor, despite being a fixture in the hall.

"Yes," she said, thinking to offer the man a drink, so miserable was his look.

Hobbs stood at attention like one of His Majesty's Yeomen of the Guard. His eyes focused somewhere on the wall above her head. He was not an old man, being perhaps five and forty years, but he was pasty-faced and stooped-shouldered and gave the impression of being unwell. He complained chiefly of rheumatism, which at least gave them common ground. Anne suspected his momentary discomfort arose less from any physical malady and more from not being sure of himself in the company of women: he had never married or spoken of sisters.

"I wish to discuss with you a matter of some delicacy." She found it difficult to mount a conversation with a person who would not look her in the eye. "I have been pondering the event the other evening, when Lady Catherine confiscated my chitty from Mrs. White. I can imagine your discomfort when approached by Lady Catherine, but I will not have my letters opened and read by anyone, including her ladyship. Do you understand me?"

"Yes, ma'am."

"Good. I expect you to serve me as mistress of this house and deliver my mail to me and no one else."

"Yes, ma'am."

"That is all, then." Anne bent to finish her letter, only to realize Hobbs still stood solemnly facing the desk. She looked up at him. Some fierce emotion rose on his face, bringing a red spot to each cheek.

"Do you realize, ma'am—" he said, clearing his throat. "Are you aware that her ladyship has been confiscating your letters for several years now? Indeed, since before Sir Lewis died." Seeing his mistress's look of frank disbelief, he puffed out his chest like a soldier called to account by his commanding officer. "Her ladyship's enterprise began shortly after your governess quit the house, which was about the time you took ill at Christmas."

"You refer to Miss Waygood?"

"Yes, ma'am. During that time, you were but a child and likely to receive letters only from your closest acquaintances, those being Miss Waygood herself and Miss Sullen or Mrs. Sparke, as she is now. Her ladyship charged me with passing to her any letters directed to you. She made clear the consequences of my not cooperating with her." His eyes searched Anne's face. "I believe she read their contents and decided which to pass on to you and which to destroy. I have no knowledge of the particulars, but I always felt the injustice of it. I still do, in fact."

"Let me understand you. Her ladyship has been confiscating my letters since Miss Waygood left Rosings?"

"Yes, ma'am."

"Good Lord, man, we are going back ten years!"

"So we are, ma'am, and I am sorry for my role in the deception."

"Do you know whether any letters were, in fact, directed to me by Miss Waygood?"

"I believe some were."

"How many? When were they delivered? I must know."

"Three, maybe four, were received from her the first year. The letters dwindled to perhaps one a year afterwards."

All these years Anne had longed to hear from Miss Waygood but received no word of her whereabouts. She recalled the trepidation she had felt when her mother announced the arrival of a new governess to replace Miss Clark, who returned to her family in York after serving the de Bourgh family for two years. At thirteen, Anne had been prepared to dislike Miss Waygood with as much passion as she had scorned Miss Clark, whose faults lay in finding no humor in anything and being secretly aligned with the Evangelicals, which fact she kept from her Anglican employers. To her surprise, Miss Waygood was funny, artistic, and elegant when dancing. Papa readily bestowed on her the affection he truly felt. From Mama, Miss Waygood wrung a concession for her hard work, but was forced to submit to her ladyship's daily demands and rebukes like any plain servant.

Anne's friendship with her favorite governess had prospered until the day Miss Waygood eloped with Henry Dighurst, the only son of the tenants living at Bardolph Hall. Anne had suspected their affection for quite some time. When word reached Hunsford, the scandal energized the villagers as few events could. The daily speculations about the couple's whereabouts peaked when Major and Mrs. Dighurst quit Bardolph Hall and moved to parts unknown. Anne had been despondent for weeks, knowing Miss Waygood's surprising departure had deeply wounded Mr. Dighurst's family. "This is truly awful," she told Hobbs. "Why, she might think me dead."

"Yes, ma'am. I understand."

"Can you recall when the last missive was delivered?"

"No letters have been received for three or four years."

Anne had not thought her mother as cruel as this. "I shall speak with her ladyship, but let me be rightly understood on this point, Hobbs: there will be no more handing over to Lady Catherine any letters or packages directed to me. I will not allow it. I am sorry to say it, but if you cannot support me in this, I shall replace you." Although he blanched at her words, she would speak her mind. "Do not be confused about my status in this house. This is *my* property. Her ladyship lives here at *my* pleasure. If she is inclined to forget the fact, you should not. I possess the power to turn you out." She looked him directly in the face with as much fierceness as she could muster, knowing he felt torn between two masters. "I hope it will not come to such a pass. Will you stand with me, Hobbs, or against me?"

To his credit, he did not hesitate: "I stand with you, ma'am."

"I am pleased to hear it." Her eyes held his in confirmation of their allegiance. "You may go."

He bowed, looking dejected as he quit the room.

She hated to call a good servant to account. One thing was certain. The morning's happiness had drained right out of her.

—⁂—

It is a maxim commonly received, that a wise man is never surprised. So wrote Samuel Johnson in one of his *Rambler* essays, which specific article took Anne the better part of an hour to locate. She read the sentence a second time, thinking she must be the stupidest person on earth not to have suspected her mother's perfidy where Miss Waygood was concerned. Her eyes drifted farther up the page.

An idle and thoughtless resignation to chance, without any struggle against calamity, or endeavor after advantage, is indeed below the dignity of a reasonable being, in whose power providence has put a great part even of his present happiness ... How can we regulate events, of which we yet know not whether they will ever happen? And why should we think, with painful anxiety, about that on which our thoughts can have no influence?

The last question now occupied her mind: Why should I fret over Mama's behavior? Her ladyship cannot be controlled. Indeed, she cannot be influenced. I would do better to cease thinking of her, if only I could. How does one work on such a person? These vexing questions kept Anne engaged as the carriage travelled to Holcombe Manor. She stared through the window at the wet fields and dripping tree branches. It was safest to remain mute while Lady Catherine sat opposite, complaining about Lady Metcalfe's invitation to tea.

"I have no interest in meeting two medical men down from Town. What amusement can either of them offer, especially in this weather? I am confident of their low connections. Truly, Lady Metcalfe can be unbelievably crass."

Anne listened to her mother's grumbling with only one ear, knowing her to be more interested in Mr. Cole and Dr. Granville than she cared to let on. As far as she could tell, her mother was annoyed at Lady Metcalfe's having advanced the invitation first.

In fact, her mother's resentment toward her younger neighbor was of long standing. Lady Metcalfe—or Mrs. Ormiston as she was styled when she first arrived in the district—possessed all the elegance and fashion of a true aristocrat, even though her family had made their money in trade and her husband was a mere second son. The glamorous couple and their children became favorites among the villagers, being naturally convivial and sincere, generous with their entertaining, and disposed to be happy in Hunsford.

Because the couple was so esteemed in the district, Lady Catherine could not say a word against them. This consternation might have been borne had Mr. Ormiston not succeeded to his father's estate, becoming the 3rd Baron Metcalfe; he entered the House of Lords shortly thereafter. Lady Catherine had hoped the couple would remove permanently to Lord Metcalfe's estate in Buckinghamshire. Instead, they enjoyed both residences and visited Kent frequently. Whenever they resided in Hunsford, the seat of power shifted from Rosings Park to Holcombe Manor, thus making Lady Catherine more bad-tempered than usual.

Anne managed to arrive at their destination without any expression of incivility.

The wind being gusty and the rain inconstant, tea was offered in the main saloon. On entering, Anne spied Dr. Granville and Dr. Bailey in deep discussion near the fireplace, while Lady Metcalfe's only daughter, Mrs. Clarinda Venables, charmed Mr. Cole near the tea table.

"Lady Catherine," said Lady Metcalfe, "I am pleased you were available to meet the medical men down from Town. Dr. Bailey is quite taken with them and, of course, you have heard of Dr. Granville's delivering Mrs. Sparke's daughter." To Anne she said, "You must be thrilled to have your god-daughter named for you."

"Indeed, I am humbled by Mrs. Sparke's generosity and do not know how we would have managed without Dr. Granville."

"Then you must tell him so. Go interrupt Dr. Bailey, who has been keeping the doctor all to himself. I believe Dr. Granville would enjoy a tour of the orangery."

Not wishing to appear too eager to talk to the young doctor, Anne said, "Forgive me, but I had not realized Mrs. Venables was expected this week."

"No, nor I. She arrived yesterday evening, a week earlier than expected, and brought Philip with her. Philip is grown quite tall for a boy of three years. You will not recognize him. I am sure my daughter will be pleased to see you and share all her news."

Anne doubted this very much, for Miss Ormiston's fickle temper seemed not much improved after her marriage to Mr. Venables and even less so after his untimely death. None the less, Anne moved to the tea table, where she accepted a cup of tea before taking a position at Mr. Cole's elbow. Mrs. Venables scowled at her intrusion.

"Ah, Miss de Bourgh," said Mr. Cole. "How do you do? I hope you are not too weary after yesterday's excitement."

"Not at all. I am thrilled to welcome a god-daughter."

"Congratulations. I hear you performed admirably."

"If you mean that I held my friend's hand and spoke words of encouragement to her, then, yes, I claim such credit. Surely, I did no more than any other lady would do for a friend."

"You might think so, but my friend Granville has told me of cases where a lady collapsed in hysterics or fainted dead away during the delivery. You are stronger than you look, I think."

"I confess a secret: I witnessed the births of piglets, calves, and puppies when I was a child."

"Our Miss de Bourgh is a regular farmer," said Mrs. Venables, a smirk sitting on her pouty lips. "She likes nothing better than to work in manure."

Anne could only smile at this paltry compliment. Mrs. Venables was loveliness itself: twinkling blue eyes; a rosy complexion, flawless in its glow; and curly blond hair secured on top of her head with a comb. A few wispy tendrils had escaped their tether and floated about her face, giving her the look of a Botticelli Madonna. How unfortunate that her character should be so contemptible.

"But farming is the very lifeblood of Kent—indeed, of all England," protested Mr. Cole. "I admire any family that can make a living farming, for it is hard work and subject to the whims of Nature."

Dr. Bailey and Dr. Granville approached them, the older doctor saying, "I am pleased to hear you speak of your respect for farming. It is an occupation to which you are ill-suited."

"Indeed, uncle, you are right. Is it not best that I acknowledge it?"

Dr. Bailey laughed. "It is. Ah, if you will excuse me, I see Lady Metcalfe waving at me."

While Mrs. Venables spoke with Mr. Cole of Town pleasures, Dr. Granville whispered to Anne, "Lady Metcalfe tells me her orange trees are blooming. I should like to see the flowers after a winter spent in London. Shall we investigate?"

"With pleasure."

He took her teacup and set it on a tray, his courtesy performed casually, as if he waited on her every day. They excused themselves, leaving Mrs. Venables looking smug on having gained the handsome surgeon for herself.

When the heavy doors closed behind them, Dr. Granville inhaled deeply. "The smell of dirt is one I miss when in Town. I do sometimes tire of London's filth and grime."

"You don't find such earthy aromas in Kensington Gardens?"

"If I put my nose right in the soil near the shrubbery, it might be so, but can you imagine the shock to my fellow Londoners to see a gentleman scratching in the dirt like a squirrel?"

"In fact, I can imagine it very well. It would make me laugh to see your face in the flowers and your coat-tails in the air."

He grinned like a man accustomed to being teased. They wound their way along the stone walk, stopping only to admire the orange trees.

"Please allow me to thank you for your service to my friend," said Anne. "Your arrival was a great comfort. We were fortunate to have your assistance."

"It was no trouble, and Cole was keen to visit his uncle." He cast a sunny smile. "You wish to ask a question, I think."

"I must be on my guard, else you prove to be a thought-reader, not a man-midwife. But you are correct: I am curious about your interest in midwifery. It is not a profession chosen often by men. What led you to consider it?"

"My sister Janet." He remained silent while they stood at the end of the aisle, surveying the garden's trembling shrubbery through the rain-soaked window panes. "Janet was eight years my senior and quite a bossy girl, full of mischief and grand ideas. She died in childbirth not a year after she married. I vowed then to study medicine, to understand how childbirth problems arise and how they might be prevented."

"I am sorry for your loss. I have no brothers or sisters, but Mrs.

Sparke is like a sister to me and well I can imagine the pain I would feel were I to lose her."

They wandered back toward the main entrance.

"Dr. Bailey spoke of you with affection. He noted your interest in physic."

"Dr. Bailey knows me well, for he and his wife moved here from Town many years ago, before I was born. I believe he hoped village life might improve his wife's health, but she died of a fever soon after they settled. He never returned to his Town practice. He and my father became great friends, and I think of him as an uncle. As for physic, I don't know why I find it so interesting. Why is one person drawn to the study of insects, while another is fascinated by rock formations? Why is one man impassioned by natural philosophy, while his neighbor writes poems? Why does one lady delight in fashion while her friend finds joy in drawing? It is a mystery to me." She paused to gather courage for an intimate query. "Do you mind my asking whether some unusual problem arose during Marianne's delivery? I perceived an unexpected development."

"Now you are the mind-reader. In truth, the navel cord was wrapped around the child's neck and several attempts were required to free it. Such an event is not unusual. Last year—"

"Miss de Bourgh? Dr. Granville?" Mrs. Venables' honeyed voice echoed down the aisle. She approached them, her arm linked through Mr. Cole's. Her superior smile was calculated to offend her rival. "Your mother asks for you, Miss de Bourgh."

Anne stifled her annoyance. "Then I had better attend to her. Please excuse me." She smiled at the medical men.

Behind her, Mrs. Venables was heard saying, "Now, gentlemen, tell me your pleasure. Do you prefer betting on horses or cards?"

On the return to Rosings, Lady Catherine sat opposite her daughter, a scowl heralding her displeasure.

What is Mama unhappy about now? Anne wondered. She has taken the forward-looking bench, which she always claims because she cannot abide the dizzying aspect of looking backward. One day I shall choose the seat by her side, if only to see whether she is made speechless by my sauciness.

"What a waste of time," said Lady Catherine before the carriage had even left the grounds. "I saw no breeding and little elegance in either man. The surgeon is well-looking, but the other, the doctor, looks rough. He told me his father and grandfather are also doctors. Medical men—they are all quacks. I cannot for the life of me understand why Lady Metcalfe is drawn to such people."

"She enjoys meeting all kinds of characters."

Lady Catherine pursed her lips and changed the subject. "Mr. Cole was quite taken with Mrs. Venables. You would do well to adopt her style. She seems naturally to possess the art of pleasing handsome young men, although it is shocking to see her cast off her widow's dress so early. Lady Metcalfe has become alarmed."

"Alarmed? But why?"

"You know her husband was carrying nearly ten thousand pounds on his person when he died. There is talk he withdrew the money to repay a gambling debt, but it cannot be proved, and no creditor has stepped forward to claim the money. Lady Metcalfe fears some nefarious creature will impose on her daughter. That is why she and her son came to Holcombe. They are likely to remain here for several months."

"But think, Mama: her situation is not a happy one. She must live daily with questions of why her young husband dropped dead on a street corner in the middle of the day. People can be vicious about such things, no matter how innocent his death."

"That is the point. His death looks suspicious. He was a handsome, vital man—the eldest son of a Viscount—with a wife and child. Why should he drop dead on Threadneedle Street, only a stone's throw from the Bank of England? There is something gauche about the case."

"Surely you don't mean to suggest Mr. Venables dropped dead to annoy the Bank."

"Don't be ridiculous. I merely point out the obvious: she should behave more discreetly because the circumstances surrounding her husband's death are peculiar." Her ladyship rearranged her coat as the carriage approached the house. "Your behavior this afternoon was likewise less than ideal."

Anne guessed where this statement was leading.

"You were alone in the orangery with Dr. Granville. An unmarried lady should not consort with an unmarried man in private as you did. It will cause talk, in addition to that created by your going alone with Mr. Sparke to Dr. Bailey's house in the dead of night. Oh, yes, I have heard of your adventure. Did you think to hide it from me?"

"Dr. Granville is too much a gentleman to make love to me behind the ferns in Lady Metcalfe's orangery, and as for Mr. Sparke—I did not care about anybody's opinion. My first thought was of Tilly's distress. But now that you raise the issue of things hidden, I wish to inform you of a change in our household affairs. There is a new system for distributing mail. Letters directed to me will no longer be given secretly to you."

Lady Catherine seemed about to speak when Galton's muted "Whoa!" was heard, after which the carriage halted at the front door.

"In this way," said Anne, "I can be confident of receiving my mail directly and privately. Thus, any letters written to me by Miss Waygood or any other person will not go astray. Hobbs understands that he serves this house at my pleasure."

A footman opened the door and lowered the step. Anne rose and, for the first time in her adult life, descended from the carriage ahead of her mother. It was rude behavior, of this she was well aware, but even so, she felt surprisingly serene. Like a renegade plotting a rebellion, she gave no thought to consequences.

Chapter 8

"She weighs no more than a newborn kitten," said Anne as she gazed on Marianne's dewy face. "Have you set a date for the churching?"

Tilly lay abed, propped against a mountain of pillows, and considered how natural her friend looked with a swaddled child cradled in her arms. "I shall be churched on the Thursday after Easter, and the christening shall occur the week following, provided I am sufficiently well."

"It is a good plan. How does John do?"

"He is more himself now the birth is behind us. I thought he might be disappointed to have a daughter, but he says it mattered not. His first hope was for a well-made child."

"That is just what I would have expected of him. He is a good man. You chose well, for he assuredly adores you."

Tilly blushed and turned the topic. "Do you suppose Dr. Granville will visit these parts again?"

"He has no reason to." Anne sighed. The doctor had lately been her favored subject of daily fantasies and retrospection. Which of his looks was most pleasing? His profile with its high sloping forehead and Grecian nose? His grin when he held Marianne, all ruddy and slippery? His brown eyes beseeching hers when he asked if she were well? Every friendly gesture during their walk in Lady Metcalfe's orangery was recalled with delight. She fell into a deep reverie broken by a curt cough. Seeing Tilly's bemused look, she said, "I had a letter from Lady Metcalfe."

"Oh? What does she write?"

"She and Mrs. Venables left Holcombe yesterday for Ramsgate, where Lord Metcalfe will join them for the Easter recess. Miss Pope remains behind with Lionel, James, and Mrs. Venables' son, Philip." Anne did not mention Lady Metcalfe's personal comments:

You know my nature. Every occasion of discovering an attraction between two young persons well suited for each other brings me joy, and I cannot but wish for the happiness of one as dear to me as my own children. Thus, I speak my mind: Dr. Granville was most impressed with your charms. I believe he will find an excuse to return soon to Hunsford.—Of course, I have been told often and often of your engagement to Mr. Darcy, but I have experienced enough of the world to know that long engagements don't always succeed. In choosing a suitable life partner, you will think first of your duty, which quality I admire in you, but I pray you will also consider your personal happiness. You are of an age to follow your own dictates and to guard against the persuasion of others.

Anne had not expected to receive a letter of such intimacy from Lady Metcalfe, for she believed her regard for Dr. Granville had been well concealed. If Lady Metcalfe detected it, was it possible her mother did as well? On considering the matter, she discovered she cared not who knew of it, for her instincts spoke: he was a good man and worthy of affection. If his manner or address gave evidence of a deeper tenderness toward her, she would reciprocate.

Tilly stifled an impulse to tease her friend, saying, "News is thin on the ground these days. I hear Sir William returned to Meryton, leaving Miss Lucas to enjoy her sister's company. I suppose the parsonage guests will settle soon to a routine. When are Mr. Darcy and Colonel Fitzwilliam expected?"

"They arrive on Tuesday. Mama is almost giddy at the prospect of entertaining her nephews. One might be excused for thinking it a Royal visit."

"Her ladyship delights in their company, which relieves you of being the object of her scrutiny. Is she likely to speak to Mr. Darcy of marriage?"

"I fear she will bedevil him about his duty to offer for me, it being high time we married. Her words, dearest."

"Mrs. Collins told me Mr. Darcy met Miss Bennet when he traveled to Hertfordshire with his friend Mr. Bingley. I hear she is considered one of the prettiest ladies in that district and wish to meet her, but, of course, I cannot leave the house until my confinement ends."

"Yes, your situation is unfortunate, for I believe you would be quite taken with her. Mama certainly is. In fact, I wonder whether she perceives a threat there. Since becoming acquainted with the charming Miss Bennet, she finds fault with me on every front: my hair is a fright, my skin too sallow, my disposition dull. I cannot hold a candle to the lively Miss Bennet."

"You must remain true to yourself."

"As if I could do otherwise," said Anne as she patted Marianne's plump cheek, "which is precisely what irritates my mother."

This conversation was a source of troubled contemplation as Anne tramped the shaded path through the Park on her return to the house. She seemed always to have felt the force of her mother's displeasure for one flaw or another: she lacked vitality; wore her clothes ill; and flaunted boyish manners, the result of trailing after her father into fields and barns when she was a child.

In recent years her greatest failing was making no effort to please Darcy, to whom she had been betrothed since infancy. In truth, she had no wish to please him, for he made little effort to win her affection. She could not imagine having amorous congress with him—the very idea brought a blush to her cheeks—and dreaded his forthcoming visit, for his presence at Rosings seemed always to provoke Lady Catherine.

Perhaps it was not fair to blame Darcy for this consequence. Anne had struggled against her mother's dominion for years, the skirmishes having begun within weeks of Sir Lewis's burial, when her ladyship announced she would not move to the dower house.

Anne recalled her mother's words with perfect clarity: "Your relations approve my remaining here at Rosings, since you are yet unmarried. Moreover, you are too inexperienced to handle the house affairs. A strong hand is needed to manage the staff now that your father is dead. Servants are a lazy, surly lot and will take advantage of so young and stupid a person as you. I shall continue to impose order on their domain, where you cannot." Her ladyship had tugged the stiff, black lace on the cuff of her mourning dress. "Go upstairs now and wash your face. You look a fright."

Not for Mama the turmoil of removing to the dower house at Guston Hill, Anne grumbled as she stepped around a pile of horse dung on the park path. Not for *her* the effort of commanding every-one—the Rosings servants, the villagers, and half the county—from a modest house in the woods. Not for her ladyship the misery of relinquishing her status as mistress of Rosings just because Sir Lewis de Bourgh died. Within weeks of Sir Lewis's burial an unusual divi-sion of labor evolved. Lady Catherine controlled the living now enjoyed by Mr. Collins—as was her right, the advowson having been conveyed to her on Sir Lewis's death—but she also ruled the house, which purview should have been Anne's.

Seeking a triumph over her mother, Anne had sought help from the family's London solicitor, Mr. Newland. Her complaints and pleadings, posted in a flurry of passionate letters, earned his sym-pathy but brought his admonition that she was still quite young and might benefit from Lady Catherine's continued residence at the Great House.

A conversation with Dr. Bailey, of all people, convinced her to tame her prejudice. In a liquor-induced haze of reminiscences, he had said: "Your mother and I are much of the same age. We are the golden lad and girl who, like chimney sweeps, are soon to come to dust. When one reaches our lofty status, Miss Anne, the future is a fearsome beast. You, young as you are, know what it is like to lose your anchor. A sudden fever, a broken neck—in a single blink, you are set adrift. No sight of shore. No compass." He paused and with a trembling hand lifted a glass of brandy to his lips and emptied its contents in one gulp. "If you can, Miss Anne, if there is any compassion in your heart, think of your mother's terror at being forced to leave the only house, the only life, she has known for more than twenty years." He dropped into a deep sleep, his head lolled forward. Anne had watched him napping in the fire light. For a heartbeat—a bare blink—she saw her father sitting in that chair, here in the parlor with the fire dying down.

She wanted to resist Dr. Bailey's gentle persuasion, to renounce his claim on her sympathetic heart, but the image of her dear Papa made her pause. If she forced her mother to move to Guston Hill, would she find herself made miserable by her ladyship's festering resentments? Would she be robbed of belief in her own goodness? What did it say about her character if she could not reach that exalted plain of Christian duty where no reward was sought for compassion freely given?

After mulling these questions for weeks and knowing beyond doubt what her father would expect of her, she had tossed her most recent letter to Mr. Newland into the fire. As the pages curled and blackened, she wondered, fleetingly, how soon she might come to regret her decision.

Since that time, mother and daughter had lived together in something like equilibrium. The pendulum swung most days in a tight arc, lurching from indifference to intolerance; it seldom swayed as far as acceptance and ease. Seeing Tilly's happy situation and snuggling little Marianne had made Anne feel bereft of affection and the hope of a happy future. Where would she find the reserves to receive her mother's sharp barbs and unkind cuts during her cousins' visit? How could she bear her ladyship's decided amiability toward her cousins? Could one heal a wound that festered for years?

"Miss de Bourgh," called George Martin Tench as he stepped out from the thicket.

"Good God! You scared me half to death," cried Anne, pressing a hand to her heart. "What do you want?"

He flourished a courtly bow. "I did not mean to startle you, but I wish to ask a question: Why do you not appoint me to Pa's office? His duties, by right, are mine to claim. I grew up on the estate, the same as Roger. I walked the fields with my father and stood at his knee while servants and tenants pleaded or complained. I listened to arguments over crop acreage, yields, and animal husbandry. I am familiar with more than you give me credit for."

"Unlike Roger, you are often absent from the estate." She tried to brush past him. "And I have much on my mind besides replacing my steward."

"You might at least listen to my arguments." He thrust one arm to block her passage.

"Very well. Meet me in the steward's office at five o'clock. Tell Roger I shall be there at half past, if he wishes to speak with me." She did not wait for his answer but broke free of the trees and reached the open grounds, feeling his dark, moody eyes marking her steps.

—⁂—

"Where do you go?" asked Lady Catherine. She was writing a letter to Lady Matlock. Corresponding with her brother's wife was a chore.

"I agreed to meet the Tench brothers in the estate office. I shall return shortly."

"It is not wise to meet them there. The men should come here to the house, as they usually do. You must at all times preserve your command, Anne. Your going to the steward's office will not elevate your rank or earn their respect, as you will one day discover."

"I think it a good idea to venture occasionally into their territory. Please give my regards to Lady Matlock," she said, hoping to deflect her mother's criticism.

The steward's office had the look of a cottage. Its plain, two-story façade fronted five windows; its roof hosted two chimneys. From the main house, the building was reached by walking east along the drive and then veering left. A stand of densely packed firs shielded visitors from this, the business side of the estate: the servants' quarters, laundry buildings, and at the furtherest point, the estate office. In a heavy rain, one could get quite wet running from the laundry across the cook's herb garden to the steward's retreat.

On this occasion she arrived well before five o'clock, feeling sad to enter the steward's domain after his recent death. The terrible impressions of her last visit hit her afresh: the cloying smell of putrefaction, the cindery odor of a dying fire, the rumpled bed-clothes, the steward's sweaty face.

A young servant, a lad with pitcher ears and lank hair, the son of a tenant, rose from his knees and bowed stiffly. "Beggin' your pardon, ma'am. The fire is lit. Will ye want anythin' else?"

"Thank you, no, Lester. Stay close by, should I need you, and leave the door open."

She inhaled the smells of leather, tobacco, and straw. This was a rustic meeting place for men: salesmen, dairymen, day laborers, traders in horse flesh, auctioneers, gardeners, tradesmen, and veterinarians. No feminine ornaments graced the shelves or adorned the desk. No feminine flourishes were welcomed: no damask-covered chairs or chintz drapery, no toile wallpaper or woven rugs. The walls and furnishings were plain. The steward's desk planted opposite the fireplace was much too large for a lady. It was a man's desk, massive in its proportions, scratched and marred in odd places by knives, short-handled scythes, skeps and surcingles, and heavy bags of oats and barley. Its only accessories were two tarnished candlesticks that stood like sentinels guarding the estate's wealth. Their candles glowed against the darkening windows.

According to her watch, the time was six minutes past five o'clock and there was no sign of George Martin Tench. She moved a straight-backed chair near the fire, sat down, and waited. She should be preparing to meet Tench's older son. She should be ready to cool his anger over Roger's appointment as interim steward. Instead, her mother's voice intruded: "It is good you returned to Rosings. There can be few demands on you here."

How obtuse her mother could be. Her ladyship knew the running of Rosings could not be left to the steward. Of course, many decisions fell within his purview, but since inheriting Rosings, Anne felt deeply the claims connected with managing the estate. As tenant for life, her signature was affixed to all deeds, leases, mortgages, and agreements. By *my* signature the estate succeeds or fails. If I'm not careful, I might deplete the cash surplus or halt works in progress. A wrong decision risks ruin in life and reputation. But if I'm smart and lucky, I shall secure the estate's income for improvements and replenishing animal stock. And I pay Mama's jointure. Lady Catherine never forgets that essential expenditure! I have enjoyed good fortune so far.

She recalled Tench's loyalty and patient counsel. He believed her to be intelligent and capable. "I have faith in you," he had said on his deathbed. To hear such words of confidence from a man she admired and respected touched her deeply.

"Working lads have no time for wool-gathering." George Martin Tench leaned against the door frame.

Anne had not heard his footfall on the path. "You are late by fifteen minutes," she said, coming to her feet.

"So I am, but my excuse is worthy. I rescued a little lamb lost near the Whitaker farm. It would have been unwise to leave her to the mercy of foxes."

Anne doubted this story, for his clothes were too fine for farm work. The darling lamb probably walked on two legs, not four. "You requested an interview. What would you say?"

He grinned. "It would be polite to offer me a drink."

"There are no spirits here. Now, speak."

George Martin stared at her before prowling the room. With sneaky looks in her direction, he opened a cabinet door, pinched a woolen cloak hanging near the door, and snapped the lid on a wooden tool box. Bored with roving, he settled himself against the desk. "Don't worry over your virtue. I shall not assault you. Come, let us think on happier times and share memories of our fathers and their rule of this land. Let us speak as friends."

"We are not friends."

His lopsided grin looked more like a sneer. "We might take advantage of our privacy," he said, pushing off the desk. He did not touch her, but his handsome face hovered close to hers. His bruised cheek gave him the look of a dashing corsair. His voice rumbled low and mellow: "If you but trust my kind intentions, I can introduce you to delights that will make your wedding night all the more satisfying—that is, should you ever marry. You are growing rather old for matrimony, are you not?"

His voice fell on her like warm honey, so smooth and bewitching was its timbre. His smile invited her confidence. She had never liked him. "I understood you to have something to say about the steward's office. If you wish to convince me of your merits, this is the time to do so." She worked to remain indifferent to his nearness. He stood so close she could smell tobacco on his shirt. Her stomach fluttered at the sight of his tousled hair and dark eyes, at his white shirt, open at the neck, at the tuft of black chest hairs curling over the white collar.

"Why so solemn, Miss de Bourgh? Why so glum? I think you are afraid of me."

"You are mistaken. I have no fear, but I grow mighty irritated."

George Martin Tench grinned, drew a finger down her cheek and kissed her quickly on the mouth. "Good. It is a beginning." He turned, laughing, and strode out into the night.

Anne pressed a hand to her lips and stared aghast into the dark beyond the door, transfixed by his tomfoolery. She could not have been more shocked had he arrived expressing his undying love for her. That avenue she could imagine him pursuing, for she had inherited a profitable estate, and he had a penchant for London life. In marrying her, he gained control of her property. Her lands, her money, virtually her every possession would be his to do with as he pleased. Even her children, the very issue of her womb, would be his in law. As his wife—as any man's wife—her property would not be hers to control during their marriage.

Yes, George Martin Tench might find a confession of love a most suitable strategy for his personal betterment, but, if so, this was hardly the way to begin.

"Ma'am," came Roger Tench's call as he tapped on the door frame and stepped over the threshold. "Has my brother come and gone?"

"He has."

"May I speak, then?"

"As you wish."

Roger twisted his cap with his hands. Some internal quarrel raged within him until he reached a resolution.

"Ma'am, I don't know what my brother said to you, but you must not heed his arguments. Certain ladies find him very persuasive, but he has ruined more than one life, I assure you. If you love Rosings, you will not yield to his demands. He will not serve you well."

Anne frowned. "Your brother's suitability for the steward's office is for me to determine. Do you wish to speak of your merits?"

"I wish to know what my father said on his deathbed. Did he issue no guidance?"

Anne recalled with perfect clarity his father's words, spoken in grief and pain in his last days. "I love both boys," Tench had said in a trembling voice, "but their differences are great. Roger is young and untried, but he loves this land as if it were his own. He can be stubborn, God knows, but he will serve you faithfully. George— George has no fixity of purpose. He cannot be trusted, it pains me to say." Speaking of this matter would wound both sons. She said gently: "Your father was in great pain when last I saw him. We had only a few minutes together, but he did say this: 'I love both boys.'"

Roger's face colored and his voice quavered before gaining ground. "I have decided that should you name my brother steward, I shall leave Rosings." To her troubled look, he added: "My resolution is strong."

"I suggest you think on the matter. It would be more productive to consider how you might assist me in improving the Park and all its holdings."

Roger Tench pressed his lips together, gave her a curt nod, and spun on his heels. She watched him disappear into the dark.

After supper she sat near the fire in her private parlor, her hand working a steady rhythm as she sketched a song thrush's nest. She recalled the brothers' words and actions and searched for nuances and true feelings. The conundrum was Roger's conduct. Some part of his behavior was hurt pride, of this she was fairly sure, but she had not foreseen his threat to leave her service if he did not get what he wanted. Was there not a danger in giving such a powerful position to a man who uttered ultimatums? Might he continue to issue threats of one sort or another if he were named steward? Should she be surprised if his character proved different from his father's? This last question could be answered, surely, for she believed—nay, prayed—her own character was nothing like her mother's.

On feeling a chill descend as the fire burned low, she thought of one task she might complete before retiring to bed. Settling at her desk, she selected a piece of writing paper. As she dipped a quill-pen in the ink pot, an image of her uncle formed. Edwin Augustus Fitzwilliam, 2nd Earl of Matlock, was very like his sister, Lady Catherine, being tall and big-boned with a strong jaw, large hands, and a sharp eye that made the proudest shopkeepers quake when challenged about the price or quality of their goods. Lord Matlock had a smart look about him and enjoyed a reputation among the Tories for his shrewd electioneering. He was a busy man but not one to resent her interference. She opened her letter with a few pleasantries and then wrote: *I have a piece of business to discuss with you, if I may so boldly impose on your time …*

Her letter, directed to Lord Matlock, would be ready for the early post. During Darcy's visit, she hoped to defend a decision.

Chapter 9

For two weeks the servants labored to bring the house to its sparkling finest. Windows were washed, silver polished, vases dusted, rugs beaten, and sheets ironed. The bustle brought a breath of excitement to an otherwise dull routine and made Anne almost look forward to her cousins' arrival. Since Tilly's delivery she had endured Lady Catherine's criticism for every little thing: consorting with the medical men, appeasing the Tench brothers, and defending a common governess. Her worst crime was resisting her ladyship's improving suggestions. Having not an ounce of patience left, Lady Catherine took the carriage out alone nearly every day to visit such villagers as needed her guidance and, when in company with the Collinses and their guests, paraded a cool civility toward her daughter.

After Darcy and Colonel Fitzwilliam arrived, her ladyship became pleasant, even gay. Anne felt the sting of her mother's torment, but was mostly armored against it by the affection of friends and neighbors and fond recollections of Dr. Granville. When supper was laid *en famille* one rainy evening, she studied her cousins, thinking, every year the same.

Colonel Richard Fitzwilliam, the second son of Lord Matlock, was in high spirits, having imbibed two glasses of a good cellared wine. In form he was stocky with broad shoulders and longish brown curls falling to his coat collar. Any deficiency in his smile arising from several crooked teeth was more than offset by the sparkle in his eyes. In character he was a hail-fellow man, greeting everyone with warmth and sincerity. He now embellished a story, his lips twisting into a sardonic grin as he pounded the table. "Then Sergeant Greengoose tripped over his feet, crying, 'Faith an' troth, ye scar'd me half to death. I thought ye was a monkey!'"

Lady Catherine twittered, only to be polite. Darcy scowled. Anne laughed at the Colonel's idea of humor. He enjoyed telling stories, mostly on himself, but sometimes about the men under his command. "Boys, they are," he once told her. "Crude and uneducated boys—'muds and bloods,' Colonel Fitchett calls them." In the candle light his impish smile belied his worry over their rations, clothing, and training.

Darcy could not be more different. He was tall and dark—dark of hair and eyes, often dark of mood. He was unfailingly proper, not given to rowdy laughter or gossip, and seemingly incapable of silliness. His character was ruled by duty and decorum braced by an intimidating intellect. Anne could not recall an instance when he lost control of himself. Although she admired his character, she seldom found ease in his company.

Every Easter the cousins drove down from London in Darcy's elegant equipage. Every Easter Anne asked herself the same question, Can you marry this man, this stranger, of whom your mother is so fond? While studying his intimidating brow she suddenly comprehended a truth she had hidden from herself: Darcy's indifference to her was exceedingly painful. Yet—was not this her pride speaking? Would she be happier if he adored her when she felt no affection for him? Surely such a derangement would make neither of them happy. Still, his aloofness begged a question: If the threat of marriage were removed from their relationship, would he show her greater affection? This question could not easily be answered, but with each passing year it became more difficult to imagine being joined with him in matrimony, no matter how deep her respect for his character. Indeed, the very idea of marriage troubled her. How does one recognize a proper partner? Oh, not proper in the sense of appropriateness of rank or income, but proper in the sense of suitable in character and temper. How does one recognize a true heart when many flaws can be hidden by good manners and a pleasing countenance?

Marriage aside, she puzzled over Darcy's enjoyment. While the Colonel seemed comfortable at Rosings, it being a pleasant diversion from the trial of training his men, Darcy was perennially unhappy in Kent. Did he resent the duty of his Easter visit? Did he come only to honor the memory of his father? Had Lady Catherine smothered his pleasure with insinuations regarding marriage?

These questions occupied Anne all through the meal. Lady Catherine, increasingly agitated as each course was laid, pursued Anne up the stairs after supper. Her ladyship banged the bedchamber door closed and bellowed, "What game do you play? Do you think Darcy does not notice your preference for Colonel Fitzwilliam? You flirt easily enough with *him* and laugh at his stories, but you hardly condescend to speak with Darcy, your future husband. It is no wonder he is sullen and distempered! He feels keenly your lack of effort. I insist you pay him the respect and attention he deserves."

With a withering stare, she stalked from the room, satisfied her command would be obeyed to the letter.

Chapter 10

Anne stared through the conservatory's tall windows, a half-empty coffee cup in hand. She contemplated her mother's authority and the strength of her cousins' allegiance to it. Their loyalty was not easily determined. Darcy revealed no peculiar susceptibility to Lady Catherine's influence and seemed much as he ever was—polite to everybody and formal in company. He spoke warmly of his much younger sister, Georgiana, and his family estate, Pemberley, but offered little in the way of personal insights or opinions on other intimate topics. He was most animated and at ease in the company of the Colonel. For his part, Colonel Fitzwilliam was attentive to her ladyship and took the trouble of pleasing her. Being naturally talkative and ebullient, he often carried the burden of conversation. If he was troubled by the duty, he did not show it.

"Here is the coffee!" exclaimed the Colonel.

"Good morning, Cousin. I was just thinking of you."

"Truly? It must tax your brain to do so before dinner. I hope you don't develop a sick headache for your trouble. May I join you?"

"Please do." Anne extended her hand toward the small sofa sitting at an angle to the one on which she sat. "Shall I pour coffee for you?"

"It is not necessary, for I am able to do so myself. We military men learn to be resourceful." He poured coffee and selected a scone from the tray. "This is a pleasant room. Do you often enjoy your coffee here?"

"Yes, the conservatory offers my favorite view. I have been watching a peacock strut across the lawn—see, there he goes behind the bushes. His tail feathers are getting wet in the morning dew."

They sat quietly while the colonel ate his scone.

"What made you think of me?" He brushed crumbs from his lap.

"I was thinking how much my mother enjoys your company."

"You jest! She constantly berates my appearance and rough manners and criticizes my haircut."

Anne laughed. Although her cousin was not a handsome man by the common standard—he was rough as an old boot compared with Darcy—his convivial disposition made him the handsomer of the two to Anne's eye. Few ladies would agree with her in this, she supposed. "Mama does no such thing. Oh, she likes to pester, true enough, but she makes allowances for your bad behavior. You must see that."

Colonel Fitzwilliam looked at her, his features softening. "I do. I also see that she is often critical of you. What mischief does she lay at your door?"

Anne stood to check the coffee urn. Seeing as the brew was still hot, she streamed coffee into her cousin's cup and replenished her own. "It is nothing—nothing to speak of, in any event. But I have a favor to ask of you, if I may." Seeing her cousin's complacent look, she said: "Would you have time to tour the park again this year? You can go farther afield than I and are likely to observe more of its changes and deficiencies. I realize it is a demanding task, since the duty cannot be completed in a single day, but your impressions of it will improve my planning. Mama has told you, I am sure, of Tench's death earlier this year."

"I was sorry to hear of it. He was a good man."

"I must replace him. Indeed, I have written your father for advice, which brings me to another matter."

"Ah, a second favor."

Anne hid a smile. "I know that look, sir. It will not do. You cut your eyes at me much as you would have done when you were four years old and trying to provoke your nurse." The Colonel grinned. "Would you tell Darcy I wish to speak to him about the Tench brothers? I cannot find the proper moment for approaching him. He seems different this visit: preoccupied or agitated or muddled or—"

"All of these things," said Colonel Fitzwilliam. "I have noticed it, too. Darcy, of course, admits to nothing. He enjoys a mystery, I think. As for your favors, don't worry. I gladly undertake these duties for you. In fact, I shall begin my tour of the park now, if it pleases you, and walk a little of it when the weather is good. Do you care to accompany me this morning?"

"Thank you, no. I am content here."

"Then I shall see you later." He gave her a curt bow and called to Hobbs as he passed the butler in the aisle.

"Good morning, sir." Hobbs carried a silver salver. "Ma'am, a letter arrived for you."

"Thank you, Hobbs." She retrieved the missive and turned it over to check the seal. It had not been forced. Cracking it carefully, she opened the letter and read:

London Thursday March —th

Dear Niece,

It was a pleasure to receive your letter. Let me assure you of the health and happiness of my own family and offer my hope of the same for yours.—The arrival of your letter was most fortuitous, for I am able to suggest a gentleman for your consideration as steward. The circumstances are these: a few weeks before your letter arrived, I learned that a friend's steward, Mr. Theophilus Arnot, had been released from his office by the new owner of my friend's estate, my friend having died a few months ago. The new owner is one of my friend's nephews, a young man named heir to my friend's property, although their acquaintance was not a close one. Having another, larger property in Cheshire, the nephew determined to reduce the staff and take other money-saving measures.—I recommend Mr. Arnot without reserve. He served as steward to my friend for roughly twelve years and is experienced in the management of an estate similar in size to Rosings. He is widowed with two grown

children, both of whom are married. His disposition is open and
agreeable; his character, steady and reliable. My friend thought
highly of him and credited him with many improvements to his
estate.—If you are willing to interview Mr. Arnot, please write
directly, advising of the dates most agreeable to you. You should
allow two or three days for the visit, which will give you time to
become acquainted with the gentleman and allow him to assess
the workings of your estate. Don't feel obligated to hire him if he
does not suit you, for you remain my own dear niece, regardless of
your decision.—Please give my regards to my sister and remind
my second son to behave with decorum during his visit with you.
Yours affectionately, Matlock

Anne was bemused by the last sentence. Colonel Fitzwilliam
must often feel the pressure of his father's thumb. How kind her
uncle was, to go to such trouble on her behalf. She would write to
him on the morrow.

When clouds drifted from the west and blocked the sunlight, she
rose to retrieve a shawl. Her thoughts shifted from the prospect of
interviewing Mr. Arnot to wondering whether she might find an
opportunity of speaking with Darcy on a personal matter. She wished
for good fortune in this but knew what the Scots would say: he that
lives on hope has but a slender diet. And, of course, there was the
worry of whether she had the nerve to speak her mind.

Chapter 11

The Rosings library was a room not much acquainted with the person of Lady Catherine and perhaps, for this reason, the more willing to bestow on tired refugees all the joys of ease and comfort. Nichol, a young parlor maid possessed of a sweet but timid disposition, had become accustomed to Anne's intrusion into this formerly masculine retreat and, in keeping with her habit, had brought in a tea tray and set it on the table at Anne's elbow. "Excuse me, ma'am," she said, nodding in the direction of the tea sweets. "Cook said to tell you the Plumb cake is fresh-baked." She curtsied and left her mistress perfectly content.

For the first time in several days Anne had the pleasure of her own company and a good book. Shutting away all thoughts of her relations, she settled to reading. Some time later the library door opened. Darcy entered and closed the door behind him. He moved to the bookcase nearest the fireplace and stood entranced by the display of leather-bound tomes. One title was sufficiently interesting to cause him to pull the book out from among its companions and open it.

Anne felt a prick of anxiety at his unexpected presence.

Darcy turned then and saw her. "Cousin Anne, forgive my intrusion. I had not realized the room was occupied." He smiled nervously. "I have come to find an amusement."

With hardly any more forethought than she might have given to choosing a scone over a tea cake, Anne blurted, "May I speak with you, Cousin?"

Being too much the gentleman to ignore her request, Darcy crossed the room, settled on a padded chair, and stretched his long legs across the carpet. "How may I serve you?"

"There are two matters about which I would speak with you. The first has to do with the steward's office."

"The Colonel informed me of your desire to discuss the Tench brothers. Lady Catherine, you must realize, supports appointing George Martin to the office."

"I am aware of her opinion. She believes him to be familiar with all aspects of the estate."

"And you disagree?"

"George Martin Tench might tell a cabbage patch from a wheat field, but he knows little of surveying or recording the tenants' rents and services. I believe he would not recognize an estate roll if it fell on his foot. He is ignorant because he spends most of his time in Town."

"I understand you met with him and his brother. What did they say for themselves?"

"Neither interview unfolded as expected," replied Anne, recoiling at the memory of George Martin's odd behavior. "Roger surprised me by vowing to quit the estate if he is not appointed steward. I do not appreciate threats and so wrote Lord Matlock, who forwarded the name of a candidate. I wish to interview the gentleman as soon as possible."

Darcy returned a pointed stare. "What, pray, do you wish me to do? It seems you have already set your course."

"I would appreciate your speaking with the Tench brothers, supposing, of course, that George Martin returns to Rosings before your visit ends. I seek confirmation of their capabilities. I don't wish to subtract from the pleasure of your visit, but I value your opinion more than any other." Although his look suggested he was not easily flattered, Anne added: "My friend Mrs. Sparke once observed that you have uncommon good sense. It is that quality of your character upon which I impose. I believe you will give me a fair assessment of each man's suitability for the steward's office. Will you assist me?"

"I believe time can be found for this purpose." A hint of a smile adorned his face. "You spoke of two matters about which you sought my counsel."

Anne's heart galloped at his words. How ironic that, for once, he was disposed to converse with her. Having gained his attention, she was now afraid of breaching his tranquility. You have spent years preparing for this day, she reminded herself. Speak! There may never be a better time. "I feel—I must—it is time to be honest with you, Cousin. I have no wish to marry you."

The shock of her inelegant pronouncement hit Darcy fiercely, judging from his furrowed brow.

"Forgive me. I did not mean to startle you. My manners are crude, the result of being confined in the country with few opportunities for enjoying polite society. I have been thinking on our situation. Would you not agree that we have both felt the pressure of our families' hope regarding our marriage? You are aware of Mama's expectation, are you not?"

Darcy's eyes darted left and right, before coming to rest on his cousin's face. He pulled his legs in, clasped his book like a talisman, and laid a restless hand on one knee. "I never thought to hear such language from you. Do you not feel bound by our mothers' heartfelt wish that we marry? Do you ignore the claims of honor and duty?"

Seeing his countenance (part puzzlement, part incredulity), Anne said simply, "I don't feel bound by duty in this instance."

"In *this* instance. Am I to understand that you recognize and act on your duty to Lady Catherine, except in the case of our marriage?"

"Where her ladyship is concerned, I assume the duty of her care. I allow her to live here, where she is comfortable, rather than insist she move to the dower house at Guston Hill; I see that her jointure is paid every year and do not interfere with her private expenditures; and I indulge her wish to manage the house, even though it is inconvenient to the staff and to me. I receive no thanks for fulfilling my duty. She does much as she pleases. But in the case of marriage, I feel no obligation to her."

Darcy looked dazed. "How can you speak so? How can you ignore her ladyship's wishes?"

"I speak from my heart, Cousin, for I don't believe submitting to duty will make me happy. Indeed, I see in you the same dilemma, even if you don't confess it."

Darcy's eyes widened at this charge.

"Allow me to speak plainly, though I fear I may wound you further," she said. "In the first few years after my father died, you and uncle Darcy came down every spring to renew family ties and offer comfort and kindness. On your father's death five years ago, you assumed the duty. But although you visit Rosings every year, I detect no joy at the prospect. Indeed, I believe you rely on the Colonel to relieve the tedium of the obligation. If duty fails to bring satisfaction for so simple a chore as visiting family, then why should we expect it to serve as a reasonable basis for felicity in marriage? I ask you to consider your own beliefs. If you agree with me, then let us throw off duty's mask and live as befits our personal wishes."

She had seldom known Darcy to be stupefied, but so he seemed. He blinked twice before coming to his feet, a wild look flickering in his eyes. "You cannot be serious."

Anne rose from her chair. "I am perfectly serious. Have you never thought on the matter?"

"What of your mother? You would wound her for your own enjoyment? You would injure her for the satisfaction of your own selfish desires?"

A jolt of anger surged through her. "*My* selfish desires? And what of my mother's? Mama would have us marry whether we care for one another or not. You—you, of all people, would demand of me the duty of marrying to please my mother? You know her character. You can barely endure it for a few weeks each spring. I must endure it daily. She pins me down with her incessant demands. She whips me for the smallest infraction or the least rebellion. I am not mistress of my own house! I have thought this through, Cousin. I have scoured my heart and tell you this: I would sooner die an old maid than marry any man my mother chooses for me."

She heard his sharp intake of breath.

His eyes pierced her own, as if he were seeing her for the first time, as if he had discovered a demon in the library—a craven, deformed beast never seen in these parts.

"You know nothing of duty." He spat the words at her, his cheeks coloring, and turned away.

"Then tell me this, Cousin—" cried Anne.

Darcy glared over his shoulder at her.

"Do you love me?"

He did not speak but strode from the room.

Anne sat down, her book forgotten. She watched the sunlight creep along the carpet and travel across the bookcase as the golden orb sank behind the trees. She felt sick on recalling their conversation. It had been a gamble to broach the subject. Clearly she had been rash to suggest each of them might secure their own happiness without regard for the wishes of parents living or long dead. After all these years, she had not penetrated his formidable armor or come to know his intimate thoughts and desires. She knew he did not love her. Some days he was barely civil, seldom bothering to see to her comfort or inquire after her interests. He might comment on her looks or health, but the effort was contrived and held little warmth. The few minutes spent in Dr. Granville's company had yielded more felicity than all her years in Darcy's presence. Surely Darcy did not intend to marry her just to please Lady Catherine and his dead parents! If he sought her hand, it would certainly not be to please himself. Colonel Fitzwilliam had the right of it, after all: Darcy was a mystery.

Chapter 12

"I hear the Easter Sunday service was well-attended, and the de Bourgh's full pew was a source of excitement," said Tilly.

"Really? In what way?" Anne was truly perplexed.

Tilly mimicked Anne's blank face. "Truly, Anne, you are sometimes remarkably dull-witted. Many young ladies in the district enjoyed seeing two such well-dressed, fine-looking, single young men as Mr. Darcy and Colonel Fitzwilliam in church. I am told even Miss Lucas is taken with their pleasing manners and dress."

"Miss Lucas? She is a mere child and much too young to be thinking of men."

Tilly laughed. "You sound like Lady Catherine. Miss Lucas is not indifferent to the charms of a handsome man. After all, considering whom her sister married, it is not surprising she should begin to consider the qualities most pleasing in a husband."

"If she would choose appearances over character, then she is much too young to be thinking of marriage. I suppose Charlotte Collins is the source of your information. How does she do?"

"She is well, but busy with her guests. When she stopped here for a visit, she shared a piece of news you will find interesting."

Anne sipped her tea. The friends had fussed over Marianne and tried fitting the baptismal dress Anne had sewn, but gave up the activity when the child turned peevish. Mrs. Beath took her charge upstairs. "News? Hmm. Does it have anything to do with Mrs. Collins herself?"

"You are thinking Mrs. Collins might be with child. No—at least, she did not confess it. Her news is to do with Mr. Darcy."

"Darcy! What has he done?"

"Mr. Darcy called at the parsonage yesterday and spoke with Miss Bennet alone. He likely thought all the ladies were at home when, in fact, Mrs. Collins and her sister had gone for a walk." Tilly paused for effect. "Mrs. Collins believes he is in love with Miss Bennet." To Anne's dumb surprise she added, "Miss Bennet herself throws cold water on the idea, but in this, Mrs. Collins disagrees with her friend. Did he express any particular interest in her when the Collinses and their guests came to Rosings on Easter Sunday?" Tilly gauged Anne's surprise. "Can you not speak?"

"I hardly know what to say. Darcy enamored of Miss Bennet?" Anne recalled the afternoon's activities. Her mother had bound Darcy to herself in a long, intimate conversation to the exclusion of their guests—that is, until she noticed Colonel Fitzwilliam's fascination with Miss Bennet. On pressing the Colonel to admit the topic of their *tête-à-tête*, he relented: they were discussing music, for which her ladyship claimed a special appreciation. After coffee was served, Miss Bennet consented to play for the Colonel. The two of them moved to the pianoforte, causing Darcy to turn a shoulder to his aunt and join them. At this unexpected sociability, Mrs. Jenkinson had leaned close to Anne's ear and whispered, "Darcy has surprised her ladyship. I have never known him to move with such deliberation. Look, he speaks with Miss Bennet. She smiles and charms. He never so much as looks at you, Miss Anne."

"Are you well, Anne? You have turned pale."

"I recall a comment Mrs. Jenkinson made."

"Mrs. Jenkinson? What piece does she add to the puzzle?"

"She can be very discerning. In fact, she perceived Darcy's interest in Miss Bennet. This is all so strange. I spoke with Darcy on Saturday. I told him I had no wish to marry him.

"You did not!"

"I told you I would do so when I had the chance of it."

"What did he say? What were his looks?"

"His reaction was not what I expected. He mostly glared at me and seemed perplexed rather than alarmed. Since we spoke, he has avoided me more assiduously than ever, but it is no surprise he is thinking of marriage. After all, we have both reached an age when we should marry—Lord knows, Mama has been giving hints to me and very likely to him—but I had not thought he would be attracted to someone of our close acquaintance. Of course, it is a long leap from attraction to marriage. Darcy is mindful of his duty, which will likely prevent him from forming a serious attachment to Miss Bennet."

"What did he say to you, after you told him of your wish?"

"He said I knew nothing of duty."

Tilly's thoughts leapt in several directions at once. "Do you believe he will pursue you out of duty alone?"

"I hope not. Still, I can imagine the dilemma he wrestles and don't envy him the choice."

"You are thinking of Lady Catherine."

"If he marries me, he must submit to Mama's whims and expectations, without hope of escape; but if he marries someone else, he exposes himself to her pitiless wrath and censure. No matter which path he chooses, he cannot win his own pleasure—at least, not in the short term. Poor Darcy."

Chapter 13

Curiosity gave way to confederation. Tilly served as the conduit, being naturally inquisitive and longing for entertainment after her confinement ended. Mrs. Collins and Anne stoked the fire, each assuming the role of spy in her own domain.

Mrs. Collins at first feared her observations might offend Anne, but Tilly reassured her. "My friend has expressed her intent of never marrying Mr. Darcy. Indeed, I sometimes fear she will never marry at all. Please speak to no one of this, for Lady Catherine will not be happy should Miss de Bourgh fail to marry her cousin." On being reassured of her trust, Tilly gave it no thought thereafter, knowing Mrs. Collins to be discreet. Now, had Mr. Collins joined their league, *The Times* might know their every action and speculation.

Anne and Mrs. Collins took their duties seriously but were hindered at every turn. At Rosings Anne endeavored to converse with Darcy, but he kept his distance, fearing further intimacy. He was tense and uncommunicative, looked splenetic when conversing with Lady Catherine, and regularly went for long walks in the park.

"What does Mrs. Collins say on the matter?" Anne asked Tilly as the friends meandered a path in the field bordering Tilly's house.

"She cannot add to your story. At the parsonage, Mr. Darcy is always in the company of the Colonel, whose lively disposition overshadows Mr. Darcy's reserve. Mrs. Collins cannot interpret his looks.

Where Colonel Fitzwilliam's delight with Miss Bennet is obvious to everybody, Mr. Darcy might be thinking as much of murder as marriage." Tilly squatted to pick several wild daisies. "The facts are these," she said, reaching for Anne's hand as she came to her feet, "Mr. Darcy and Miss Bennet were introduced in Hertfordshire. Mr. Darcy has been ill-tempered this visit, which condition might be due to almost anything. Why, a foul tooth would make anybody bad-tempered. Neither party shows any particular regard for the other when in company."

"We have not made much progress." Anne pulled her shawl close against the morning's chill.

"It is exasperating to have so little information. You must make more effort," Tilly demanded.

"I *have* made an effort, but I cannot trap the man in a closet and coerce a confession. Indeed, Darcy's aloofness led me to befriend Miss Bennet. I endeavored to engage her attention whenever I had the opportunity—no easy goal when Mama dominates every conversation. I tried once to coax from her an opinion on Darcy and even asked her about the Hertfordshire plough."

"What does ploughing have to do with anything?"

"I thought to find a common interest," replied Anne, her voice sinking.

Tilly shook her head at Anne's idea of polite conversation. "Has nothing of import happened?"

"Something unusual occurred yesterday." Anne grinned at Tilly's alert look. "You must have your news! Fair enough. I shall indulge you, since you have been confined indoors this past month. Miss Bennet was indisposed with a sick headache and did not join the rest of her party at Rosings. Darcy looked discomforted on learning of her absence and, after a few minutes, quit the room. He was absent for the remainder of the Collinses' visit. I was never more astonished. Of course, he might have been distressed by the painful twinge of a kidney stone or a sore tooth."

"Where did he go? Did he say anything?"

"He simply left our company, saying not a word, not even to Mama."

"What do you make of his behavior?"

"I am at a loss to explain it. Shaw told me he quit the estate."

After contemplating her impressions of the participants, Tilly said, "Servants know everything. If I were a tyrant, I would badger them all until the cause of his strange behavior became known. As it is, I am muddled. So, what other news do you bring? When will Lady Metcalfe return from Ramsgate?"

"She wrote to say the family intends to return to Holcombe next week."

"And Mr. Darcy and Colonel Fitzwilliam leave on Saturday?"

"Yes, that is their plan."

"Everybody is running hither and yon. You are not planning to leave Hunsford, I hope."

"No. Mama and I have no travel plans, but a new face is expected in our village. Mr. Arnot arrives next week."

"I had quite forgotten about him. Are you prepared for his visit?"

"I am curious about him. I daresay the Tench brothers will not be pleased to meet him."

Tilly was lost in thought for several minutes until she remembered wishing to ask Anne's opinion. "What did you think of the churching? Marianne looked quite sweet in her baptismal dress, did she not?"

"So she did, and the service was charming."

"You are joking! Mr. Collins was mortified when she cried during the baptismal."

"True," said Anne, "but don't let his embarrassment upset you. God took no offense, I am sure. She is such a little thing."

"Mr. Collins is not partial to children, I think."

"It appears so, which will make for very interesting times if Mrs. Collins ever forms a family."

Tilly gasped. "Mr. and Mrs. Collins enjoying a little basket-making—I cannot bear to think on such a thing."

"Tilly! You are the devil's own some days."

The friends laughed as if they were girls again, and entwining their arms, they hurried back to the house before the chill penetrated their bones.

Chapter 14

The cousins departed early. Darcy was anxious to be gone and grew irritated with Colonel Fitzwilliam for dawdling. When the carriage pulled away from the house, he stared at Anne standing on the step. His eyes held hers, seeming to send her a message whose form she could not interpret. There was pain in those dark orbs, but also something else: Regret? Grief? Whatever his intent, she did not comprehend his meaning.

Anne and Lady Catherine hardly had time to settle themselves in the drawing room when Mr. Collins arrived to console them on the loss of such agreeable company. He remained long enough to apply the balm of kindly condescension to Lady Catherine's wounds and secure an invitation to dinner. When he returned with Mrs. Collins, Miss Bennet, and Miss Lucas, Lady Catherine opened the conversation with a long lament about her dear nephews. "They were excessively sorry to go! But so they always are. The dear Colonel rallied his spirits tolerably till just at last; but Darcy seemed to feel it most acutely, more I think than last year. His attachment to Rosings, certainly increases."

"How could he not feel keenly the sad prospect of leaving Rosings, especially given the felicity of his relations?" asked Mr. Collins with great dignity. "And he carries away the hope of a deeper, more intimate connection in the future."

Anne all but rolled her eyes and barely managed a thin smile.

After dinner Lady Catherine pressed Miss Bennet to stay with the Collinses another two weeks, to which suggestion Miss Bennet replied that her father could not spare her and, in fact, had written to speed her return to Hertfordshire.

"Oh!" said Lady Catherine, "your father of course may spare you, if your mother can.—Daughters are never of so much consequence to a father. And if you will stay another *month* complete, it will be in my power to take one of you as far as London, for I am going there early in June, for a week; and as Dawson does not object to the Barouche box, there will be very good room for one of you—and indeed, if the weather should happen to be cool, I should not object to taking you both, as you are neither of you large."

Anne barely hid her astonishment. Mama is going to Town for a week! Whatever would draw her to London at this time of year? And with only her maid for company? For the rest of the evening, she could think of hardly anything else. On retiring she said to Shaw, "Tell me what you know of Lady Catherine's travel to Town. I only heard mention of it this evening."

"I am as fog-bound as anybody, ma'am. Dawson is well schooled at keeping her ladyship's secrets, as you know."

Chapter 15

Mr. Arnot's arrival at the White Horse Inn was known at Rosings within the hour of his being admitted to his room. He came on horseback two days early, hired a carriage, and spent his leisure time driving around the district. Being naturally reticent, he spoke hardly a word to any clerk, customer, or busybody while he inspected every shop along Hunsford's high street and sipped beer in the Hare in Hand. He offended nigh on everybody with his Northern manners.

"I glimpsed Mr. Arnot crossing the road near the inn," said Mr. Collins, who was visiting Rosings for the purpose of conferring with Lady Catherine on various parish matters. "He is an ill-formed man with a disagreeable countenance. Mrs. Gallows says he is a widower, which likely accounts for his miserable state. The absence of a helpmeet must be felt deeply."

"Can you speak to his character?" asked Anne.

"Not at all. I have not been introduced to the man. My time has rightly been devoted to more spiritual matters."

It was as she supposed: Mr. Collins embraced his first impression. Like as not, Mr. Arnot had indigestion after eating one of Mr. Garvie's beef-steaks. On the appointed day, Anne formed her own impression when she met him in her parlor. Thinking he might feel uncomfortable to find himself the subject of close scrutiny, like an animalcule trapped under a water-microscope, she sought to put him at ease. "My uncle wrote of your experience managing an estate in Wiltshire. Are you from that part of the country?"

"I have lived in Wiltshire for many years." His voice carried traces of a midlands accent still untamed.

"I understand you have two grown children. Do they live in Wiltshire as well?"

"They live in the southern part of the county."

Anne disliked admitting it, but she agreed with Mr. Collins. Mr. Arnot was not a well looking man. His rough visage owed much to his pock-marked skin, the likely result of his having been infected with the smallpox. The scars were mostly disguised by a rough beard, clipped short, that grew up his cheeks and lent him the unkempt look of a lowly ploughman or wagoner. He was of medium height and powerfully built. His weathered face and close-set eyes gave him a hawkish look, as befitted a man who spent much of his time out of doors. Nor could his temper be fixed—he was polite but restrained, his manner suggesting a degree of indifference. Five minutes of stilted conversation left her hardly better acquainted with the man than when he introduced himself. Tiring of his reticence, she posed a more pertinent question: "Where do you care to begin, Mr. Arnot?"

"If you please, I am interested in hearing your plans for improving your estate." His face settled into a mask of repose.

Anne suspected he was pleased to fix *her* under the microscope, but consented to describe her ideas, the most critical being that of replacing the dairy roof. "The estate has a small herd of dairy cows—ten altogether. Most dairies in this part of the county produce milk, butter, and cheese for local use. The same is true of Rosings." Next she described the scheduled improvements on several tenant farms.

"All worthy projects," he said.

Anne was sure he thought no such thing.

He next asked about the properties that fell to the steward's management. "Also, I wish to know the income they generate."

"The seat itself is close to three hundred acres," she said, sensing he was not in the least impressed with this fact. "Eleven small farms lie in this part of the district, close to the seat, and produce vegetables—mainly beans and peas—for Sevenoaks and Tunbridge and also for the London markets. The remaining fourteen farms lie east of here, a distance of some fifteen miles. Farms near the villages of East Peckam, Yalding, and Hunton produce corn and hops for the London markets. The total farm acreage amounts to roughly four thousand acres. The estate counts one hundred and twenty-two tenants. Most years it yields an annual income close to five thousand pounds."

She felt a prick of pleasure at seeing the surprise in his eyes. "I shall show you the operations of the local farms. The former steward's son, Roger Tench, shall travel with you to visit the distant farms in Middle Kent, since an overnight stay is required."

"I understand," he said kindly.

They fell into a pattern by mutual agreement. Mr. Arnot took command of the carriage as they traveled about the western farms with Mrs. Jenkinson. Anne described the size and success of each enterprise; the number of head of cattle and hogs; and the acreage planted in vegetables. She sat in the carriage while he conversed with the tenants. He was keen to inspect every barn and field and seemed not to mind how long he kept his prospective employer waiting.

On Thursday she asked Roger Tench to serve as guide. He bridled at the request. "Why should I assist the man who will likely take the office that should, by rights, come to me?"

"Because I expect you to do your duty," she replied. "Your father would expect no less of you. See that Mr. Arnot is returned to the house by four o'clock, so that I may introduce him to Lady Catherine. Tomorrow you shall accompany him to East Peckham."

When the candidate was shown into the drawing room Anne introduced him to her mother. "I understand you are from Nottinghamshire," said Lady Catherine. "I have never visited that county, but I imagine its beauty is nothing to Kent's. Would you agree?"

"Yes, my lady. During my short visit I have discovered many Kentish beauties."

Mr. Arnot gave the impression of being in his natural element. He replied to Lady Catherine's penetrating queries and sometimes insulting remarks with the calm spirit of a true gallant. He took no offense, was not overly fawning, and expressed an honest delight in the grounds and environs of Rosings. Anne was piqued by his apparent ease during Lady Catherine's interrogation, when he had been aloof and unfriendly during her own interview. When he left to meet Mrs. James and tour the dairy, Lady Catherine said, "His looks are not so pleasing as those of George Martin Tench, but I daresay he is more knowledgeable. Whether his Northern manners will succeed here remains to be seen."

Chapter 16

Anne reread the letter Darcy had dashed off before departing Rosings. His handwriting was elegant and proper, if a little cramped in style. It was devoid of curls and flourishes:

Rosings Park Friday May —th

Dear Cousin Anne,

I regret having no opportunity of interviewing Mr. George Martin Tench during my stay at Rosings. I was told he was in Town and not expected to return for several weeks. The servants and tenants admit he is often absent from the estate, which fact is a prejudice against him in considering his suitability for the steward's office.—As for his brother, Mr. Roger Tench, I found him mostly well informed about the estate and its holdings and on good terms with the servants and tenants. His chief deficiency is a lack of imagination. He readily sees himself in the role of steward, but his ideas for improving the estate are vague. I sensed in him a discomfort, if not a downright suspicion, of innovation. Of course, my assessment of him is likely biased by my own prejudice in favor of continual agricultural improvement. Thus, I asked myself the question you most want answered: Would I hire this man as steward of Pemberley? I do not waver in my opinion: No. He has potential, but he also has much to learn. He may serve you well

*in the near term, but his fear of seeking agricultural innovations
may hamper the estate's long-term success.*

Yours in family affection, Darcy

Anne examined the closing: *Yours in family affection.* Not, *Yours
Ever.* Not, *Yours most affectionately.* Not, *Your affectionate cousin.* So,
he did not forgive her impudence in the library. Had she erred in
thinking he could be approached for advice? He had never appeared
to resent her ownership of Rosings, as some relatives might do, but
his letter was so impersonal, so analytical, that she wondered: Did
he think her unsuited to the job of choosing a new steward? If that
were true, then he must think her incapable of managing her estate.
She thought back over his visit. His behavior had been unusual, to
say the least. He seemed preoccupied with his own thoughts and was
testy in his dealings with nearly everybody, including the Colonel,
which was most unlike him. A troubling realization struck: her
understanding of his character was so meagre that she had imposed
on him without realizing how much he disliked her doing so. In
truth, they had never discussed farming methods and agricultural
innovations in all the years since Sir Lewis died. Was it not odd
that while they were both landowners, their willingness to share
their ideas and encourage each other was virtually nil? She shook
her head as if to clear cobwebs. She must accept that he did his
duty by writing the letter, but was saddened to know he took no
pleasure in assisting her. Surely a man who held so little regard for
her would not seek her hand in marriage. Well, if he should ever
ask, she would not waver in her answer: No.

A knock came on her parlor door.

"Enter." She folded the letter and shoved it into a drawer.

"Excuse me, ma'am. I wish to share with you my impressions of
the tenant farms in Middle Kent," said Mr. Arnot.

"Come in. Do you care to be seated?" She waved her hand in the
direction of the settee and moved to join him. Although she could
not warm to him, her instincts and common sense led her to invite
him to assume the steward's office, which invitation he accepted with
alacrity on hearing the salary. They parted with the understanding

that he would move into West Lodge within the month and assume his duties immediately thereafter. As he stood to take his leave, he noticed the watercolors on the wall near the door.

"Are these your paintings?"

"Yes," she said simply, being surprised he would comment on them, their composition being mere weeds. At the top was a painting of a plain wild daisy; the lower one, a simple bindweed flower. She had thought nothing could be more challenging than detailing the daisy's dense yellow florets, until she tried to master the bindweed's delicately ruffled rim and bugle-like hollow. Done for her own amusement, she had not anticipated anyone taking notice of them.

"Very good," he said, smiling. "I shall return within the month."

After he departed Anne made her way to the drawing room, where she was greeted by news of the Collinses' expected arrival with their guests, Miss Bennet and Miss Lucas. She told her mother, "I engaged Mr. Arnot as steward. He will serve the estate well, I believe."

"His manners are mostly agreeable for one of his station, but you would have done better to hire George Martin. Arnot will prove a challenge."

Anne had no opportunity to query her meaning, for their guests entered the saloon. Mr. Collins came first, all but clucking like a mother duck, and seated himself in his usual place near her ladyship. He lamented his guests' leave-taking scheduled in two days' time, on Saturday. "Such felicity we have known these past weeks," the rector said as he made a wheezing noise and glanced at Miss Bennet.

Lady Catherine pressed Miss Bennet for detailed information about their travel to Hertfordshire and cautioned against haste in packing. "Nobody these days knows how to pack a trunk properly. You must layer your gowns at the bottom. Next add stockings and undergarments ..."

Is there any topic on which Mama has no opinion? Anne asked herself as she listened to her mother's boring discourse on packing. What next? Remarks on the Royal Assent for the Kent Road Bill?

How did their guests endure her ladyship's unending persuasions? Clearly, Mr. Collins possessed a healthy endurance. After a year's acquaintance, he rushed to approve her ladyship's opinions and advice; indeed, her every banal comment pleased him. Mrs. Collins, in contrast, seemed always to espouse her ladyship's instructions and entreaties, but Anne knew her respectful countenance was a ruse— she found Lady Catherine's manners insufferable. Miss Lucas, a sweet, shy girl who only ever spoke when spoken to, ventured now to ask her ladyship a question about packing a Wellington mantle and Spanish hat.

What of Miss Bennet? She had recovered some of her animation since her last visit to Rosings, owing perhaps to her excitement at the thought of returning to her family at Longbourn. Her conversation suggested a closeness to her father, which Anne understood and envied. She tried picturing Miss Bennet married to her cousin. When Miss Bennet's style and dress were improved by Darcy's ready income, they would make a handsome couple. Even so, their tempers seemed too dissimilar to promote marital felicity, although there was no accounting for the mysteries of attraction, the proof of the puzzle being exemplified by the Collinses' marriage.

But if they did marry, Miss Bennet would become a sister. Hazy mental images of Mr. and Mrs. Darcy at Rosings flickered dimly— conversations in the conservatory, table talk over dinner, walks in the Park. Anne could not imagine a sisterly confidence between them, especially since Miss Bennet's manner toward her had been mostly one of indifference. In truth, engaging Miss Bennet in conversation had been hard going, every effort thwarted by one distraction or another: the Colonel's joke turned Miss Bennet's head, Lady Catherine demanded the lady's attention, Darcy interposed at the tea table, Mrs. Jenkinson cut across their conversation to speak a concern or ask a question.

Anne could not recall an instance when so much effort had been expended for so little effect. Yet, she knew how things stood. She saw herself through Miss Bennet's fine eyes: plain but rich—bookish— ill-favored in health and disposition—boring and dull. She was not vivacious or pretty or talented. Instead, she looked a mouse sitting in the cat's shadow, not moving too quickly, not drawing attention to herself, but gravely favoring a quiet repose.

She wished to be charitable toward Miss Bennet in this, for the lady knew very little of her life at Rosings. Miss Bennet had not buried a dear father, did not suffer from severe rheumatic complaints, had no experience of life without the comfort and liveliness of siblings, and was not responsible for managing a good-sized estate.

A slight smile played across Anne's lips. Of course, Miss Bennet might already have formed an opinion of the heiress of Rosings and found her character wanting. But should Darcy ask for her hand, does Miss Bennet possess the nerve to marry him despite his disagreeable relations? And if she marries him, does she do so for money or love? What will Mr. Collins say if his pretty cousin marries the illustrious Fitzwilliam Darcy?

The thought of Mr. Collins squeezed between his lowly family connections and his aristocratic benefactress amused Anne; but since the possibility of a marriage seemed remote and could not be predicted in any event, she chose to overlook Miss Bennet's aloofness, for she found much to admire in the lady. Miss Bennet claimed no pretension to rank or privilege and met the world as herself—with confidence and a natural vivacity. A second realization struck. Without ever intending to, Miss Bennet had served as a guide in her dealings with Lady Catherine, for she seemed naturally to know how to deflect her ladyship's sharp slings and biting criticism. Perhaps Miss Bennet's style might be adopted as her own.

Yes, Rosings would be dull when Miss Bennet and Miss Lucas left Hunsford, for they had been agreeable guests. Indeed, when they rose to leave, Anne curtsied and shook their hands.

Volume II

Chapter 17

"Has Dawson come downstairs? The woman keeps me waiting."

"She sits in the carriage, your ladyship," said Hobbs.

Lady Catherine fussed with her shawl, threw the butler a stormy look, and strode across the pebbled drive. She refused help climbing into the barouche.

Anne stood on the step from whence she had observed Darcy's departure. She did not so much seek, as hope, for a confidence regarding the purpose of her ladyship's trip to London, but none was forthcoming. As the coach occupants settled themselves, she called, "Safe journey, Mama." Neither her ladyship nor Dawson glanced in her direction as a footman stowed the step, closed the door, and gave the nod to Galton.

It was not in Anne's nature to be morose, and so she returned to the house, feeling more cheerful than she thought she should. For the first time in days she felt well after the trial of her cousins' visit and a bout of rheumatism, the latter having kept her confined until the tenderness in her swollen joints subsided. The dreary days of May with their showers, hail storms, and cooling wind belonged to the past, and the June morning's sunshine made her alive to the joy of summer and the rare prospect of being mistress of the house. She hastened to her parlor, where she spent a pleasant hour organizing gifts for Tilly and Mrs. Purkess. To the latter she penned a long letter in which she reminded her friend to read *Sense and Sensibility*: *I hope the lady will write another novel, for her manner is quite lively and her understanding exceptional.* The missive was laid atop the white cartridge paper and the parcel wrapped for the post.

"May I interrupt, ma'am?" asked Arnot.

"Of course. I was expecting you," she replied, pointing to a wing-backed chair placed near the desk for her steward's use. This being only his second week as steward, they had no fixed routine, but with each meeting Anne felt increasingly that his will prevailed. When she opened her mouth to take charge, he said, "I wish to speak this morning of muck." He removed his turn-pin spectacles and rubbed the bridge of his nose.

"Manure? Surely there are more important matters to be discussed. We have not yet reviewed the rent receipts for the past quarter. Three families—the Owens, the Joyces and the Dawbers—are several months in arrears on their rents."

He took no offense, but balanced his spectacles on his nose with great care. "There is no more important topic, in my opinion."

Anne resigned herself. "Very well. Let us talk of manure. What would you say of it?"

"There is an old Norfolk proverb: 'Muck is the mother of money.' I believe the estate is not so careful with its muck as it could be. Much of it is wasted. I wish to begin a new regimen for increasing the production of muck, for storing it, and for spreading it on fields to improve the crops."

"Cow dung is collected, on the instructions of the former steward. Is this not sufficient?"

"It is sufficient as far as it goes, but the plan does not go far enough toward improving the soil."

"What other actions should be taken?"

"It is good you take an interest in the topic. Are you familiar with the writings of Sir Humphry Davy?"

"I have heard of the man," rejoined Anne.

"Then you know Sir Humphry has very particular and quite scientific ideas about muck, tillage, the planting of turnips and grasses, and the rotation of crops. I also ascribe to the principles laid down by Lord Townshend and Coke of Norfolk, whom I met a few years ago. We shall implement their ideas here."

"Many modern ideas are being used on the estate's farms," she said in defense of Tench. "What is your opinion of Mr. Coke?"

"A smart man. Innovative. He inherited some thirty thousand acres when he was but two and twenty, so he told me, and has served in Parliament for many years. He made his reputation experimenting with grasses and husbandry. Very fond of sheep, he is."

"Will his methods increase the estate's profits?"

"They stand to double your profits at least."

"Double my profits! Surely you jest."

"I do not. It is a proven fact. I have need of your help in this matter, however, for the tenants will resist any change." Arnot was methodical. About each of the estate's natural divisions—the tenant properties and the Home Farm, which included the house, pleasure gardens, vegetable gardens, orchards, stables, dairy, livestock, and woods—he asked pointed questions, wrote notes in a pocket-book, and inquired about those endeavors that had been successful and those that had not.

Did she have the nerve to trust his judgment? Did she trust her own? What was the point of hiring the man if she ignored his suggestions? "I agree to support you," Anne told him, "but I expect to be involved in your decisions."

He bowed stiffly and left her to recall her mother's prediction about his proving a challenge to manage. *His tenure has only just begun,* she reminded herself. *What is his turn today may be mine tomorrow.*

—⁂—

After Arnot departed, Hobbs appeared in the doorway. "Excuse me, Miss. A chitty for you has arrived."

Anne recognized Dr. Bailey's scrawl. He invited her for tea—an event as rare as a comet trail. His hosting a gathering of neighbors was a welcome diversion and suggested the presence of a guest. Her heart raced to think Dr. Granville might have traveled down from Town to call on his friend's uncle. When Mrs. Killick ushered her into the doctor's comfortable parlor, she searched for her heart's desire. Dr. Bailey's garrulous self stood near the window talking to Mr. Collins, Squire Rivers, and another gentleman, hidden from view. The doctor guffawed, clapped Mr. Collins on the back, causing the sober rector to splutter, and turned at perceiving a new arrival. He bowed to Anne, giving her a glimpse of his nephew. It was Mr. Cole, not Dr. Granville, who attended. Had it not been for Tilly taking her arm and pulling her over to the tea table, her disappointment might have been visible to everyone.

Mrs. Collins and Mrs. Roberts welcomed her to their circle and asked after her ladyship's health. While they conversed Mr. Cole approached, his demeanor inviting a conversation. The other ladies drifted toward the lattice window but eyed the couple discreetly.

"I am pleased to see you looking well." His smile radiated warmth, putting Anne at ease.

"Thank you. Have you come to Hunsford to visit your uncle?"

"I rode down yesterday from Chatham. Uncle Bailey wrote me of his interest in poisons."

"Poisons!"

"Yes, he desires information about the effects of vegetable poisons on the respiration of animals. I thought he might like to hear of Mr. Brodie's lecture describing his experiments on how vegetable poisons cause death in rabbits and guinea pigs."

"The poor creatures. How ignoble to torture them."

"You are kind to express compassion for his victims, but surely you appreciate that his studies advance our knowledge of science. His lecture on animal chemistry at the Royal Society in February was most invigorating, for he described the effects of woorara."

"Woorara? What does this odd word mean?"

"Woorara is a plant poison used by certain Indians of South America. The savages coat the points of their spears with this poison to improve their game hunting."

"But what effect does it have on the unfortunate animal? Surely the meat of a poisoned animal would not be safe to eat."

"Brodie found that woorara rubbed into a skin wound on a young cat caused the animal to stop breathing. In fact, the cat appeared quite dead. Yet, so long as its lungs were inflated artificially—to imitate the actions of breathing—the cat lived and recovered. As to how it tasted, I don't believe Brodie investigated that aspect of the cat's character." He raised one eyebrow.

"I should imagine not, but I wonder: Is Dr. Bailey planning some nefarious woorara treatment for his most troublesome patients? I should like to know so that I may introduce myself to another doctor. I might need to travel as far as Canterbury for a medical opinion."

Mr. Cole laughed. "Do not be alarmed. I believe uncle Bailey's interest in woorara is purely scientific."

"That is a great relief."

"I heard my name mentioned. What complaint is being laid at my door?" asked Dr. Bailey, approaching them. His ruddy face was clean-shaven, his eyes clear and bright.

"I have reassured Miss de Bourgh of your clinical soundness, uncle. She no longer fears seeing you sneak about the village with a woorara-tipped spear."

"Of course not. Miss Anne knows I am inclined to choose another poison when I have the chance of it."

Anne gasped at the doctor's frankness, but Mr. Cole merely winked. She had not noticed before how blue were his eyes, how dark his lashes. She returned his silly grin.

Chapter 18

The next afternoon, being balmy, proved a good one for visiting Tilly's local gossips. At Mrs. White's cottage Anne feared she would not be welcomed. "Thank you for handling a difficult situation," she said as she handed over a gift basket of cheese, sausage, wheaten bread, and good long-acre honey from the Rosings kitchen. She collected herself in advance of an apology. "It struck me how utterly alone you were. I came to appreciate the magnitude of the burden you accepted in service to Mrs. Sparke and her family and wish you every success in your practice."

Mrs. White blushed at the tribute. "Thank you. Have you seen Dr. Granville since he delivered Mrs. Sparke's child? I so admired him. He wore no London airs."

"No—no, I have not had that pleasure, but Mr. Cole told me he was quite busy in Town."

Not much remained to be said. Before leaving Mrs. White's cottage, Anne was introduced to James, who protested being removed from his warm crib. Like any nine-month-old child, he bellowed his complaint for the remainder of the visit.

Now Young Kitson maneuvered the phaeton down a narrow, rutted lane strewn with rocks and weeds. An unruly hedge bordered the lane on the left, while the field on the right was wild with scraggly shrubs and tall grasses. Mrs. Beath's cottage was situated in the country past Bardolph Hall, off the main road, where Anne had never ventured. She was unnerved by the land's unrestrained abundance and relieved to have the company of Young Kitson. His equine skills were needed, for the horse became excited by the peculiar smells emanating from the cottage grounds, where animal skins cured on wooden lattices. Mrs. Beath's physic garden lay in irregular plots near the dark abode.

Young Kitson stopped the carriage. A short, thick-set youth with peculiar eyes stirred the contents of a large cauldron with a wooden paddle. Steam encircled his bare arms, but he seemed not to mind the heat.

Anne nodded to him as she carried her basket to the front door. She knocked on the thick oak and stood watching the youth swish the paddle back and forth in the hot pot. The door jerked open. Mrs. Beath's large form filled the doorway. She wiped her hands on a stained apron, saying, "Miss d' Bourgh! Do ye come for more ointment?"

"No, but thank you again for it. My leech bites have healed. I've come in gratitude for your help during Mrs. Sparke's delivery." Anne hesitated, unsure of the proper course.

Mrs. Beath conquered her surprise, stood aside, and waved her hand, giving Anne leave to enter. The single-room cottage was made dark by small windows set beneath a fringe of thatched roof. A ragged curtain separated the beds from the eating area. Tangles of half-dead plants and bundles of dried herbs hung from the rafters.

"Ye find me on wash day. Neddy helps. He is a good lad. Here, sit."

Anne sat on a wobbly chair near the fireplace. "I brought food from the Rosings pantry." She set a basket on the floor at her feet. "Little Marianne thrives and Mrs. Sparke has recovered well. Your poultice did the trick, I think."

"Yes, ma'am," said Mrs. Beath as she picked up a dirty shirt and sat on the only other chair. "I use it often for one thin' or another. It worked for ye mother."

Anne blinked. "Excuse me, it worked for my mother?"

"Aye. It was many years ago, before ye was born. She miscarried a child early in her marriage, ye must know, an' lost two children when they was deliver'd—both boys, one right after the other. Sad times, they were. Before her first birthin' the midwife broke her arm and the village had no apothecary or surgeon, so Dr. Bailey was call'd—Dr. Bailey, him as still lives 'n the village. It was a hard birth. He tried to pull the child through the womb with a long-handl'd tool—I do not know its name—but he struggled mightily. The boy 'ad a large head and tore the lady's privities when he was deliver'd. Ye mother wept like a child when the boy died the next day. She blamed the doctor. I remember her screamin' at him: she wouldna' ever let him touch her ag'in." She paused, her thoughts wandering. "I used the poultice then."

Mrs. Beath moved abruptly to the door to watch Neddy. Being satisfied he was safe, she took her chair, which creaked as she sat down. "For her second birthin', two midwives served, but ye mother suffered a great floodin' until her waters broke. I hear'd it said the navel-string slipp'd low in the womb an' the child was born dead. Reckon the afta'birth came before the child, which mayhap caused its death, poor thing. Her ladyship was weak, very weak, and could hardly walk abou' the room for weeks afta'wards. Both boys are buried in the family plot in Herne Green. Ye might ha' seen their little graves."

"No—no, I have not," stuttered Anne.

"We all thought it great luck when ye was born, for her lady-ship be violent sick wi' a fever. There was quite a bit o' fever that autumn—some folks died 'round these parts. On ye birthday she still sweated a bit and convulsed once. Scar'd us all half to death."

While Mrs. Beath talked of the remedies for stopping convul-sions, Anne absorbed the news. She had brothers buried on land elsewhere. Why had these events been kept secret from her? Did these facts explain her ladyship's resentment of Dr. Bailey? What had her mother said that evening when she confiscated Mrs. White's letter? Her words hinted that if Tilly or her child died, Dr. Bailey was to blame. So, Lady Catherine held Dr. Bailey responsible for her son's death. No wonder she was barely civil to him.

Dr. Bailey's good looks and joking demeanor the previous evening were a reminder of his inconstancy. Some days he resisted the gin spinner's call; other days he succumbed. Who knew what demons tortured him? The sudden death of a child—the son of Sir Lewis, his good friend, and delivered by his own hand—might have driven the doctor to drink. No wonder he would have nothing to do with Tilly's delivery. The doctor had chosen the comfort of ale rather than risk the unpredictable dangers of childbirth.

"Convulsions are not so common as other problems but they c'n carry off a lady right quick," Mrs. Beath was saying.

Anne listened with only one ear, offered little conversation in return, and left the cottage when manners permitted. Her surprise at this news had more handles to it than one.

Chapter 19

The household shuddered when her ladyship returned to Rosings. The parlor maids straightened their caps and stifled their giggles. The cook, who had been stirring her mirth like a roiling stew for a week, hollered at the scullery maids and rapped her spoon on the kettle at the slightest provocation; all ease drained right out of her.

Anne felt a chill wind blow through the house from the moment her mother's strident voice carried up the stairs. She was none the wiser regarding the purpose of her mother's London trip, but did not dwell on the mystery. Many estate duties occupied her time. It being near the end of June, she and Arnot had settled to a routine. One humid morning Arnot led the conversation, as usual: "I will commission a four-coultered plough from a ploughwright in Sevenoaks and hire a Tunbridge fellow to fashion a new drill-box for the sowing of seeds. The estate's implements are outdated. Newer ones should be tried by one or two tenant farmers—Joyce and Dawber might do—as a means of increasing yield."

While acknowledging his expertise, Anne sometimes could not abide his confidence. "How familiar are you with the turn-wrest plough, which has long been used in Kent?" she asked.

"I have not seen one working the fields. Newer ploughs have the advantages of achieving good furrow depth and making the soil more friable."

"New ploughs often perform poorly in West Kentish soil," she explained. "The Suffolk plough, for instance, has been tried here repeatedly without much success."

"I thought you wished to make improvements."

"I do, but before we rush to commission a new plough, I believe there is merit in talking with tenant farmers about their experiences in the fields with the turn-wrest plough."

He cocked his eyebrows. "You are prepared to accompany me into the fields?"

"I wish to hear firsthand the farmers' comments on their plough-ing experiences. Tell me why you choose Joyce and Dawber. Why do you begin with the most irascible farmers on the worst land? The fact that they are behind on their rents is proof of their laziness, is it not?"

"Joyce and Dawber are behind on their rents because their farming habits are poor, not because they are lazy or because their land is inferior to land farmed by more successful tenants. Their land's yield is low because they have not used muck properly and their ploughs are old-fashioned. They still sow seed by hand!" He sketched his ideas for helping them adopt his innovations.

Anne declined to be conquered by his sudden ill temper. "Do you have any particular instructions for our visit to the Joyce and Dawber farms?" she asked, returning his cool gaze.

Arnot looked over her person quite frankly. "Be agreeable and wear a simple gown and sturdy boots—nothing so pretty as what you wear this morning. You are liable to be dirty by the time you return to the house." At Anne's offended look, he stood suddenly, his chair legs scraping the floor. "We shall leave tomorrow morning at nine o'clock, if that suits you. Tench will accompany us."

"Roger Tench? Does he have an interest in these new methods?"

"I am not certain of it, but I am determined to find the proper role for him on the estate."

"What is your opinion of George Martin Tench?"

"I have yet to meet the man."

Anne wondered, not for the first time, what Arnot thought of her capabilities. Since he gave no hint of his opinion, she was not likely ever to know.

Chapter 20

"Why are you dressed like a dairy maid?" Lady Catherine tossed an icy look at her daughter. "You look ridiculous. Whose hat is that?"

Anne had hoped to escape the house before her mother came downstairs for breakfast. "Arnot and I are traveling to the Joyce and Dawber farms today. I am dressed for walking in the fields. The hat belongs to Tilly and will serve me well."

"Miss, excuse me," said Hobbs. "Arnot has brought the carriage around front."

"Then I had best join him." She took a sip of tea. "I shall return in a few hours, Mama. Don't wait luncheon for me."

"Have you lost your wits? You cannot roam the countryside unchaperoned."

"Roger Tench accompanies us. He can chaperon me."

"You cannot be serious. Mrs. Jenkinson must accompany you. Vaughn, fetch Mrs. Jenkinson at once."

Vaughn nodded, annoyed at being forced out just as the excitement began.

"I will not allow Mrs. Jenkinson to join me." Anne tied the hat ribbons under her chin. "She is noisy and impatient. She tires quickly of outdoor activities and will be cross, whether she sits in the carriage or joins us in the fields. Her presence will annoy everybody—me, most of all."

"I brook no disagreement. She shall accompany you."

"There is no cause to disturb her, Mama. I travel on estate business with my steward, just as Papa did. Anyone seeing us together on the road will understand."

"You will find, my dear, that most people are perfectly pleased to misunderstand."

"Then I cannot be held accountable for their willful twisting of the facts," she rejoined, rising to follow Hobbs.

"In the end, you will be held accountable, whether you care to be or not. Mrs. Jenkinson will join you," said Lady Catherine to her daughter's retreating figure.

Her ladyship is too conscious of propriety. I have half a mind to act a harlot, at least until Mrs. Jenkinson catches up with me. Her frowning face exposed her thoughts, for Arnot's smile vanished as she approached the carriage. He handed her up onto the bench and climbed up after her, wondering what the old ogre had said to upset his mistress. *Best not dwell on it.* A call to the horse put the wheels in motion. Roger Tench trailed behind on horse.

The drive to Dawber's farm took the trio north, away from Hunsford, and then east into the dale. Farms, interspersed with thick stands of old-growth trees, lay on either side of the road. The sun's warmth grew, giving promise to the prospect of a glorious summer day. At the Dawber farm, Anne greeted the farmer, a wiry man whose smile revealed a missing tooth.

"Show us your plough," commanded Arnot.

The farmer and his visitors gathered around the implement. Roger Tench kicked the share, as if he might startle it to life.

Arnot gave him a fierce look before saying, "Tell me about this plough."

"Well, sir, this plough be drawn by six horses. So many be needed 'cause the earth does not yield easy-like to the share." When nobody said anything, he went on: "This here be the beam—the chep—the gallows—the tow." He patted the parts, almost with affection.

"Yes, yes, I can name a plough's parts. Have you tried other ploughs?" Arnott asked.

"Nay, but some 'ave."

Arnot's look was ambiguous. "Where is your field?"

Dawber led them through a thin stand of trees to his plot. The sun was nearly directly overhead and the air was hot and drowsy with bees. A grasshopper leaped ahead with each step of Anne's boot, its hurried antics bringing her joy. She felt a thrill of satisfaction at being landowner and Master as she she stood at the field's edge and watched the hay mowers and tedders working the long rows.

"How long have you been farming this land?"

"Goin' on twelve years." Dawber gave Anne a gap-toothed grin and tugged his forelock.

When the group returned to the farm house, they found Mrs. Jenkinson sitting in the phaeton, looking none too pleased. Anne smiled at her but stood next to the carriage, waiting for Arnot to hand her in. She would not give up the chance to learn about ploughing merely to satisfy her mother's honor and appease her companion.

Arnot settled his mistress in the carriage, as was clearly her wish, and climbed up next to her. When they reached the road, Anne asked, "What is your assessment of Dawber?"

"He is confident, but the fact remains: his yields are low. A new type of plough will improve his situation."

"Ploughing methods differ across Kent. In the east, four horses are sufficient and most farmers plough more than an acre a day. Our western soil is full of flint and clay, which makes it hard to work."

Arnot held his peace, not being a man to discount a woman's opinion out of hand. Not many young ladies could speak so confidently about farming practices; still fewer had the wherewithal or drive to conquer the landowner's business. If he wanted to make a success of it here, he must be prudent. Little would be gained by getting his back up over ploughs, but he might risk a tease. "Dawber likes you well enough."

"I am no fiend," Anne said, grinning.

On their return to the house, her thanks were sincerely meant.

"You did well today, Miss de Bourgh. We shall make a farmer of you yet."

"It would make me proud," she called.

Chapter 21

The weather proved disagreeable following Anne's tour of the farms. Nearly every day was marked by a cool, steady drizzle or sudden storm. The damp aggravated her rheumatism. She took refuge in her bedchamber, her knees and ankles swollen and tender, her body weak, her spirit made low by a general malaise. She lay in bed, the sweat trickling down her temples; every leg movement brought an agony. Her disposition soured with pain and fever and the fear she might be confined for several weeks.

Dr. Bailey came to the house. His treatment consisted of purgatives and alkaline salts interspersed with doses of lemon juice, sulphur, and mercury.

"I was afraid your mother might not allow me to come upstairs," he said, his eyes red and rheumy. "But I warned her: the rheumatic poison might carry you off to the graveyard if you were forced downstairs on my account."

Anne nearly joked in return: Mama would not shed a tear at my passing, for then she would be rid of a troublesome child. When Shaw returned from escorting the doctor downstairs, Anne advised cutting each dose in half, since she was not sure his mind was quite right. A few days later she applied for help to Mrs. Beath, who advised a daily gruel of softened oats and linseed for reducing the joint swelling and redness. Whether her mealy concoction or the return of fair weather did the trick, Anne could not say, but she was pleased to return to the world and the serene rhythm of summer.

When showers swept across the land, she spent hours in the conservatory painting flowers and fruit or visited Tilly and Mrs. Collins. In fair weather she joined Arnot in his tour of the estate farms. They queried tenant farmers and gauged the crop growth and argued good-naturedly over farming innovations. Like as not, they traveled alone, for Mrs. Jenkinson had grown tired of trailing behind in the phaeton. Ploughing and planting bored her. It being such agreeable weather and her having the advantage of a carriage all to herself, she found excuses for pursuing her own interests. If Lady Catherine should ever demand a report, she would offer reassurance: she detected no inappropriate regard or flirtatious glances between the daughter of the house and the estate steward. Indeed, the twosome were decidedly dull, finding hardly anything to speak of except the crops and weather.

Near summer's end Anne joined Arnot one hot and muggy morning. Billowing clouds rose overhead as mistress and steward stood in the farmer's field and discussed the virtues of planting lucerne and sainfoin. On the return to Rosings they traveled a narrow road bordering an open field, all the while debating Sutton's willingness to plant grasses for enriching the soil. Dark clouds overtook them. Low rumblings of thunder, at first faint, grew urgent, and the light became tinged an odd greenish color. Tree limbs heaved suddenly as the wind launched a strong assault. The clouds released a rain shower so dense the horse was spooked.

"Take the reins, while I calm the horse," cried Arnot, standing up in the carriage.

Anne struggled to slow the horse's wild stamps. The mare reared up, her head tossing wildly, her eyes rolled back in alarm. She settled only when Arnot grabbed the harness ribbons. "Let me lead her," he shouted over a crash of thunder.

Anne relaxed her grip and peered through the slashing rain. The steward pulled the animal into the field under the wind-tossed trees. "I see a lean-to. Let us shelter there," he shouted as lightning blazed overhead. Arnot wrested the horse forward as the wind thrashed the trees and rain ran in rivulets across the field. They were both soaked to the skin before they reached shelter. He looked up at her. "Are you well?"

"I'm drenched but hale."

As the rain marched in sheets across the field, she observed Arnot tending quietly to the horse. He patted the animal's neck and rubbed her forehead, all the while murmuring in her twitching ear. The mare whickered as if agreeing with his view of the situation. While calming her, Arnot appeared not in the least self-conscious about his clinging clothes.

Anne had never seen a vigorous, well-formed man wet to the skin. She admired his physique—his strong shoulders and muscled arms—and watched his hand play over the mare's neck and mane. He had a working man's hands, rough and suntanned; yet they were gentle and caressing, too. When he lifted his eyes to hers, she feared he might have guessed what she was thinking and shifted her gaze across the wet grasses. He had kind eyes.

"Are you chilled, Miss Anne?"

"Not yet."

When the rain eased, he patted the mare's flank and checked the harness. "My daughter, Eliza, would not have been half so calm as you in this squall. She is easily spooked by wild storms." He climbed into the carriage. "The rain has subsided. Let us return to Rosings."

Anne considered what she had heard. What did it mean that he had called her 'Miss Anne'? Only a handful of men called her so—her uncle, her cousins, Dr. Bailey and Mr. Sullen, while he lived. Did Arnot speak from affection or had he forgotten himself? She was careful not to read too much into it, but equally she was alert to the event's being unusual. In truth, she was not sure how she felt about it.

Chapter 22

"Leave us," ordered Lady Catherine, giving Shaw a piercing look.

"Did you not think to knock, Mama?" Anne sat at her dressing table. She caught Shaw's wary eye in her looking glass before the maid curtsied and left them alone.

Lady Catherine said, "I come to tell you I depart for Town on Wednesday. I shall return next week."

"Would you like me to accompany you?" What concern would take her mother to London for the second time this summer?

"No. I am perfectly able to travel alone. My reason for speaking privately has to do with your wanton behavior." Her ladyship scowled. "I hear reports of your traveling alone with Arnot. Mrs. Whitfield told me yesterday her son saw the two of you on the road to Smockden. I at first believed the report nothing more than the vicious fancy of a village gossip, until I interrogated Mrs. Jenkinson, who confessed she has not always accompanied you on these excursions. What is worse, Mr. Collins saw you and Arnot pass the parsonage last week. He was scandalized to observe my daughter frolicking with a male servant. Have you no shame? Heaven forbid if Darcy should hear of it. He would be deeply offended to know his intended bride paraded her wantonness before half the county."

"Frolicking? Is that the word he used? Really, Mama, you know Mr. Collins well enough to recognize his love of a good exaggeration.

And what business is it of his? He is not my protector. I go with my steward to evaluate the agricultural progress made on the estate's holdings. Do you not wish me to enhance our income? Are you not pleased to enjoy the estate's profits? After all, its success ensures your comfort."

Lady Catherine frowned at this ploy. "You might well smirk, but what would Sir Lewis say of your behavior if he were alive?"

Anne felt her blood quicken at the mention of her father.

"As you give no thought to your reputation," Lady Catherine continued, "I intend to thwart your wishes. I shall speak with Arnot and demand of him a vow to refuse your company on future ventures." She looked triumphant.

Anne stifled a laugh. Surely her mother was not so naive as to think she could persuade Arnot to go against his employer's wishes.

"You are amused by this scandal?"

Anne rose from her bench and turned her back to the looking glass. "Whether you are happy on this point or not, the fact remains: Papa appointed *me* tenant for life. He did not pass the estate to any son of the de Bourgh family." She let her brutish words sink in. "He bequeathed his property to me, his only child, with the expectation that I marry and have children. Until Rosings passes to my son, Papa would expect me to perform all the duties of a Master. If I do not accompany Arnot—especially now, when he is meeting the tenants and building his reputation in the district—I risk losing control of my own affairs. My being in the fields with him is the best way of learning his character. I must be assured that he is of the same moral persuasion as Tench—a man I trusted with my life. Only by pursuing this course can I sustain the estate's reputation, even if, in the process, I diminish my own."

"How selfish of you to give so little thought to our family's reputation," said Lady Catherine.

"What choice do I have? If I succeed as Master, I am derided for wearing a man's boots. If I fail, I am scorned for being an empty-headed woman. Which path would you pursue?"

Lady Catherine looked half a mind to say something, but instead she swept up her gown and stormed from the room.

Chapter 23

A cock crowed in the distance, its raspy call awakening Anne. The room was dark, a sure sign the approaching dawn was far from imminent, as was only to be expected in September. Anne settled herself under the heavy covers and sought a return to dreamy depths, but sleep eluded her. After a few minutes, she rose, pulled on a wrapper, and poked the ashes in the grate. The coals were too cold to come to life. It being early to ring for Shaw, she eased open the heavy door and tripped down the hall past her mother's empty bedchamber. At the last door she paused to listen to the creaks and groans of an aging house before turning the heavy handle and entering her father's bedchamber. This was a place of solace and contemplation, a sanctum her mother had avoided since Sir Lewis's burial.

Anne took her bearings in the gloom. An ornate four-post bedstead shrouded with blue damask curtains dominated the room. Nearby stood a tall chest of drawers in the French style. She moved to it, turned the key, and opened the top doors. Inside, her father's banyan lay folded neatly. She lifted it and smelled the fabric. No lingering traces of him remained. She slipped it on, feeling the silk brocade swallow her petite frame. She fingered the wooden buttons and probed the small empty pocket. Her father had worn the garment nearly every day when he came down to breakfast, and it was a comfort to feel its warmth about her.

Next she moved to the handsome mahogany writing table positioned near the east-facing windows. She opened a drawer, removed a tinder-box, and struck a candle.

Despite the room's chill, she was prepared to linger here and so sank into the desk chair where her father had spent his mornings contemplating the day's scheduled events. As always, her first thought was of him. The particulars of his accident would never be known. Dr. Bailey believed his horse had shied at a slithering snake underfoot or the nearby crack of gunshot. In its terror the animal reared and tossed its rider into a pile of felled wood. Sir Lewis's neck was broken. For many weeks after his burial the pain of his death lay heavy as an elephant's foot on her heart. His passing was everywhere felt. Hunsford residents recalled his calmness of temper. The Rosings tenants and staff missed his laconic humor and fair-mindedness. His friends regretted the loss of one who could laugh at himself. Anne missed his steady affection, but time had dulled the ache and his memory could be recalled without distress.

The recollection of the events of this day—the anniversary of his death—brought Anne to this room. She pulled a worn book bound in red leather from a drawer. It was his diary—a ramshackle collection of thoughts, queries, and decisions regarding the running of the estate since the new century's beginning. His notations were sometimes itemized neatly in lists; elsewhere, fragments were scribbled in his slanting script, dashed off before he forgot, a jumble of hurried ideas. His last entry was dated 10 Septr 1807, two days before his death.

She turned to the first few pages. It was as she remembered: there was no mention of sons, no record of graves.

Here is a mystery, she said to herself as she gazed at the east-facing window, where a pink-tinged sky heralded the dawn. Lord Matlock once told her the de Bourgh family's residence had been situated near Herne Greene but was destroyed by a lightning-sparked fire only a year after her parents married. Lord Matlock recalled his sister's unending complaints about the many inconveniences of living with her husband's sister while a new residence was being built near Hunsford: "Catherine said it was the worst year of her life." Indeed, it must have been so, for her ladyship never spoke of that time. Being very curious about the place and since her mother was in Town, Anne had approached Arnot for a favor: "Would you drive me to Herne Green?"

"If it is important to you, I shall do so," he had said.

A muffled clang reached her from somewhere below. She set the room to right and left her father's sanctum. There was plenty of time to dress for the drive.

—m—

A prettier autumn day could not be conjured from the imagination. The sky sparkled, its blue hue so bright it burned the eyes. Birches and oaks waved their greens and golds, while the sun shed its warmth like a summer's day. The drive to Herne Green took them north along the post road toward Bromley and then east through densely forested land. They rode in companionable silence until arriving in Wartsbury Hill, where Anne queried the curate about the location of the graveyard. "We are within two miles of the old church," she told Arnot.

They continued along the road and took the right branch of a fork down an ill-used lane. Woods encroached from both sides, the tree branches forming a canopy that provided a cooling shade. When the lane ended, Arnot maneuvered the mare in a tight turn and called "Whoa!" All was quiet. The harness jingled when the mare snorted.

"According to the curate, that is the shortest trail," said Anne, pointing to the left. "Will the mare be safe while we walk the trail?"

"It seems quiet enough. We shall trust to Providence." He led the way into the woods, his musket resting on his arm as if he hunted quail or pheasant. The trail was worn in some places and overgrown in others. When the path narrowed, he pulled her through the brambles, stopping to wrestle her gown from their thorny clutches; later, he steadied her as she climbed over a fallen tree. They had been walking for perhaps ten minutes when the trail took an abrupt turn into a shady clearing, where the hard packed earth had no tolerance for grass. Two men leaned against a decayed tree. One man jumped to his feet, his knife at the ready.

"Easy, gentlemen," Arnot said. "We are searching for an old grave-yard in these parts."

The men, both now on their feet, said nothing but stared as if seeing ghosts. Their homespuns were filthy and ragged. The taller man cradled his arm against his chest, his face a grimace of pain. Dried blood specked the cuff and sleeve of his shirt.

"We kno' nothin' of graves," said the knife-holder. His eyes flicked to Anne's face. "You got a pretty miss there."

"We want no trouble," said Arnot. He stood facing the men, his left hand folded over his musket, his eyes boring into theirs. The gimblet-eyed man waved his knife and jerked his head toward the trail head; his confederate, understanding the mute command, stumbled toward the path. Arnot raised his musket. "Leave the carriage alone."

The injured man stopped in his tracks.

Anne's heart thumped in her chest. Her legs quivered. Let me not faint!

Nobody moved or spoke. The armed man lurched forward, a sneer showing sickly teeth. Arnot pointed his musket at the man's chest.

"Beath, leave 'em be," said the injured man wearily. "We need to be movin' on."

"Beath?" croaked Anne. "Are you kin to Mrs. Mary Agnes Beath of Hunsford?" Seeing the leader's startled look, she asked, "You are Neddy's brother, then?"

The leader was thrown off by her questions. In the awkward silence, Arnot spoke: "Put your knife away. You shall show us the graveyard and earn a shilling for your trouble."

Their progress was slow, since Beath was obliged to support his friend. Arnot walked behind the pair, his musket pointed at their backs; he left his mistress to fend for herself, which Anne thought prudent. A hundred yards farther along, the crumbling remnants of the old church and its graveyard rested under ancient trees, the stones and decayed timbers protected by tall seedlings and fallen tree limbs. Arnot motioned the men off to one side.

Anne pushed through tangled grasses in search of her family's plot. Many headstones could not be read, the inscriptions marred by wind and rain or covered by lichen and moss. Some tilted precariously; one lay cracked upon the uneven ground. Eventually, she found a tall, pointed monument whose chiseled inscription read: *To the Memory of John Edward de Bourgh, who died the 15th of February, 1776, Aged 57 Years, and of His Wife Henrietta Evans de Bourgh, who died the 7th of November, 1800, Aged 71 Years.* These were her grandparents, two souls about whom she knew almost nothing. Her grandmother's death was not that long ago, yet she had not been told of her passing.

A small gravestone nearby was buried by debris. She tossed several rotted branches aside and shoved a cluster of faded cow parsley to one side. The inscribed names read *To the Memory of John Lewis de Bourgh, who died on the 24th of April, 1783, Aged 1 Day, and Joshua Walter de Bourgh, who died on the 30th of August, 1784—His Sweet Lips Never Drew Breath. Beloved and Lamented.*

Her brothers: John and Joshua.

A bubble of grief rose in her throat to picture her father standing in this spot, looking down on the newly-mounded soil. What heartache he must have felt on losing two sons to the whims of Fate. Had he felt disappointed to have only a daughter survive? No, she could not believe it. Despite what her mother had said to Miss Bennet—"Daughters are never so much consequence to a father …"—she knew he had adored her.

How different might her life have been with brothers in the house. She preferred to believe she would have found in them the ease of companionship she knew with Colonel Fitzwilliam, but, like as not, she might have felt estranged from their realm, much as she did with Darcy.

Of course, had either of them lived, Rosings would not be hers.

The boys' names played through her head as she followed Arnot through the forest. True to his word Arnot tossed a coin at Beath. On the return to Rosings Anne considered Lady Catherine's trials. Her mother's character seemed fixed as irascible and mean-spirited, but, surely, she had not always been so. She had once been young and newly married. Had she been happy in her married life or did she endure Sir Lewis out of duty? Had the loss of two sons fueled her bitterness? Did she resent her sister, Lady Anne, for delivering a son, the Darcy heir? The questions swarmed like hornets, each flinging a sting. So engrossed was she by thoughts of her mother that she lost all sense of time.

Arnot held his peace until they reached the Bromley road and turned south toward Hunsford. His kind words fell on a tender heart: "I have been told your father was an excellent man, a generous man, and good to his tenants."

Tears pricked her eyes but she could not speak, merely nodding in mute appreciation.

Chapter 24

"What goes on here?" rasped Lady Catherine as she swept into the morning room with all the éclat of a duchess. Her indignation at being ignorant of the proceedings was palpable.

"I invited our neighbors for supper this evening," replied Anne as she studied the menu. "I wish to visit with Lady Metcalfe, and it has been an age since we last entertained Squire Rivers. I invited Mrs. Venables, of course, and the Sparkes, the Collinses, and Dr. Bailey, along with the Mostyns and Admiral Powlett and his wife, the tenants of Bardolph Hall."

"This idea is ridicu—"

"Dessert will be served on the terrace," said Anne, cutting across her ladyship's objection, "for the weather is favorable—perhaps the last good weather we shall have this autumn. Had I known your travel plans, I would have chosen a different evening, but as you did not share with me the date of your return, I proceeded according to my own wishes."

"Surely you realize it is not proper to introduce the Mostyns to Lady Metcalfe. They are mere tenants, and Squire Rivers is eccentric, to say the least."

"Squire Rivers *is* an odd body, but the fact remains: he and the Mostyns are our neighbors. The Mostyns have lived at Guston Hill for six months, and it is time we became acquainted. Did you know

Mr. Mostyn served by royal patent as chief engineer of England until he retired in the county? Surely a man who served at the King's request is worthy of friendship, and we seldom include Squire Rivers in our activities, which reflects poorly on us. Thank you, Mrs. Faber. I make no changes to the menu. Please set aside a bottle of spiritous liquor for Dr. Bailey; he prefers something a little stronger than tea in the evening."

"Yes, ma'am." Mrs. Faber's smile lent support.

Lady Catherine settled at her writing table. "I cannot approve your inviting Dr. Bailey to the house. The man is despicable."

"I enjoy his company."

The trip to Herne Green had sparked memories of how the estate anchored the district during her father's lifetime. Sir Lewis was fond of a good party and opened the house regularly to friends and neighbors. The idea for the supper came to her after realizing how decidedly odd were her mother's ideas about entertaining. Her ladyship rushed to invite the Collinses and their guests ("mere commoners") to Rosings, but seldom hosted Lord and Lady Metcalfe or other notable neighbors. Anne decided it was time to improve their standing in the neighborhood.

It proved to be a pleasant September evening. Nearly everybody was in high spirits and disposed to be kind and tolerant.

The Mostyns seemed a typical middle-aged couple. Mr. Mostyn was a soft-spoken, unassuming sort of fellow with a gentle smile. He was deliberate in his speech, as might be expected of an engineer used to ruminating on the least little thing, whereas Mrs. Mostyn hardly drew breath. True to the navy, Admiral Powlett's commanding voice could be heard across the lawn, the volume best suited to carry over the boom of cannon fire and the confused shouts of subalterns. He interrogated Squire Rivers about the decline of game in the district due to poaching, while Mrs. Powlett looked on her husband with stalwart affection and sipped her tea.

Anne assumed her duties with grace, facilitated the introductions and conversations, and anticipated her guests' comfort. The simple act of performing as mistress of the house made her happy. Teacup in hand, she joined her neighbor near the potted orange trees.

"Lady Catherine does not seem herself today," said Lady Metcalfe. "Is she quite well?"

"So far as I know, my mother is well. Perhaps she struggles to adjust to our local fellowship after spending a week among London's more rarified society."

"Miss Anne, I don't care for that tone of voice. A lady does not disparage her family in public, although I know you think of me as family." Lady Metcalfe looked determined to speak her mind. "I believe Lady Catherine is concerned for your welfare and with reason. Indeed, I hear talk of you and none of it good."

Anne gave her a sly look.

"I see you understand me. You were seen frequently this summer traveling alone with Arnot to visit your properties. I know you too well to suspect you of any tender feelings toward him, but many people in the district will believe the worst about your character. You must be more discreet. If you were a man it would not make a whit of difference, but as you are unmarried, it behooves you to be circumspect, and you cannot be sure of his intentions. You are a wealthy young lady and fair game for any fortune-hunter who cares to dishonor your engagement to Darcy." Lady Metcalfe pulled Anne's arm through hers. "Now, I have a proposal to make, one that meets with Lady Catherine's approval."

Anne listened while her neighbor expounded on the benefits to herself of agreeing to the idea. When Squire Rivers interrupted their discourse to inquire after Lord Metcalfe, she excused herself to speak with Tilly. "What a lovely shawl, Mrs. Sparke. It complements your violet eyes."

"Thank you. It is a gift from a rational creature."

Anne laughed. "You have not called me a rational creature in years. I am sure I don't deserve it."

"That may well be true," Tilly teased, "particularly when I consider a certain report I heard about you."

"What report?"

"Arnot is a suitor."

"Not you, too! I am plagued by innuendoes and insinuations on every side. He is my steward. We have done nothing more than conduct estate business. One would think the banns were being posted even as we speak."

"You don't hold a special affection for him?"

"Goodness, no. What makes you think such a thing?"

"Mrs. Venables spoke of it."

"Truly?" Anne turned to stare at the lady. "I had not imagined Mrs. Venables so taken with local gossip, but she likes to believe the worst of me. Would it be so bad if I did?"

Tilly gasped. "You joke, surely. I accept that you don't wish to marry Mr. Darcy, but you cannot marry your steward. The whole county would be convulsed."

"I must disagree with you. The county would be in a twitter for a few days or weeks but then return to its own selfish concerns. My mother, I concede, might require a doctor's care."

"Be serious, Anne. Are you developing feelings for Arnot?"

"Not amorous feelings, no, although I admire him. He is a good man, Tilly—steady in his estate duties and fair in his dealings with my tenants and staff. Mrs. Faber speaks highly of him."

"Mrs. Faber might be setting her cap at him herself."

"I had not considered it, but you may be right. Tell me, how are you feeling these days?" Anne asked, eager to direct the conversation down a different path.

"I am mostly well, but some days feel a general malaise. Perhaps it is the weather, so hot and sticky for September." She fanned herself lazily. "Lady Metcalfe looks very well today."

"Yes, and she has invited me to visit Dodford Meare. Apparently, Lady Catherine readily supported the idea. I believe the ladies conspire to remove me from Arnot's influence."

"Will you go?"

"I am sorely tempted, but I do hate to give my mother pleasure."

Chapter 25

"Welcome, Miss de Bourgh. My name is Ross. Please follow me while Conner assists your maid and companion." He marched sedately up the steps, not a hair in his powdered wig jiggling.

Anne struggled to match his gait as they crossed the reception hall on the *piano nobile* of Dodford Meare. "This is the Marble Room," the butler told her, as if she could not surmise the fact herself from the black and white marbled floor and oversized Greek and Roman statues arranged artfully about the space. She tried not to gape as they passed under the domed, frescoed ceiling and proceeded up the carved, red-carpeted staircase into the guest wing. The size, opulence, and beauty of the house was astonishing: soaring windows and high ceilings, faded wall tapestries and polished armor, ancestral portraits, and everywhere, marble statuary, ornate pedestals, heraldic emblems, and magnificent sprays of fresh-cut flowers. This was a seat of money and power to rival her uncle's estate in Wiltshire. She felt a twinge of sympathy for Miss Lucas, who had been intimidated by the grand drawing room at Rosings Park.

"Lady Metcalfe has placed you here," said Ross as he opened a door and allowed her to enter the bedchamber. "If something is not to your liking, please inform me or the housekeeper, Mrs. Mitchell. Your maid shall attend you directly. Lady Metcalfe anticipates welcoming you at supper, which will be held in the Gold dining room at six o'clock. If you are recovered from your journey before that time, you may join the other guests on the south lawn." He bowed and closed the door.

The room, though not large, was nicely apportioned. A toile pattern of French design decorated the walls, and the ornate French furniture was delicate and feminine. The fireplace was stunning, its mantel and surround being ornately carved and polished to a high gloss; the mantel itself was a work of art: three narrow shelves stepped up from its base, each displaying a collection of blue and white Delft earthenware teapots, cups, and vases. She thought of Hunsford's rector. What price would Mr. Collins place on such luxury?

Her bedchamber overlooked the broad south lawn and formal gardens, which gave way to thick woods framing a small but pretty lake. A dozen guests milled around a white tent stationed on the lawn. She watched them pair and part. Only Mrs. Venables and Lady Metcalfe were recognizable from where she stood. The prospect of introducing herself into this society was daunting, for she knew Mrs. Venables and her set moved in the most fashionable London circles and would not be much impressed with a plain country miss, even if the lady was an heiress. Well, now that she had arrived she must proceed. "All travel has its advantages," she said aloud, believing Dr. Johnson's insight proved a reminder of her long-held desire to be out more in the world.

The door opened behind her.

"Lor', Miss, this is a pretty room," cried Shaw. "Lowrie, the upstairs maid who is helping me get organized, said this is Lady Metcalfe's favorite guest room."

Anne admitted its charm and, after the hot water arrived, submitted to Shaw's ministrations. The layering on of clean white sarcenet removed all traces of grime and ill-humor. Leaving Shaw to finish unpacking the trunks, she made her way to the south side of the house. Liveried servants opened the French windows for her, giving access to the stone terrace, which she crossed quickly. As she started down the steps to the lawn, her eyes roved the crowd in search of her hosts. She need not have worried about going unnoticed, for Lord Metcalfe advanced in her direction, a grin on his face.

"Ah, Miss de Bourgh. Welcome to Dodford Meare. Your travel was not too onerous, I trust? No highwaymen on the road?" He took her hands and kissed her cheek.

Anne curtsied, laughing. "None, sir. Only a very talkative maid who drove Mrs. Jenkinson and me quite mad."

"Better a garrulous maid than a pertinacious valet or a masked robber, I say. Now, my lady has been asking for you, as has Lawrence. Let us find them. But first, you must have a glass of champagne." On sensing a protest, he said, "I insist, especially as much trouble was taken to smuggle the stuff to England and across the southern counties. No mean feat, I warn you. Ah, there is Lawrence. Lawrence," he shouted, "I have found our Kentish neighbor." He pulled Anne across the lawn.

—m—

Lawrence Ormiston, the family's second son, possessed golden curls, a ready smile, and a pleasing manner. He added his warm welcome before taking her to greet Lady Metcalfe, who expressed every delight in having her dear neighbor at Dodford Meare. He next introduced her to two of his closest friends, a Mr. Nelkins and one Mr. Palmer.

"They traveled down from London to breathe our fine air and perfect their shooting," said Mr. Ormiston with mock seriousness.

Mr. Palmer protested immediately, claiming the fine food as his main purpose for traveling to Buckinghamshire, whereas Mr Nelkins joked it was the comfortable beds he sought, for he knew the company was uncertain. Their unabashed nonsense reminded her of Colonel Fitzwilliam.

"You are from Kent," said Mr. Nelkins, "the Garden of England. Do you have a pretty garden, then?"

"I have a garden that requires constant pruning and replanting, which activities seem to require a dozen gardeners. Is not that the way of most gardens?"

"That has been my experience," said Mr. Nelkins. "Palmer here knows nothing of gardening. Why, he could not tell a forget-me-not from a fence post."

Mr. Palmer raised his champagne glass. "True. But I can tell a pheasant from pepperwort, which is a damn sight more useful."

"Gentlemen, gentlemen," said Mr. Ormiston in a warning tone, "mind your language. A lady is present." The men bowed their half-hearted contrition for misbehaving. "Come, I shall introduce you to her ladyship's sister." With these words he escorted Anne under the canopy's shade. "Don't be offended by my friends. They are harmless sorts."

"I am not insulted. They are in high spirits."

"Yes, well—they often are." He grinned as he accepted a chilled glass of champagne from a servant and handed it to her. "You are looking very well, if I may say so."

"Thank you. I feel refreshed. Has Mrs. Ormiston come to Dodford Meare as well?"

"She wished to accompany me, but I forbade it. She is in the family way, and I thought she should not attempt the rigors of travel." His coloring heightened in response to her sincere well wishes. "I anticipate your next question. Clarinda and William are here; Charles and his family will join us in a few days. Come, you will enjoy meeting my aunt." He escorted her to the far side of the tent where several guests stood talking.

"Aunt, may I introduce our Kentish neighbor? This is Miss de Bourgh."

Anne curtsied to the lady and offered a greeting. She liked Mrs. Goodall's appearance, her being a handsome, elegant woman, perhaps a little older than Lady Metcalfe, and the very model of respectability.

"I understand you are a keen gardener. If the weather holds fair, I hope you will allow me to show you the knot garden. It is quite charming."

Anne expressed her delight in the idea. She was then introduced to the other guests in the circle: Lady Braybrooke, a petite, older woman with wavy white hair whose deportment hinted at a strong personality; Mr. Filbert, the parish vicar, and his wife and daughter; Lady Coldham, who hailed from the southern part of the county near High Wycombe; and Mr. Worthington, who hardly acknowledged the introduction, his attention being diverted across the lawn.

Common pleasantries gave way to a chat about the beauty of the Chiltern Hills and the Vale of Aylesbury until a gong sounded for supper.

As they mounted the steps, Anne greeted Mrs. Venables, who introduced her friends, Mrs. Linwood and Mr. and Mrs. Egerton. Mrs. Linwood was Mr. Egerton's sister, which fact had not been hard to guess, for they favored each other strongly.

"Miss de Bourgh is a most progressive young lady," Mrs. Venables told her companions. "She is a lady farmer who has formed an affection for her steward. Any day we anticipate the banns being posted." She turned to Anne, her white teeth sparkling in a sneery smile. "What joy your family will know when your betrothal is announced."

Anne saw surprised looks on several faces and Lady Braybrooke's creased brow. "You forget that I am engaged to my cousin," she said, reasoning that although she did not consider the statement true, it was prudent to report a widely known belief rather than rouse speculation about Arnot. "Indeed, your report is a vile rumor. I shall be grateful if you tell me its source."

Her tormentor laughed. "Oh, I forgot about Mr. Darcy. Come, let us not tarry or we shall be the last seated at table."

Anne followed her up the steps, her teeth clenched at the idea of her visit being ruined by the likes of Clarinda Ormiston Venables.

Her mood lifted somewhat during supper. Seated between Mr. Nelkins and Lady Coldham, she found ample opportunity to enjoy the company of more agreeable persons. On asking Mr. Nelkins about his interests, she learned of his being a Gentleman Antiquarian, much as his grandfather had been. "I am particularly formed for studying churches and their histories," he said. "Of late I have been exploring the history of the pointed arch in England. A fine example of it can be found at Winchester Cathedral, I have read. I intend to travel there to assess the claim myself."

Hearing his remark, Lady Coldham whispered a different view into Anne's ear. "Never mind his smooth manners, he is is a gamester and nothing like his grandfather."

From the head of the table Lord Metcalfe announced the evening's plan. "At your leisure, make your way to the Gainsborough saloon for cards. Those of you not familiar with the saloon will soon understand how it acquired its name: a very fine portrait of my mother, painted by the great artist, hangs above the mantel."

When the guests left the table, Lady Coldham whispered to Anne, "Watch your purse tonight. Mrs. Venables has an instinct for the sport."

Chapter 26

"You are the first up, Miss. The other quality will not rise until noon." Shaw helped Anne remove her nightclothes. "There's to be a ball tonight. People from all 'round the neighborhood are invited. Downstairs everybody is scurrying around like bedlamites, polishing silver and ironin' linens. Lowrie said we might use flowers from the conservatory for the ladies' hair."

Fortified by Shaw's excitement and hungry for breakfast, Anne made her way to the Court Room, so named because it overlooked a small courtyard ornamented with stone benches, rose bushes, and a little pond. On entering, she greeted the only other guest seated at table and helped herself to the generous repast laid on the sideboard. As she took a chair near Lady Braybrooke, Mr. Worthington strode in, his cane tapping the marble floor. He stopped, a scowl flashing across his face. His look suggested he might bolt for the woods, but he seemed to change his mind and nodded a greeting to the ladies. He hooked his cane on a chair back, helped himself to the breakfast viands, and sat down across from Lady Braybrooke. The only sounds in the cavernous room were the clinks of silverware on plate.

"What have you to say for yourself after last evening's performance?" asked Lady Braybrooke, her coal-black eyes glinting like sharp obsidian points.

A lump rose in Anne's throat on seeing the lady's arch leer. She feared Mrs. Venables' fabrication regarding Arnot lay at the root of the question.

"You placed a poor bet more than once, I noticed. You will never play cards really well if you do not attend to the game."

Anne's features relaxed. "I am no card player."

"Card games don't interest you?"

"Not particularly. On a rainy day when there is nothing else to do, I sometimes enjoy a hand or two, but I tire of the activity quickly."

"Besides farming, what interests occupy your time?"

Anne glanced at Mr. Worthington, whose mouth twitched. He busied himself cracking an eggshell.

"I read and draw." She did not dignify the comment about farming with a reply.

"Do you play or sing?"

"No, ma'am."

"That is very odd. Your father was a baronet. Did he not think it important that you learn to play a musical instrument? Surely, even in Kent, a good piano master can be had. Musical training bestows grace and provides evidence of discipline and passion. A man's status is enhanced by an accomplished wife."

Anne suppressed a rebuke, recalling Miss Bennet's calmness of temper when held to account by Lady Catherine.

"My governess was an accomplished pianist and taught me to play the pianoforte. Under her kind instruction, I made excellent progress, even though I had no special aptitude for the instrument. The lessons ended when I was laid low by a putrid infection at the age of seventeen. My recovery was deemed a miracle."

"I have in recent years suffered from rheumatism brought on by our disagreeable weather," said Lady Braybrooke, "but as a child, I was exceptionally sturdy, hardly being sick a day. Young people today don't eat properly, and they spend too much time out of doors in the filthy air, which renders them susceptible to every passing ailment."

Anne could think of no worthy reply, but was tempted to ask her ladyship whether *she* played a musical instrument. Any further discussion of the topic ended, however, when Mr. Worthington excused himself from the table.

"If that young man continues to bolt his food," observed Lady Braybrooke, "I fear he shall have dyspepsia before he reaches the age of thirty."

—m—

The country dance, as Lord Metcalfe called it, proved to be a grand affair. The ballroom was decorated with kentia palms and planters of boxwood festooned with garlands of roses. Long ribbons of flowers adorned the wall sconces, their fragrance perfuming the night air.

"Enchanting!" exclaimed Anne. She was approached almost immediately by Mr. Ormiston, who invited her to stand up with him at the opening. The music and elegant dancing of her partner was a fitting start to the evening's festivity. By ten o'clock a large crowd had gathered. Several dozen guests partook of champagne and punch, partnered for the cotillions, or sought the cool air on the terrace, where tall torches lit stone benches and shrubbery alike.

"I would so like to dance," said Miss Filbert, her heartfelt wish bringing something like beauty to her plain, round face. She had taken the seat next to Anne near the French windows. "Have you sampled the punch? It is very good."

"Yes, thank you." Anne raised her half-empty cup. She hoped to have a few minutes alone to recover. She had been listening to Mr. Egerton joke about his idiot neighbor when she heard a lady behind her say, "She is no beauty, but owning property in Kent might compensate for her personal deficiencies. I shall not encourage my Abel to pursue her, for it is said she is engaged to a cousin in Derbyshire."

The woman must be speaking of her. On hearing the complaint, her impulse was to round on the gadfly and deliver a pointed question: *What personal deficiencies? I am not so pretty as Tilly or Mrs. Venables or Miss Bennet, but I am no hag either. The gall of the woman to express her opinions so decidedly to half the county.* Did knowledge of her supposed engagement to her cousin explain why she was seldom asked to dance? In her heart, she was not engaged to Darcy, but because the engagement was widely reported—thanks to Lady Catherine's industry—she could not be more forward in furthering the acquaintance of any man she found attractive. Or worse—had Mrs. Venables put it about that she was set to marry her steward? It was disconcerting to be the object of such blatant speculation.

Miss Filbert intruded on her troubles. "Lord Metcalfe is a tease, is he not?"

"Yes, but he is good-natured about it. Do you know Lord and Lady Metcalfe well?"

"Oh, yes. They are fine people—Lady Metcalfe, especially. And the sons are all handsome and agreeable. Mr. Ormiston is very popular in the district. All the single ladies in these parts lamented his marriage last year. Do you know the daughter well? I don't believe Mrs. Venables has spoken more than five words to me all evening."

"I have been acquainted with Mrs. Venables for many years. Even so, I don't know her well."

"She is too pretty to be widowed," said Miss Filbert. "I must say, she behaves nothing like Widow Crowder, whose husband died while out hunting on their estate." She sighed heavily. "We were all insensible on hearing the news, for he was killed accidental-like by his brother—shot in the stomach. So young he was, not yet five and thirty, and handsome, too. Can you imagine the horror?" Miss Filbert paused, seemingly overwhelmed by the memory, but then brightened. "Mrs. Venables is very popular with the gentlemen."

Anne's eye fell on the lady in question. She was standing close to Mr. Egerton, a mischievous grin lighting her face. In profile she had the look of a Roman statue carved in marble, so aquiline was her nose, so pale and unblemished her complexion. A single camellia adorned her blond curls. Its beauty attracted Mr. Egerton's attention. He planted his nose in its petals.

"She has a smart way about her and is elegant in her dress and appearance," said Anne as she observed a drama unfold. Mr. Egerton rocked back on his heels, seemingly overpowered by the flower's fragrance. The lady placed her hand on his arm and laughed a reproof. Mrs. Egerton, standing at her husband's elbow, looked decidedly uncomfortable at their play, as did Mr. Worthington, who stood several yards away, his brow knitted in contemplation of the scene.

"I should like to be pretty and accomplished like Mrs. Venables," opined Miss Filbert. "Mama chastises me for eating too many sweets, but Papa says I am pretty just as I am. He believes virtue and goodness make the true beauty. What do you think, Miss de Bourgh?"

"I can agree with the sentiment. I also think superior finery often implies superior breeding. Whether it should or not is another question entirely."

Chapter 27

Two days after the country dance, Anne endured being dressed by a disgruntled maid. "I fear you shall be the only one partaking of an early breakfast," complained Shaw. "Most of his lordship's guests are late risers, I'm told."

"Yesterday Lady Braybrooke had eaten nearly half a plate of eggs and sausages before ever I sat down," said Anne, "and I have been an early riser since I was a child, as you well know."

"Yes, ma'am. Do you go to the service this morning?" asked Shaw as she dressed her mistress.

"Of course, and you should as well." To her ready assent, Anne said, "Good. I shall go down to breakfast now."

All was much the same when Anne entered the Court Room, for Lady Braybrooke and Mr. Worthington were already seated. Determining that a routine had been established, she prepared a small plate of fruit, bread, and cold meats and took the same chair as before. Nobody spoke and several minutes passed while each guest enjoyed their host's bounty. Quick, furtive glances passed among them.

Mr. Worthington cleared his throat before speaking: "What have you to say for yourself this morning?" He stared at Anne briefly before casting down his eyes to butter a piece of bread.

Lady Braybrooke jerked around to stare at him.

Anne detected no insult in his manner, but wondered at his meaning. Did his question, so similar in form to Lady Braybrooke's, have to do with the country dance? She had partnered Lord Metcalfe and his sons and also Mr. Nelkins, Mr. Palmer, and the son of a neighboring family; she had conversed with a good twenty guests. She met no lovers in the shrubbery or assaulted any servants. Nothing remarkable had happened.

Thinking it must be a challenge of sorts, she cast about for an answer, finally saying, "My father taught me to carve a turkey at table."

Mr. Worthington laughed. "Are you any good at the endeavor?"

"I am very good, thank you. When I was fourteen, I carved a large roasted turkey for Lord Norford, who was mightily impressed."

He grinned. "Excellent," he said before resuming his breakfast.

When Mr. Worthington quit the room, Lady Braybrooke asked, "Whatever is that young man about?"

"I have no idea. It seems he likes a joke."

—∾—

The chapel was small but beautifully lit by golden rays piercing the stained glass windows. An elderly gentleman stood in the amber light, a Bible clasped to his chest.

Anne entered the dim chamber, her shoes flapping softly on the stone floor. Before taking a seat she moved to greet Lady Metcalfe, who took her hand, saying, "I believe you shall enjoy listening to Mr. Tweedy. He is retired now, but still has a lively manner."

"I look forward to his sermon." Anne returned up the aisle, nodding a 'good morning' to her host. Mrs. Egerton entered a moment later on Mr. Worthington's arm and settled into the pew in front of Anne.

Mr. Tweedy had two rare gifts: perfect diction and a sonorous voice that resonated to the farthest reaches of the chapel. "This day's lesson is from Zechariah." After a pregnant pause, he read verses 6:1 through 6:5. His voice thundered across the chapel, much like God might sound if any of His congregation dared to fall asleep during His sermon.

*"And I turned, and lifted up mine eyes, and looked, and, behold,
there came four chariots out from between two mountains ..."*

While Mr. Tweedy read the scripture, Anne's thoughts wandered,
for she was not much impassioned by the reading of the Prophet's
visions. Her eyes beheld the scenes of Jesus's life in stained glass: wise
men and angels gathered around his manger; supplicants attended
his Sermon on the Mount; cherubs surrounded a divine Christ. She
was contemplating the age and beauty of the glasswork when Mr.
Tweedy's voice recalled her to his words.

"Zechariah quails at the meaning of his visions. In confusion he
asks the angel: 'What are these, my lord?'" The retired reverend's
voice dropped almost to a whisper. "The angel's answer reveals God's
power: the chariots went forth on *His* command. Zechariah's vision
reminds us that God's hand governs all things: chariot and horse,
fish and fowl, wind and sun, spirit and flesh, man and child. As
Almighty God commanded the spirits, so He commands each of
us. We are instruments of His will. Like Zechariah the prophet,
we cannot comprehend God's will, but we are instructed to listen
to and heed His message. Like Zechariah, a mere man, we cannot
comprehend the awful calamities that befall us, but we are instructed
to accept God's will and to believe in our hearts that His goodness
directs our every breath. Only in submitting to His divine will shall
we be blessed."

Anne bent her head as Mr. Tweedy began his worshipful prayer.
Her thoughts dwelled very little on the obligatory offers of atone-
ment for earthly sins and more on Mrs. Egerton, whom she had
seen wiping her cheek. What aspect of the sermon, Anne wondered,
had moved the young lady to tears?

—⁂—

"I am glad you took the trouble of attending our chapel service this
morning," said Mrs. Goodall to Anne as they crossed the gravel
drive with due deliberation. "What did you think of Mr. Tweedy?"

"I enjoyed listening to his exceptional voice and interpretation of
Zechariah's visions. I cannot imagine the rector of Hunsford's parish

being so forward in his thinking." Anne did not care to elaborate on Mr. Tweedy's counsel to accept God's will in the face of life's calamities, for privately she questioned this tenet of faith. In what way was her father's untimely death a manifestation of God's will? What instruction, other than the lessons of grief and forbearance, had she received from it? And what of Tilly's sorrow at her mother's death? How did Mrs. Sullen's sad passing represent God's goodness? Such questions perplexed her whenever she thought of the myriad awful, heart-wrenching events in people's lives: war, pestilence, pain, betrayal, death.

"Mr. Tweedy's reputation as an ecclesiastical scholar is built on his published papers, but not everyone embraces his views." Mrs. Good-all shifted her parasol. "The knot garden is just beyond those trees."

Their dignified pace gave Anne time to think how best to broach a topic that interested her. "Mrs. Egerton has a sweetness and reserve about her that is very attractive. What do you know of her?" Anne pictured the young lady's high forehead, rosy lips, and fair hair, which was not so curly and brassy as Mrs. Venables' golden tresses.

"She is unhappy in her marriage, I am told, but nothing can be done to improve her situation."

"I am sorry to hear it. Has she been married long?"

"Not quite six months, which can seem a lifetime when one is truly discontented. Lady Metcalfe told me that before her marriage, Mrs. Egerton was in love with a man of the family's long acquaintance. He returned her love and wished to marry her. Although her father admired the youth, he could not support their marriage because his daughter's suitor was a sixth or seventh son and not likely to inherit property. When a rumor reached him that the couple might elope, he pressed her to marry Mr. Egerton, the son of Viscount Clerkenwell and heir to a grand estate."

"She seems very young," said Anne. "Perhaps the couple will find ease together in time."

"Perhaps." Mrs. Goodall snorted. "Mr. Egerton is a man of the world, which fact must try them both, for he is nearly ten years older than she—Mrs. Egerton is not yet eighteen." She stopped and closed her parasol. "We have arrived at the knot garden."

Anne could hardly appreciate its intricate beauty, so absorbed was she in contemplating Mrs. Egerton's sad situation. The garden was laid in a large square. At its heart stood a water fountain dominated by a tall statue in the classical Greek style. Arranged around it were interwoven braids of boxwood interspersed with herbs, aubretia, and grey cotton lavender. Four paths led toward the fountain, near which stood Mr. Worthington, unaware of their approach.

Mrs. Goodall called out, "Good evening, Mr. Worthington."

The gentleman turned in their direction and bowed, a bare hint of irritation on his face. He closed his pocket-book and exited through the far pathway.

"Mr. Worthington is a singular man in his habits." Mrs. Goodall watched him disappear into the trees. "He always carries a book when he is out of doors. Mrs. Egerton described him as a naturalist. She is his cousin and must be qualified to speak of him so."

"Oh, they are cousins. I had not understood their connection."

"He takes prodigious care of her. Some people speculate it was Mr. Worthington with whom the young lady fell in love prior to her marriage, but the fact is not certain. The cousins are as close as some siblings."

"Did they grow up near one another, then?"

"On the death of his mother, Mr. Worthington went to live with his uncle, Mrs. Egerton's father, Sir William Rawlins. Mr. Worthington was only a child at the time, perhaps ten or eleven years old. He and Miss Rawlins, as she was known then, grew up in the same household, which explains their familiarity."

Anne believed it possible that Mrs. Egerton's tears had been ones of grief at being in the company of her former lover. How would Mr. Tweedy explain God's goodness to a couple whose affectionate hearts were torn asunder by earthly matters of money and property?

Chapter 28

Anne felt a flutter of nerves at the prospect of breakfast. A game was afoot and she feared it was her turn to open the play. Her anxiety was for nought, for when she entered the Court Room boisterous laughter greeted her. Mr. Nelkins, Mr. Palmer, Mr. Egerton, and the Ormiston men occupied the center section of the table, their breakfasts nearly finished. Mr. Worthington sat apart. Lady Braybrooke was nowhere in sight, perhaps preferring a tray in her bedchamber, since the morning was rather chilly.

The men stood on seeing her. Mr. Worthington was the last to come to his feet.

"Good morning, gentlemen," Anne said. "You are at breakfast early today."

"We go hunting, the weather being nearly perfect," said Mr. Ormiston as he reclaimed his seat.

"Come, Worthy, join us," Mr. Palmer called down the long table. "It would do you good to escape the ladies. Fresh air and the thrill of the hunt, that is the thing for you."

Mr. Worthington would not be goaded. "There is plenty of fresh air here. I shall keep myself occupied."

Shortly after Anne served herself, the hunters departed in a flurry of scraped chairs, tossed napkins, and teasing jokes. All was calm in the aftermath. The servants quietly cleared the table and righted the chairs. Anne called for another cup of tea. When sated, she excused herself and left Mr. Worthington to his musings.

—⁓—

A path led from the terrace past the west wing into a thin grove of trees. Any walker might pause, as Anne did, and look back at the three-story house which rose grandly on a modest hill. The manor stood ready to withstand any assault. One could image dozens of armored men positioned along the battlements, ready to release their arrows at intruding knights who dared to cross the vast lawn now sparkling with dew.

Traversing the grove, she emerged onto open ground, where the path skirted a ribbon of hawthorne trees before sloping down to a dark wood. Here the foliage was dense and the quiet welcoming. She slowed her pace, happy to be free of company and the effort of conversation. The scent of fallen leaves and pine needles was strong. A rustle nearby made her pause. Her eyes searched the forest floor for some small vole or skink, but the creature proved too clever by half and avoided detection.

At the lake, she stopped to admire the view. The sun's brilliance, surprisingly warm for an autumn morning, made her glad to have brought a parasol. She raised it above her head and walked along the lake's edge. Ahead she spied another trail, which would take her back to the house.

On pursuing the trail into a region of tall grass, she saw Mr. Worthington poised on the path, his back to her. He hunkered down on his haunches, a tablet steadied on one knee, his cane laid to one side. His longish, umber-colored curls gleamed in the sunlight. He was a model of concentration. When she stepped forward, taking great effort to be quiet, he heard her footfall and thrust his hand out to one side—a clear signal for any trespasser to stop. He never glanced over his shoulder but focused on some sight in the reeds lining the lake. After a minute or two, he picked up his cane and stood. When he turned in her direction, his expression changed from surprise to chagrin.

"Miss de Bourgh! I had no idea it was you on the path. I thought it was the gardener's young sons, who dog me nearly every day. Please forgive my rudeness."

"It was no torment to wait in this lovely spot. What was the subject of your study?"

"I spied a grass snake crossing the trail toward the water. It slowed when I approached and gave me a chance to sketch its likeness." He showed her a pretty graphite drawing.

"You captured its forked tongue perfectly. It seems to smile."

"Yes, it is a clever creature. You don't fear snakes, then?"

They turned together and proceeded along the path.

"Not particularly. I saw quite a few as a child when I joined my father in the fields or in the barn."

"Your father took you with him into the fields? Did you not resent the effort? My sisters played in the house and were seldom parted from their dolls and crayons."

"In this, I am an odd specimen, even among my friends. I enjoyed many girlish amusements, but I wished always to accompany my father, no matter where his duties took him—into hay field, orchard, stables, barn, woods, or park."

"I suppose that is why Mrs. Venables called you a lady farmer."

"Mrs. Venables has a teasing manner," she said carefully, "and her thinking is naturally influenced by her father's ideas. Lord Metcalfe holds a traditional view of women, notwithstanding his wife's lively opinions. My father's views must have been unusual during his lifetime and would not be appreciated even now. He simply saw no reason to forbid my learning any function that one day might be used to manage and improve the estate. Of course, he warred with my mother in this."

Mr. Worthington proved a good listener and as they ambled through the woods, Anne told him of her worries in the months after Tench died and of the gossip she excited by venturing out with her new steward. "I came to rely on Tench for all decisions related to running the estate. Since his death, I am sometimes thrilled, but mostly terrified, by the responsibility of protecting Rosings. The decisions are now all mine."

"Not entirely," said Mr. Worthington. "You have hired a new

steward to guide you and you have in your neighbor Lord Metcalfe a successful landowner. Do not allow idle talk to undermine your determination."

"Would that I could. Few people tolerate the idea of a woman managing her property. If I were married and my husband approved my stewardship, I might be subjected to less criticism."

Mr. Worthington kicked a pine cone with his cane. "It is true— few women enjoy such independence, even among the gentry, but there must be some few men who pass the running of their estates to a wife, provided she has the wherewithal, the inclination and, above all, the skill. Why, I might be tempted to do so myself, if I were given the chance."

"You would? I am astonished to hear it. The prejudice against women owning land is entrenched in the public mind and virtually enshrined in law. Few men think it proper; even fewer are prepared to relinquish their power."

"I am not insensible to the broad belief, but I am also aware of the dangers that accrue when women are not allowed to direct their own lives. They can be coerced—their wishes thwarted—their happiness ..." He shook his head, scowling, and swiped the weeds along the path with his cane. "Frankly, I think an industrious wife might make me happy. She would mind the dairy and cull the deer and argue with tenant farmers, as was her wont, while I remained free to study Nature and never think on sick horses or ruined crops or disgruntled servants. Yes, such a plan might suit me very well." He paused, fearing he had been impolite. "You must think me a most irascible character."

"Not at all," said Anne. "You are a man of passion. What is life, without passion?"

His grey eyes studied her face. "You think on such things?"

A sudden shyness overtook her. "I lead a quiet life in the country and enjoy a small circle of friends. I see passion in their humble lives and seek it in my own."

He kept his own counsel until they arrived at the path fork.

"Oh, we are returned to the house," said Anne. "I shall leave you here. Thank you for accompanying me on a most enjoyable walk.

I wish you good fortune in your plan for happiness."

"I shall have need of it," he said with surprising grace. He bowed smoothly before continuing on through the woods.

Anne crossed the lawn, swinging her parasol in a very unladylike manner, and climbed the steps to the terrace. Mrs. Venables and Mrs. Linwood observed her progress. "Good morning, ladies," she said as she passed them.

—⁂—

At supper Mr. Ormiston regaled their end of the table with tales of the morning's shoot.

"I object, Friend," said Mr. Palmer, "to your insinuation that I am not steady on my feet. The rock concealed its slipperiness until I stepped on it."

"Evil rock, that," muttered Mr. Nelkins.

"Yes, a vile rock in a mean stream. The ladies will think me a blunderbuss. Thanks to you, I shall lack a partner at every dance."

"The ladies know you to be a fool, Palmer," said Mr. Egerton *sotto voce*.

Mr. Ormiston, alert to Mr. Egerton's scorn, said gallantly, "I consider it a great stroke of luck that you fell without discharging your gun. Ladies, picture this: the confident step, the great wobble, the cry of dismay, the absurd tumble—his gun thrust high above his head—and, finally, the vigorous splash."

When the female cohort giggled, Mr. Palmer protested. "You laugh! As did all my friends standing on the bank."

"I will speak on Mr. Palmer's behalf," said Mr. Ormiston. "After he doused himself, his skill improved greatly. Indeed, he dropped more birds soaking wet than all the rest of us combined, though we were dry as deserts."

One hunting story led to another and the convivial atmosphere put everybody in the mood for the evening's program of music. On advancing into the music room, Anne took her bearings. The men clustered around Lord Metcalfe at the far end, where the joking persisted. Lady Metcalfe and the other *belle dames* found comfort in large, plush chairs pushed together; they waited patiently for the evening's diversion. Mrs. Venables and Mrs. Linwood sat whispering, their heads close together. When Anne moved to take a seat somewhat removed from them, Mrs. Venables called to her, "Do you intend to perform this evening, Miss de Bourgh? I recall last hearing you play the pianoforte a good ten years ago. 'Greensleeves,' I think it was."

"You have an excellent memory. I did play 'Greensleeves.'" She was annoyed to hear Mrs. Venables snigger, for the folk tune was virtually the only piece she played well, which prompted her to add, "You, I recall, played a simple rondo, but neither of our performances matched Miss Derrythorpe's vivid skill that evening. Who would have thought the rustic village of Clun could nourish such beauty and talent?" She gave a tight smile. Insufferable woman.

Anne approached Mrs. Egerton. "This seems a comfortable sofa. Do you mind if I join you?"

"Not at all." Mrs. Egerton's look was more tentative than confident.

Anne seated herself and wrestled inelegantly with her shawl.

Mrs. Egerton kindly pulled the fabric over Anne's shoulder, saying, "Will you play for us this evening?"

"I wish I could—thank you—but my lessons ended when I was seventeen and nearly succumbed to a feverish infection. I have not attempted to play since that time, the more the pity. Do you play?"

"I don't enjoy playing for company." Mrs. Egerton faltered. "You must think me odd, for what is the purpose of learning a musical instrument if not to perform for others?"

"By God's good graces we are allowed to amuse ourselves, in so far as our amusements do not harm others. I played best when I had the music room to myself and no one who listened or criticized. I never developed the confidence my governess had, for she performed easily in company. I cannot explain why that should be, but so it was."

Lord Metcalfe stepped to the center of the room and rubbed his hands together. "We have an interesting program this evening. Mrs. Linwood offered to please us first."

There was polite clapping when Mrs. Linwood and Mrs. Venables rose and went to the pianoforte. The former sat down on the bench with a flourish and stood her sheet music in place, while the latter prepared to turn pages. The ladies made a pretty pair: Mrs. Venables so fair with her halo of blond curls; Mrs. Linwood so dark, her wavy hair as black as coal. Her selection was the Andante cantabile con espressione of Mozart's sonata No. 8 in A Minor, which she played beautifully. The applause was generous. When it died away, Mrs. Venables took the bench. From the first notes, Anne recognized her choice: the simple Prelude in C Major from Bach's Well-Tempered Clavier, after which she played a sonatina. Her skill had improved over the years, but even so, her hands were rather heavy on the keys.

Next, Mr. Nelkins and Mr. Palmer sang in harmony two ballads, the last more suited to a gentlemen's club than a private gathering of mixed company. Lord Metcalfe calmed the laughter and invited Mrs. Egerton to come forward. "We have been told you play very well," he said, smiling his encouragement. "Would it be too much to ask you to play for us?"

Mrs. Egerton stiffened. Her countenance, pale enough in the candle light, seemed suddenly bled of all color.

Goodness, will she faint? Anne thought to clasp the lady's hand, but stilled her movement when she saw Mr. Egerton advance in their direction.

Mr. Egerton's stride brought him to his wife's side. Bending close, he grasped her wrist and whispered into her ear. His ebon curls flopped forward, covering most of his face. When he pulled back, he cupped her chin in his hand, a hard glint in his cerulean eyes. With a perfectly pleasant countenance he turned to his host: "Mrs. Egerton is delighted to accommodate your request, sir." A mask settled over Mrs. Egerton's features.

Anne felt an unnatural dread as Mrs. Egerton rose and went to the pianoforte. The young lady settled herself and poised her hands above the keys. From memory, she began the somber harmonies of the second movement of the *Pathétique*. Her performance was flawless.

Here is beauty and artistry; here is sublime passion. Anne blinked back tears.

When the last chord faded away, Mrs. Egerton seemed not to hear the vigorous applause, but stared across the piano strings as if her heart were dead to the world.

Chapter 29

"Good morning, Miss de Bourgh," called the housekeeper, who approached carrying a large spray of lilies and gladioli. "A fine day for the picnic."

"Indeed, I look forward to it," replied Anne with more cheer than she felt. She was not in the mood for jovial company at breakfast, having woken in the night from a horrible dream whose sinister shadows still haunted her thoughts. With luck she might have the Court Room to herself. Instead, she found not only Lady Braybrooke, but also Mr. Worthington, seated in their customary places, as if by appointment.

She settled at the table, noting Mr. Worthington's disgruntled look. Lady Braybrooke's eyes flitted from one fellow guest to the other. A servant entered, bearing a silver slaver. "Miss de Bourgh, there are two letters for you this morning."

She lifted the missives. Lady Metcalfe's handwriting was easily discerned on the one, while the other was from Kent. She opened her ladyship's first.

Good morning, Miss Anne.

I write to suggest that you invite Mrs. Jenkinson to join today's picnic, if it suits you. She might enjoy seeing more of the country-side in the company of Mrs. and Miss Filbert and Miss Attemore,

whom I also invited. The Filberts you have already met. Miss Attemore is an older but delightful woman who lives in the village. I believe Mrs. Jenkinson will enjoy their company and also our trip to Highlough. Still, the decision to include her is entirely yours.
                    Yours in true affection, Felicia Metcalfe

How kind, Anne said to herself as she laid it aside and picked up the other letter. She glanced at her companions absorbed in their nourishment. This letter was from Arnot.

                              Rosings Sept' —th
Dear Miss de Bourgh,
    A circumstance has arisen on the estate that I thought proper to bring to your attention. It is nothing to worry over, but I wish to make known to you a certain fact, in case you have particular instructions.—Last week I was surprised to have Beath—him, whom we met in Herne Green—approach me for a job. He expressed a willingness to do any steady work. My opinion of the man is low, which fact will not surprise you, and my reluctance to hire him even lower. But I cannot in good conscience deny a man the opportunity of working when he proves himself willing to do so.—Accordingly, I expressed my reluctance but agreed to give him a trial working with the dairy cows under Mrs. James's supervision. Kitson and his son also agree to keep an eye on him. In these last few days he has performed well, but I made it clear to him that your judgment on the matter is final.—Please write and let me know whether you are comfortable to accept his presence on the estate. Anyone familiar with the particulars of that day would not fault you for denying him employment.
                    Your faithful servant, Theophilus Arnot

Anne never thought to see Beath again and vividly recollected his leery grin and dirty knife. Would she feel unsafe with such a man working on the estate? She frowned to realize she must think on the matter.

"I trust your letters bring no bad news," said Lady Braybrooke.

"No, ma'am. Lady Metcalfe invites me to bring my companion along on today's picnic, which I shall do, and my steward writes on an estate matter—nothing of consequence."

"Your steward writes often, does he?"

"He writes when he has reason to do so. I appreciate being kept well informed."

"I am told you are deeply involved in managing your estate."

"I must be."

"Indeed? I hear you travel about the countryside with your steward unchaperoned and meet tenants in the fields. These are highly unusual activities for a lady." To Anne's forced smile, her ladyship said, "Your reputation will be stained beyond repair if you do not take steps to amend it. No man of good sense will marry a woman who flouts her independence."

"He will, if her property is profitable."

"Bah! When you marry, your husband will not tolerate such behavior. You must realize this, surely. As it is, your behavior offends all members of the nobler sex and undermines the modesty and exquisite sensibility of every feeling lady."

Mr. Worthington stopped eating.

"I daresay your ladyship is correct, but in the absence of a husband, I must oversee my property as any man would do. If I don't take the reins, who will? My steward? The gardeners? The stable master? Any landowner who does not manage his staff and tenants can fall prey to a dishonest servant or conniving gamester, and more can be lost than mere gold and silver. One can waste one's reputation and land. I shall not let that happen. I love Rosings too well to be intimidated by claims that I cannot control my estate merely because I'm a woman." She stabbed an orange slice. "As for marriage—I would sooner not marry than put the prosperity of Rosings in the hands of a brigand or buffoon. In fact, my constant worry is this: any man seeking my hand will feast his eyes on my land while ignoring my exquisite sensibilities." Her exuberance had gotten the best of her, judging by the startled looks on her companions' faces. One or two of the servants looked alert, as well. "Excuse me," she said, "I am in a foul mood this morning. I did not sleep well." She caught

Mr. Worthington's sly smile. His sympathy for her situation seemed to have evaporated since their walk in the woods. "What have you to say for yourself this morning, Mr. Worthington?"

The gentleman pushed back his chair and stood, his grey eyes flashing. "I say, I have never before witnessed at breakfast so spirited a defense of the landowner's duty and prerogative." He laid his folded napkin on the table and bowed. "Pray excuse me, ladies."

The silence lingered in his absence. Lady Braybrooke's pursed lips revealed her displeasure.

Anne berated herself for not being more compliant, but she resented the prejudice against her as an heiress. She had not begged or schemed for the indulgence; it came to her by law. In a calmer mood she might have soothed her opponent, but this morning she was ready to thrust and parry. Here was one consequence of being abroad in the world: a skulking derision was as likely to be found in the breakfast room at Dodford Meare as hiding in the lanes of Hunsford.

—॰॰—

An open carriage ride in the country on a lovely autumn day must be the surest cure for a bad temper. Anne joined Lady Metcalfe in her carriage. Her heart sank on seeing Lady Braybrooke's quelling look. The morning's imbroglio at breakfast was neither forgotten nor forgiven. Mrs. Egerton appeared distracted, but managed a weak smile as she made room for Anne on the bench. Every guest being accounted for, the carriages rolled down the long drive and entered the main road. Lady Metcalfe and Lady Braybrooke settled themselves like old friends, speaking of accidents, illnesses, and other travails.

The men rode their horses alongside. Anne watched Mr. Egerton sitting tall in the saddle, her thoughts returning to his wife's sad situation. How much pressure had she endured before yielding to her parents' wish? What sort of coercion had her father wielded— the loss of family affection? Physical threats? Now that she had married, how could she bear to see her lover—if Mr. Worthington was, indeed, that person—knowing she could never be united with him? God forbid if Mrs. Egerton's tender soul could not recover from the wound. What a pity if she became sad and embittered. Lady Braybrooke's gravelly voice intruded on her thoughts.

"Your cousin Mr. Worthington is a good horseman," said her ladyship, speaking to Mrs. Egerton. "Does he ride to hounds?"

"Occasionally, ma'am," came the soft reply. "The activity brings him little pleasure."

"He objects to the sport? That is surely odd in a country-bred man."

"He is a naturalist and prefers to sketch his subjects, not kill them. Such amusements as bear-baiting, cock-fighting, and goose-throwing disgust him. He has a tender heart."

"He is the youngest of seven sons," interposed Lady Metcalfe, "and is a congenial, studious sort of fellow. His drawings are very fine and suggest a rare talent." She shielded her eyes from the sun. "Our picnic site is not much farther along. Look, there is Metcalfe, guarding the food."

Hungry guests spilled out of the carriages or dismounted from their horses and moved toward the buffet tables. Liveried servants stood ready to please as the guests helped themselves to a generous repast before settling on large blankets spread on the mowed grass. The day was perfect for a picnic. High clouds filtered the autumn sun, and a lazy breeze refreshed rather than chilled. After luncheon, the men were all for climbing the grand hill.

"There is a trail, just there," said Mr. Ormiston, pointing across the field, "that wanders through the beech trees. A fine view of the valley can be had from the summit. Ladies, don't be intimidated by the height, for you are all fit to climb it."

The men were off like a shot. Several ladies followed at a more sedate pace. Anne caught up with Mrs. Jenkinson and her carriage companions. Behind them, Mrs. Venables and Mrs. Linwood teased Mrs. Egerton about her tiresome gait, but soon wearied of cajoling and pushed ahead until they were lost from sight. Anne lagged, keeping one eye on Mrs. Egerton, who seemed content to fall behind, perhaps relishing a few moments of peace and quiet. When she was lost from view, Anne waited.

"It is cool and quiet in the woods, is it not?" asked Mrs. Egerton, coming up the trail. She appeared to have slept poorly, for her pretty face lacked animation. Her blue eyes, the color of cornflowers, were shielded by puffy eyelids; her rosebud mouth turned down at the corners. "I have been thinking about the feverish infection you had when you were a child. Was it very bad?"

"It nearly killed me," Anne told her. "All I remember is fainting with fever, my father carrying me upstairs to bed, and my maid holding me down for cupping. My stamina has not been good since then, and I succumb sometimes to rheumatic attacks. But who among us has not suffered such ailments?"

"No, indeed. I am told I suffer from nervous anxiety, which affliction apparently resides only in my mind. It seems my *amour propre* has been touched, and if I would only exert myself a little, I could conquer it." Mrs. Egerton lifted her gown to step over a tree root. "In truth, I do not know how to conquer myself and so must muddle through. I suppose Providence challenges us, each in a separate way."

Anne cast about for a more pleasant topic when Mrs. Egerton introduced a new theme: "I am told you are engaged to your cousin who lives in Derbyshire. Have you planned a wedding?"

"Alas, no. Our engagement is of a peculiar kind. Indeed, I hardly know the man and often doubt whether we shall ever stand together at the altar."

"You are wise to be cautious. What is said of it? 'Marriage, with peace, is the world's paradise; with strife, this life's purgatory.'"

Anne was searching for a favorable comment on the institution— she dare not speak the other homily: marriage and hanging go by destiny—when they stepped into a clearing. Below them, the valley lay dotted with autumn greens, yellows, and reds. Here at the hill top, the breeze had a bite to it.

"We shall have rain tomorrow," said Mrs. Egerton, as if there could be hardly anything worse.

Chapter 30

For two days rain and wind storms buffeted the house. The men kept to the billiards room, where they sampled his lordship's wine and port, told ribald jokes, and bet on their games. The ladies chafed during the inclement weather. The mood in the Gainsborough saloon on the third day was rather desultory. Candles had been lit and a fire laid to ward off the dark and damp, but even so, the ladies could not settle to any agreeable activity. Lady Metcalfe and Lady Coldham played cards half-heartedly with Mrs. Venables and Mrs. Linwood, while Mrs. Egerton and Anne sat reading near the fireplace. There was not much conversation and even less animation.

"Oh, I hate this rain," complained Mrs. Linwood, "for it curls my hair awfully. When shall the men return?"

"Any moment, I should think," replied Lady Metcalfe. "They shall be soaked through. Metcalfe must visit our neighbor to see his new carriage, and he *will* have the company of his sons and their friends. He never minds the rain—no, nor snow either. I fear one day he shall take a serious ague, though he only laughs at my worry."

A parlor maid entered then and said, "His lordship has returned to the house, ma'am."

"Good. I shall hunt him down. Excuse me, ladies." She folded her cards and led her maid into the hall. The remaining card players quit the game.

"Are you hungry?" Anne asked her fireside companion.

"Not particularly." Mrs. Egerton had spent the past hour staring into the flames rather than reading the book laid across her lap.

"I believe I shall excuse myself and call for a tray from the kitchen. The rain and damp have begun to aggravate my rheumatism. Shall I see you for tea?"

Mrs. Egerton sat stone-faced, swathed by morose spirits. She had not heard the question, and so Anne let her be.

The evening turned gloomy. Low clouds perched on the chimney tops and battlements while the rain ran in wide rivulets down the windowpanes. Anne drew a shawl over her shoulders and plodded down the hall to the staircase, her knees stiff and achy from the cold and damp. Angry voices, women's voices, made her pause. A door flew open on her left. Mrs. Linwood stood in the candlelight, her back to the hall, and warned a half-dressed Mrs. Venables: "Whatever game you play, you shall not win."

Mrs. Venable's reply was lost when Mrs. Linwood yanked the door closed. She cut Anne a malignant look and stamped down the hall to her bedchamber, where she slammed the door.

Anne stood frozen, lest a sudden movement excite more violence, then crept down the stairs to the Gainsborough saloon, where maids were laying teacups and platters of biscuits. Not wishing to interrupt their work, she sought his lordship's library. A new book would be the very thing to lift her spirits. She pushed open the library's tall, carved door and stepped into the dim light. No candles glowed; no fire roared.

She moved to a bookcase near a tall window and was perusing a collection of travel books when a man's voice reached her from the far recesses of the vast reserve. Stepping farther into the room, she discovered a private conversation.

Mr. Worthington sat next to Mrs. Egerton on a long sofa. His hands cupped one of hers. He rubbed her fingers while earnestly entreating her on some delicate matter. The lady sniffled and patted her check with a handkerchief. He seemed determined to persuade or comfort, but his efforts failed, for Mrs. Egerton released a heavy sob. His shoulders slumped.

Anne quietly retreated to the hall, still holding a book opened at random. She was very much the interloper this evening.

—ᴍ—

Supper was a dull affair. The talk was mostly of neighbors—Lord Metcalfe's and everybody else's. Anne stubbornly refused to make any disparaging remark about her Kentish neighbors, instead saying, "My neighbors are exceptionally congenial and never troublesome, with the possible exception of the rector."

Several men scorned her politeness.

"Now, gentlemen," said Lady Metcalfe, her eyes shining. "I charge you to respect the lady, for she is entitled to her just opinion. Moreover, she speaks true: I know the rector well." Chuckling at her little joke, she rose and led the ladies into the main saloon, where they waited for the men to finish their port. Rain pelted the tall windows, but the fire vanquished the night.

"We have decided on our entertainment," his lordship announced when his guests had settled. "The men agree to read or recite for us. Our talents are not so refined as those of you ladies, but we shall have some fun. This is no simple reading, for you ladies shall be divided into teams. When any lady recognizes the poet or author attached to the reading, call out the name. Extra points shall be awarded for stating the work. Prizes can be won. Ladies, sort yourselves and then we shall begin."

There was a moment's hesitation. Mrs. Linwood, determined in her retaliation, grabbed Mrs. Egerton's arm and allied herself with Lady Metcalfe. Mrs. Venables, glaring at her friend, called to Anne and Lady Coldham to join her on the opposite sofa. Lady Braybrooke preferred to observe.

Lord Metcalfe, satisfied with the groupings, said, "I shall keep score. Ready, ladies?"

Mr. Nelkins chose a familiar poem: "It is an ancient Mariner, and he stoppeth one of three …" As the readings progressed the ladies rose to their challenge, calling out: Cowper, Wordsworth, Shakespeare, Robert Burns, William Blake, Richard Glover, Wordsworth again. After Mr. Egerton read a passage to test their wits, the team members conferred among themselves with much whispering and shaking of heads. Lady Metcalfe's team put forth an answer, which proved incorrect. Mrs. Venables turned to Anne, who said, "I believe the reading is from Peter Teuthold's *The Necromancer*, but I would not wage a guinea on it."

"Very good," said Lord Metcalfe. "Your team wins. Each of you shall receive a wirework necklace. Don't be distressed, my ladies on the losing team. You shall each receive a lovely hair ornament."

Mrs. Venables whooped in a very unladylike manner and bestowed on Anne a rare smile of genuine appreciation. Everyone applauded their host's generosity, after which tea was laid. While the guests refreshed themselves, Mr. Nelkins proposed to read an essay. "The night is stormy and a long reading might soothe us." His idea was enthusiastically supported and the group settled in advance of a quiet performance. "I choose to read from *The Spectator*." He began: "It is an inexpressible pleasure to know a little of the world, and be of no character or significancy in it ..."

While he read in a pleasant, somewhat high voice, Anne's attention was drawn to her fellow creatures: Mrs. Venables' flushed cheeks as she charmed Mr. Egerton; Mrs. Linwood's deepening scowl on observing her brother's reckless behavior; Mrs. Egerton's rigid posture as she stared at the carpet; Lady Metcalfe's thoughtful brow. Only Mr. Worthington seemed disinterested in the evening's proceedings. While the eaves creaked in the gale and a steady rain glazed the windows, he slouched in a deep chair near the fire, an empty wine glass in one hand; he did not stir when a sooty log crashed in the grate, sending sparks flying up the chimney.

Chapter 31

The desk in Lord Metcalfe's library was massive and ornate. Shortly after arriving at Dodford Meare, Anne sought his lordship's permission to use it, causing him to comment, "Please do so whenever it suits you—everybody does. You will find writing paper in the drawers and all other accessories for penning private letters." His eyes gleamed. "Surely you have a lover or two waiting anxiously to hear how you do."

She laughed at his silliness and availed herself of his desk nearly every day. Now she bent to her letter, rereading her lines.

> *Dodford Meare Wednesday Sept' —*
> *Dearest Tilly,*
>   *Your letter revived me, for I have grown morose in this gloomy weather, although much has happened since my last letter to you. Yesterday Charles Ormiston and his family arrived from Town. They traveled in a drizzle, arrived chilled, and were met with every kindness. The house seemed to awaken suddenly as if from a dreary slumber, and most guests found their spirits enlivened by the new arrivals. I write "most" because there was one exception. I last wrote of a new acquaintance. Mrs. Egerton—*

Anne peered through the potted palms to where the object of her discussion sat near the fire. The lady's head was bowed as if in prayer. A book lay opened on her lap, but Anne had yet to see her turn a page.

> *—is sweet and shy but wears a heavy cloak of melancholy for one so young. The other night Lord Metcalfe asked her most graciously to play the pianoforte—you know his heart: he would not have been offended had she refused—but the lady shrank from his invitation in terror. Mr. Egerton rushed to her side and whispered to her. I at first thought he meant to offer encouragement, but then I saw such a look of malicious intent on his face that I trembled for her. I have relived that moment a hundred times and believe he threatened her with some fierce punishment, for she was pale as a ghost then and has been unwell since. Two days ago I discovered her and her cousin here in the library. Mr. Worthington appeared to use every persuasion in his address to her, but at his kind words, she only sobbed and could not be comforted. I cannot imagine—*

Movement caught her eye. She looked up to see Mr. Egerton striding across the library, his hands clinched. Anne saw panic rise in Mrs. Egerton's face, but no look of dread impeded her husband's naked anger. Grabbing one arm, he yanked his wife to her feet and slapped her. His voice seethed with emotion, although his words could not be discerned across the library's vastness. While he ranted, Mrs. Egerton cowered, her arms raised to protect her face from more blows. Having said all he wished to, he shoved her back onto the sofa. "This business does not concern you," he shouted as he stabbed his finger at her.

If Anne thought to avoid his censure, she was mistaken in the idea, for the scoundrel, startled to discover a witness to the scene, stormed in her direction. She stood, her knees wobbling, and placed her quivering hands on the edge of the desk.

"You!" he spat at her. "Stay away from my wife." He glared at her, his nostrils flaring, before quitting the room.

Mrs. Egerton burst into tears.

Anne's heart raced so fast she could hardly breathe. Seeing the lady's distress, she helped herself to his lordship's brandy, pouring the bracing elixir into two goblets. She took a deep draught from one, set the pair on a table, and wrapped her arms around Mrs. Egerton, who shuddered and sobbed against her shoulder.

Anne soothed her as she would a child. Eventually, the sobs eased. Mrs. Egerton pulled back, gulping, "I am sorry, so sorry—"

Anne hushed her. "There is no need to speak. It would be please me greatly, however, if you would sip a little brandy."

For a long while they sat together, sipping brandy and watching the room grow dark. Mrs. Egerton's sniffles lessened and she became more composed. "I must dress for supper," she said. "Please know that I appreciate your kindness." Through red-rimmed eyes she gave Anne a brave look.

Anne sat alone for a few minutes and then returned to her letter. After what she had witnessed, she could not finish it. Crushing the paper into a ball, she tossed it into the fire and waited while it burned.

Chapter 32

"I thought you did not enjoy cards," said Lady Braybrooke as she laid down a queen of hearts.

"I seldom do, but it suits me today," replied Anne. In truth, she could not settle to anything. She had talked with Mr. Palmer over dinner about the appalling state of London's hospitals, of which neither had any experience, though both were ready to draw on hearsay. "If you are not sick when you go in," he said, "you will certainly be very ill, or dead, coming out."

Later in the drawing room Mr. Nelkins pined for a sweet and pretty neighbor. "She is a vision of virtue and loveliness," he said, looking at Anne with luminous eyes. "Just to be near her makes me feel more alive than ever I feel when visiting churches or combing through dusty manuscripts. Her father is against the match." He shook his head forlornly. "She is not yet fourteen, and I am not a wealthy man."

A break in the clouds called nearly everyone out of doors to the stable or garden paths or woods. Anne joined Lady Metcalfe on the terrace.

"Mrs. Egerton has taken ill," said her ladyship, a worried frown on her face. "Lady Coldham believes she might be in the family way, but the signs are vague. It would do her good to start a family, for she seems to enjoy children—or, at least, the idea of them—and a child would animate her. She is much too melancholy for one so young." She turned the conversation. "Shall you stay with us for another week or two?"

"I had thought to enjoy your company another week, but with this damp weather, I believe I should do better at Rosings."

"I am not surprised to hear it. You don't seem yourself today. Are the aches very bad?"

"My knees have become quite stiff. When my rheumatism flares, the question is whether a carriage ride can be better endured now or later."

"I understand. When you decide on a day, tell Ross. He will arrange everything for you."

"Thank you. I appreciate your kindness."

Lady Metcalfe's eyes sparkled. "Did you meet any lovers? I had thought Mr. Nelkins might be growing fond of you."

Anne laughed. "Mr. Nelkins is besotted with the thirteen-year-old daughter of his neighbor."

"Ah, it can be hard to tell what a young man is thinking—or if, in fact, he *does* think. There is, then, no threat to Mr. Darcy's claim. Lady Catherine will be happy to hear it." Lady Metcalfe was distracted by the approach of Mrs. Mitchell, who spoke to her in a low voice. "Excuse me, Miss Anne. I must speak with the cook."

Not being dressed for standing in a chill wind, Anne sought solace in the library. Candles had been lit and a fire laid. Only Mr. Worthington was at work. He occupied the desk where she had sat the previous day and confronted Mr. Egerton. Book in hand, she took a wing-backed chair near the fire. Time was lost to her.

"Miss de Bourgh, may I interrupt your reading?" Mr. Worthington appeared weary-eyed and a haggard look haunted his tanned face. His lanky frame stood somewhat intimidatingly over her.

"Of course."

He sat down on the edge of the chair opposite. "I wish—that is, Amelia … Mrs. Egerton told me of your kindness to her yesterday. She was quite distraught and found your presence reassuring. Would it be too much trouble to tell me what happened?" His eyes pleaded his case. "She will not speak of it."

Anne had not expected to be asked such a question. Should she speak honestly? Would such terrible language only anger and wound the man? How could it possibly comfort him? "I prefer not to describe it."

"It is vital that you do so."

In his look she saw affection for his cousin written plain. "I will say only that her husband assaulted her with the most violent language."

"He did not assault her physically, then?"

She cast down her eyes, refusing to reply. She did not wish to be rude, but likewise she would not speak openly of Mr. Egerton's utter baseness.

"I find my answer in your demeanor."

Her face colored at his perception.

"My cousin said she found a friend in you. Your thoughtfulness—"

From the doorway, Mr. Palmer rapped the oaken door and called, "Worthy, come. Lord Metcalfe wishes to ride."

When he stood, Anne said, "Mr. Worthington, would you ask Mrs. Egerton if I might write to her? It would be my pleasure to do so."

"Worthy!" Mr. Palmer was impatient to be off.

"Coming, Palmer," Mr. Worthington said as he strode to the desk. He scribbled a few lines along the bottom of his drawing and returned to her, saying, "She will enjoy hearing from you, but take care in how you write." His implication was clear. "Thank you," he said with great sincerity before turning to follow his friend.

Anne thought he had fine eyes and wondered how it would feel to enjoy, if only for a moment, their affectionate gaze upon herself.

Chapter 33

"He slapped her!" cried Tilly.

"Yes. I never thought to see such violence or experience such menace myself. No wonder the poor lady looks ill. She must live daily with the threat of force."

"How is such a thing to be borne?" Tilly shook her head. "No wife should be expected to endure such malice."

"Since women cannot claim for themselves the freedoms men enjoy, Mrs. Egerton has few options."

"I wonder at his being so brazen as to assault her in a public setting. Why anybody, even his lordship, might have been there. Only think what the cad might do in private." Tilly checked her watch. "Oh, the time! I must return to the house and check on Marianne. She has been feverish these past few days—another tooth is erupting. I am glad you returned safely. Do you think Lady Metcalfe is aware of the goings-on in her house?"

Anne walked her out. "I cannot say. She has a good deal of intuition, but she cannot be everywhere at once in such a house."

"I shall pray for Mrs. Egerton's safety and strength," said Tilly before kissing her friend's cheek.

Anne watched her friend run across the lawn and enter the trees. The chill October wind rustled the leaves and thick clouds darkened the sky. Anne retreated to the library. She requested a pot of tea and began a letter to Lady Metcalfe. The exercise proved a trial, for Mrs. Egerton's sad situation intruded on her thoughts. Her letter finished, she pulled Mr. Worthington's drawing from her writing box and studied it again. He had redrawn the grass snake, placing it in its natural setting among the weeds. Her focus lingered on the snake's flicked tongue and alert eye. Even in graphite, the creature seemed to breathe. At the bottom he had written Mrs. Egerton's direction in a neat but tight hand. She would write to Mrs. Egerton, but first she was in want of a shawl.

As she traversed the hall, a cry reached her ears: "No!"

The shout came from the front of the house. Its unearthly sound made Anne pause. She listened for further utterances, and hearing none, but fearing some monstrous catastrophe, hurried through the antechamber and entered the drawing room. Lady Catherine gaped at the rector, her face a rictus of anguish. Mr. Collins stood pale as a graveyard specter.

"What has happened? Mama, are you unwell?" Anne went to her side. "Please, sit. Let me fetch a glass of wine for you."

Lady Catherine stared right through her daughter.

Anne knew not how to comfort her, but reached out to touch her mother's arm, at which action Lady Catherine spun away and charged from the room, nearly colliding with Nichol, who carried a laden tea tray. Nichol shied at her passing.

"Shall I serve the tea now, Miss?" the maid asked in confusion.

Anne recalled herself. "Yes, tea is the very thing. Mr. Collins, are you quite well? You look stricken. Please be seated and allow me to pour you some refreshment. Nichol, see that her ladyship wants for nothing. If the apothecary is needed, ask Hobbs to send for him directly."

"Yes, ma'am." Nichol set the tray down and hastened away upstairs.

Mr. Collins sank heavily onto the sofa. Anne had never found much to admire in the rector, but she felt truly sorry for him at the moment. She poured a cup of tea and added two lumps of sugar, per the rector's usual habit. Fearing he could not handle anything so delicate as a porcelain teacup, she set the refreshment on the table at his elbow.

When he looked more in control of himself, she said, "Mr. Collins, I wish to understand what happened here."

"I shared with her ladyship some news that has distressed her." Mr. Collins sat hunched forward, his shoulders sagging. He pulled a handkerchief from his coat pocket and patted his forehead. "Mrs. Collins received a letter from her sister, Miss Lucas, informing her of an engagement: Miss Elizabeth Bennet's older sister is engaged to be married."

Anne hoped this news was a delight to the Bennet family, but its implications were obscure. "Excuse me, Mr. Collins, but I am no more knowledgeable than when I sat down. Why would this news affect her ladyship so severely?"

Mr. Collins took a long draught of tea. His nerves were so rattled the teacup shook when he set it down. "The man Miss Bennet is engaged to marry is a close friend of your cousin." His look pleaded with her to forgive him for imparting bad news. "Her letter hinted at the probability of Miss Elizabeth Bennet being soon engaged to—to Mr. Darcy." He let out a long breath at having conveyed the worst of it.

Anne's thoughts whirled at the supposition. The image of Darcy towering over her, growling "You know nothing of duty," mingled with his dark look the morning he departed Rosings. Had their conversation in the library given him rein to align his ideas of duty with his desire for felicity in marriage? Could he have taken so bold a step?

"Mr. Collins, the information about Mr. Darcy and Miss Bennet appears to be pure speculation. It is not known in fact. Why would this conjecture so affect her ladyship?"

"Her ladyship was prepared to believe it true, but as to why that should be, I don't know. If you will excuse me, I must return to the parsonage. I am not feeling well."

"Of course. Let me walk you out."

Anne was surprised at Mr. Collins. He quit the house quite insensible to his surroundings and never commented on her apparent lack of offense at the news. He would be annoyed with himself later for this lapse, she was sure.

Chapter 34

"Miss—excuse me, Miss," whispered Shaw. Not being able to stir her mistress with words, she poked her arm. "Miss, wake up."

Anne awakened groggily. "Shaw?"

"Her ladyship is fixing to leave the house, ma'am. I thought you might like to know."

"Her ladyship? Leave the house? Now?" Anne's eyes searched the darkness. "The sun is not up. Mama does not like to rise in the dark."

"Yes, ma'am, I know. If you wish to see her before she leaves the grounds, you must get out o' your bed now. You have no time to dress."

"Gracious heaven, what is she about? Here, fetch my wrapper." Anne pulled her braided hair over one shoulder while Shaw helped her into her robe. On descending the staircase, her mother could be seen crossing the Great Hall. Her coat swirled around her legs as she strode forward with purpose; her muff was wrapped around one arm.

"Mama! Mama!" cried Anne as she rushed down the stairs. Her mother could not help but hear her call, for the house was quiet as a tomb, and yet she marched straight through the door, down the front step, and across the gravel drive to the carriage, as if she were deaf to the world.

The barouche stood ready. Two liveried men wrestled a trunk

onto the rack, while another held the lead horse's reins. Dawson sat perched atop, his whip in hand, while Galton checked the harnesses. Hobbs rushed to assist Lady Catherine into the carriage, where Mrs. Dawson sat primly.

"Mama, where do you go? If you delay your departure an hour or two, I shall come with you," called Anne as she approached the carriage.

Lady Catherine signaled Hobbs to close the door and pulled the check-string. The horses strained forward, even as a footman struggled to jump onto the back step. Anne trotted alongside, shouting, "Mama, wait." After a few paces she gave up the chase and watched the carriage disappear behind the rhododendrons and head toward the Bromley road.

"Come, Hobbs, let us return to the house. Oh, the morning is chilly." Anne shivered as she led the way. Over the course of the morning she made no progress identifying her mother's compulsion. The servants, each questioned privately, could state no reason for her ladyship's unexpected travel. Anne believed Darcy stood at the heart of it, but confirmation must wait for her ladyship's return or a letter from a confederate.

At Tilly's, speculations about Lady Catherine's mysterious absence took precedence. "She must have traveled to London to accost Mr. Darcy, given the rumors of his engagement to Miss Bennet," said Tilly. "Where else would she go in such a hurry?"

Mrs. Collins, for one, could imagine her ladyship journeying all the way to Longbourn to challenge Lizzie directly, but she wisely kept her own counsel. Likewise she refrained from confessing her hope of the match, fearing Anne would be wounded by it.

"I believe you are right," Anne interposed, guessing what her companions were thinking. "I shall be mortified if Lady Catherine tries to interfere with Darcy's wishes, but you know her character. She is most happy when she is organizing everybody. For years she has pictured me marrying her favorite nephew and may lose all reason if Darcy challenges her plan. For my part, I hope the rumor proves true."

"Do you, truly?" asked a startled Mrs. Collins.

"Why, yes. If Darcy has the nerve to marry Miss Bennet against my mother's wishes, I applaud him and wish them both very happy. Indeed, I believe Miss Bennet will do him good. She will improve him. Where he is aloof and introspective, she is lively and companionable. It says much about his character and understanding that he seeks a wife who will help him overcome his personal deficiencies."

"Don't let Lady Catherine hear you speak of Mr. Darcy's deficiencies," warned Tilly.

"Of course not, but we are none of us perfect. Darcy is a man of good character and high principles, but he can be proud and disagreeable and bad-tempered. Miss Bennet will smooth his rough edges, soften his manners, and plague him with her wit and vivacity. I wonder if he quite understands what sort of woman she is."

"Surely he must, or he would not have lost his heart to her, if so be the case," declared Tilly. "They will make a handsome couple. Picture their charming children—all dark-eyed beauties." She lost her composure briefly. "Speaking of children, I wish to share my news: I am in the family way. John is pleased, but I had hoped to avoid another pregnancy for at least a year. It seems Providence decided otherwise."

Anne was about to offer her congratulations when Mrs. Collins spoke shyly: "Providence has blessed me as well, for I am also in the family way."

Every good wish and encouragement was shared among them. Anne listened to their happy chatter but could add nothing to their speculations about birthing dates and laments about morning sickness. She was not resentful. Rather, with the news that Darcy may have engaged himself to Miss Bennet, a kernel of hope rose in her breast: she might, at last, set a new course for her life.

Chapter 35

Lady Catherine could not be satisfied. A difficult, demanding woman at the best of times, she had become rude and imperious since returning from her third mysterious trip of the year.

"You stupid girl! Not this one, the other one," she complained to Letty when the wrong shawl had been fetched.

The entire household felt imperiled; its servants retreated to the shadows, tread the halls quietly, and spoke in hushed tones. Anne knew better than to speak a word on the topic of berating the staff.

"The servants have become slovenly in my absence," said her ladyship as she cut into a duck pie. "I would replace the lot of them tomorrow if I could. But to what end? Servants drawn from the country cannot be trained, and those in Town are no better."

Anne glanced at Vaughn standing next to the sideboard, prepared as always to help his mistresses. His face reddened.

"Shall you meet with Mr. Collins this evening, Mama? I daresay he has many parish problems to share with you."

"Very likely. We shall finalize the service for Sunday—St. Crispin's Day. Mr. Collins shall admonish us to reflect on whether we labor for the good of our Lord or toil in vain. I should think the latter is the more common among his parishioners."

Hobbs approached. "Excuse me, ma'am. There is a letter for you." He extended a silver salver.

Lady Catherine reached for it, broke the wafer, and read the short missive. Her face drained of color. "Oh! No!" she cried, pushing her dinner plate, which clinked against her half-full teacup, upsetting its contents. She stared across the table at her daughter while her mouth worked in vain. Finally she blurted, "This—this is *your* fault."

Anne reached across the widening stain and righted the cup. "Whatever is the matter?"

"You! You are the matter." Her ladyship's hands trembled. "Slovenly, disagreeable girl—you made no effort, tried no arts, formed no plan. You have ruined us. I shall never forgive you."

Anne's stomach lurched. "Tell me what has happened."

"Darcy writes to say he has engaged himself to Miss Elizabeth Bennet! I long suspected the girl's pretensions but had not imagined her success. Your indifference toward my nephew has crushed our hope for a secure future."

"Mama—"

"If you had not been so ill-natured, this would never have happened." She jumped to her feet, crumpling the letter in her hands. "Selfish, selfish girl. You think only of yourself." Lady Catherine stalked from the room. A shout rang down the hall. A door slammed. The house held its breath and dared not exhale for hours.

Anne sought solace in the conservatory, her thoughts whirling. So Darcy has made his choice. The die is cast. How can it be otherwise? I do not love him; he does not love me. It is natural and just that he should choose another, and I believe he will be happy with Miss Bennet. But why do I feel unsettled?

A childhood memory burst to life: a chill day in May, a promise fulfilled, Papa rowing a small boat, herself shrieking when he whacked the water with a paddle, cold drops sprinkling her face, and later, his pulling to the water's edge—she could not say what stream or river—where he tied the boat to a low-hanging tree branch and climbed ashore; turning, he shouted, "Oy!" and charged into the rushing depths, making a frantic plunge to catch a trailing rope as the boat parted company with the weedy bank. She had felt no fear. Papa would rescue her, even at his own peril. And so he did. But Darcy would not. She pictured her cousin standing in the tall weeds. His dark eyes caught her surprise: he did not care where the wee boat carried her. His tall form retreated behind the overhanging shrubbery as the water rippled, gathering speed as it swept downstream. Her bowels churned. With fear? Perhaps at first, with the shock of the news, but now with a wondrous excitement. She was free—no longer chained to her engagement, no longer bound by expectations and duty. Was her decision foolish? No. She made this choice, anticipating the consequences, acting on impulses that felt right and good. Her fate was not tied to his. Her future was her own.

A throb of pleasure nearly made her laugh aloud. She was free.

—⁂—

In the drawing room Lady Catherine tortured a piece of writing paper. She dipped a quill in her ink pot and scribbled hurriedly.

"Mama, may I ask to whom you are writing?"

"I'm not on speaking terms with you, it pains me to say. But since you ask, I write to Darcy. I shall give him my thoughts on his engagement. He would not listen when I stopped in London—young men can be utterly stupid. Perhaps a letter, written by one of his nearest relations and pointing out the evils of his choice of wife, will be better received. I shall remind him again of his mother's wish and his father's expectation that he fulfill his duty to our family. Bah! This quill pen is worthless." She combed through her writing implements and chose a fresh one. "Miss Bennet is pretty, but she has no connections and brings no dowry. She and her notorious family—especially that scandalous sister of hers—will be the ruin of him. He must be prevented from throwing himself away on a chit, a nobody, from the wilds of Hertfordshire."

Anne had been horrified to hear of Miss Bennet's youngest sister having eloped with uncle Darcy's god-son, George Wickham. His treachery was easily imagined, for she recalled several nasty experiences at Wickham's hand when she was a girl. Foremost among them was the evening she had succumbed to his charm; in a fit of passion her animal spirits had overpowered her common sense and led to disgrace. She pitied Miss Bennet's sister for having so little sense as to tie her future to his base character.

"Please don't send Darcy this letter," pleaded Anne. "It will offend him. I fear it may estrange him from you, who hold him so dearly."

"I shall not thank you for your advice, as I did not seek it and have no use of it." Lady Catherine all but stabbed a hole in the writing paper, so distressed was her style.

"Mama, take a moment to think about what you are doing. He has made his choice. Do you not want him to be happy?"

"Happy? Whatever does happiness have to do with it? Felicity in marriage comes from honoring one's duty. He would do better to marry you, despite your disagreeable nature, and thereby unite the family estates. I write to predict his regret one day, when he realizes his wife is beneath him in character and situation. That day will come, for he will soon be embarrassed at his folly in succumbing to the allurements of a scheming, low-class girl."

"How can you speak so unfeelingly of Miss Bennet?"

"Very easily. She refused to marry Mr. Collins, believing herself above the dignity of the clergy. I was not surprised to learn of her refusal, for her eyes were always set higher. Well, she shall not have Darcy."

Anne wondered at her mother's intent, for Darcy would never break an engagement, especially when he was in love with the lady. "I don't comprehend how you can condemn either party. Darcy is a gentleman; Miss Bennet is a gentleman's daughter. Their engagement is not shameful, for both are commoners and stand equal in marriage. Consider your own union. In marrying Papa, you fell from the realm of the peer to that of the baronetcy. How can Darcy's situation be more demeaning than yours?"

Lady Catherine returned a hateful stare. "As usual, you comprehend nothing."

Volume III

Chapter 36

"You look distressed, dear Anne. What troubles you?"

"Mama is maddening. She plans to embark on a matrimonial scheme and speaks of traveling to London, where she will introduce me to the single sons of her friends. Why can she not leave me alone? I am determined to refuse her."

Tilly smiled at Anne's complaint, thinking how familiar its tone.

"You find my situation diverting?"

"Of course not. I only wonder why you don't bend a little when the wind blows hard. If you struggle against your mother's determination, it will only make you ill. Better to keep to your own course but endeavor to accommodate her wishes when you have an opportunity of doing so. Your being agreeable to the idea of a trip to London is sure to improve her temper. Is not that desirable? Do you not wish for a good-tempered mother?"

Anne barked a laugh. "How sweetly you speak while holding a knife to my throat."

Tilly overlooked this outburst. "I appreciate that you cannot ignore the source of Lady Catherine's misery. She is cast down by Mr. Darcy's marriage."

Anne fiddled with the fringe on her shawl. "It's Mama's own fault. After receiving her letter, I cannot blame Darcy for refusing to invite us to his wedding. I fear any mention of his happy day shall always rankle her."

"Go to London," said Tilly. "Your mother will feel useful at a time when all her fondest wishes lie in ruins. As it is now, she worries over your future and hers. Mr. Darcy's marriage has affected her deeply. Few men are as perfect in her eyes as he, for he combines integrity with a handsome visage and a mighty estate. His being lost to your family is a source of great pain to her. An unmanned river boat could be no more adrift than your mother is at present."

Anne frowned at Tilly's understanding. "Yours is a sensible suggestion, I allow. But do you think I can hold to my own course?" This was the perennial question. Could she grant her mother's wishes without throwing over her own? And what exactly did she want? Her list of longings began respectably enough—an affectionate husband, loving children, a happy household, one true talent—but then slid fairly quickly into the ordinary (wealth, ease, good health) and the peculiar (travel and adventure, when possible; peace and quietude, when needed; a surfeit of good books, always), before descending to petty frivolity (pretty hair, a more womanly figure, long eyelashes like Tilly's). At seven and twenty years of age, she could not state the one thing she most desired in life. No, that was not true. Her one genuine desire was so awful, so unspeakable, she would not share it with anyone, not even Tilly.

"You found your voice this past year," Tilly was saying. "It took courage to tell Mr. Darcy you did not wish to marry him, knowing your action would thwart your mother's wishes. Not every daughter can stand her ground against so formidable a force. Go to London. Her ladyship will gain the satisfaction of believing herself in charge of your future, while you experience the pleasures of London and keep to your own path. Who knows? Whilst in London, you might chance to meet a handsome doctor with fine eyes."

"Dr. Granville." Anne sighed. "It has been a year since he delivered Marianne. He cannot think of me at all after so many months. Frankly, I don't expect to renew our acquaintance, there being a multitude of people in London, even in March." Shyly she added, "I do wish to see him again."

The next week found Anne supervising the packing of two clothing trunks.

"Good Heaven, Miss, I am very excited to travel to London," said Shaw. "Emily is jealous. She longs to visit Town. Indeed, she dreams of sailing to America, of all places. I am not so adventuresome. Indeed, I wonder at our nerve for traveling in this sleet."

"All will be well, Shaw. The sleet is not likely to last long and you don't travel alone. Mrs. Jenkinson and Dawson accompany you."

"Mrs. Jenkinson! She complains at having to travel in the second coach. Dawson is quite put out with her. As for myself, I am quivering, for I have never seen Chidham House. I hear it is very grand."

Shaw's excitement was infectious. At the appointed hour, Anne was dressed in her finest, warm coat, her hands tucked into a white muff. She stood in the Great Hall, waiting for her mother. Lady Catherine started down the staircase, still issuing orders to Letty, whose look betrayed exasperation at her mistress's final demands.

"Hobbs, see that the second coach leaves within the hour," ordered her ladyship while pulling on her gloves.

Anne proceeded to the waiting barouche. When the footman opened the door, she stepped into the coach and took a seat at the farthest end of the forward-facing bench. Her hands, clasped inside her muff, were cold, more from anxiety than from the frosty morning air. Her mother paused on being handed up, but settled herself on the bench, not speaking a word, but making a point of the inconvenience by tucking her coat close on that side nearest her daughter. When she pulled the check-string, their conveyance jerked forward.

Anne's heart fluttered at her mother's rude move, but any worry about the consequences of her own saucy action was overturned by the time the coach turned north. Happy scenes crowded her thoughts, and her imagination cheerfully tortured itself recalling Dr. Granville's looks and gentle voice. As the coach rumbled toward London, she reminded herself that their meeting in Town was unlikely, for the Great Metropolis was densely populated, and Lady Catherine would restrict her introductions to aristocratic sons. A lowly doctor, no matter how admirable his character, could not stand against the slings of money, title, and power.

Chapter 37

Lady Catherine's matrimonial campaign began as soon as the knocker was placed on the door, heralding their arrival at Chidham House. Over breakfast that first cold morning, she announced her intention of applying for admission to Almack's.

"I will not go," said Anne.

"You will." Lady Catherine signaled the servant to refill her teacup. "You seem not to appreciate, silly as it sounds, that our status as a family depends upon obtaining tickets to Almack's. A family's fortunes can be ruined in a single stroke by the Lady Patronesses, all gathered around their silly table in King Street. That cruel cabal may deny our application for whatever reason suits them and without explanation. They exert absolute power over our situation in society."

"I am too old to dance at Almack's and will appear ridiculous standing next to girls ten years my junior. To attend now, at my age, would be a travesty of decorum."

"I agree with you there. It is unfortunate we are forced to pursue this course. Had you won Darcy's affection, we would not find ourselves at the mercy of Countess Lieven and the other Shallow Seductresses, who, without exception, are pertinacious and vindictive. If we don't succeed in securing tickets from these fickle arbiters of fashion, then we are lost. We cannot hold our heads high as members of a noble, ancient family. We will be snubbed, and you stand no chance of making a suitable marriage." On seeing her daughter's challenging stare, she stood and threw her napkin on the table. "If I must grovel like a common cur, if I must prostrate myself like a slave before these self-appointed rulers of style, if I succeed in obtaining tickets, then *you* will attend." She quit the breakfast room looking more haughty than usual.

"I will not," whispered Anne under her breath when her mother was out of hearing.

Later that morning Lady Catherine quit the house to call on Lady Cowper and present her case for an Almack's subscription. Anne and Mrs. Jenkinson walked to Hyde Park; on their return Anne observed the butler's grim expression. "Has her ladyship returned, Juggins?"

"Yes, ma'am. She is in the drawing room."

Anne found Lady Catherine standing before the well-stoked fire. "Did you find Lady Cowper agreeable?"

"I was received," replied Lady Catherine.

But not welcomed, Anne surmised.

"We are invited to meet the Committee tomorrow," said Lady Catherine. "Next week we shall know our success."

"Invited? Is that how the command was worded?"

Chapter 38

At precisely three o'clock, Anne followed her mother into the lionesses' den. The Lady Patronesses sat in chairs arranged around a large table covered with a red cloth. Their demeanors did not encourage pleasantries. As soon as Anne and her mother were seated, one of the Shallow Seductresses spoke, addressing her questions directly to Anne.

"You are rather old to apply to Almack's, are you not?"

"I am, Lady Castlereagh."

This admission seemed to surprise the inquisitor, who covered her reaction with another question: "Why did you not apply for admission to Almack's years ago?"

"I nearly succumbed to a putrid infection at the age of seventeen. Since that time my health might best be described as indifferent." Anne saw Lady Castlereagh's little moue. None of this intelligence would be fresh, for Lady Cowper would have shared Lady Catherine's conversation regarding her daughter with all the Patronesses.

"Are you engaged to be married?"

"Not at present, your ladyship. For many years I was promised to my cousin, the son of Lady Catherine's deceased sister—a handsome man of good character with a large property in Derbyshire. Sadly, his affection was never mine to claim. You must allow: it is harder to marry a daughter well than to bring her up well."

Lady Castlereagh ignored this last remark. "Why do you deserve a ticket?"

Aye, there's the rub, Anne said to herself. She had been pondering the proper attitude to convey during this trial. She looked from lady to lady. Each eye judged her beauty and style, her worth and position in society. In her favor were her ownership of Rosings and her connection to Lord Matlock; against her were her plain face and advanced age. The outcome of this match mattered little to her. If the verdict was Nay, she would not be ashamed of herself and her family. Since her character was fixed, her being an adult and not a simpering chit of seventeen, the fact of being denied entry to Almack's might be a disappointment, but it would not destroy her. The *ton* was a merciless crowd, like hounds on the hunt. She did not care to play its game, and the Lady Patronesses knew it.

"I seek admittance to Almack's to please Lady Catherine," replied Anne. "Since my cousin married another lady, Lady Catherine now bears the unexpected duty of making a marriage for her grown daughter. Surely every feeling mother dreads this circumstance. Would you not do the same for your daughters?"

The Countess of Jersey's eyebrow twitched.

Lady Castlereagh cleared her throat. "We pose the questions here. Can you dance? Country girls are rudely ignorant of the steps and have no style. Indeed, the débutantes to whom we award tickets are, without exception, elegant and modest and worthy of attending our exclusive little club." She nodded to her fellow conspirators and received their ready affirmations in return.

"I dance very well and know the German waltz." Anne raised her chin to the height of haughtiness. "Monsieur Bourchier was my instructor for all but the waltz, in which I was trained by Herr Schröder." This last part was a lie. She had not been instructed by anybody in the waltz, but knew London society was animated with talk of the dancing sensation. Although lying was not a habit with her, she refused to be intimidated by these powerful peacocks and proved her mettle by returning their pointed stares.

Lady Catherine was subdued on the return to Chidham House. On entering the front hall, she said, "All hope is lost after your shameful lies and confessions. As with Darcy, you have ruined our chance of success."

"Quite the contrary, Mama. We shall receive tickets. I am sure of it." Anne lifted her gown and mounted the stairs to the upper floor, knowing her insight to be true, but not understanding how she came to know it.

Chapter 39

Anne sat at her desk in the morning room. Lady Catherine was not yet dressed, which allowed her to enjoy a few minutes alone. She settled to her task:

Chidham House Wednesday March —th

Dearest Tilly,

Thank you for writing of Charlotte's good health and of your own. I am relieved to know my friends thrive in this cold weather. And how does my god-daughter do? I demand news of her smiles and babbles!—Mama and I are not so much thriving as surviving. I believe she is exhausted after only two weeks in Town. Poor creature. She applied to Almack's for tickets, having first called on Lady Cowper, who received her without much enthusiasm. Mama said she was forced to grovel, which idea intrigues me, for I have never known her to abase herself to anybody. The Lady Patronesses invited (nay, ordered) us to meet with them. They were haughty but civil. Yesterday, Mama sent Corby, attired in his finest livery, to learn our fate. He hurried back, waving a three-cornered note that confirmed our acceptance for a set of balls. My prediction of acceptance having proved true, I shall garb myself in rags and make my way in the world as a fortune-teller.—I cannot think why the Lady Patronesses consented to our attendance and wonder at the schemes that brought them to support us. Of course, Mama is the daughter of an earl and sister to Lord Matlock, whose powers might have smoothed her way. Frankly, I believe the Lady Patronesses approved my admission for spite. They delight in my being conspicuously mature. They anticipate my embarrassment at being ignored and forced to watch the dancing from the perimeter. They shall relish my fall from grace. Still, Mama is jolly as a sandboy and disposed to be kinder toward me than usual; and although I at first resisted the idea, I am sufficiently curious about the entire affair as to consent to go.—The next chapter in her ladyship's book is set: we have appointments with Madame Chaumond, one of London's best dressmakers. Mama vows we will adorn Almack's in style, never betraying our origins as country bumpkins (my words, dearest, not hers). I fear my vanity exceeds all bounds, for an Almack's ticket means I am not the quiz I thought I was.—Write at once. I long to hear from you.

Yours very affectionately, Anne

Chapter 40

The days leading up to the ball at Almack's were exhausting and exhilarating. Anne's ball gown was fitted three times in as many days, until Madame Chaumond at last pronounced the fit perfect. It was a beautiful dress: silk the color of French champagne over a sheer white slip. A green sash, the color of an avocado, encircled the bodice.

Now at half past nine o'clock Anne and her mother waited impatiently in the carriage as it inched its way to the hall's entrance.

"What a shocking crush," said Lady Catherine. "There must be a hundred coaches in line. I should think we have another half hour at least to wait."

"Is it always thus, do you suppose?" asked Anne as she looked toward the entrance where a throng of ladies and gentlemen pushed their way into the hall

"I cannot say, but I trust we arrive before the doors are locked."

"The doors are locked?"

"Oh, yes—at precisely eleven o'clock. Not even a member of Parliament can enter. Why, the Duke of Norfolk himself would be turned away should he apply for admittance even five minutes after eleven. It seems a stupid rule to me, but so it is. Ah, I believe we are close enough to quit the carriage and not be accused of approaching the ball on foot."

They joined the excited mass and gave their tickets to the door-man, who inspected each one with care. After relieving themselves of their coats, they entered the spacious, high-ceilinged hall. Two rows of sofas ranged all around the room and faced the dance floor. At the upper end of the saloon, the Lady Patronesses sat on their particular sofa; their ruby- and diamond-bedecked head-dresses glinted in the candle light. Nearby the orchestra rail was hung with garlands of flowers. Anne followed her mother until she stopped at an empty sofa in the second row.

"We shall sit here," said Lady Catherine. "It is not, perhaps, the best location, but our late arrival prevented us from obtaining a better situation."

"I have never seen such fashion and glitter." Anne stared across the crowd. "There must be several hundred people here."

"I should say five or six hundred, at least." Her ladyship gave her daughter a determined look and said in a low voice, "Let me remind you of your duty. I expect you to make an effort."

Anne chose to ignore her mother's directive, knowing the thrill of the new was a far greater stimulus to happy participation than duty.

A fashionably dressed woman with sharp eyes approached. "Good evening, Lady Catherine. I heard you were in Town. It has been many years since our families enjoyed one another's company in Wiltshire, when we were mere girls. How does Lord Matlock do?"

"I am pleased to see you after so many years," said Lady Catherine with little joy, for she remembered many dreary afternoons spent in the company of Miss Dodderick, as she was then. "Matlock does very well and is busy with parliamentary affairs. You are not acquainted, I believe, with my daughter, Miss de Bourgh. Anne, allow me to introduce you to Lady Milcombe."

Said lady tucked her chin in acknowledgement before introducing her youngest daughter, Miss Williams, who smiled shyly. "I see you have positioned yourselves close to my nephew and his friends," said Lady Milcombe. On these words, a youngish portly man turned to greet his aunt. "Mr. Hathorn, permit me to introduce Lady Cath-erine de Bourgh and her daughter, Miss de Bourgh. Mr. Hathorn is my sister Jane's son."

"At your service," he said, bowing in a courtly manner. "My friends and I claimed the sofa in the front row and are delighted to share this location with you. Should you find yourself free to dance, Miss de Bourgh, I would be pleased to claim your hand."

"Thank you, sir. It would be my pleasure."

Mr. Hathorn gave her a curt nod before taking his aunt's arm and moving away.

Lady Catherine whispered, "She was always ambitious—a pompous, ingratiating woman who married into the aristocracy despite being the daughter of a squire. Well, you will not dance with her nephew. I am sure he is neither an eligible suitor nor worthy of your time."

"Why should you say so?"

"He is a second son. I expect you to aim for a prize."

"You insisted I attend Almack's. You went to considerable mortification to apply for the opportunity. Now I am here, I will dance with any man who asks me, whether he is an heir or not, whether his belly is as broad as an ox's rump, or though he stands on three legs. You wish me to meet eligible men, and this is the market for doing so. In fact, I hope to dance every set."

Just then the orchestra struck the notes for the opening dance, and couples by the hundreds surged onto the dance floor. Two dances finished and Anne had not been approached or even acknowledged.

"There is Lady Lavendon. Come," said Lady Catherine.

They squeezed their way through the crush of couples standing near the ropes and approached the lady, who readily acknowledged their acquaintance. Her ladyship was a petite woman with bright brown eyes and a quick manner. Her velvet hat, topped with a short, white feather, bobbed with every jerk of her head.

"Lady Lavendon, you may remember my daughter, Miss de Bourgh."

Anne curtsied to the lady's discriminating eye, which priced her dress and adornment to within a guinea, no doubt.

Lady Lavendon introduced her youngest daughter but one and her son. She sent Reginald a sharp look, who said to Anne, "Would you care to dance?"

"I would be honored, sir."

He pushed ahead of her onto the dance floor and chose a position. Anne thought him a passable dancer, but not exceptional. He had sweaty palms and eyed the crowd closely, fearing his friends might see him dancing with a relic. She understood he acted on his mother's command.

When the dance ended, he introduced her to his friend Mr. Dickerson, who took her hand for the next dance. He was an enthusiastic dancer and inclined to overspeaking, relating all he had seen during his visit to London—the clubs! the pubs! the crowds at Vauxhall!—before telling her of his family seat in Staffordshire, of his father having broken his leg while hunting ("he was disguised, you know—drunk as an emperor"), of his sister's recent marriage to a man of no consequence, of his jackanapes of a brother who had lost a fortune (eight thousand pounds!) at the gaming tables and would surely ruin his family, all confessed in a gush. When the dance ended, he bowed to her, saying, "You are an excellent dancer, if not much of a conversationalist."

On circling through the mob to find her mother, she bumped into Mr. Hathorn, who invited her to stand up with him next. As they groped their way to a suitable spot, they edged a group of revelers; the press of the crowd caused two men to lose their footing on the slippery floor. Amid shrieks and cries, they pitched into several dancers, tripping six or seven, including Anne and Mr. Hathorn, who fell in a heap. Two ladies were in tears, one having cracked her elbow badly. Anne blushed at having her gown crumpled up around her knees and her leg pinned by a red-faced man who stammered his apology.

"Goodness," said Mr. Hathorn as he lifted her to her feet. "You are durable to have survived an accident at Almack's."

"What happened?" she asked as she rearranged her gown. "It seemed we were about to begin the dance when we were knocked down."

"It is the floor wax—some odd French concoction that makes the floor as slippery as eels."

"I have never seen an eel, sir, but I now have a profound respect for the species." Several dancers pushed past them, all agog to be dancing.

"Might I suggest we venture into the tea-room? We can endure a cup of truly awful tea and sit for a few minutes in recovery." He led her through the crowd and found an empty sofa, where he insisted she rest while he fetched refreshment. "If the dancing doesn't kill you," he said as he handed her a glass, "the lemonade will."

She took a sip, her face puckering in disgust. "This is lemonade?"

"So they say. I guess the ladies-patronesses spend their money on decorations and the orchestra and never trouble themselves over the refreshment."

"You appear knowledgeable about the club. Have you attended other balls at Almack's?"

"This is my second and last season. If I cannot beguile a lover, then I shall not return. Indeed, I shall not be allowed to, for the Important Personages who rule this fiefdom will turn me away like a one-eyed pauper. In truth, I tire of the race."

"Do you mean you have thrown over every hope of matrimony? You are young and vigorous and likely to meet a suitable lady any day."

"Perhaps you are right, but it is such effort. Observe the couples here in the tea-room. They laugh and flirt and charm. After a few dances and a little conversation, they agree to marry or elope, the decision requiring less thought than might be given to buying a brood mare. The men fall easily before a pretty face and shapely figure. The ladies are smitten by manly looks and visions of a large estate. I have yet to meet a lady who did not first rate the size of my purse before giving a thought to my character."

Anne clutched her glass, never taking another sip, and considered how to respond to thoughts so in agreement with her own. "I believe the lemonade is making you morose," she said. "Assuredly, there is much truth to the proverb 'Marry in haste, and repent at leisure.' Bad marriages are made every day, but happy marriages exist. People sometimes meet at a ball, marry, and make a fine marriage." Mrs. Collins's story of Darcy's meeting his future wife at a Meryton assembly was readily recalled. "When you find the right lady, you will wonder that you ever felt so jaded as to assume women are interested only in money."

"So, you are a philosopher." He grinned. "I had not expected to find such a creature here, but I am returned to my senses by your kindness. Shall we dance?"

"With pleasure," she replied, giving him her hand. They joined the swirl of silk and the bubble of soft laughs.

Chapter 41

The clock on the mantel struck one o'clock when Anne sat down to breakfast, fagged to death. Lady Catherine had insisted on leaving Almack's at half past three, claiming no lady of any age looked good at four o'clock in the morning.

The town-house was quiet. Lady Catherine still lay abed and would not rise for another hour. Anne thought her mother had never looked so haggard as she did when they returned to Chidham House only a few hours ago. Of course, her mother was no longer young, but it was unsettling to see her looking frail. Something about her person was not quite right.

Anne pushed aside her now empty plate, having enjoyed her breakfast of eggs, sausage, and toast, and sat sipping tea. She stared out the window and recalled the evening's adventure: the dazzle of diamonds, the rustle of silk and muslin, the familiar tunes directing the dances, the throng of aristocrats and hopefuls. One country dance had been perfection, for her partner had been confident and graceful and entertaining with his many witticisms about the Lady Patronesses. She had met an agreeable soul or two but no lovers.

Juggins entered the breakfast room. "There are letters for you, Miss."

"Thank you. Tell Mrs. Juggins her eggs were cooked to perfection."

"She will be pleased to hear it," he said, closing the door.

The first letter was from Tilly and full of news about Marianne's antics: she crawled and squatted, pulled herself up next to the tea table, and gurgled at the sound of the door-bell. She nearly swallowed a button, but the nurse's quick action prevented a calamity. As for herself, she was still bedeviled by a persistent sickness nearly every morning, but she was otherwise well. "Did you win any lovers at Almack's? Write soon," Tilly commanded in her handsome script, "for Hunsford is dreadfully boring these days."

Mrs. Collins's letter opened with the hope of Anne's enjoying her visit in London and ended with her thanks for introducing her to Tilly, whose friendship was particularly important now that she was in the family way.

Next was a lengthy letter from Arnot, reassuring her that all was well at Rosings and advising her of the winter wheat crop's looking quite promising. Being too tired to pay close attention to his estimates for crop growth, she picked up the last letter. The handwriting was Mrs. Egerton's. Anne had not heard from her new friend for several weeks. Since being introduced at Dodford Meare the previous September, their correspondence had been regular but rather bland. Predicting another insipid letter about Mrs. Egerton's latest embroidered sampler, she read:

> *Seighford Place Tuesday April —th*
>
> *Dear Miss de Bourgh,*
>
> *I must take care writing to you, for my every action is watched. A horrible event forces me to prevail upon your kind heart, to entreat you to assist me, even though you are a friend I would not wish to offend or harm in any way. But I need a confederate in this desperate hour. You will find enclosed a letter directed to my cousin. Would you be willing—do you have the courage—to forward it to him? I would not impose on you if I could communicate with him directly, but my husband forbids him to enter our house. When Worthy last applied to see me, claiming all the affection and rights of family, he was bodily removed from the hall and thrown upon the drive. The door was locked against him. Please, please, never mention my secret plot, for I tremble to think what*

*evil might befall my faithful servant, who risks her livelihood to
help a poor, secluded soul.*

Your grateful friend, Amelia Egerton

Anne sat up straight. What sort of man denies his wife the pleasure of receiving the affection of family? What sort of man holds
his wife a prisoner? She examined the enclosed letter, especially Mr.
Worthington's direction written in haste, and had no qualms about
the proper course: the letter must be posted. But in what manner
should she communicate with Mr. Worthington? Their connection
was tenuous at best, being founded on a few exchanges at Dodford
Meare. How should she address him?

An idea occurred to her. It was unusual, to say the least, but it
might prove proper or, at least, not improper. She carried the letters
upstairs and retrieved Mr. Worthington's drawing from her sketch
book. She hated to part with it, but nevertheless gathered several
crayons in green, brown, and yellow. After adding the barest hint
of color to his original drawing, she blended the colors along the
snake's back with the tip of her little finger. Considerable care was
required not to smudge the graphite. The overall effect pleased her
eye; she hoped it would please his. At the bottom of the sheet she
wrote: *in service to your cousin and my friend.* Mrs. Egerton's letter was
tucked inside, the missive sealed, and Mr. Worthington's direction
written boldly. Her nerves were alive with the realization that this
was the first personal letter she had ever posted to a man who was
not a relative. She wondered what he would think on receiving it.

Chapter 42

"Lady Lavendon invites us to a private ball on Thursday," said Lady Catherine, pleased with the number of invitations to dinner, carriage rides in Hyde Park, card games, and exhibits. "That son of hers is nothing to look at, but he stands to inherit property in Suffolk. There is talk his great aunt intends to bequeath her estate in Lancashire to him as well, although why anybody would care to live that far north is beyond comprehension. Still, we shall make what we can of the invitation. You need a new gown. I shall write Madame Chaumond." She rose from her *table à écrire*, an odd grimace on her face. "I ordered the carriage for six o'clock. Although I am not fond of Lady Milcombe, we cannot decline her supper invitation."

Anne was tired of Town. She missed the vista from her bedchamber at Rosings, the library's beloved haunts, the sunlight falling on ferns in the conservatory, and the earthy smells of the stables. The gardens would be alive with blooms on tree and bush alike. She missed Tilly and Mrs. Collins, Dr. Bailey, and Arnot. So deep was her longing for the sedate comfort of Rosings that she felt peeved all through Lady Milcombe's raucous supper, the food being indifferent and the company worse.

Days later she endured the frivolity of a ball. After an hour of dancing she escaped to the window seat in Lady Lavendon's ballroom, from whence she could observe the actors in the evening's romantic comedy. The hostess had invited perhaps forty young people and their parents or chaperons to this smallish ball, where the music was lively and the dancers were giddy and energetic.

When the musicians took a break to whet their whistles, the dancers did the same, forming small groups of mostly silly young ladies on one side of the saloon and awkward, boisterous men on the other. One gentleman, to whom she had been introduced earlier, joined her in the alcove.

"The man is a veritable bacon-brain. No, worse: a pompous fool." said Mr. Urson. "I never heard such nonsense in my life. He will not listen to reason. I join you in this alcove to elude his hallucinations, ere they be catching." Leaning close he whispered, "I would be interested in your opinion. The question being debated is this: Are vegetables capable of sensation?" His dark eyes sparkled under a fringe of heavy eyebrows.

"I confess to having given the idea no thought," replied Anne. Her eyes were drawn to the short, slender scar high on one cheek, which gave him the look of a plundering buccaneer. "What principles form the basis of his argument?"

"Laroche there claims inspiration from a Fellow of the Linnean Society who argues that because animals are irritable, then vegetables, being subject to the same irritability as animals, are also capable of sensation." Mr. Urson turned to her with a quizzical look. "Did you ever meet an onion with instinct?"

Anne laughed. "If I did, I was not aware of it. But what is instinct? If it be the property that propels Animal life to act with pure motivation unconnected to reason—that is, without thought, without any mental power that supports logic and the creation of ideas—then vegetables might be said to possess instinct."

"Don't tell me you are persuaded by his logic." His expression was mocking, but his eyes looked jolly.

"I believe a defense can be mounted. Some actions of plants must be instinctual. Saplings seek the sunlight; ivy vines twist and climb in search of a proper anchor. Plants are sensitive to heat and cold, just as animals are. Mr. Darwin wrote on the irritability of plants, which he claimed was proof of their sensation, albeit, an inferior power compared with that possessed by animals."

Mr. Urson's brow crinkled. "Has this Mr. Darwin published a book?"

"He wrote *Zoonomia*."

"Of course. No man is considered great unless he has published a book," he joked. "I have no time for such intellectual enterprises, being better suited to the out of doors. Are you fond of gardening?"

"Oh, yes, I enjoy my rose bushes and also paint fruit and flowers."

"Truly? I once spent a morning sketching the vista from Box Hill, but I was not satisfied with my success."

"I often find myself in the same muddle," said Anne, pleased to find a kindred soul. "Why can I not capture what I see? I should be able, with practice, to render faithfully a simple flower, tree, or piece of statuary. Yet, I cannot."

"My drawings of the vineyards on Mt. Etna were so disgusting I burned them."

"Were you taking the Tour? I should like to travel to foreign lands. I have never visited Italy or France or any foreign port. Indeed, I have never sailed from England's shores and rarely travel outside of Kent."

"I have seen many interesting cities," he said with little enthusiasm, "including Rome, Athens, and Paris."

"Paris? I would love to visit Paris. What was your impression of it?"

His nose wrinkled. "Paris stinks and is full of Frenchmen."

As the topic appeared to offend him, she refrained from querying him further. Just then Mr. Lavendon, standing across the saloon in a circle of lanky youth, guffawed rudely and grabbed a friend's shoulder. A harsh comment mortified the friend, whose face reddened.

"Now there is a puppy." Mr. Urson nodded toward his host, a sneer sitting on his lips.

"How is it that you know him?"

"I once performed a favor for him."

Anne wondered whether the favor had to do with a gambling debt, for it was rumored that Lord Lavendon's eldest son was a shameless spendthrift. Indeed, when the rumor reached Chidham House, she informed her mother of her intent to avoid Mr. Lavendon in company; she certainly would not encourage him by any romantic arts, never mind marry him, for she could not bear the idea of relinquishing control of Rosings to a scattergood. Lady Catherine did not hesitate to relay her opinion: "I cannot express much sympathy for you. Had you troubled yourself to secure Darcy's affections, you would not now be faced with settling for a lesser man." Their argument had escalated until Juggins announced their morning callers.

Mr. Urson recalled her to the moment: "And you? When did you meet the noisy cur?"

"I was introduced to Mr. Lavendon a few weeks ago at Almack's."

"Yes, of course. Almack's. Did Brummell attend?"

"I was introduced to him but did not meet with his approval. I had been knocked to the floor earlier in the evening, and my dress was somewhat *en désordre*."

Mr. Urson smiled down on her. "You are uncommonly direct. The other ladies here appear interested only in fashion and gossip; the men find delight in stories of their exploits in the field. Muskets and hounds, that is the thing: the mad chase across dangerous terrain, the thundering herd of horses, the dogs barking and panting, hot on the scent of a tired fox. It is wearying."

"You are not a sporting man, then?"

"I am not fond of country sport. Town Clubs are my sanctuary."

When the musicians took up their instruments, Mr. Urson said, "It seems the vegetable debate has been thrown over in favor of dancing." His tone was dismissive.

"You dislike dancing as well?"

He grinned. "Not if you will be my partner."

On the return to Chidham House, Anne recalled Mr. Urson's pleasing form. He gave the appearance of being quite tall, when, in fact, he was only a few inches taller than herself. His comportment was manly and his dress stylish enough to warrant even Mr. Brummell's regard. Although he appeared a little stiff-necked, his penetrating gaze seemed to hide a light-hearted soul. Whatever faults he might claim, he had been an agreeable dancer.

Chapter 43

"A letter has arrived, Miss."

"Thank you," Anne said, reaching for the lone missive.

"Shall I open a window? The room is stuffy."

"Oh no. I am perfectly comfortable. It is dreary today and I enjoy the warmth. Is not this disagreeable weather so odd in April?" As she spoke a cold, slashing rain pelted the windows.

"The chill will not last long, ma'am," Juggins said, retiring.

Anne recognized Mrs. Collins's handwriting. She held the letter in her hand but made no move to open it; instead, she drooped onto the sofa pillow and stared at the coal grate. In truth, the room was overly warm, but the heat soothed her aches. Her body was lethargic, her energy spent by too much dancing and the steady effort of making herself attractive to arrogant young men who took little interest in her. She resented their idle efforts, knowing they were pushed by calculating mothers who reminded them that Miss de Bourgh was an heiress with a fine estate in Kent. The clodpoles were all boorish and uninteresting. Mr. Lavendon, for instance, was an intemperate man with hardly a solid thought in his head. When asked for an opinion on the four-coultered plough, he said derisively, "I leave the ploughing to my tenants."

Anne saw how easily her mother was swayed by friendly manners and a pleasant countenance. Lady Catherine had surveyed the crop of eligible men and seen three that might suit: Mr. Lavendon (his being a prize), Mr. Laroche (whose silliness and fawning affection easily recommended him), and Mr. Gilbert (who had nice teeth and no wit and was the son of a Viscount). Tradition ruled Lady Catherine's thinking—her daughter would marry for rank and title. Anne feared her ladyship did not appreciate how quickly an imprudent man might plunder the riches of Rosings, might mortgage properties to pay for his bets at Ascot, might destroy in months what had taken years to build. She could not, would not, marry any of the men to whom she had been introduced. She would rather die an old maid.

Was Mr. Urson an exception? She knew little of his situation, other than hearing Lady Lavendon say he had been adopted by his titled uncle. His air bespoke something of the dandy, which could not please; but he was courteous, capable of stimulating conversation, and nothing like the young buffoons. She found him attractive, but could she feel a deeper affection for him?

Here was the puzzle. How did one sort a sincere regard or mere infatuation (such as she had felt for the roguish Mr. Wickham when she was still quite young) from true and lasting affection? Having never been allowed to become acquainted with many single young men, other than her cousins, she had never been in love. She knew not how to separate the whimsical from the enduring or how to refine the skill to do so.

When the wind rattled the window panes, she vowed to think on the matter later, pulled her shawl tighter around her shoulders, and opened Mrs. Collins's letter:

Hunsford Friday April —

Dear Miss de Bourgh,

I trust this letter finds you well and not overly tired of London. Mrs. Sparke has shared your letters with me, and I, mine with her. Your adventures have entertained us wonderfully and we thank you for sharing them.—I write to inform you of a concern that arose a few days ago regarding Marianne. Mrs. Sparke was not at first alarmed by this situation, but is now every day more worried and unhappy. You, who know her so well, can imagine how fiercely she pressured me not to write, for she feared interfering with your happy time in Town and knows how little there is to excite you here. As you see, she failed to extract from me an agreement to her wishes.—Thus I tell you that Marianne has been ill with a feculent diarrhea. We understand the condition is common among children her age and often occurs during teething, which painful process sets her mouth and teeth in sympathy with her liver and stomach. Dr. Bailey was surprised to be informed of the child's distress, as this form arises most frequently during the summer heat and the autumn cold. At first he believed a dose of castor oil would stem the malodorous discharge, but this has not been the case. Yesterday, on being informed of the child's recurring tendency to puke, he gave her a dose of calomel, which thoroughly cleansed her stomach, poor thing, and left her weak and disagreeable.—This morning he confessed his fear the condition may prove stubborn to treatment, especially if the bowels over-sympathize with the gums. Should this prove true, he advises cutting the swollen gums down to the teeth to relieve any inflammation. Mrs. Sparke cannot bear the thought and charged Mrs. Beath with preparing linseed tea to soothe the child's tender gums.—In short, the situation is fretful but not threatening. Because you look on Marianne almost as your own daughter, your inclination will be to return immediately to Rosings. I know not how to advise you, other than to suggest you search your heart. It has the power to inform your best decision.

Your affectionate friend, Charlotte Collins

With surprising quickness for a body so lethargic, Anne moved to tug the bell-rope. She knew exactly what she wished to do. When Juggins answered her summons, she said, "Find Shaw and send her to my bedchamber. I have need of her help."

"Yes, ma'am. Right away."

Anne next knocked on her ladyship's door. "Mama? Are you dressed?" Her nerves jangled at the prospect of challenging Lady Catherine, who would resist the idea of removing to Rosings before the Season ended. She would argue that nothing more could be done for Marianne and, in any case, all children succumbed to such ailments at one time or another and recovered quickly. There was truth in this view, but Anne wished to leave London, first, because the month of May was nearly upon them, and every prudent land-owner would hurry to survey his properties and oversee his tenants now that the crops had been sown, and also because she had met no lovers and secured no man's affection. She had not—would not—find a suitable husband in Town: the air was too polluted; the parties, too vapid; the distractions, overpowering. Hardly a snip of sincerity had been met with anywhere. Nothing could be gained by prolonging their stay at Chidham House. In every respect, Marianne's illness was a suitable pretext for leaving Town.

Anne knocked again.

Muffled sounds could be heard through the door.

"Mama," she said on opening the door and advancing into the room, "I have received an urgent letter from Mrs. Collins regarding Marianne. It appears the child is quite ill. I have decided to return to Rosings to comfort Tilly." All the while she spoke, she observed Dawson's rigid stance. Some private endeavor had been interrupted, but its nature could not be readily perceived. Thinking she imagined it, she continued: "I plan to leave in two days time, if you care to accompany me. I shall arrange one or two appointments for tomorrow and direct the staff to ready the house for closing."

Her mother's face, reflected in the looking glass, was pale.

"Shaw and Mrs. Jenkinson shall travel with me in the smaller coach," Anne added, "and leave you to travel in the barouche, should you choose to stay in Town."

"Allow me to think on it," said Lady Catherine.

"Of course," replied Anne. She stood her ground for a few seconds, being surprised at so careless a reply, before returning to the drawing room to implement her plan. She must write Tilly and Charlotte of her intention to return to Rosings and seek an appointment with Mr. Newland.

Her letters finished and passed to Juggins with instructions as to their urgency, she removed upstairs to direct Shaw on packing. Her heart harbored a secret hope that her mother would choose to remain in Town.

Chapter 44

"Has Lady Catherine returned to Rosings?" asked Tilly. She sat near the casement window, as she had done frequently during her first confinement. Her hands pillowed her large belly, while a gentle May breeze caressed her neck. A fire had been laid, in keeping with the custom.

"She arrived last evening." Anne cooed at Marianne, who sat on her lap being very entertained with trying to touch the wirework necklace around her godmother's neck. Her little fingers grabbed the delicate filigree and gave it a good twig; when it did not yield, she pulled it toward her mouth, but the chain was too short to give way. Her lips puckered, leading Anne to distract her with a small stuffed doll, else she take to wailing and upsetting their peace. On seizing the soft toy, Marianne put one of its arms in her mouth.

Anne laughed at her playful pranks. "You silly goose." On being squeezed affectionately, Marianne tossed the doll to the floor, a daring look in her eyes. "I thank Providence for Marianne's recovery," she said as she bent to retrieve the doll, "but now worry about her ladyship's health. Some aspect of her person is altered, but I cannot define the change. She is more private than usual and has taken to wearing shawls nearly every day, which is unlike her. Letty is likewise ignorant and complains of being refused entry to Mama's bedchamber while she dresses. Only Dawson is permitted to dress her."

"That is odd, particularly as Dawson is quite elderly now. I should think she would be pleased to have Letty's help."

"As you say." Anne studied Tilly in the filtered light. A calmness had settled over her friend. There was no anxiety at the prospect of delivering a second child, her confidence being increased by the fact of Mrs. Roberts and Mrs. White being ready to manage her delivery. "I visited Charlotte yesterday," she told Tilly. "Lady Lucas and Miss Lucas have arrived to attend her. I enjoyed seeing Miss Lucas again and meeting her mother. Charlotte invited me to sit as a gossip, which I shall do, provided her delivery does not interfere with yours. She says Mr. Collins is puffed up with pride and predicts she will deliver a son, despite her admonishments to the contrary. 'No one, excepting God, knows whether the child will be a boy or girl,' Charlotte said. You can hear her voice, I imagine."

"Poor Charlotte. She must keep Mr. Collins calm while curbing her own concerns." Tilly risked mentioning a sensitive topic. "So you never saw Dr. Granville in Town."

"I looked for him during all my walks and rides in the parks, but it was not to be."

"The best remedy of affliction is submitting to Providence. Your feelings for Dr. Granville were not meant to take root. Don't despair. God's plan will be revealed to you in time."

These words were little comfort, but Anne knew Tilly meant well. "I have one bit of intelligence. George Martin Tench has returned to Rosings. It has been nearly a year since he set foot on the estate." Remembering their last encounter heightened the color in her cheeks. She had not told anybody of his stolen kiss.

Tilly spied Anne's discomfort. "The thought of him unsettles you? I suppose since Dr. Granville remains elusive, you now set your hopes on a new lover, although I am shocked to think your heart beats wildly for Tench."

"Believe me, I want nothing to do with him. I only wonder what woe brought the rascal down from Town."

"Your confession is a great relief. For a moment I feared he had some claim on you. Surely, when you were in Town, you met at least one dashing and agreeable man who caught your fancy. What of Mr. Urson?" Tilly fluttered her eyelashes, looking a very pregnant but silly coquette.

Anne tapped Marianne on the nose. "Your mother is a foolish fowl, just like you." Marianne's loud gurgle made both ladies laugh. "I enjoyed Mr. Urson's company while in Town. All good so far, except Mama spoke with him at one of Lady Milcombe's dinners and hinted at my being agreeable to the idea of an engagement. Yes, I see your surprise. I never gave her ladyship cause to think such a thing and wonder at his response."

Tilly silently gave thanks for never having lived under so odious a parent. "Aside from Lady Catherine's hope, does Mr. Urson have matrimonial potential?"

Anne let Marianne slip off her lap. "I cannot say, for I know so little about him. He talks with enthusiasm on almost any topic, except France: he cannot abide the French, which is no uncommon sentiment these days. He is eccentric in some ways, but attractive in his countenance and manners. Can hope be built on such a flimsy foundation?"

"I dare say, it can and has."

"I am exceedingly annoyed with Mama for inventing stories about me. As usual, she acted on her own feelings without regard for mine."

"It will be all the same a hundred years hence," said Tilly, her eyes bright with mischief.

Chapter 45

The best-laid schemes o' mice an' men | Gang aft a-gley. | An' lea'e us nought but grief an' pain | For promis'd joy!

Anne hoped Robert Burns did not speak true.

Believing the poet's words might be prophetic, every precaution had been taken to ensure a good outcome: the two midwives stood ready, the lying-in chambers were well stocked, the gossips gathered, the caudles simmered. All that could be done, had been done. The outcome lay in God's hands. Fortune smiled. On Monday Tilly gave birth to a son—Patrick John Sparke—whose square chin put all the gossips in mind of his proud Papa. On the Thursday following, Mrs. Collins also birthed a son, William Joseph Collins, whose indignant cry at being exposed so barbarously to the cold night air was heard by Mr. Collins in the church chancel next door.

Anne was tired but happy as she sat in the de Bourgh pew on Sunday. When Mr. Collins took the pulpit, his feverish eye raked the expectant faces of his congregation. His whole person seemed powered by some inner Light: "'Unto the woman he said, I will greatly multiply thy sorrow and thy conception; in sorrow thou shalt bring forth children; and thy desire shall be to thy husband, and he shall rule over thee.' Genesis, verse 3:16."

Anne was struck by the unusual nature of his reading, for this passage hailed from one of the most devastating events in the Christian canon—the casting out from Eden of Adam and Eve. Mr. Collins's fervency captured the congregation's attention as he wove the story of Adam and Eve's downfall into a reflection on the purity of new-born children: "Before a child is birthed into the world, he has eyes but cannot see the sun and stars; he has ears but cannot hear the rushing brook or merry thrush; he has a tongue but has never tasted sweet fruit or wine or the bitter dregs of sorrow and remorse. He knows nothing of this world. He enters this realm wrapped in God's grace. He embodies the perfection of a natural state that is without sin, without blame. Would that we might all live lives as pure as a newborn child."

Mr. Collins felt his good fortune. Kind Providence had given him a son. He appeared genuinely humbled by the experience and in his humility, savored the affection of his flock. Indeed, on perceiving his rapture, Anne felt yet again that it was she alone who stood apart from life's experiences. She seemed destined to pass through life untouched by the ordinary and expected events of love found, of marriage celebrated, of children birthed and reared. During Mr. Collins's benediction, she admonished herself: you cannot know God's will for the path you walk. Instead, live in thanks for the safety of Tilly and Charlotte and their children. Rejoice, for they are all healthy this day.

After the service she told Mr. Collins, "I have never known you to speak so eloquently."

For once he was at a loss for words.

Chapter 46

Mr. Worthington had sketched a turtle sunning itself on a log. Its long neck stretched toward the sky; its eyes fixed closed in contentment. The likeness showed considerable skill. He had written no words of friendship or posed any queries regarding her health.

"Mornin', Hobbs," called Arnot.

Anne stuffed the drawing into a drawer and pretended to study the steward's monthly figures just as the man himself pushed open the door to her parlor.

"Good morning, Miss."

"Good morning. Are you for Faversham today?"

"Yes, ma'am. I shall meet the owners of the Helden Bigsey Brewery." Arnot settled himself in the chair he now thought of as his own and began to discuss leases, mortgages, expected acreages planted in hops and corn. "As for the Faversham brewery, I believe it might suit Roger Tench, who continues to resent my presence on the estate. He has become more disgruntled since his brother returned. I don't understand the basis for their enmity. What do you know of it?"

"Very little. As boys they were tutored by a friend of my father's, a Mr. Cripps—a retired clergyman, but no fribble by any means. Neither was good at book-learning, as I recall. I once heard my father observe that George Martin was jealous of Roger's steady determination. If it were true then, it is likely so now."

"George Martin strikes me as something of a mischief-maker. Have you heard any serious reports of him?"

"No. A house maid has sometimes complained of his unwelcome advances."

Arnot raised an eyebrow. "I should have thought a few might be pleased by his attention. I shall keep an eye on him. Well, I best leave, for it is a long ride to Faversham."

—⁂—

"What is this I hear of your attempt to purchase a brewery?" asked Lady Catherine from her writing table in the drawing room. Two letters had been sealed for posting. A third lay under her determined hand. "You have lost your wits if you think any commercialist will sell his operation to a chit of a girl."

"When he sees there is money to be made in the transaction, he will agree to it," retorted Anne.

"You can play at being a gentleman farmer here in the district, where our neighbors indulge your proclivity, but the commercial world has no patience for fools." Beneath rumpled brows her ladyship's keen eyes fastened on her daughter. "Now were you your father's son, you would enjoy the privileges of title that arise from being a true heir. Instead, your femaleness is an impediment to success. Once again, you care not whether you embarrass me. Would that Arnot had the spine to check you."

"I am sorry my efforts to enhance the estate's income insult you."

"Do not speak of income, for you are forever throwing that in my face. I see what you are about. You are in competition with Darcy, who has enjoyed success exploiting the mineral rights on his lands. His business acumen shall always exceed yours. Where he has an eye for the promising opportunity, you are ignorant and lack finesse."

Anne was surprised to hear Darcy's name on her mother's lips, for she had not spoken of him above three times since his marriage.

"Thomas, post these letters immediately," commanded Lady Catherine as she pressed hot wax onto the last folded white paper. To Anne she said, "I invited Mr. Urson to pay us a visit, for he has never been in these parts, although he has an acquaintance living near Ashford. I wrote to suggest he bring a friend and stay for a week or two. I also invited Lady Milcombe and her daughter Miss Williams. The daughter is an insipid little thing. She will be no threat to you, if you will only put forth some effort."

"You have no right to invite Mr. Urson here without my consent, Mama. You seem to think I will yield to any handsome man. Let me be understood: on the matter of marriage, I shall choose a man to please myself and no one else."

"I have the right to pursue your interests, particularly when you are too lazy to do so."

Anne knew it was futile to argue against the idea. Instead, she said, "You don't even like Lady Milcombe."

"True, but I believe she will prove useful—for once in her life."

Chapter 47

"Do sit down, Anne. I am getting a migraine."

Anne sat with a flounce on the straight-backed chair near Tilly's bed. "I cannot believe my mother invited Mr. Urson to Rosings without my consent. The woman is insufferable."

Although Tilly was in complete agreement with her friend, she tried applying the balm of reason. "With a little effort, we might think on this development with optimism."

"You mean, I might do so," declared Anne with some vehemence.

"Possibly a divine intervention has occurred," said Tilly. "You know what Cowper wrote: 'God moves in a mysterious way.'"

"I see that gleam in your eye, dear friend. You know I detest Cowper."

Tilly only smiled. "You said yourself: Mr. Urson was handsome and charming on every occasion. You can have no cause for thinking he will be otherwise here."

"You know young men. They are as changeable as a summer sky." Anne pictured Mr. Urson's flashing eyes and the mysterious scar on one cheek. The prospect of his visiting Rosings unsettled her.

"How can you speak so? We are none of us constant, and it would do you good to take a lover, if only to soften the sting of her ladyship's lingering resentment over Mr. Darcy's marriage."

Anne rose to Tilly's charge. "I am constant in my wish not to be bullied into marriage. Mama thinks she can govern every aspect of my life. Predictably, she warned me to be on my best behavior. 'He is quite the thing and worth winning,' she said."

"Oh? How so? Does he own a large estate in Derbyshire, like Mr. Darcy?"

"Mr. Urson is the nephew and heir of the second Baron Nortleigh and will inherit a large estate in Lincolnshire. Mama has been conjuring matrimonial visions, I am sure of it. How quickly she forgets that I cannot be forced into marriage."

"You enjoyed Mr. Urson's company in Town. There can be no danger in making yourself agreeable during his visit."

"No danger? Mama's intent is about as thinly veiled as a spider's web. Mr. Urson would have to be dense as a cedar plank not to be aware of it."

"Let us not fret over her ladyship's schemes. It will all unfold as it should."

Chapter 48

Extra candles had been lit in the library. Rumbles of thunder and the sound of rain tapping the panes overruled the crackle and hiss of the hearth fire.

Anne sketched in crayon a still life of a simple nosegay. Her hands worked purposefully while her mind fastened on scenes of pleasure or pain. As had been her wont of late, Dr. Granville's happy countenance featured prominently. His voice and look came to her with perfect clarity: "Women are frightened half to death by obstetrical instruments—fair enough, I say ..." The look on his face was so sweet, so earnest, she had wanted to press her hands to his cheeks, pull him close, and kiss his lips. Flushing at the memory, she remembered being so unnerved by her unruly thoughts that she had pulled back, fearing to act on her impulse. Had Dr. Granville sensed her desire? She thought his eye revealed an equally powerful emotion. Had she imagined it? The urge to kiss him had felt proper, as if she knew he would not object. She shuddered to realize these thoughts had nearly impelled her to hasty action. She had chastised herself then for amorous musings about a London doctor just met, when she should have been thinking of Tilly. She chastised herself now for giving her tender heart free rein to recall his jaunty grin and confidence. He was lost to her. How easy it was to fabricate a future built on little more than a *tête-à-tête* over tea.

She had been introduced to a surfeit of single men in the past year: Dr. Granville, perhaps the finest man of her acquaintance; Mr. Cole, a handsome man whose passion for Science, while admirable, might make him a sort of medical connoisseur, too devoted to scientific study to be a good companion; Arnot, a steady, honest man whose rough manners grew familiar, but for whom she felt no improper regard; Mr. Haworth, congenial and ready to forswear marriage altogether; Mr. Lavendon, a gambler whose flinty eyes held little true mirth; Mr. Worthington, a decent sort who had given his heart to his married cousin; Mr. Urson, well-formed, charming, and fashionably attired, if a little dour.

Mr. Urson. His was an interesting character. He appeared to read widely, which activity counted in his favor, but he disliked dancing, which counted against him. He claimed to enjoy sketching, a point in his favor, but sometimes wore a sneering smile, which suggested a mocking personality. She wondered whether his visit would advance her affection or thwart it.

The tinkle of china interrupted her musings. She looked up to see Nichol standing at her elbow, her expression one of frank admiration for her mistress's skill. "Where shall I place the tea tray, Miss?"

"Over by my chair." Anne stepped away from the desk. "Oh, my knees have grown stiff." She jumped when a flash of lightning sparked a thundering boom that made the house shudder.

"Gracious!" screeched Nichol. "Is that hail?" She set the tray on the table with a clatter.

"I believe so. It has been a wild day for weather and nothing like what is expected in June."

"I shouldn't like to be traveling this evening." Nichol jerked her head up as rain and hail hammered the window panes.

"No, our guests chose an unfortunate day for their journey. Thank you, Nichol. I shall pour my tea."

"Yes, ma'am," said Nichol, her curtsy rushed.

Anne packed her drawing materials, poured a cup of hot brew, and opened a travel book about Turkey. A good while later a heavy pounding could be heard elsewhere in the house. Shouts and hurried footfalls reached her ear. In the hall she beheld a wild spectacle.

"Here, sir," Hobbs called to George Martin Tench. "Sit him down here." He positioned a chair near the door.

Tench struggled to hold onto a wet and muddied man, whose knees buckled beneath him. The scene was lit from behind by lightning, while rain slashed through the doorway and puddled on the floor. "I cannot hold him," cried George Martin. Two footmen rushed forward to assist the injured man, who yelped in pain.

"What has happened?" Anne called.

"An accident on the road into Hunsford, ma'am," Tench told her. "I came upon a coach that had skiffed ow'r the road. I brought the gentlemen here."

Another man, equally wet and disheveled, stepped into the hall, shaking out his muddy greatcoat. When he took off his hat and gloves, Anne said, "Mr. Urson! We thought you must have put up at an inn in this awful weather."

"We would have done so had we any notion of the storm's severity." He looked disconcerted amid all the hubbub, but he recalled himself and bowed to his hostess.

"Are you injured, sir?"

"No. My friend there, Mr. Pantley, took the brunt of the crash."

"Let me send a servant to fetch Dr. Bailey. Hobbs—"

"Thank you," said Mr. Urson, "but it is not necessary. My friend is in no danger. He wrenched his shoulder, but nothing is broken."

Mr. Pantley added huskily, "I am fine, only having the breath knocked out of me." He rubbed his sore shoulder.

Anne turned to Hobbs. "Take these gentlemen upstairs and ask Mrs. Faber to see to their comfort." Hobbs signaled a footman.

"I apologize for causing such work for your household," said Mr. Urson.

"It is only mud and water. I am relieved you and your friend are not injured." There was an awkward pause, after which Anne said, "I shall see you in the morning."

She watched two footmen help Mr. Pantley up the stairs, with Mr. Urson following stately behind. Before the group disappeared into the guest wing, George Martin Tench faded into the rain-swept night.

Chapter 49

Lady Catherine and her daughter sat with Mrs. Jenkinson in the drawing room, awaiting their guests. Anne leaned over her writing table, Mr. Worthington's latest drawing laid before her. She had added colors. The turtle's back wore dusky rings of amber and brown, a blue-striped damsel-fly with twin dots of red for eyes hovered above the log, and a black water bug danced on the murky green water. On impulse, she wrote these lines underneath the drawing: *Does Mrs. Egerton enjoy good health? I worry about her.* And then: *Are you well?*

Should she sign her name and, if so, how should she write it? Never having encountered this problem, she could not decide on the proper form. Her given name was too intimate and her initials too strange. She left the space blank and wrote Mr. Worthington's direction from memory. Would he write back or send another drawing? They had exchanged six drawings since the previous autumn, but could not be said to have corresponded. She rose from her chair, wondering at the wisdom of taking up this intimacy. No matter. Mr. Worthington likely would not respond in kind.

"I expect you to be agreeable during Mr. Urson's visit," said Lady Catherine. "Do not give me that quelling look, for it carries no weight with me. Let me remind you: it is time you married. Mr. Urson is an eligible man from a noble family. He may be your last hope to rescue this estate from obscurity and pass its fortune to an heir. Use every flirtatious art you possess, meagre though your female wiles be. I expect you to fulfill your duty. Your father would expect the same."

Anne bristled at the idea her dear father would expect her to use feminine guile or be insincere. Papa would never wring duty from me, she grumbled to herself as she pulled the bell-rope and handed Hobbs her letter.

Shortly thereafter the gentlemen were announced. Mr. Urson's manner and appearance were everything the ladies desired. He bowed low over Lady Catherine's hand and introduced his friend Mr. Pantley before speaking to Anne. "It is a pleasure to see you looking well."

"Thank you. Was your journey difficult?"

"It was a wild night."

Sitting down next to his friend, Mr. Pantley added: "One horse threw a shoe near Three Chimneys, forcing us to retire to the local tavern for dinner, where a great big oaf of a serving girl dropped a platter, thus splattering our clothes." He flicked an imaginary bit of dirt from his knee-breeches. "We found fleas there, did we not, Urs?"

"Perhaps one or two, but no more than anybody might expect when traveling in the country. At least the Wealden roads were not too onerous, although the storm made our travel extremely arduous."

"Travel is dangerous at the best of times," said Lady Catherine, smiling at Mr. Urson. "Did you find any amusements in Ashford?"

"We boated on the Great Stour nearly every day, the Stour being a lazy river in that part of Kent. I believe I prefer boating on the Stour to traveling on the Thames. What say you, Pan?"

Mr. Pantley's smile puffed his freckled cheeks. "The Stour is more rustic and gave us some exercise, but the Thames can be very sporting. I enjoy watching a good wherry competition on London's water road, for the wherrymen must keep their wits, else they be swamped by a colly coal-barge." He stood and burst into song: "The Sleeping Thames one Morn I cross'd, by two contending Charons tost; I Landed and I found, by one of Neptune's juggling Tricks, enchanted Thames was turn'd to Sytx, Lambeth th' Elysian Ground …"

Anne was entranced, having never had a guest perform spontaneously. His rich tenor seemed to make the furniture quake. When the last note faded he bowed, sweeping his good arm in a long stroke as if flourishing a plumed tricornered hat. Mrs. Jenkinson joined Anne in rich applause, their glee bringing a flush to his cherubic face.

"You have a fine singing voice," Anne said. "I am not acquainted with that song."

"It is of very old stock. There are more verses, but I shall not torture you with them. Would you like to hear another? I have a large repertoire."

"That will not be necessary," said Lady Catherine. "You have a flair for the dramatic. Are you an actor?"

"No, ma'am," he replied, darting a glance at Mr. Urson, "although I have a great love of the theatre."

"What of your family, Mr. Urson? Are there actors lurking in your pedigree?"

"I was raised by my uncle, whose people are rather plain. My sisters play the piano and draw a little. They show no remarkable interest in the theatre."

"I am acquainted with Lord Nortleigh," said Lady Catherine.

"I was not aware of the fact, ma'am."

"Our acquaintance was of short duration. I hope he and Lady Nortleigh are well."

"Yes, ma'am. They enjoy excellent health."

"I recall a scandal there—an elopement. A hushed and hurried marriage often ends badly, but it seems your aunt and uncle have been steadfast in their duty." Looking quite smug, her ladyship turned to Anne. "Our guests might like to check their horses. Afterwards take them for a walk around the Park, it being a fine day."

When the men followed Anne and Mrs. Jenkinson out onto the terrace, Mr. Pantley quipped, "I say, Urs, you never mentioned a connection with this family."

Chapter 50

Mr. Urson and Mr. Pantley proved to be agreeable. Every amusement was their delight: cards in the evenings, carriage rides around the neighborhood, walks in the Park. On Sunday, they accompanied the ladies to the church. The parish's single ladies were all agog on seeing such a handsome specimen as Mr. Urson—why, he favored Mr. Darcy in his coloring and air of self-confidence. Moreover, he was the nephew of a baron, which enhanced his charm. Even Tilly commented on his fine eyes and striking attire.

Under their kind regard, Lady Catherine became nearly as animated as when Darcy and Colonel Fitzwilliam were in the house, while Anne grew easy in their presence. Mr. Urson entertained them every evening by reading poetry, letters, and articles from *The Gentleman's Magazine*. His voice had a rich timbre, deep and clear, with no traces of the distinctive Lincolnshire accent. Mr. Pantley often sang, his strong tenor lulling them into a happy complaisance, or challenged Mrs. Jenkinson to a game of piquet. Their calls of points and hands—Ten! Forty! Blank!—sometimes grew boisterous. One evening Mrs. Jenkinson was heard saying, "I give you fair warning, sir, I shall anoint you with the oil of gladness."

Mr. Pantley protested. "Dear lady, I am not the sly-boots you think me. I am no varlet and you are no badger. It is only my luck running high this evening."

Lady Catherine, who watched them from the comfort of her favorite chair, said, "Your language is very colorful. Despite your protestation to the contrary, I believe you are connected with the theatre."

"Not precisely, ma'am," said Mr. Pantley. "I am acquainted with several persons at Astley's. Have you attended a performance there?"

"I have not had that pleasure," replied her ladyship, a note of scorn in her voice.

"My friend Turner helps train the horses," he explained, going on to describe the acts and the new rider named Ducrow, who was also a rope-dancer. Mrs. Jenkinson praised the tumblers.

Mr. Urson leaned toward Anne and whispered, "Lady Catherine is not much impressed with Astley's. She is offended, I think, by my friend's pursuits. Pantley is quite child-like in his pleasures. He loves the circus and is a superb rider."

"Then I hope he will avail himself of the cattle in the Rosings stable," she replied. "I shall instruct Kitson to help him choose a mount. You must speak with the stable master as well, if you are inclined to ride."

"You are very kind," he said. "I recall Lady Catherine saying she knew my uncle. Has she ever spoken of him to you?"

"No, I did not know she was acquainted with your family until she mentioned it."

"Perhaps she was introduced to him through your father," he said indifferently.

"It is possible. My father knew a great many people."

His eyes roved her face. "You are in good looks this evening. Your hair is quite pretty in the firelight."

She was disquieted by his flattery, knowing herself to be rather plain. Her hair, in particular, was nothing to remark on, it being a dull brown and straight as a stool leg. No amount of curling gave her a fashionable look.

Oblivious to her heightened color, he said casually, "Lady Catherine told me of your cousin's infamy. The man is a scab to disavow his promise to you and marry another lady. I would not wonder at your being pained by his betrayal."

"You wound my cousin, sir," she was quick to say. "Mr. Darcy is a good man. I have no injuries to report. Indeed, I wish him very happy and believe he married a lady whose style and character suit him."

"If you speak truly, then your sweetness and gentle nature are all the more to be admired. I cannot recall meeting another lady whose liberality matches yours. Most ladies would be quite cast down on having an engagement broken—and by so close a family member as a dear cousin. Indeed, after being jilted before all the world, a few would plot revenge." He leaned forward, his husky voice spilling into her ear. "Do you plan to punish him?"

"I have no grounds for retribution. Indeed, I am fond of my cousin and would not consciously injure his character or reputation. Excuse me, I shall refresh my coffee." She left him to sit by himself.

Chapter 51

Mr. Urson looked as smug as a barrister whose guilty client has escaped the gallows. He stood at the side table and streamed hot tea into a cup. Addressing the fireside group, a smile on his lips, he said, "Her ladyship asked me to inform you that Lady Milcombe and her daughter shall remain in Town for another week. It seems Miss Williams is sick with the ague, which she contracted after being exposed to the evening dews in Vauxhall."

"What? That's stupid," said Mr. Pantley. "The lady must have slept upon the damp grounds to take a fever there."

"So it seems. She is tiresome in any event."

"Do you know her?" asked Anne.

Mr. Urson's look suggested he knew he had spoken intemperately. "We were introduced at Almack's. She is extremely shy and dances poorly."

"I thought you did not dance."

"I only enjoy dancing when my partner is especially agreeable. Come, let us take some air. Shall we all walk to the Folly?" He set down his teacup with a clatter, enlisted the somewhat reluctant participants, and led the way across the terrace and into the trees. He kept pace with Anne while Mr. Pantley teased Mrs. Jenkinson some distance behind. "I find the district quite bucolic and your estate is charming," he said. "Indeed, Rosings puts me in mind of my uncle's property in Lincolnshire. Edenworth is less wooded and can boast of more fields planted in corn and vegetables, but it is equally successful. It would please me greatly if you would come to Edenworth for two or three weeks. Lady Catherine finds the idea agreeable, but her opinion is nothing to yours."

Anne offered a polite "thank you" but seethed inwardly at learning her mother had advanced her position before the principals were even sure of their regard for each other. She found the growing intimacy between Lady Catherine and Mr. Urson disturbing, and she did not like the high-handed way in which he relayed intelligence that should have come first to her.

Mr. Urson, being insensible to her distress, mistook her humble reply for encouragement and elaborated on Edenworth's many charms, speaking lyrically of his uncle's cabbage and onion crops. When they passed beneath the Folly's stone arch, he paused in admiration. "Each time I visit this place I am struck by its beauty. I have never seen a Roman ruin so happily situated."

Anne was soothed by his approval. The Folly was her favorite retreat, built by her father when she was a girl. It consisted of hardly more than a stone arch connected to a series of columns topped by a classical architrave; two niches were set in a short wall abutting the line of columns. She had enjoyed many childish adventures among its crannies. "Sir Lewis called it the Temple of Apollo Palatinus, after the ancient Roman building. I daresay it looks nothing like the original, but I love the wild roses tumbling down that stone wall, and the benches are particularly fine, being tooled to resemble fragments of Corinthian columns. Sir Lewis enjoyed a good joke and told me the columns had been felled by a strong quake when imperial Rome ruled Britannia, thus making me think they have lain on this Kentish soil for more than a thousand years—a fantasy I believed until my governess corrected my misimpression."

Footfalls on the path caused them to turn. Jones was running in their direction.

"Mrs. Faber asked me to find you, Miss," panted the young footman. "Her ladyship has fallen. It is not fatal, but Mrs. Faber believes you would wish to return to the house."

"I shall come directly. Excuse me, Mr. Urson."

In Lady Catherine's bedchamber, Dawson and Letty hovered near the bed. Mrs. Faber tucked the covers on one side and whispered, "Hobbs heard a cry in the hall and found her ladyship at the foot of the main staircase. She was insensible. The footmen brought her upstairs."

Lady Catherine thrashed and moaned under the bedcovers.

"Tell Hobbs to send for the apothecary," said Anne, laying a hand on her mother's shoulder.

—⁂—

Dr. Bailey crossed the drawing room, a calm gracing his features. "Mr. Gordon has been called away into the country, Miss Anne, and so I stand in his place. Let me reassure you. Her ladyship is bruised and rattled, having taken a hard knock to the head, but no bones are broken. She must stay abed for a few days."

"That is a great relief. Did she fight you tooth and nail?"

"Sharp pain can make anyone disagreeable."

Anne smiled at his diplomatic circumlocution. "Then she will recover completely."

"I expect her to do so, although once, long before your time, Lady Catherine told me of an accident she suffered when she was a young woman. She fell on stepping into a carriage and received a blow against her breast. The wound turned black and grew troublesome, as might be expected from a hard knock against tender tissues. Leeches were applied, but a small lump remained. It was not particularly uncomfortable, she said, although it could be felt if pressure was applied. Her ladyship told me the breast has now swollen considerably. It seems the wound has erupted afresh."

Anne grew alarmed. "Has a tumor formed?"

"It might be a scirrhus tumor or possibly something else. I wish she would allow me to examine her, but since she will not, I shall write my nephew Cole for an opinion. I am confident he will agree to see her and then we shall have an expert report."

Anne consented to the idea. "Can you stay for dinner? It seems a long age since we enjoyed a little time together, and you shall have an opportunity to meet my guests. I would be pleased to know your opinion of them."

"You know me too well, dear girl," replied Dr. Bailey, patting his ample belly.

Conversation proved a trial across the dinner table, for Dr. Bailey showered the gentlemen with questions. Mr. Pantley took no offense and shared all matter of stories about himself, his family, and his politics and pursuits. Mr. Urson, however, bristled at having his habits queried. He spoke in monosyllables and was barely civil. Afterwards Anne walked the doctor to the front hall and was surprised to see dark clouds racing across the sky, pushed by a strong wind. The threat of rain was imminent.

"Shall I call a carriage for you?" she asked.

"No. I am sturdy in a gale." He took her hands in his. "Thank you. I have had no Lenten fare today, and it has done me good to see you looking well. Keep your wits about you with those two men in the house. You know my thoughts: too much courtesy, too much craft."

"You need not worry," she said, patting his arm.

Chapter 52

"Mama, you cannot come downstairs. You are in need of rest, not amusement. Besides, Mr. Cole is expected shortly."

"Mr. Cole can have nothing to say to me."

"I insist on your receiving medical care. If you will not allow Dr. Bailey or Mr. Gordon to examine you, then you must endure Mr. Cole." An hour later Anne escorted the surgeon upstairs. Lady Catherine sat in a Chinese chair near the window, while Dawson hovered nearby. Her ladyship's downturned mouth and knotted brow was a sign she would cooperate only if prodded from behind with a stick. Anne pulled the door closed and put one ear to the wood, but heard only polite murmurings. When Mr. Cole reappeared downstairs, she motioned him to sit. "What is your opinion?"

"Lady Catherine has a large swelling in one breast, the apparent result of an injury received when she was a girl. The tumor began increasing about two years ago and changed shape. The veins feeding the swelling also enlarged and the skin is discolored." To Anne's pale look, he said, "It is tender and likely to grow more so. Last June and again in September her ladyship saw a Town doctor who applied leeches to shrink the veins."

So this was the reason for Mama's mysterious travels. How like her to be so stubborn in her habits as to say nothing of the matter. Recalling herself, she said, "The treatment did not work, then."

"No. Despite being an acceptable course, the leeching did not decrease the swelling. The tumor has reached a weight of perhaps four pounds."

"Four pounds! How can she endure such discomfort?"

"She has a stout constitution and claims to feel well. I applied a mercurial plaster and prescribed a strict vegetable diet, as recommended by Dr. Lambe for the treatment of scirrhous tumors. Whether this be a scirrhous tumor or not, her ladyship will benefit from avoiding animal foods and noxious liquids. She told me such a course will prove difficult, but you must pressure her to pursue it. Dr. Lambe believes strongly that a vegetarian diet is useful in these cases." His blue-eyed stare signaled a challenge to her resourcefulness. "Her ladyship is prepared to endure her present condition, but if the tumor grows larger she will need surgery."

Surgery. The word struck fear. Stories of mutilation and excruciating death at the hands of a surgeon abounded. Anne recalled dear Dobbie's tears on learning of her brother's death from coach driver's knee. The poor man had few choices. He might endure the painful, swollen aneurysm situated at the back of his knee—the condition due to wearing tall, tight-fitting boots—and die an early death when it burst, or he might risk a surgeon's knife to remove the leg, in which case he stood to lose his livelihood. A bloody amputation had killed him on the table.

Mr. Cole smiled reassuringly, as if reading her thoughts. "Her ladyship experiences no great discomfort because of it, other than the bruising she suffered when she fell. There is no harm in waiting." When he determined Anne's relief, he said, "I have a bit of news for you regarding my friend Granville: he is engaged to be married. My friends and I tease him without mercy, for he is quite smitten. Miss Watkins is charming and very pretty. She is the daughter of a London physician and is used to a doctor's odd hours, which bodes well for their happiness. Granville cannot stop smiling at his good fortune."

Anne schooled her face. "Please assure him that I wish him very happy, and tell him Mrs. Sparke's daughter thrives."

Mr. Cole beamed his approval and for the next half-hour described the couple's wedding plans in great detail.

Chapter 53

"I hear her ladyship is improving," said Mr. Pantley.

"She shall come downstairs in a day or two." Anne looked up at his cherubic face.

"I am glad to hear it." His smile blessed everybody before next he challenged Mrs. Jenkinson to a game of backgammon. Mr. Urson joined his hostess before the fire.

Anne mostly stared into the flames, a travel book open on her lap. The day had been hard-going. First she struggled to accept Dr. Granville's betrothal, which fact was to be expected but depressed her spirits none the less, and then she ran about at her mother's command. Her ladyship was difficult to please on the best of days and nearly impossible when invalided. They had argued over the housekeeping. "Mama, you must rest. Mrs. Faber and I can manage until you recover." Her ladyship was barely mollified by any assurance of her resuming her duties when she felt stronger.

"How fortunate your family can claim a doctor's expertise in so small a village as Hunsford," said Mr. Urson, imposing on her reverie. "Can you imagine the horror of the desperate indigent who must submit to a Town hospital, surrounded by all sorts of diseased persons, coughing and spewing and moaning?"

"Country life has its challenges, assuredly, but it also has many benefits."

"I am every day more appreciative of it, but do you not sometimes miss the liveliness of London?"

Anne realized Mr. Urson's understanding was not so good as his friend's. Mr. Pantley, being an able reader of nuances, would recognize her need for peace. "Might I trouble you to pour me a glass of sherry?" she asked.

"Of course."

She watched him cross the room to the sideboard, where he lifted a small goblet to the candlelight. Convinced the glass had no fault, he unstoppered a crystal decanter and poured a stream of sherry. In profile he had a strong chin, good cheekbones, and a slightly overlong nose. He was fastidious and confident, projecting an assurance born of wealth and good looks. He poured brandy for himself.

"This will enliven you." He handed her the goblet and sat down, taking care to adjust his coat. "Lady Catherine told me she enjoys Town immensely. She is stimulated by its many amusements while also relishing the beauty and peace of Rosings. After you marry, you shall be glad of her presence here. When you depart for your husband's house, you can say goodbye to your former life knowing your property is secure." He sipped his drink.

Anne felt the force of his implications. "I may never marry. Who among us knows God's plan?"

"Miss de Bourgh, what a tease you are. Of course, you will marry. What a shame to waste such sweetness, such beauty and reserve. You must choose well, however. You would not care to relinquish your estate to a scoundrel."

"On that we can agree, at least," she replied, fixing a stare on his cheerful face.

Chapter 54

Mr. Pantley had sipped gleefully of the rosy god all through supper and jousted with Mrs. Jenkinson over London's best gardens and ale-houses. Mr. Urson inserted his own view a time or two. When the men later joined the ladies in the drawing room, Mr. Pantley challenged Mrs. Jenkinson to a game of piquet, while Mr. Urson settled himself next to Anne on the sofa. "I had hoped to see Lady Catherine and yourself at Edenworth in a few weeks, but I fear her ladyship is not well enough to travel. Still, it is of no consequence, for she will recover soon, and then we may pursue our plan."

"To what plan do you refer?"

"Why, our marriage, of course. Her ladyship has written your uncle, informing him that you and I agree to wed. It is joyous, is it not?"

Anne stared open-mouthed, not believing she had heard him correctly. "Did I understand you to say that you have spoken to Lady Catherine about marriage?"

"Yes. We had a delightful conversation on Sunday. I was a little intimidated on approaching her, for she is a rather grand and imposing lady, but I found her to be delightful in her praise of you and congenial in her attitude toward our marriage."

"Have you taken leave of your senses? You must realize it was wrong of you to approach her ladyship without first consulting me."

"I considered whether my approach was proper, but believe it was expedient to consult her ladyship first, for she stands in the place of Sir Lewis, and it is always wise to obtain a mother's blessing. Indeed, our conversation was providential, for it was on Monday that she injured herself."

"Let me speak plainly, sir: you can have no claim, for I have not consented to marriage." The scar on his cheek suddenly looked more sinister than gallant.

He took her hand and stroked her arm. "I appreciate your confusion, but I cannot have misinterpreted your kindness. All that remains to secure our happy plan is the approval of Lord Matlock. My uncle will offer no impediment."

"Your reasoning is flawed," said Anne coldly. She tried to withdraw her hand.

He would not release it.

She glared at him. "My feelings oppose the match in every particular, and my uncle's approval, which you deem so worthy, is not required by law."

He gave her a fulsome smile and squeezed her hand. "Don't worry. Lady Catherine and I are of one mind—the match is suitable and desirable. Your uncle will support his sister's wish."

Anne wrenched her hand from his grip and jumped to her feet. "I have no wish to marry you, Mr. Urson. Good evening."

He stood and laid one hand on her arm, stopping her progress. His face wore a bemused look, as if he coddled a child, but his eyes were flinty. "You will agree to the marriage."

"I will not."

Mr. Urson merely smiled and released her. She raised her chin and stalked from the room.

What madness is this? she asked herself. The pretentious toad. How did Mr. Urson insinuate himself so easily into Lady Catherine's graces? Of course, her ladyship must be flattered and admired; she must have her pound of adoration, and he is prepared to serve her. When she thought back to their first meeting, Mr. Urson had been entertaining, almost silly, at Lady Lavendon's ball and afterward, more reserved but pleasant whenever they were in company together.

At Rosings his friendly and agreeable manner seemed natural. How badly she had misjudged him. This would never have happened if Papa were alive, she told herself, for he would shield me from harm. Mama is worse than useless.

Anne needed a man to stand in her father's place. Would Lord Matlock serve? Lord Metcalfe? Dr. Bailey? Darcy?

In her bedchamber she pulled the bell-rope for Shaw.

She must remain calm. After all, she was not without friends.

Chapter 55

"Are the gentlemen in residence, Hobbs?"

"No, ma'am. They rode to Tunbridge and expect to return this evening."

This intelligence suited Anne very well, for she was in no mood to argue with Mr. Urson. She entered her parlor with a particular purpose. No sooner had she retrieved several sheets of her finest writing paper than Arnot knocked on the door. "Can you spare a few minutes, ma'am?"

"Of course." She moved to the settee while Arnot took his customary chair opposite. "I had not realized you were on the estate today."

"I am meeting Knevett, who has come down to examine Mrs. James's best milking cow." He opened his pocket-book and riffled the pages until he found what he wanted. "As you know, I traveled to Faversham," he said as he positioned his glasses, "where I met the owners of the brewery. Mr. Helden and Mr. Bigsey have been partners for roughly five and twenty years, but Mr. Bigsey retired recently because his health is poor. Thus, Helden seeks a new partner."

"What is your impression of his operation?"

"It's a small brewery, but produces a popular ale, which is no mean feat in a town dominated by the Shepherd brewery." Arnot read the figures from his notes: number of staff; weekly income; expenses for hops, wood, barrels, wagons, and the like; size of the district, etc.

"What do you say of Helden's character?"

"I like him," Arnot said without hesitation. "He is gruff and unpolished, but he knows his business. He recognizes the threat of Shepherd's success but keeps to his plan for expanding his operation. His ideas are sound."

"And Roger Tench?"

"Tench accompanied me and claims an interest in becoming a maltster. Helden will hire an experienced maltster to replace Bigsey, but he is willing to consider Tench as an apprentice, provided the new maltster approves of him. The next step is to ensure ourselves of the soundness of his operation, which requires a man with a good head for numbers and a sound understanding of the brewing business."

She stared at him thoughtfully for several seconds. "How confident are you about Roger's interest?"

"He may change his mind, but he has shown more animation in this venture than in any other. If Tench should quit—" He shrugged. "Your investment in the brewery itself is the important thing. Do you remain confident of your decision to become a partner in a brewery?"

"Some people will criticize me for the decision, but I see a future in it. I shall write my family's solicitor, Mr. Newland, this morning. He can send one of his agents to Faversham."

"Good." Arnot moved to take his leave.

Anne delayed him, asking, "What do you know of George Martin's activities on the estate? I have seen him several times in the stables or walking the Park paths when my guests were exploring the grounds. I cannot imagine what interests him here."

"He is mostly a lingerer and comes and goes as he pleases."

"Would you keep your eye on him? Not in any overt way, of course, but discreetly."

"I shall continue to do so." He seemed about to add something, but changed his mind and left to meet the veterinarian.

Anne turned her mind from the excitement of a new business adventure and her worry over George Martin's pursuits to writing letters. The first was directed to Mr. Newland in London, asking him to send an agent to investigate the brewery's operation. The next was to Lord Matlock, in which she first assured him of Lady Catherine's recovery and then described Mr. Urson's surprising behavior.

He claims Lady Catherine wrote to you of our engagement. Is this true? Did you receive a letter from Mama?—My nerves are disquieted by this unexpected development, for I have not given this gentleman reason to think me willing to engage myself. In fact, I told him outright I did not wish to marry him. Considering his apparent ardor, I must prevail upon you to tell all you know of this man and his family.—Please forgive my urgent demands but write directly to me, for I don't wish to add to Mama's distress. Know that I rely on your kind and intelligent guidance …

The letter was rough, but she had no time to polish it. To Hobbs she said, "I want this delivered directly into Mr. Garvie's hands for the post, and hold on your person any letter directed to me. Don't allow my correspondence to lie about. Do you understand?"

"Yes, ma'am," he said, his eyes widening.

Anne wondered how Mr. Urson would behave when next they were in company together. The time came too soon, for the gentlemen joined her for tea.

"You must think me lacking in every refined feeling," Mr. Urson said as he settled himself in the chair opposite Anne near the fireplace. "I am not insensible to your surprise, but I believe you can be convinced of the rightness of our marriage." His eyes held hers while he swirled brandy in a goblet. "Being responsible for Rosings and its staff must often over-power you, given your delicate health. In truth, managing an estate as large and diverse as Rosings would be exhausting for any lady. Men, after all, are superior to ladies in strength and stamina. We are favored with the ability to reason dispassionately, and we possess wisdom that produces sound decisions. We are formed for action and thinking. You are formed for affection and grace." He looked pleased with himself.

"I must disagree with you," said Anne. "My duties are not onerous, and I am as capable of reason as any man."

His lips puckered as if his drink were sour. "Your perfection as a member of the gentler sex lies in your modesty and virtue, and in your beauty and tender feelings. When we are married, you shall find joy in our children. You shall submit to those finer domestic duties that rightly belong to the purview of women."

She could think of only one reason why a man would bully a woman into marriage: money. Did Mr. Urson have gambling debts that spurred his ardor? Would he escape some terrible calamity by marrying her? Had Lady Catherine told him of Sir Lewis's bequest (fifteen thousand pounds, advanced when she had turned five and twenty)? No matter the reason, why would any thinking, feeling man approach a potential wife with vinegar on his tongue and a whip in his hand? And since he was sufficiently skilled to gain Lady Catherine's approval, what honeyed language had he used in presenting his case? Did her mother have no suspicion of his principles, or was she merely desperate to marry a difficult daughter? Mr. Urson's overweening manner goaded Anne to fling a barb of her own. "Have you always favored a narrow view of women, or does your contempt for female dignity arise from some recently acquired prejudice?"

His features hardened. "Let us consider your most recent scandalous idea to purchase a brewery. Your steward is a fool to think he can negotiate a partnership for you. No right-thinking man will choose a female partner for such an enterprise. The idea is laughable. I wonder at the power you hold over Arnot. Perhaps he eagerly does your bidding because he is in love with you—or you with him."

Anne hid her sensibility under a mantle of self-control. "I am not obliged to explain myself to you."

Mr. Urson's look grew dark. "You seem to delight in a challenge, but you will find no husband tolerates liberal sensibilities in a wife."

"That very much depends on the man."

He twisted in his chair and laid his claim baldly. "You can have no objection to an alliance that suits both our needs."

"Your need for cash, perhaps—" Anne's lips curled into a sneer.

"My need for steady companionship and an heir. Your need for security and respectability and for relief from the daily drudge of managing the estate. It might be possible to revive Sir Lewis's baronetcy, which would please her ladyship." His false smile looked decidedly sinister.

"I don't think I should like your plan at all. You would squeeze my profits to cover your debts and fund any number of egregious enterprises that might interfere with my plans." Anne merely guessed he had debts, which his sullen glare confirmed. "Most importantly, I am not prepared to enter into marriage where there is no affection. Are you willing to do so?"

He puffed out his chest. "I am prepared to do my duty."

"You are a man after Lady Catherine's own heart, then." Anne gave him a proud look. "Your opinion does not signify, for I tell you this: I would sooner die an old maid than marry without affection. We shall never find common ground. Your manners are offensive. In fact, you are no longer welcome here. I suggest you pack your bags. Hobbs will bring your carriage around front and see you safely on your way."

His eyes glinted. "Don't trouble yourself. I have no intention of leaving Rosings until you consent to marriage. Besides which, Lady Catherine invited me to Rosings and it is to her that I owe a duty to remain. I remind you that she expects you to submit to duty."

"You are impertinent."

"You are as well. Does Lady Catherine know your thoughts on marriage?"

He did not stop her when she quit the room.

Chapter 56

"Where do you go, Miss de Bourgh?" called Mr. Urson as he strode across the drive, a riding crop in one hand.

"I have several morning calls to make," Anne replied with feigned disinterest. Her heart thudded in her chest at the mere sight of him. To Hobbs she said, "Yes, the basket can sit there."

"Shall I accompany you? It would be my pleasure."

"If you are fond of crying children, then you are welcome to join me. I go to visit my lady friends in the village." She took a calculated risk in sharing her plan and did not wait for his answer. Young Kitson helped her into the phaeton and climbed up after her. When the carriage approached the Hunsford road, she said, "I must speak plainly and I wish you to speak so to me. What is your impression of Mr. Urson?" When Young Kitson remained mute, seemingly too busy managing horses that were perfectly able to pace the drive by themselves, she added: "I don't care for the man myself. Indeed, I begin to suspect he is not a gentleman."

Young Kitson slowed the horses as he wended their way through the village. "I don't trust him."

"Do you have any particular reason for your distrust? Has he assaulted a stable boy or abused the horses?"

"No, ma'am, not exactly. He likes to order the boys around." Young Kitson smirked. "He orders everybody around. Bossy, he is. Like an old woman—beggin' your pardon, ma'am." He gave her a sideways glance. "'Course, he takes care to mind his manners when he comes to the stables 'cause Pa keeps a close eye on him, and he knows it."

Anne mulled over these words. "But there has been no particular incident to make you distrust him?"

As he halted the phaeton in front of Tilly's house, Young Kitson said, "He was seen over in Tunbridge with Tench."

"Roger Tench?"

"George Martin. Thick as thieves they were, so Ham said."

"Mr. Urson knows George Martin Tench. How interesting," she said as she climbed down and retrieved the basket.

Her wait was not long, for Tilly tramped down the stairs none too quietly, being pleased to have company. Seeing consternation on Anne's face, she said: "You look a determined woman. What concerns you? Is it Lady Catherine?"

"No. It is something I never expected to experience in my whole life. At Dodford Meare I discovered that a man can be one sort of person in public and quite someone else in private. I fear Mr. Urson may be cut from the same cloth as Mr. Egerton."

"He has not assaulted you, surely."

"No, not physically, but he threatens me in other ways." Anne told Tilly all that had happened since last she visited Rosings.

"This is dreadful. Fortunately, you are of age and cannot be coerced into marriage."

Anne shook her head. "It should be so, but I never thought to experience such relentless condescension. In company, he is all charm and courtesy, particularly toward Mama. More than once I have seen her watching us with satisfaction. Mr. Urson must congratulate himself on securing her support for our marriage."

"Mr. Urson is all politeness."

"Not *all* politeness. Yesterday morning I chanced to look out a library window and saw him arguing with Mr. Pantley. Mr. Urson rounded on his friend, shoved him against a tree, and made a fist as if to strike him. Poor Mr. Pantley looked ready to retreat. I cannot help wondering if I was the spur to their argument."

"What a vile creature. His behavior is shameful, and his refusal to leave Rosings beggars belief. What shall you do?" Tilly asked.

"I have written Lord Matlock and shall ask Lady Metcalfe for help. I must know more about him. I welcome your guidance too."

Tilly hugged Anne. "I shall think on it. Write if you want me to come to Rosings. We shall not let this man have his way."

—⁓—

"Welcome, dear Anne. How do you do?" Lady Metcalfe was enjoying a late breakfast. "Let Mills pour you a cup of tea, or do you prefer coffee?"

"I am well, thank you, and coffee would be welcome."

"How is Lady Catherine? Has her recovery been a terrible ordeal for you?"

"Her ladyship has kept to her bedchamber for several days, but her spirit has improved. She has never been one to lie abed and, with guests in the house, desires amusement." She smiled at Mills when he handed her a pretty cup. "Are Lord Metcalfe and Mrs. Venables here in Kent?"

"I expect them soon. Clarinda is staying with Metcalfe in Town." She frowned as she ladled a spoonful of marmalade on a butter scone. "I hoped she would come down with me, but she was not ready to leave her friends. The Egertons and the Linwoods occupy much of her time. I wish she had your steady nature, Anne, but she has grown quite wild. There must be balls and routs and plays and carriage rides in Hyde Park—it all takes a toll on her health and disposition." She stopped and studied her young neighbor. "What brings you here this morning?"

Anne smiled. "You read me better than anyone other than Mrs. Sparke. I have a favor to ask of you, a personal favor and one I wish to keep secret."

Lady Metcalfe sat back in her chair. "How extraordinary. Please explain yourself."

And so Anne relayed every circumstance involving Mr. Urson, from their meeting at Lady Lavendon's ball to his apparent argument with his friend.

"Have you written your uncle?"

"Yes. I thought it prudent to do so."

"Good. It is right and proper to call upon your family. Lord Matlock, being a man of sense and strong character, can advise you."

"I have asked one or two trusted servants to alert me to any actions that appear suspicious. Was it imprudent to do so?"

"Not at all. Be careful, however, for it would be unwise to risk injuring his reputation. False accusations will harm you more than him. I know you too well to believe he has any power over you, but tread cautiously. His actions are mischievous. I shall write a dear friend, a woman I trust explicitly. She is acquainted with that family and can advise us." To Anne's heartfelt thanks, she said, "It is no trouble. I wish Clarinda had as much forethought as you."

Chapter 57

Anne surveyed the occupants of the drawing room. Mrs. Jenkinson, and Mr. Pantley played cards, seemingly sincere in their enjoyment of each other's company. Mr. Urson entertained Lady Catherine, who smiled and twittered like a school girl. Their intimate conversation would nauseate any daughter forced to observe her mother flirting with a man half her age. The main doors opened and Hobbs approached. He whispered to her. She laid her book down and went with him into the antechamber, where he handed over a letter. Standing near a window for better light, she scanned the first part of Lord Matlock's letter, which offered the hope of his sister's complete recovery. Next came the point regarding Mr. Urson:

> ... I received a letter from Catherine a few days ago. I must remind you that although you are of age and have the right under law to marry whomever you please, it is your duty to involve your nearest relations in the decision. Marriage is a contract between two persons and their families; it is not to be entered without careful thought and preparation. Youth are easily blinded by passion and beauty and seldom appreciate the importance of good character, simple affection, and family interests.—I know a little about the Ursons. Some eight years ago, the family endured a tragedy: their twin sons were seized with a vicious brain fever and died. Having

no other sons, Lord Nortleigh resolved to bestow his estate on his nephew Hugh Rusbridge and so brought the young man to Eden-worth. The young man took the family surname of Urson and was educated at Oxford. I seem to recall … well, perhaps it is best to withhold further comment until I am certain of the situation.—In any event, I cannot agree that your present circumstance is worri-some. A match between you and Mr. Urson is suitable, if it pleases you. Since it does not appear to do so, I shall query a friend or two in the hope of obtaining more information about the man and his family. Knowledge may bring you comfort.—Meanwhile, conduct yourself with dignity and propriety. A virtuous heart is your best defense against an unsavory character, if so he proves to be.

With true affection, Matlock

The lines about Anne's mouth deepened. Here was an unexpected and not altogether desirable wrinkle. Lord Matlock danced a merry jig, caught between sister and niece.

Chapter 58

Anne felt armored against Mr. Urson's slings and arrows. Each time he cornered her, she listened demurely while he rebuked her for being overly friendly with her servants, criticized her unladylike behavior in managing the estate, and denigrated her dealings with Arnot. He threatened or cajoled, as suited his whim, and became increasingly quarrelsome in the face of her resistance. She did not allow herself to be alone with him.

In Lady Catherine's company, he was the perfect gentleman and an agreeable guest, which made Anne's effort to reason with her mother all the more difficult.

"You can have no grounds for refusing his offer," said Lady Catherine as Dawson dressed her for dinner. "He comes from a noble family, has a cheerful disposition, and confesses every sentiment conducive to marital happiness. He is not as handsome as Darcy, but his charms are equal to any man's."

"Mama, the man is a blackguard. He—"

"What notions you have," said her ladyship. "I cannot credit the source of your strange imaginings, other than your indulgence for romantic novels. Where Mr. Urson is concerned, allow me the dignity of claiming some experience in these matters. The match is suitable and I expect you to fulfill your duty. You will marry him. Now leave me to finish dressing."

Anne returned to her bedchamber, exasperated with her mother's hare-brained thinking. How can Mama be blind to the man's superficial charm? Why is she determined to have him for a son-in-law?

Shaw was laying her mistress's dress and stockings on the bed, going to and fro about the room, grumbling to herself all the while.

"Shaw, why are you so disagreeable this evening?"

"I better not say, ma'am." Shaw dropped several ribbons and bent to retrieve them.

"I would rather hear the worst than endure your bad temper. What troubles you?"

"Did you hear about Nichol, ma'am? Mr. Urson roughed her up yesterday. Caught her running an errand for Mrs. Faber and tried to kiss her. When Nichol punched him, he grabbed her so hard she dropped a pretty yellow vase and broke it all to pieces. And before that he went after Sarah in the dairy barn while Mrs. James sorted cows in the paddock. The rake pinned her down in the straw and nearly had his way with her, with Beath looking on, grinning. Sarah wanted to smack them both hard—"

"Did he injure her?" cried Anne.

"Oh, her clothes were mucked up in a fair way, but Arnot happened upon them and pulled Mr. Urson off, pushed him up against the wall, and laid his arm across the man's throat, like to choke him. Mr. Urson will not be visiting the dairy any time soon."

"I had not thought him as bad as this. Why was I not told of his actions?"

"Beggin' your pardon, ma'am, but her ladyship was told. Arnot saw to that."

"Arnot spoke with Lady Catherine?" blurted Anne. Had she so lost control of her affairs that her steward would speak directly with her ladyship before informing her, his employer? Worse, what good could be said of her mother's behavior? Lady Catherine had been told Mr. Urson was a scoundrel, and yet she did not scruple to accept him into the de Bourgh family. This, from a woman who criticized Elizabeth Bennet for no greater fault than being a commoner!

Shaw, for all her country ways, instantly appreciated her mistress's distress and defended the steward. "Arnot made sure us servants were alert to his nasty ways. Mr. Urson is no gentleman—he'd like to be an oak, but he's a noddy, for all his fancy dress. 'Course, he's ogled all us women at one time or another, but the men are watching out for us, and Arnot is watching over *you*. Mr. Urson will not dare take advantage since Arnot warned Lady Catherine about the joker's evil deeds. That scoundrel George Martin Tench had his hand in this mess, you can be sure. I bet a guinea he told Mr. Urson you was ripe for picking, beggin' your pardon, ma'am, and all he had to do was work on her ladyship, which he did sure enough and met no resistance. I'll hold my tongue now, except to say to you what I say to everybody: Miss Anne's not going to marry any dangler, no matter what her ladyship says. Mr. Pantley is the one I feel sorry for. He is kind to us servants."

Anne was trying to sort this confused rambling when a knock on the door interrupted them. Nichol entered. "Excuse me, Miss. Hobbs sent me to tell you Colonel Fitzwilliam has arrived and is asking for you."

"Colonel Fitzwilliam! Here at Rosings? I was not expecting him, but tell him I shall be down in a few minutes."

When Nichol closed the door, Shaw grinned. "Thank goodness. The militia has arrived."

Chapter 59

Colonel Fitzwilliam was easily enlisted in Anne's cause. "I am given leave to guard your honor."

"Thank you, gallant sir."

"Understand—my father expects you to choose a suitable husband. He is traditional in his thinking, but he would not wish you to marry a rook."

"It is not your father who worries me. It is my mother. She will hear no word against Mr. Urson. Speak with her, Cousin. She may listen to you."

"Give me a day or two to study the principals. The truest wealth is that of the understanding."

Colonel Fitzwilliam's military mind and convivial person were ideal for sorting the problem. He laughed and joked with the gentlemen, flattered Mrs. Jenkinson, and was attentive to his aunt when she came downstairs for dinner or tea. He did not hover over his cousin or appear unusually sensitive to her situation. He was exactly as he seemed—a dutiful nephew and amiable cousin.

Several days later the cousins met in the conservatory.

"I have made little progress," said Colonel Fitzwilliam. "Lady Catherine resists any hint the man may be a scoundrel."

"Mama will hear no evil of him. She supports his offer of marriage and cannot countenance my refusal."

"In her own words, she sees in Mr. Urson a suitable candidate for marriage."

Anne paused in digging over a plot to plant a fern and gave him a frank look. "You are withholding an opinion," she said irritably as she brushed black dirt from her finger tips.

The Colonel chuckled. "I should have stood *en garde*, for you read me very well. I was merely thinking how best to speak my observation: he does not appear to be a villain."

"Do you doubt my word?"

He blanched imperceptibly at so direct a challenge. "You are no simpering, moon-faced school girl. I have never known you to be anything other than rational in your thinking. Is there another candidate, then?"

"No. I begin to believe there never shall be."

The Colonel's look turned tender. "You must realize Lady Catherine seeks only your happiness."

"Does she?" Anne snorted. "I wonder."

Colonel Fitzwilliam frowned at her sauciness.

She could imagine his dilemma: Which character in this drama was deserving of trust? His aunt? His cousin? Mr. Urson? A sadness rose on realizing that, for once, the Colonel was not in complete sympathy with her. "Do you ever think about the source of Lady Catherine's unhappiness?" she asked as she settled the fern and mounded dirt around it.

The Colonel sighed. "It is a question Darcy and I often ask when we visit Rosings. I believe none of us shall ever know the spur to her discontent. What is it you wish me to do? I am ready to perform any service for you."

She wiped her hands on her apron. "I will not marry Mr. Urson. It pains me to admit it, but I need your help removing him from this house."

"Then let us speak with Lady Catherine." He offered her a hand.

Anne found comfort in his strong hand-hold and allowed him to lead her through the potted palms to a reckoning with her mother.

—⁂—

"These flowers are dead." Lady Catherine fussed with the arrange-
ment and dead-headed three or four drooping roses. Desiccated
petals fell from the table to the floor. "A fresh vase should have been
placed here this morning."

"I—I shall see to it right away, ma'am," mumbled Nichol as she
laid her hand against the table's oaken edge and swept floral debris
into her palm. Relief flashed in her eyes when the Colonel and Anne
entered the drawing room.

"I wonder whether we might speak with you privately, Aunt?"
asked the Colonel.

Something in her nephew's tone made Lady Catherine pause
before frowning at Nichol who squatted to gather loose petals. "Must
you crawl about the floor? Fetch a broom and do the job properly."

"No, ma'am. Yes, ma'am," stuttered Nichol.

"Leave us," she commanded. "You, too, Thomas."

Nichol gave Anne a sympathetic glance in her rush to escape.

When the footman closed the door, Lady Catherine took her
favorite chair and observed first her daughter before giving her
nephew a level stare. "Well? Have you something to say?"

"Please be seated, Cousin," said the Colonel, sweeping his hand
toward a sofa.

Anne did as she was bid.

The Colonel clasped his hands behind his back and cleared his
throat. He was not insensible to the unusual nature of this event.
In fact, he could not count an instance when he had been moved to
challenge her ladyship directly over a matter of such import. Until
this moment he had never cared to be anyone other than who he
was, but gazing on her ladyship's lizard-like smile made him wish
for Darcy's confidence and stature.

"Matlock shared with me the contents of your letter—" he began.

"So I surmised. You have come to Rosings, I believe, out of some
misplaced affection for your cousin, but your journey was for nought,
for I see no cause to yield on the point of her marriage to Mr. Urson."

"Anne does not wish to marry him."

"What does that signify? She was indulged by her father when she
was a child and now reaps what has been sown. She never learned

the lesson of duty and gives no thought to what she owes the family."

"Duty takes different forms," the Colonel said carefully, "but it need not dictate every decision. Anne has the duty to involve her relations in her decision to marry, but she can choose whom she shall marry, having long ago reached her majority. She cannot be forced into marriage."

"No, but she should be open to persuasion from those closest to her. As her mother, I claim the right of influence. I have her interests at heart and believe her marriage to Mr. Urson is all for the good. It will secure her future and advance the interests of his family as well as hers."

Colonel Fitzwilliam seemed to relax when he saw a truth that must be stated. "If you value Anne's happiness, Aunt, then you will acknowledge her right to marry whom she chooses."

"I was not aware she disliked Mr. Urson," said her ladyship. "I saw them happily engaged in conversation, walking together in the Park, and laughing over trifles, as any courting couple would do. In every respect, they seem well matched."

The Colonel glanced at Anne. "Be that as it may, she has told her uncle and me that he does not suit."

Lady Catherine's temper flared. "Then allow her to make her own decision. She will make a mess of it. I wash my hands of her." She came to her feet, her bearing as regal as ever. "Let hers be the duty of informing our guests they are no longer welcome." With these words, she stalked from the room.

Chapter 60

"Come, Colonel Fitzwilliam, I shall show you my new fountain," said Lady Metcalfe. "It is not so grand as the willow tree fountain at Chatsworth, but it may amuse you."

"I am open to every amusement," he replied, offering his arm.

"Truly? You astonish me."

Anne watched them cross the lawn. She cast an eye at her sole companion, who sat stiff-backed, her head erect, her bearing more condescending than usual.

"I understand Mr. Urson left the district," said Lady Braybrooke in a business-like manner.

"Colonel Fitzwilliam"—Anne nodded across the lawn to where her cousin was fixing a great hairy rudbeckia bloom in Lady Metcalfe's hat—"convinced him to do so."

"It is good you rebuffed his charm, although I imagine Lady Catherine is not pleased."

"My refusal of his marriage offer seemed to cause her ladyship some consternation, for she told the Colonel she had not been aware I disliked the man. I find myself in the uncomfortable situation of either naming her a liar or pretending that I am both hysterical and imprudent."

Lady Braybrooke turned a critical eye on Anne. Choosing not to respond to this last ill-conceived remark, she said, "Lady Metcalfe asked me to share with you what I know of Mr. Urson. In doing so, I must address a delicate matter—a family tragedy. I charge you with the utmost discretion."

Anne realized Lady Braybrooke was the family friend whose help Lady Metcalfe sought. Remembering the last time they were in company together, she said, "I shall be discreet."

Lady Braybrooke snapped closed her fan as if to seal their pact. "The unhappy event I speak of occurred a few years after Hugh Rusbridge, now Hugh Urson, arrived at Edenworth. Having no moral compass, he forced himself first on two maids-of-all-work, one of whom bore him a child. Stern lectures from his uncle did little to deter him. Since servants were no longer fair game, he sought satisfaction seducing one of his cousins. He settled on the youngest of his uncle's daughters, a sweet girl of fourteen. She also became with child." Lady Braybrooke's voice quavered slightly, but she did not flinch. "They might have married and no one would have been the wiser, but Baron Nortleigh could not wed his favorite daughter to a rapscallion. He sent Mr. Urson away to school and has never permitted him to step foot on the estate."

Anne imagined the Baron's ire and his family's sorrow. Knowing a beloved daughter had been seduced by an unprincipled nephew must create a heartache that could not heal. "And the young lady?"

"Miss Urson was sent away to the country, to a good family, to bear her child." A grimace distorted her ladyship's handsome features as she recalled painful scenes.

"I am relieved to be told the truth of the matter," said Anne. Here was proof, as if she needed it, that appearances often deceive and show is not substance. "May I ask: What happened to her?"

"She and the child died in childbirth," said Lady Braybrooke with a tremulous voice. "I shall always hold Mr. Urson responsible for her sad fate. He has the morals of a tom cat. If it were a crime to be a dissolute scoundrel, he would qualify for permanent residence in Newgate." A look of remorse crossed the lady's face. "There is one other matter of which you may not be aware: the Ursons have a connection with your family."

Surprise rose in Anne's eyes.

"Your mother nearly married Hugh Urson's uncle John, now the second Baron Nortleigh." Lady Braybrooke fought to master her emotions, being reluctant to open old wounds. "When he was four and twenty years old, John Urson fell in love with the pretty, sweet daughter of a London alderman—my youngest sister, Frances. They enjoyed a deep affection, but John's father was against the match. No pleading moved him. Deaf to their wishes, Baron Nortleigh pressed for a more advantageous marriage, settling on Lady Catherine. The principals were introduced. Lady Catherine's family agreed to the marriage. The settlement was drafted. But John Urson would not be bound by duty. He convinced Frances to elope before the papers were signed. Baron Nortleigh could not be reconciled to their marriage and vowed never to see his son again. He kept his word. John felt the estrangement keenly but never regretted the marriage. When Baron Nortleigh died ten months later, John succeeded to the estate."

Anne observed Lady Braybrooke's rigid profile. Her lips were pressed into a hard line, and her gaze did not waver as she stared across the lawn to where Lady Metcalfe and the Colonel stood admiring the new fountain. "I cannot help speculating that my mother wished to marry John Urson," she said. "When her wish was thwarted, she married my father, Sir Lewis, instead. She must have believed it was her duty."

"For a woman as proud as Lady Catherine, the fact that John Urson chose a young lady with no dowry or connections over the daughter of an earl must have been galling."

"And she cannot be happy knowing your sister's marriage still thrives." No wonder Darcy's decision to marry Miss Bennet enraged Lady Catherine. He refused to marry the grand-daughter of an earl and chose to marry a lady very like Lady Braybrooke's youngest sister.

"There is one other connection." Lady Braybrooke turned to Anne. "Hugh Urson's great-grandparents, Walter and Elizabeth Evans, are your great-grandparents. He is your second cousin on your father's side."

Anne recoiled at the idea such a man was a relative. Why had she not been told of this connection? Her mother's resentment at being coerced to marry Sir Lewis de Bourgh must have disordered her mind all those years ago, for she never spoke of Sir Lewis's family, not even when pressed for information about them. The Fitzwilliams could not have realized how their plan for Lady Catherine to marry John Urson would spur her discontent when the engagement fell through. And what of Sir Lewis? Was he a willing participant or was he resentful as well? Some questions had no answers, but one truth emerged: bitterness had sat on her mother's tongue for so many years that she tasted no sweetness anywhere.

"Do you think Lady Catherine knows of Hugh Urson's infamy?" asked Anne.

"She may know of it. A family secret can be difficult to keep."

A monstrous thought occurred to Anne. Had her mother's insistence that she marry Mr. Urson been an honest effort to claim the moral high ground or was it a despicable act of revenge? By her own twisted thinking, Lady Catherine might feel vindicated to see her only daughter, a de Bourgh, marry into the Urson family. "I wonder whether Lady Catherine encouraged his advances on purpose," she blurted.

"If she knows of his character, it is a shocking indiscretion," said Lady Braybrooke. "The Urson family would be little harmed by your marriage to him, for the fact of his having seduced his cousin might remain secret. The greater wound would be to your person and happiness. Such action on Lady Catherine's part would be unconscionable."

Anne could well imagine her mother knowing exactly what she was about when she agreed to Mr. Urson's marriage offer. "What motivation would Mr. Urson have for pursuing me against my wishes, even if my mother inspired him to do so?"

"Money," Lady Braybrooke said simply. "His uncle cut him off completely last year because he has a newly born grandson to inherit Edenworth. For Mr. Urson—a man with no income—Rosings is a very pretty property, indeed."

"Money. I guessed as much."

"You handled yourself well. I believe you have nothing to fear from him. Tomorrow I shall call on Lady Catherine."

Chapter 61

"Did you hear me, Anne?"

"Hmm?" Anne shook her head. "Forgive me. I dozed off."

Tilly swallowed her bite of biscuit. "Has Lady Braybrooke left Hunsford?"

"She departed yesterday, shortly after the Colonel left for London. I shall miss her."

"Really? You surprise me. I understood you were not too fond of her after the house party at Dodford Meare."

"She is overbearing, true, but she discouraged my mother, as someone only of Lady Braybrooke's standing can do."

"Did Lady Catherine say anything to you of their conversation?"

"No, nor do I expect her to do so. She has been in high dudgeon. By her reckoning, I have destroyed, yet again, our prospect for happiness and comfort."

"Is she as bad as the horse-lipped Mrs. Jewkes, then?"

For the first time in days, Anne laughed—a true, heartfelt laugh. "Who? Mama or Lady Braybrooke? Not even my mother is as bad as Mrs. Jewkes." She closed her eyes and recalled girlish pleasures when she and Tilly read aloud from Richardson's novel *Pamela*. "I could lie here for hours, listening to the tent flaps rustling and the hum of bees and your dear voice. I shall want nothing more."

"Somehow I doubt that."

The friends each occupied a pillowed chaise longue in the shade of a white tent. Between them rested a low table, on which Nichol had placed lemonade, sweet biscuits, cheese, and fruit. They sampled as they pleased.

"Are you recovered from Mr. Urson's mischief?"

"Tell me: Which should offend more—Mr. Urson's deceit or his conceit? I fell prey to both. I laughed with him, flirted, flushed at his smile, and thought him gallant. I believed he suffered that scar dueling to protect a lady's honor. More likely, he got it in a mill over cards. For all his fine clothes and handsome air my heart remained untouched, which perhaps is just as well. I am not formed for love, I think."

"Oh, Anne. You love me, do you not?"

"I do, and I receive love from you and Mr. Sparke and from Dr. Bailey, Lady Metcalfe, the Colonel, and even Mrs. Beath. My weakness is that I have longed too desperately for love. I should do better to give up the quest. If love is only a frail tendril, I shall never recognize it."

Tilly chuckled.

"Does my weakness amuse you?"

"I believe you have succumbed to the charms of Mr. Pantley—such drama and passion on display this afternoon." When Anne tossed a grape across the grassy span between them, Tilly retrieved it from the folds of her gown and rolled it on her palm. "We all of us have trouble knowing love. It comes to us, not when we demand it, but when we neither expect nor look for it. It is a rare gift of trust and joy." She blushed at the thought of Mr. Sparke's fond embrace and tossed the grape onto the lawn.

"Did Macbeth misspeak, then?" asked Anne, overlooking Tilly's bloom. "With the death of each day's life, is it love, not sleep, that knits up the raveled sleeve of care, that soothes the hurt mind and nourishes life's feast?"

"That is a question for keener minds than mine, but I know you are as deserving of love as anyone."

"It is kind of you to say so, but I've grown ridiculous. Mr. Urson is not entirely to blame, although he contributed to my understanding.

I had a revelation, Tilly—two, actually." Anne stared across the lawn as if the sight of verdant grass and masses of blooming rose bushes might fortify her. "One evening I observed Lady Catherine sitting with him on the terrace. She flirted shamelessly: giggling and tapping his arm with her fan. In her playful glances, I saw happiness and delight. Her eyes were amiable in their cast and grew tender when they settled on me. How rare was such a look. In a flash I saw that for days I had basked in her approval. It hurt to realize how deeply I desired it. I understood then the price demanded for receiving her affection: I must marry Mr. Urson. Having refused to do so, I am not likely to enjoy peace in this house."

"And your second revelation?" asked Tilly.

"I cannot marry a man who seeks my mother's affection before securing my own. And there is the issue of Mr. Urson's being willing to submit to Mama's scheme regarding our marriage. His behavior was loathsome." She forced a smile. "Do not worry. I shall recover from my injuries as soon as I have forgotten them; and now that I have refused one offer of marriage and fear I shall never have another, I shall find comfort teaching your ten children to draw."

Tilly huffed, seeing in her friend rather too much self-pity. "You are becoming maudlin and would do better to think on the charity of forgiveness."

Anne smirked. "I am not inclined to forgive. How consoling it would be to know of God's just punishment for Mr. Urson—nothing so vile as hanging or transporting—but some small penalty that overturns his vanity. That is not very charitable of me, is it?"

"No, but it is understandable. Did he apologize?"

"The Colonel made him do so, but his words rang insincere. Mr. Pantley's words and actions were quite the opposite. He apologized for the pain he caused me and said he would recall my kindness all his days. His disgrace was etched on his face. Him, I forgave. Why could I readily absolve him, when I cannot pardon Mr. Urson? Perhaps Mr. Collins could be enticed to speak to my deficiencies, of which there are many."

"Anne, time is all you need to get yourself sorted. Eventually you will forgive both Mr. Urson and your mother."

"I fear I need quite a bit of sorting, for I have proof of my ignorance—I clearly know nothing of men. Did I tell you? George Martin Tench met Mr. Urson at the gaming tables in London. The two of them led me on a merry dance. Mr. Urson lied about his inheritance and invited Mama and me to Edenworth, knowing he was barred from his uncle's estate. When it came to the day he would have had an explanation for why our invitation had been rescinded, which makes me both resent and marvel at his ingenuity. Few men would have the nerve to sustain such a ruse. And Tench is no better, for he guided Urson here and provided advice on my situation and interests. How abominable! Both men have been warned off Rosings. Roger Tench is pleased as punch, his being the one person who finds satisfaction in this mess."

"At least you were not alone in your troubles. Your family and friends came to your aid. There is joy in knowing they are loyal to you."

Anne felt a surge of affection for her friend. "As usual, you remind me of life's goodness, and one other virtue emerged from this sorry tale: I am grateful to Darcy. In seeking Miss Bennet's hand he pursued his own interests without regard for mine. Had he been made of the same stuff as Mr. Urson, he would have married me for my property and I would now be bereft of hope."

Thinking it wise to turn the conversation, Tilly said, "Do you go to the Powlett's party?"

"Yes, a little dancing might do me good."

"The Powlett's nephew will attend, I hear. Perhaps you shall find a new lover."

Anne loosed a low laugh. "There is no chance of it, for I forswear all men."

Chapter 62

Anne took no special care in dressing for the Powlett's party. It would be a trial to force herself to smile and converse; but by the time Mrs. Powlett finished playing the first lively piece on the pianoforte, she was surprised to find joy dancing with the lady's nephew Mr. Johnson. He was a short, rotund man with reddish hair, a fleshy chin, and a penchant for telling funny stories. Anne was absorbed in his description of the Harmonists' settlement near Pittsburg when a servant approached.

"Excuse me, ma'am," he said, "but a lad is asking for you."

"Oh, I shall come directly."

Tilly's worried look followed her into the hall where she found Lester, looking a little lost.

"Pardon me, ma'am, but a genman and a lady arrived at Rosings a short while ago."

"Who are they?"

"Mr. Worthington and his cousin. The genman wrote ye." Henry offered her a letter, which she opened and read:

> *Dear Miss de Bourgh,*
>
> *I hope you can forgive my imposing on you. I dared not give you warning—not out of concern for myself, but in fear for my cousin. I await your return.*
>
> *Worthy*

Anne's eye lingered over his signature while the gravity of the situation settled on her. She turned to Mrs. Powlett's servant. "I wish to write a reply." In a small library the maid gave her a fresh quill-pen. Underneath Mr. Worthington's words she wrote instructions to Hobbs and Mrs. Faber and took her reply into the hall.

"The genman said he would not wish ye to give up your pleasure."

"I shall not do so. Thank you, Lester." On returning to the party, Anne could hardly attend to any conversation or receive pleasure from dancing. She was anxious to know why the cousins had come to Rosings in the dead of night.

Tilly expressed her own view: "You have experienced more commotion this season than during all the years you were engaged to Darcy!"

"Yes, and I wonder how much of it is for the good, although sometimes I feel stimulated by my new adventures."

—⁊⁊—

"Mr. Worthington is in the library with Dr. Bailey," said Hobbs solemnly.

"The doctor was called?"

"Aye, ma'am. The gentleman was most insistent on having a doctor attend the lady."

From the library door, the gentlemen were seen sitting before the hearth, where a low fire burned. Mr. Worthington's profile brought to mind his sombre look that evening at Dodford Meare when a storm beset the house.

"Miss Anne," said Dr. Bailey, pushing himself to his feet.

Mr. Worthington set down his half-drunk glass of port and stood, alert to criticism.

"Welcome to you both. How does Mrs. Egerton do?"

Dr. Bailey's look was grave. "Mrs. Egerton was assaulted by her husband and suffered a disjointed shoulder, which was repaired by a surgeon in London, and a bruised eye. The swollen orb has turned a nasty purple." A scowl rose on his lips. "She is young and will recover. I gave her a draught of laudanum to ensure a good night's sleep. All she needs now is rest."

Anne studied Mr. Worthington. He appeared almost gaunt and his clothes were disheveled. Giving him a frank look, she said, "I shall instruct the maids to allow you and Mrs. Egerton to rest as long as you like. Tomorrow will come soon enough and we can speak of this situation. Good night, sir." She spoke to the man-servant: "Ibson, show Mr. Worthington to the Green room and ask Hobbs to bring the carriage around front for Dr. Bailey."

Mr. Worthington was too dismal to argue. He offered his thanks and followed Ibson out into the hall.

When the footman closed the door, Anne said, "Is Mrs. Egerton's condition very bad?"

Dr. Bailey eased himself down onto the upholstered chair. "Sorry, Miss Anne. My joints ache today." He sighed. "Are you confident the lady was not assaulted by her cousin? He might be a villain."

"Mr. Worthington is no churl. Indeed, he is quite in love with her. The villain is the lady's husband. I have observed his anger first hand and fear Mrs. Egerton has long suffered his abuse."

"Then I won't worry over your safety with the man in residence."

Anne thought the doctor might be joking, but his look said otherwise.

"I wonder that he did not remove her to her family's residence," he said sternly. "That would have been the proper action."

"It is a good question. I don't know him well, but Lady Metcalfe can speak to his character. We shall have an explanation tomorrow."

"Fair enough. As for the lady upstairs, it pains me to see such beauty suffer at the hands of a gentleman—I use the word with reservation." He drained the port from his glass. "Now I am for bed, Miss, and I shall not let anybody impede my progress."

Chapter 63

Luncheon the next day was a disagreeable affair. Lady Catherine complained about the guests. "The least you might have done was tell me of your invitation. I am in no mood for company. This lamb has a funny taste. Take this plate, Vaughn, and serve me some beef."

"I had no knowledge of Mr. Worthington's plan until I received word of his arrival," said Anne calmly. "Their presence will not inconvenience you."

"Humph. They are likely to stay for several weeks, judging by Mrs. Egerton's condition."

"Then we may be as hospitable toward them as we were to Mr. Urson and his friend."

A pretty summer morning lengthened into early afternoon and still there was no sign of Mr. Worthington. Long after luncheon he appeared in the drawing room.

"You are rested, then?" asked Anne as he crossed the rug toward her, a questioning look in his eyes.

"Thank you, yes."

There was an unnatural stillness about his face. He did not smile, which was unfortunate, Anne thought, for he had a wide, expressive mouth designed more for laughing than scowling. One dark curl fell over his forehead, forming a peak above his intelligent, grey eyes. He was not handsome in the classical sense—he was less striking in his physical form than Darcy and less congenial in his manner than Colonel Fitzwilliam—but he was attractive none the less.

"I apologize for imposing on you without notice, but I had no other choice."

Anne could not countenance his standing like a soldier addressing his commanding officer. "Will you sit?"

He sank onto a chair, a furrow settling on his brow. "You are owed an explanation. Egerton refused to receive me. The rake thwarted my every move. I could not put a foot on his property. I could not waylay his carriage on the road. He led me on several wild-goose chases about the county, sometimes sending out two or three carriages, thus forcing me to choose which to follow." The chair being too confining, he set to pacing the carpet. "Amelia—Mrs. Egerton—was forbidden to write to me. Her father paid her a visit, presumably to call her to duty. He is as much a blackguard as Egerton himself! Two days ago Amelia's former maid Millie learned of the assault; she still has friends at Seighford and called on a footman to help remove her former charge. They took a great risk but brought her to me. We traveled straight to London, stopping for one night, and then came here." He ran his hand through his hair. "You do see my dilemma: I could not release Amelia to her family. She would find no support there." His eyes held hers. "I thought of you. Amelia spoke often of your kindness to her and I thought perhaps—" He sighed. "I hoped you might—"

"—offer Mrs. Egerton shelter. I am pleased to do so."

He bowed to her. "I aim to rescue Amelia from her marriage. Her freedom is my only goal."

Chapter 64

"I cannot risk anyone knowing where she is," protested a scowling Mr. Worthington.

Anne had enticed him into the gardens, thinking their beauty would calm him while she convinced him to inform Lord and Lady Metcalfe of Mrs. Egerton's situation. Alas, he strode along the path, whipping his cane about and stabbing the earth with it, all the while offering objections to her idea. He accidentally lopped a rose from its thorny spike. The sight of the soft, sweet-smelling bloom lying in the dirt startled him. He picked it up, gently brushed away the soil bits, and handed it to her.

"Forgive me. I am not myself today. I received a letter from my oldest brother. He writes to say I must take Amelia to her father's estate. He believes I have little choice since my actions look hostile to Mr. Egerton and his family, which, indeed, they are."

Anne stroked the bloom's pink petals. "I understand your wish to keep her situation secret from as many people as possible, but already her presence at Rosings is known in the village. Mr. Egerton will learn of it soon enough. All the more reason to gather allies in your fight." His scowl was nearly as forbidding as Darcy's, but she was not deterred. "What is your plan for rescuing her?"

"Divorce would be the rightful thing, the only way of protecting her, but—I know—" His voice trailed off.

Anne knew better than to encourage any hope of divorce. "Let us seek Lady Metcalfe's advice. She has a tender heart."

They walked the two miles to Holcombe Manor. Hardly any small-talk passed between them, although they exchanged speaking looks.

"You have few choices," said Lady Metcalfe. "Divorce is out of the question. I see you bridle at the thought, but I speak frankly. Nothing can be gained by ignoring the fact: marriage is an indissoluble contract, ended only by death."

"But a Divorce Bill can be obtained by any man!" cried Mr. Worthington. "If a husband can seek redress, why not a wife?"

"A man need only prove damages for criminal conversation. If he can prove his wife is guilty of adultery, then he can secure the Private Act of Parliament that will grant him a divorce and allow him to remarry. A wife has a greater hurdle: she must prove her husband's adultery *and* his mistreatment of her. It can be difficult to prove either. Mrs. Egerton might claim physical mistreatment at his hands, but can she prove adultery?"

"Why should a man's adulterous infamy be any different from a woman's? If one sins before God, the other should claim restitution." Mr. Worthington's eyes blazed at the injustice.

"Think on it, sir. A husband wants assurance that every child is his own and not some philandering fool's. Under the Law, a husband holds the rights to his wife's body. If her issue is a son, he must be confident the boy is *his*—his heir. For this reason, adultery can be forgiven in a husband, but not in a wife." Seeing his forlorn look, Lady Metcalfe said gently, "Mrs. Egerton might be able to obtain a separation—a divorce from bed to board. She could not remarry but she might obtain peace by removing to her own house. Would this serve her purpose?"

"I don't know. We have never spoken on the matter, but nearly everybody knows she is unhappy in her present circumstances."

"You must speak to her immediately. You cannot act until you know her wishes."

Mr. Worthington cut his eyes at Anne. "Would you speak with her? I don't trust myself to be dispassionate."

"Of course. In return, will you allow Lady Metcalfe to visit her? There may come a time when Lady Metcalfe's influence would serve you well."

He agreed reluctantly to this proposal.

—⁂—

"Please call me Amelia. You have become a sister to me these last days."

Anne patted Mrs. Egerton's good arm. "If you will call me Anne."

Mrs. Egerton smiled feebly and settled herself against the head-board. Two large pillows placed at her back eased her shoulder pain.

Anne observed her guest's bruised cheek, swollen eye, and listless person. She could hardly bring herself to follow through on her promise. "There is something I must discuss with you, even though I fear I shall disturb your peace. Mr. Worthington is willing to pursue any course to protect you. Indeed, he is somewhat incautious in his planning and intolerant of the delay imposed by your recovery—men are easily wearied by the sick bed, be it theirs or someone else's. You, more than anyone, know his nature: he will do anything, but must first know your wishes. Can you speak of the future? What course do you wish to follow?"

"Worthy is a good man. I have come to rely on him more than I should. Tell him I must return to Seighford. My husband and father expect it. I don't want to go, but I have no other choice." Her eyes grew dull.

"Amelia, you might pursue a legal separation. You could not remarry, but you would be removed from harm."

"I am aware of this possibility, but cannot pursue it. I have not the will to disclose my husband's base character to the world. The danger is not only to me, but to anyone involved in the case. He has a vengeful heart. He can neither forgive nor forget."

"You might not be safe in his house!" cried Anne, forgetting herself. Since arguing would do no good, she said, "Forgive me. I spoke rashly. If you applied for a separation, your friends would support your case. Dr. Bailey and myself, Lady Metcalfe, Mr. Worthington—even the London surgeon who treated your shoulder, I am sure—will step forward to speak of all that has befallen you. You would not be alone in this trial."

Mrs. Egerton smiled as one might favor a simpleton. "Do you remember Mr. Tweedy's sermon at Dodford Meare? He quoted Zechariah the Prophet, saying we are instructed to accept God's will and believe in His goodness. His words made me cry, so resentful had I become. I railed then against God for demanding obedience to Egerton's torture and preventing me from marrying a man I truly love. Now I question His goodness and His plan, even as I believe He guided me to Rosings, where your friendship sustains me. I am fickle in my understanding, am I not?"

"You are struggling to make sense of a monstrosity most of us can only imagine."

"Then forgive me for being weak and selfish, but offer comfort, when you can."

—m—

By the light of blazing candles, Anne drew veins on a dozen obovate leaves sketched on artist's paper. Her eyes darted repeatedly to the drawing in *Curtis's Botanical Magazine*, which was the subject of her effort. The species was the blunt-leaved *Fothergilla*, a native shrub of Carolina. The veins completed, she began shading the leaves to give them depth. The activity was a mere stop-gap to settle her mind while she considered how best to convince Amelia to adopt another course. A rustle caused her to look up.

"Mama, you have decided to join us this evening." Her comment alerted Mr. Worthington, who was absorbed in a book borrowed from the Rosings library. He came to his feet.

Lady Catherine's look made known her displeasure on finding the two of them unchaperoned, however industrious and innocent their present occupations. She raised one eyebrow and moved to the sofa, where she released a 'humph' when she sat down.

"Shall I pour some tea for you?" asked Anne.

Lady Catherine inclined her head, but stared at Mr. Worthington, who was obliged to sit. He laid his book on his knee, his fingers marking his place.

"I hear you are from Leicestershire. Do you still have family in that county?" Lady Catherine accepted a cup of steaming tea from her daughter.

"Yes, ma'am."

"I don't know any Worthingtons. It would be too much to expect a connection with the peerage, those esteemed individuals being the most illustrious in the country, but your surname might reasonably appear in *The Baronetage of England*. Alas, I do not find it there."

"I am not surprised to hear it. My father, like his father before him, was a bootmaker. When he died his estate passed to my eldest brother, Harley."

Lady Catherine squinted. "Is your brother also a bootmaker?"

"Yes, he directs a thriving Leicestershire enterprise."

"His operation is not located in London? How peculiar. London is recognized throughout the world as the seat of the Empire and the heart of commerce. I should think he would seek the largest possible market for his … boots, in which case a shop in London is *nécessaire*."

"It would not be practical to situate the operation in London."

Having nothing to say to this bald report, Lady Catherine asked, "Do you have other siblings?"

"I am the youngest of ten children. Three brothers manage the family business, another is a vicar, and the other two are in the navy. My three sisters are all married. I am an uncle to a large brood."

"I understand you were raised by your uncle, which explains your closeness to Mrs. Egerton."

"After my mother died, her brother offered to raise me, seeing how my father was busy with his business and numerous other children."

"Your uncle was kind in his offer, which does him credit. How do you occupy yourself—that is, when you are not protecting Mrs. Egerton from her husband?"

"I am a naturalist," said Mr. Worthington with perfect aplomb. "I am drawn to observations of birds and reptiles but also study plants, particularly trees and shrubs." He had taken Lady Catherine's measure soon after his arrival and counted himself fortunate: no ladies in his family tree, whether placed there by blood or marriage, had been struck with her ladyship's stamp. In her brittle disposition he found little to admire and much to dislike. There being no hope of gaining support for his profession, he readily defended himself against her blatant hostility by speaking as though he believed her curious. A quick glance at Miss de Bourgh revealed her view of his position: kind approval spiced with amusement. "I have been studying the coot, a common bird found in most parts of the kingdom. For all its rather plain demeanor, the coot is interesting in its habits. It is a water bird, but it is more fastidious in its choice of habitat than, say, the gallinule. Where the gallinule can sometimes be found some distance from water—on a country lane, for example, or near cottages—the coot is seldom seen on land, but prefers to ride the surface of a lake or large pond. Almost nothing is known about its pairing habits. Earlier this year I spent a week in Derbyshire studying the coot."

"I suppose every man seeks an amusement. Yours is no worse than some." Lady Catherine set her teacup on the side-table. "I shall send Mrs. Jenkinson down immediately."

When her ladyship left the room, Mr. Worthington bestowed on Anne a dazzling smile that hinted at some devilment. She responded readily in kind.

Chapter 65

"Listen to this." Mr. Worthington sat in the chair opposite Anne, reading aloud from the *Philosophical Magazine*. "'*At five o'clock in the afternoon, the first commotion took place. The air was calm, the heat excessive: nothing preceded or announced such a catastrophe. A shaking was first perceived, strong enough to set the bells of the churches a-ringing.*' Can you imagine the horror? A Frenchman writes here about the earthquake, saying the earth seemed to boil like water. It is incredible he survived."

"Was the damage truly awful?"

"In an instant, eighty thousand people lost their lives and thousands were wounded." His eyes scanned the page. "Many residents were in the churches, it being Good Friday, and so were entombed. It says here that two churches were originally more than one hundred and fifty feet high, but afterwards, their ruins did not exceed five or six feet."

"I have never experienced an earthquake and can only imagine their terror. I should not know what to do first."

"If you survived, you would gather your wits, count your arms and legs, and then rescue your family and neighbors," he said, peering over the magazine.

Anne smiled. How pleasant to imagine listening to him read every evening. They had spent considerable time in each other's company. Nearly every day they walked in the Park—he with his pocket-book and pencil, she with her art paper and crayons, Mrs. Jenkinson with a sulky pout on her lips at having to play chaperon amongst insects and other wild creatures—and found some flower or shrub or frog to sketch. More than once they drew the Folly's aspects, lamenting the difficulties they encountered with perspective or shading. Criticism was given and taken in good faith, each recognizing the other's skill. On their walks they spoke of artists and painting techniques, of their favorite poets and novels, of childhood pleasures and memories. He told her of his mother's sad death: "Our carriage turned over; its weight crushed her petite form and I was tossed against an earthen bank. The hard landing thus damaged my hip. I have only the haziest memories of her but recall that she always smelled of lavender." Anne began to count him a friend and dreaded the day he departed Rosings.

"This will interest you," he said. "Some fathers lost five or six children and their entire property, yet shed not a tear. Others married."

"Married!"

"It says here that about two thousand persons were married over the course of two days." His eyes glinted. "It suggests a rare form of optimism, does it not? When the earth trembles and buildings crumble, when your very life is torn asunder, why not marry?"

"You would never be so irrational," she said.

A subtle change came over his features. He seemed about to speak but instead his eyebrows bunched as he took up his place.

Anne turned a page in her book, knowing he thought of his cousin.

Chapter 66

"How dare you presume to impose on us," said Lady Catherine, her shrill voice piercing the breakfast room.

Anne traded a look with Mr. Worthington. They put down their forks and hurried into the hall where a barrel-chested, red-faced man stood his ground.

"I have every right to do so, ma'am," exclaimed the visitor. The man's pudgy fingers waved a letter under her ladyship's nose. "Mr. Egerton charges with me determining his wife's suitability for travel. You shall not bar my way." His cheeks turned pink from an excited blood pressure.

"I am the owner of this property, sir," Anne cut in. "What is your purpose?"

"My name is Skirving," he said, patting his upper lip with a large handkerchief. "Lord Kennderby's solicitor hired me on behalf of his son Mr. Egerton. The gentleman worries about his wife, as any attentive husband would. He seeks her safe return to Seighford Place. Madam, I shall determine for myself—"

"You shall leave my cousin alone," warned Mr. Worthington with clenched fists.

Anne laid a hand on his arm to halt his glowering charge. "I shall take you to her," she said to the visitor. "Ibson, follow us upstairs." She adopted her mother's imperious attitude and rudely ascended the stairs. When the threesome reached the upper floor, she said to Ibson, "Wait here with Mr. Skirving while I determine Mrs. Egerton's state of dress."

When all was ready, Mr. Skirving tiptoed into the room. It being nearly eleven o'clock, the drapes were still drawn against the morning sun. Anne gently secured one drape open and signaled his approach. Even in the gloom, she saw alarm cross his florid face when he beheld Mrs. Egerton's bruises.

"What has happened to her?" whispered Skirving.

"She was assaulted by her husband and suffered a a disjointed shoulder and a black eye, which swelling has diminished considerably in the past week. The village doctor checks her progress every day. She suffers pain even when she sits up to eat and needs rest, not the aggravation of travel."

"I had not expected—he led me to believe—" Mr. Skirving shook his head. "I shall have trouble explaining this to Lord Kennderby."

"Mrs. Egerton told me she intends to return to Seighford. I don't support her decision, but I accept it. When she is ready to travel, she will contact her husband."

Mr. Skirving frowned. "May I speak with the local doctor?"

"Of course. I shall write a note to Dr. Bailey on your behalf."

After Mr. Skirving departed, Anne went in search of Mr. Worthington but encountered Lady Catherine.

"You damage our reputation by harboring a gentleman's wife. I insist you inform Mrs. Egerton and her common cousin that they are no longer welcome here."

"Mrs. Egerton is in no condition to travel, Mama. Are you not aware of her condition?"

"What does that matter to me? I am no friend of hers. If she has tangled herself with a headstrong, unruly husband, that is her problem. Our status in the district is threatened by her presence on the estate. We are the talk of the village. Why, news of her flight may already be known to half the *ton*."

"I don't care what the villagers or your friends say or think. Any decent Christian would offer comfort to one so badly abused."

"We shall see about that. I shall write her father."

"Please do! Invite him here to look upon his daughter's bruised face. We shall then measure his Christian charity."

With those words, Anne went in search of Mr. Worthington, whose patience had also worn thin. "You should not have allowed that despicable man to visit Amelia. You did her no good. Next we shall have Egerton himself on the doorstep."

"I had no other choice. Skirving would have skulked about the village for days and alarmed everyone with false claims of our refusal to allow Amelia to return to Seighford. I thought it better to let him see her for himself."

His outrage simmered a little. "What did he say, then?"

"He could not hide his alarm, the damage to her person being undeniable."

"I cannot credit his claim to have been sent here on behalf of Mr. Egerton, but perhaps we have seen the last of him."

"I doubt it. Does it matter? Amelia is determined to return to her husband. Not much can be done to stop her."

His mouth pressed into a thin line. "I would take her overseas if she would go. Otherwise, what is to be done?"

The question hung heavily between them.

Chapter 67

"I cannot countenance her decision," Mr. Worthington confessed, "for it mocks every sympathetic feeling."

"It would be far less distressing for Amelia if you would support her," said Anne. "She is well aware of your resistance and would take any measure to placate you, if she could."

They strolled leisurely, if not quite companionably, toward the Folly. For once, they had the path to themselves, Mrs. Jenkinson having declined to join them on their walk as she usually did. On his side, Mr. Worthington took care to keep the proprieties, for he did not wish to antagonize Lady Catherine with any suspicious, impolitic behavior toward her daughter. He knew her ladyship found fault with his decision to bring Amelia to Rosings uninvited and, being a gentleman in the truest sense of the word, took care to avoid giving offense. This evening, however, he could not help being gratified at having Anne's company.

Anne herself felt little modesty, for walking in the Park with Mr. Worthington felt proper and right. She had ignored her mother's scold about indecorous behavior and claimed that being alone with him was no more shocking or offensive than being alone with Darcy or Colonel Fitzwilliam. In the face of Lady Catherine's thunderous protest, she had retorted, "You never objected to my being alone with Mr. Urson."

Mr. Worthington contemplated Anne's comment. "The problem is that she has every right to pursue a divorce but will not act on her knowledge." He caught Anne's startled look. "I trust your confidence and so speak without reservation. It will shock you, I fear, to hear that Mr. Egerton has not upheld his marriage vow for close to a year."

Anne released a telling sigh. "I cannot say that I am surprised. He struck me as the sort of man who would seek a bit of comfort on the sly."

"It is worse than that. The lady whom he admires is Mrs. Venables."

"Mrs. Venables!" Anne's thoughts reeled like larks at this intelligence. Mr. Egerton enamored of Mrs. Venables? Their behavior at Dodford Meare suddenly suggested a different meaning. They were not merely flirtatious friends; they were lovers. Had Mrs. Linwood become disgusted by the relations between her brother and her dearest friend? Was this the basis for her quarrel with Mrs. Venables at Dodford Meare? Although Anne had never considered her a friend, she would not wish the lady to be in physical danger. If Mr. Egerton assaulted his wife, what principle would prevent him from beating a mistress? "Is it certain?" she asked, finding sympathy for the young widow.

"Indeed, their affair has been one of the most enduring *on dits* in Town."

"This grows worse and worse. Poor Amelia. Poor Lady Metcalfe. I wonder if her ladyship is aware of the talk about Town. She will be deeply pained by this intelligence when she learns of it."

"She knows of it and has sequestered Mrs. Venables at Dodford Meare."

"Oh, that explains her sudden departure from Hunsford. To hear of this affair only underscores Amelia's desperate situation."

Mr. Worthington knew he had not underestimated her. She would not swoon or faint at unpleasant news. "You have wicked eyes when you are all out of countenance."

Anne gazed up at him. His eyes were teasing but kind. "You are quite beyond impudent, Mr. Worthington."

His features softened. "Please call me Worthy, as my friends do. You are a friend, are you not?"

She gave her assent, feeling the thrill of so intimate a request. Recovering her composure, she said, "It is foolish of me to provoke you when we are suddenly in accord with one another, but for Amelia's sake, I urge you to accept her decision. There is little to be done if the law will not protect her."

He shook his head. "The girl is a saint. Not a word will she say against her brute of a husband. I have a mind to call him out."

"You cannot. Only think how awful it would be for Amelia if you were injured or killed. Still more so if Mr. Egerton fell to the sword. Amelia might never recover from such infamy."

"I cannot but agree with you," he said with surprising charity, "but it pains me to see such sweetness abused." He looked down on her, a quizzical glint in his eye. "Would you come to the same decision in her place?"

"I think not. I can be unyielding, which would endanger me if I were married to a man with Mr. Egerton's proclivity. God protect me from such a one. As it is, I battle with Lady Catherine's resolution on the subject of marriage. You may know my cousin Darcy and I were engaged in our infancy, his mother and my own being of one mind. Since his marriage last year Lady Catherine pursues a husband for me. We are engaged in a battle royal."

"I know of your situation."

His comment threw her emotions into confusion, and it was some minutes before she could master them. "I believe—I hope—Amelia knows her own heart, whether her guiding principle is duty or some other feeling."

"She is good-natured and unselfish. Those parts of her character make me fear for her, especially as she has always been a person to accept the strictures laid down by her father and now, her husband."

"Is there someone else in her family who might offer her protection? A grandfather or uncle?"

"It is interesting you ask the question. Yesterday I wrote Amelia's aunt, Lady De Ponte, to ask whether she might invite Amelia to visit for a few months. Lady De Ponte is an eccentric but amiable character who is happily married. It would do Amelia good to enjoy such a pleasing situation."

"Will she agree to it?" Anne asked as they approached the Folly's tall archway.

"I believe so. I hope so," Worthy said, as they halted on the path. "Enough fretting over Amelia. I promise to consider her wishes. Does that satisfy you?" At Anne's nod, he said, "Now, what is your pleasure today? Shall we draw the roses?"

Forcing her confidence, Anne asked, "Would you mind if I took your likeness?"

"Not at all—if you will allow me the same pleasure."

They settled comfortably, each on a stone bench and began their sketches. No words, only studious glances, passed. After a time, Worthy asked, "May I see your drawing?"

Anne showed it to him. "I am not particularly skilled at drawing faces. The mouth is not quite right, but I believe I have captured your eyes. Would you agree?"

"You have given me a strong face. It is a good likeness."

"Let me see your drawing."

Worthy pressed his pocket-book to his chest as if to hide it from her.

"What mischief have you done?"

"It is a true likeness," he said, "but I fear it will not suit you."

"Let me determine the truth of it for myself." One look made her laugh. "You goose. It is a perfect likeness."

He had drawn her boots and the lacy hem of her muslin gown. An ant meandered across one toe, while in the foreground a black beetle pushed its way up a tiny hillock of soil in pursuit of a distant tuft of grass.

Chapter 68

"Did Worthy leave this morning?" Amelia noticed Anne's distracted stare. Her patience was rewarded with a reply.

"He received a letter yesterday—a letter of some import, I believe, for I have never seen him so perturbed. He left for London after breakfast."

"He did not describe its contents?"

Anne shook her head. "It's a mystery. According to Hobbs, Worthy receives more letters than any other visitor, and Hobbs would know, for he has served Rosings for decades."

"Worthy corresponds with fellow enthusiasts in England and also on the Continent. I never imagined there was so much to say about newts and hedgehogs and blackthorns, but he gathers intelligence on all sorts of creatures and plants. One day he will make his mark on the world." On seeing Anne's shy delight at such praise of him, Amelia added: "Worthy has grown fond of you, Anne. I see it. Indeed, I have never known him to speak with such admiration of a lady's drawing skill. He says you have quite a good eye for detail and color, which I know well enough, having seen several of your compositions."

A bubble of hope rose in Anne's heart but was pricked by a hard reality: the man was besotted with his cousin. Since nothing could be gained by discussing her feelings, she said with false cheer, "You are looking more yourself this morning. I am pleased you are coming downstairs. Shall you try playing the pianoforte today?"

"Thank you. I wish to do so, if it will not trouble Lady Catherine."

"You will bother no one in the music room. There is sheet music in the cabinet, but I fear it will not challenge you."

"Do not worry. My music teacher was a tyrant. He forced me to memorize dozens of pieces."

After Amelia escaped to the music room, Anne studied the drizzle through the conservatory windows. She knew Worthy could not long reside at Rosings. Where would she find the fortitude to bid him goodbye? Surely a sickness would descend on her if she was left alone with only Lady Catherine for company. She feared she would go mad.

Chapter 69

"Gibbons, I thought we had an understanding," cried Anne as she approached the old gardener. "You agreed to lay down your hoe. Carter is taking up your duties."

The old man grinned, two teeth missing in his smile. "Aye, Miss. Carter is plenty ready to take over, but I canna' sit by the fire all day. The roses be needin' attention." His blue eyes sparkled in a tanned face wrinkled by time, sun, and wind.

"See that you don't overdo it, then. You have worked these gardens since before I was born and deserve a rest."

"There'll be plenty o' time to rest when I am laid in th' ground."

She gave him a rueful look and left him to work. There was no keeping him out of the rose garden. It was his first love and only comfort. He had no family living and would be happy to suffer a fatal apoplectic fit among his roses.

Would that I could achieve such simplicity in life, Anne reflected as she followed the shaded path into the woods. Fern fronds glistened, the soil was spongy underfoot, and the smell of rain lingered. As she trod the damp path she recalled skipping the trail alongside her father. He had loved and sheltered her in ways she only now appreciated. Darcy, too. For all that she had resented their engagement, Darcy had been a steady force in her life. Since his marriage, she was surprised to feel buffeted by strange new desires and unsure of herself. Only a handful of men made her feel truly comfortable: Dr. Bailey, Mr. Sparke, Lord Metcalfe and his sons, Colonel Fitzwilliam, Arnot, Dr. Granville, and now Worthy.

At the Folly she took her favorite bench. Worthy. In form and figure he was much like Darcy—tall, manly, confident. But his eyes differed. Where Darcy's shown with an intensity that could sometimes be overpowering, Worthy's welcomed and challenged, but playfully; where Darcy's eyes held little true mirth, Worthy's sparkled and teased. She liked watching him read or draw. She liked waiting for the sudden spark, the brilliant glint of whim or fancy that fired his imagination. With him, she felt the possibilities of life, of joy, of the new and exciting. Without intending it to happen, she had formed an affection for him, but feared her heart could never charm his. It was no secret. His first duty was to Amelia and his only goal to help her escape her marriage. Providence was cruel, indeed, to place in her path two eligible men—Mr. Urson, an unscrupulous man offering marriage, and Worthy, a good man in love with his cousin. There was nothing for it: she must tame her heart and accept this miserable situation. Perhaps solace might be found in friendship.

A noise behind her caused her to turn. There stood George Martin Tench. The weasel Beath squatted nearby, rolling a weed across his lips with his tongue.

"Did we interrupt your reverie, Miss de Bourgh?" asked Tench. "We should hate to disturb your peace."

At these words she pulled her shawl tighter around her shoulders. A frisson of fear gripped her belly.

Beath moved off to her right, while Tench stepped around the bench. "Are you not happy to see me after so many months? It seems you don't recognize your friends. Even Urson said you were not so compliant and friendly as when you were in Town. He was surprised to find you so disagreeable." He circled behind her and whispered, "Have you nothing to say?"

"Cold weather and knaves come out of the north."

Tench roared. "That's a good joke!" His fingers brushed her neck. "You were always more nice than wise. Only think, it might improve your situation to be a little familiar, for I have a message for you."

"What sort of message?"

He blew in her ear. "Urson cannot countenance your rebellion. When you withheld your affection he said to me, 'Teach her a lesson, George, one she is not likely to forget.' You understand, I only do as I am told."

"You don't think for yourself, then?" Her heart was fit to burst.

Tench grinned as he loomed over her. "Oh, yes. I think you are terribly alone here in the woods." He looked off through the trees. "Nobody shall hear your cry, is that not so?"

"Arnot is—" cried Anne when Tench grasped her arms, jerked her to her feet, and laid wet kisses on her face and neck. Reacting with every animal instinct, she pummeled his chest and squirmed.

"Hold her arms, Beath," Tench wheezed as he forced her down onto the path.

Beath charged forward and pinned her arms to the damp pebbled soil. A few stones dug into her back while her pulse throbbed violently. She was too terrified to yell.

Tench stood over her, a sick grin on his face, his fingers working the buttons on his britches. "I would do as I like, to honor my friend Urson and shame you for hiring Arnot. By rights, his office should be mine."

When she spat at him Beath stuffed a foul-tasting rag into her mouth. Tench sat astride her leg and clutched her dress. She bucked and kicked and thrashed, but he was too heavy to heave over. The brute worked one hand up her gown.

"You don't like that very much, do you?"

Anne felt his naked, throbbing member bump against her leg and push against her privities. She would not be ravished, not while there was breath in her. She bucked and rolled sideways to throw him off.

"I like a girl with spirit," he panted, pinching her throat.

She could not breathe. Suddenly her arms were free, giving her rein to slap him about the head. A loud crack rang out, after which Tench collapsed on top of her, a dead weight. When strong hands dragged him off, she pulled the rag from her mouth and retched onto the weeds.

When next she came to her senses, she was sitting on a chair in the Great Hall. Servants milled about. Shaw, Nichol, and Cooper clustered around her. Mrs. Faber laid a blanket across her shoulders and whispered to Arnot.

"What do you all do here?" asked Lady Catherine as she parted the crowd. "Out, out," she shouted at the groundsmen. "Gardeners are not allowed in the hall."

"Mama, please," rasped Anne

"Lady Catherine," bellowed Arnot, "Miss de Bourgh was assaulted by George Martin Tench in the woods. Gibbons and two under-gardeners rescued her."

Lady Catherine was too startled by Arnot's tone to speak.

"Gibbons," said Anne. Her eyes searched the crowd. When he stepped forward, hat in hand, she said, "Thank you, sir, for your bravery."

"I knew the men were up t' no good, Miss. When I spied them headin' into the woods, I called to Cory and John. I whack'd Tench pretty hard with my hoe handle. T'was no more than he deserved."

"Let me carry you upstairs, Miss. Lester has run to fetch Dr. Bailey." Arnot lifted her as though she were a child and mounted the stairs with ease.

—⁓—

"Miss Anne, tell me truly: Are you well?"

"I am mostly sore and bruised and shocked. You were good to come, Dr. Bailey."

"How could I not? Such villainy. George Tench would rise from his grave if he could. That his son would lay a hand on you is unspeakable. Well, he shall not trouble you again, for Squire Rivers took hold of him." He chuckled softly. "Tench was out cold for more than an hour. Who would think old Gibbons had the strength to knock him unconscious with a hoe handle?" He patted her arm. "The laudanum will help you sleep, but before you get too groggy, I gave Mrs. Sparke permission to see you. She came running from the parsonage when she heard of the assault. I cannot deny her. You rest. I shall calm your mother." He winked and tiptoed into the hall. Anne heard the pad of satin shoes.

"Anne?" whispered Tilly.

"Have you come to inspect this piece of bruised goods?" asked Anne, her voice fading.

Tilly snorted. "I am reassured by your silliness. What can I do for you, friend?"

"Come back tomorrow, at which time I hope to be more myself. We shall have a nice visit."

"So I shall do, but I mean to sit with you a while." Tilly set a small bowl on the bedside table and squeezed vinegar water from a soft cloth. She patted Anne's forehead. "Would you take a little broth?"

"No, I cannot eat." Anne struggled to focus on her friend's face as the room began to tilt and whirl. "Would you do me a favor? Tell Dr. Bailey I am still a maiden. He frets about such things." With those words, she fell asleep.

Chapter 70

"May I join you?"

"Of course." Anne could not tame her smile. "Do you care for coffee or tea?" She longed to ask Worthy about his London trip. Judging by his happy demeanor it had pleased him well.

"Don't trouble yourself." Since returning to Rosings, he had been solicitous in seeking her comfort, sometimes fetching her shawl or adding a biscuit to her plate. Coffee cup in hand, he sat down on the sofa opposite, a big grin on his face. "Amelia still lies abed?" he asked.

"She seldom rises before noon."

"How well I know it. Her looks have improved. We are both indebted to you. I cannot imagine her recovering so quickly anywhere else."

"We are quiet here, true enough."

"Excepting last week. I was distressed to learn of the attack. Are you beginning to recover yourself?"

Anne could not speak of the horror with any degree of tranquility. At odd moments the memory of Tench's leery grin, his rough tumbling and animal grunts, his hot breath on her face, trampled her equanimity. Every fusty odor recalled the taste of Beath's foul rag. Even acknowledging her good fortune at being rescued did not prevent her sometimes feeling sullen and lethargic. "My friends and neighbors are a comfort—so kind they have been, writing letters and sending sweetmeats and jars of jelly to the house—and Dr. Bailey assured me of a swift recovery. He was perhaps a little heavy-handed with the laudanum the first day or two, but I never doubted his concern. It is Arnot I worry about, for he holds himself responsible for the mishap, not only because he hired Beath but because he failed to watch Tench 'like a hawk,' as he put it to me."

"He will torture himself for a while, but will eventually develop some perspective when he sees you more like yourself. And what could he have done? He cannot be everywhere on the estate at once. I understand Beath disappeared into the woods and has not been found. Tench, however, has been taken to Maidstone for the next Assize Court. Your family must be pained by his treachery, given his father's reputation in the district. I would call him out, but you would probably object, much as you did when I threatened to duel Mr. Egerton."

"True." An air of quiet gratitude settled over her to think he would rush to her defense. "I had not expected such violence from Tench," she confessed. "He always played the dandy, but I never thought him dangerous."

"I hope you will not worry. Even should he escape being transported, he won't set foot in the district again, the general feelings in the neighborhood running decidedly against him." Mr. Worthington eyed her closely before setting down his coffee cup. "If you are feeling up to it, I would seek your opinion on a decision I must make."

She studied his eager expression. He looked quite boyish with his tousled hair and tanned face, although his dress was that of a gentleman: ginger-colored breeches, a blue waistcoat, and a starched neckcloth, carelessly tied. She liked that he was not overly refined in his appearance, his dress and accoutrements being not all that important to him. "Is it not true that too much consulting confounds the simplest decision?" she asked. A light touch was needed to depress her fear of hearing bad news.

"Not in this case." He smiled. "I have been offered an opportunity to serve the Company. I was invited to London for the purpose of meeting with Mr. Cuthbert, who has been empowered to hire another naturalist to help catalogue the flora of India—"

"India!" exclaimed Anne.

"If I take up the East India Company's offer, I shall be sent to Sibpur near Calcutta for the purpose of collecting and cataloging native plants for the Company's Botanic Garden. It is the opportunity of a lifetime, although the work will have its challenges. The present Superintendent, Dr. Roxburgh, has been unwell and removed in August to St. Helena to recover his health. Since the work must continue, two naturalists, myself included, have been hired to further his work."

"You would leave Amelia?"

"It would be difficult, I allow, but she has always supported my passion. Indeed, she encourages me to accept."

"You told her of the offer?"

"Oh, yes. She knows how to prise news out of me. But what do you think?"

Knowing she had no claim on him, she said, "Of course, you must follow your heart."

"Then it is settled. I am for India." He had the look of a contented cat with a belly full of spilt cream.

Anne's heart sank.

—⁕—

"Worthy appreciated your warm support of his plan," Amelia told Anne.

"He was so excited by the prospect, it would have been impossible to deny his enthusiasm." Anne did not look at Amelia for fear of revealing her true feelings.

"I know you worry about me, but there is no need to do so. Worthy has seen to my comfort. I shall not impose on you much longer."

Anne looked up from her sewing at these words. A clammy fear gripped her bowels to think Amelia and Worthy might be planning to leave England together. "I wish—I hope you feel welcome to remain here as long as you like," she stammered.

Amelia reached over and squeezed Anne's hand. "You are a dear friend. I knew from our first meeting that you would do me good.

But I am recovered sufficiently to travel. I have written Egerton, informing him that I intend to stay with my aunt for a few months. Worthy made the arrangements while he was in London. Egerton will not be pleased, but he can hardly accost Lady De Ponte."

"Your father will object, surely."

"My father has not the nerve to challenge his older sister. The point is that I shall regret leaving you." Seeing the look on Anne's face, she said, "In truth, I would rather travel with Worthy to India than live with Lady De Ponte, but we don't always find satisfaction in our choices, do we?"

Anne smiled weakly. "No, it seems not."

"If we were allowed our heart's desire in this life, I would now be married—happily, I think—to Mr. Madison, the former vicar of Little Newbold."

"Mr. Madison? I had thought—"

"Did you think I was in love with Worthy or he with me? The answer is No, on both counts. I fell in love with a lowly vicar—a gentle and humble soul, a scholar of quiet habits, a man devoted to his parishioners. When my father perceived the affection between us, he forced Mr. Madison out of the living. After our plan to elope was crushed, Mr. Madison left the district and I married Egerton." She saw Anne's surprise at her words. "Worthy and I are closer than some siblings, but we share a family's affection. It would please me greatly to see him marry."

"I—I cannot see him married. Can you?"

"Oh yes. He wants to marry but is cautious. And like any true naturalist, his vision is obscured because his eye is on the skink sunning on the rock or the owl hunting on the wing. One day he will shift his sight and behold a lady worthy of love."

Chapter 71

Anne nearly made herself ill as Worthy's departure approached. She could hardly bear the thought of his not being at Rosings. She would miss his laugh, his grin, the lanky curl falling over his forehead, the gleam in his eye. She tried not to picture his leave-taking.

On the afternoon before his departure, he invited her to walk in the Park. The day was chilly, with low clouds and the threat of rain. Out in the freshening air, they skirted the gardens before veering onto the track that led to the Folly. He was not insensible to her discomfort. He knew her heart was bruised and her mind disquieted; her fondness for the Folly's solitude had been dirtied and diminished by Tench's monstrous deed. He sought to restore its sweetness to her. Drawing her arm through his, he began to speak, his voice low and caressing. Her ears, her heart, her very being resonated at his words. Reaching the Folly in due time, they stood for a moment admiring the tumbling roses, their words spent. He lifted her chin, leaned down, and kissed her. The kiss, their first, was sweet but tentative. Anne's eyes roved his face, searching for clues that he thought her fragile or delicate. She would not have it so! Pulling him to her, she kissed him the way she wanted to be kissed. His passion met her own. At last he pulled away, laughing. "My little volcano!" By the time a slashing rain forced them to run back to the house, their fate was fixed.

The next morning Anne and Amelia stood in a late morning mizzle, their arms linked as they watched Worthy and Hobbs direct the loading of trunks and parcels. Neither could speak. All that needed to be said, had been said. When Worthy approached to assist his cousin into the carriage, Amelia's eyes brimmed with tears.

"I thank you again, dear sister. Your kindness sustains me. I shall write as soon as I am settled."

"Nothing would please me more than to hear that you are happily situated."

Amelia snuffled before taking Worthy's arm and ascending into the carriage.

Worthy turned, a look of pain crossing his face as he took Anne's hands. "Have you changed your mind?" he asked, his eyes beseeching hers, afraid of what he might read there.

Anne shook her head, a swift smile fading in the face of their sad goodbye.

He kissed her fingers and pulled her close. A shiver shot through her when he laid his chin against her forehead.

"I left a gift for you," he whispered. "It is hidden behind the flower brick in your parlor. I hope you will think well of me."

With those words he climbed into the coach and signaled Hobbs to close the door. Anne watched the carriage disappear down the drive, every turn of the wheels a wrenching loss. When tears threatened to spill she entered the house before Hobbs spied her woebegone look. Her impulse to search for Worthy's gift was thwarted first by Arnot, who inquired after Mr. Newland's assessment of the brewery operation, and then by Lady Catherine's call to luncheon.

"I am pleased our guests have departed," said her ladyship, looking more cheerful than usual. "They were becoming a nuisance, especially Mr. Worthington, whose attentions to you were improper, and so I told him."

"He was as solicitous of your comfort as mine, Mama," said Anne. "I recall your commenting on his polite condescension one evening, to which he informed you of his being accustomed to waiting on his sisters and aunts."

Lady Catherine's mouth pulled into a sneering line. "He is puffed up with his talk of coots and wood pigeons, but nothing shall come of his endeavors. What use does the world have for a naturalist?"

"I believe Mr. Worthington told you of his being hired to help record the flora of India on behalf of the Honorable East India Company."

"So he said, but he shall sail without you, for I do not give permission for you to marry. We need think of him no more, for we shall have a new amusement: Lady Milcombe wrote to invite us to visit. She is expecting a large party of friends, including Lord Dinmore, who is said to be dangling for an heiress. We shall depart on the sixth."

Anne took no notice of her ladyship's directive on marriage but excused herself and hurried down the hall to her parlor. She crossed to her writing table and retrieved a flat package the size of a small book. Hiding the treasure in the folds of her shawl, she could not help smiling as she ran lightly up the stairs and gained the privacy of her bedchamber.

Chapter 72

Hobbs thrust his head into Anne's private parlor. "Another letter has arrived, Miss."

"Has it, indeed? It seems no day passes without some missive from parts unknown." Hobbs grinned and closed the door.

Anne glowed to see the now familiar handwriting. Worthy wrote every day. Posted from Leicestershire, Warwickshire, Cambridgeshire, and now Suffolk—all counties where he had brothers or sisters or aunts and uncles—his letters abounded with affection, news of his family, suggestions for organizing themselves, and questions about her wishes. A true correspondence had been established, beginning with his gift—a small journal depicting life at Rosings. Her breath had caught in her throat when she saw his simple drawings of wild dog roses tumbling over the Folly's crumbled wall and purple tufted vetch blooming near the stables. In one, a baby rabbit hid in the shadow of a cabbage in Cook's garden, looking ready to bolt. Here were sketches of Kitson and his son brushing a mare, old Gibbons hoeing among the rose bushes, and Lady Catherine frowning over her household ledger in the morning room. Several were of Anne herself, caught reading or sewing or drawing. Tears spilled when she read his words: *Do not think me so mean-spirited as to seek your affection merely to gain an advantage over you. I appreciate your business acumen, but it is your love I value. It is your heart I hope to possess.*

How strange to realize she had not resisted his proposal to travel to India, even though she could not imagine the voyage or picture disembarking in Calcutta or form an image of their living quarters or activities. She could not imagine being absent from Rosings for two years. Could she bear not tasting the estate's pears or smelling the sweet summer roses? Would she not miss Tilly and Dr. Bailey and Lady Metcalfe? Was the voyage not dangerous? Was the climate not injurious? All objections fell to a simple truth: she would follow Worthy anywhere.

—⁂—

"Your eyes betray you, friend. What devilment have you done?" asked Tilly.

"It is not what I have done, but what I am about to do," replied Anne. She had been dreading this interview, knowing Tilly would resist her plan. "I leave soon for London where I shall meet Mr. Worthington. We shall be married next week and sail for India on the Friday se'night following. Mr. Purkess has kindly agreed to officiate."

"I—I—" stammered Tilly. "I cannot speak."

Anne laughed. "So it seems."

"You cannot be serious. You would leave Rosings? You would abandon Lady Catherine? You would sail to the ends of the earth with a man you hardly know? I believe Tench's assault has befuddled you."

Even though Tilly's words bruised like hail stones and rattled her composure, Anne knew this was no hasty decision. She had held fast to Pope's advice to know herself. Her heart had spoken. The one danger to her enterprise was leaving Rosings. It was her home and anchor, her comfort and treasure. Every image of that final carriage ride down the long drive toward the Bromley road pierced her soul. She could well imagine sobbing the entire journey to London, the tears starting before she left the house. But so be it.

"I have had weeks to think on the matter," she said in a quavering voice.

"Have you told Lady Catherine?"

"Yes. She is afraid, more for herself than for me," said Anne, recovering her confidence. "One thing is clear—I can no longer live to please my mother. I can no longer bear to live alone with her. My actions are selfish, but, in the case of marriage, I aim to please myself. If it brings you joy, then know that I have received two very sharp letters from Lord and Lady Matlock, a cryptic note from Darcy, and fretful pleadings from Colonel Fitzwilliam, all chastising me for not involving them in my decision. They admonish me to rethink the matter and implore me to consider my reputation and the responsibility I place on the Rosings staff. The servants I trust without reservation. They shall carry on. I also trust Mr. Worthington. I trust him as I trust you and Mr. Sparke."

"But you said a few weeks ago how leery you were of marriage, and then to agree to marry so suddenly, when you have known the man for only a short while, when you have not met his family—are these not negative considerations?"

"None of that matters, Tilly. I know this man."

"How can it be so? By your own admission you spent little time together at Dodford Meare and believed him to be besotted with his cousin during most of his residence at Rosings."

"What you say is true, but when I am with him, I feel his goodness and kindness. He is dear to me."

"How can you feel so confident in your decision? It is all so sudden, so unexpected."

Anne studied the teacup resting on her lap while her thoughts traveled back to her last walk with Worthy in the Park. The raindrops wetting his face, the lock of hair falling over his forehead, and his gentle smile had all bewitched her. Lifting her eyes to Tilly's, she said: "When did you know in your heart that you would marry Mr. Sparke, and the world be damned?"

Confusion played across Tilly's features. "Our situations are not the same. I knew his family. My father counted Mr. Sparke's parents among his closest friends. We had our families' approval before we married. By your own admission, your family is unsettled by your decision. You cannot claim their support—and you leave England. You leave Rosings! Surely you can admit your relations have cause for worry."

A shy smile graced Anne's face. "You cannot imagine how difficult this is. How many times have I sat on this sofa, holding this, my favorite teacup, while talking to you, my dearest friend, my sister? I can hardly bear to wrench myself from you or from Rosings, but I cannot continue on my present course. Since my father died, I have lived these many years in that house with my mother—a woman whose every action is driven by resentment and malice. Something you said months ago is fresh in my mind: *It will be all the same a hundred years hence.* You were right. My mother and I shall never find ease with one another. She cannot approve my actions, whether I live at Rosings or travel in India, whether I marry or remain a spinster. I shall always chafe under her critical eye. And what does it matter? In fifty years, my name may be known only to some distant offspring who kneels at my headstone and wonders what sort of person I was. In one hundred years it will be as though I never lived. Why should I not marry the man I love?"

Tears welled in Tilly's eyes. "Oh, Anne."

Chapter 73

"I do not need your permission to marry, Mama."

Lady Catherine fumed. "I have made my wishes known. You cannot marry him. Why, he has no rank or title. He is a plain commoner, the son of a bootmaker!"

"Darcy is also a commoner, but his low status did not deter you from expecting us to marry. You must know I care nothing for rank. It is the man himself, his character, that matters. Mr. Worthington is a good man, and he cares for me. As for his being the son of a bootmaker, he was joking when he described his brother's business."

"Joking? In what manner?"

"He is the youngest son in a large family, that I must allow, but to describe his brother as a mere bootmaker can be likened to saying the Prince Regent lives in a fine house. Mr. Worthington's family supplies the leather used to manufacture most of England's boots. His family's estate, which also supplies London with mutton, is easily twenty times the size of Rosings Park and all its holdings. Mr. Worthington himself expects to inherit a modest estate on the death of his godmother."

"Oh, he will inherit a country manor? I am pleased to learn he will have some small property to his credit."

"Mama, Mr. Worthington will inherit Warnford Manor, a nice piece of land in Warwickshire. It has been in his godmother's family since the Dissolution." Her mother's annoying smirk led her to keep silent about Mr. Worthington's main income: nearly four thousand pounds in annual rents from London commercial properties, an inheritance bequeathed by a beloved uncle. It would be well to remain silent on the topic, for she knew Worthy was a reserved, unassuming man who did not care to have his personal life laid bare to all and sundry.

"You paint a pretty picture," said her ladyship, "but we are ruined none the less. The de Bourgh name shall be tarnished forever if you marry this commoner. We shall never hold our heads high in society if you pursue this folly."

"You mean, you shall feel you cannot do so. It is of no consequence to me."

"Then think what Lady Milcombe will say of your headstrong behavior. I must write to her and explain why I must decline her attractive invitation." Seeing Anne's smirk, she continued, "Unfeeling girl! Think how it will look to our friends and all your relations. You marry a nobody, a man you have known only a few weeks, and you cannot be bothered to send the *Gazette* a notice of your engagement, as is proper and expected. Shameful behavior! I know not how I shall bear the scandal."

"I am confident you will rise to the challenge, and a notice of our marriage will be submitted before we leave England."

Lady Catherine wore a proud pout. "You must know your father would be ashamed of you, were he still living. He would expect you to honor your duty to this family."

Anne was not wounded by the insult, knowing she spoke true when she said, "My father would want me to be happy, above all things."

Her ladyship tried a new tack. "Travel to a foreign country is dangerous. You might be tossed into the sea during the passage or succumb to a fever among diseased natives."

Anne hid a wry smile. "Everything you say is true, but I am not deterred. Since you are concerned about your future, let me remind you that Papa deeded the dower house and its land to you for the remainder of your life. Of course, if you die while I am out of the country, the dower property will revert to Rosings. Should I die overseas, with no son to inherit, Rosings will pass in tail male to Papa's nephew, Edward de Bourgh—a man I never met in my life, but so it is."

Lady Catherine's mouth formed a perfect O. "In tail male?"

"It was to be expected, Mama. Mr. Newland reassured me of the papers all being quite proper when last I was in London." To Lady Catherine's stricken look, she added, "I should think this intelligence would give you ease. So long as I live whilst in India, you may continue to live here and enjoy the fruits of the estate without worry, but when Worthy and I return to England, you will move to the dower house. Let us be hopeful! I may yet produce a son and heir."

Anne saw desperation in her mother's eyes. Knowing the past year had been difficult, she said, "There is one other consideration. I hope you will make an effort to regain Darcy's affection. He has always been dear to you. It is time, Mama, to accept his marriage to Elizabeth. You only wound yourself by refusing to accept the fact." She ignored Lady Catherine's mulish stare. "I invite you to join Mr. Worthington and me in London. Several of his siblings shall travel there for the purpose of meeting me and, I hope, you. We shall host a party at Chidham House and then be married by special license. Our vessel sails on the sixteenth."

"Already the man takes advantage of you. He would have you pay for every trifling, I am sure."

"He does no such thing, and it is none of your concern in any event."

Lady Catherine raised her chin. "Then hear this: I take no part in your foolish scheme."

"As you wish. Pray excuse me now. I must meet Arnot, and there is much to organize before I join Mr. Worthington in Town."

Chapter 74

The press of people on the Gravesend dock was nearly suffocating. Anne held her reticule tightly while Worthy marshaled their luggage. Emily stood wide-eyed at Anne's side, her hand gripping a leather valise.

"The ship is frightfully tall," said Emily tremulously, her head cocked to view the tip of the main mast. Her eyes were wild, but whether with excitement or dread was hard to tell.

Anne merely nodded, the din filling her ears. Her rheumatism had returned with the damp autumn weather. The aches had kept her awake during the previous night's storm, and now a sharp wind whipped her coat about her legs and aggravated her joints. It was not the most propitious beginning to their adventure: *mais il en va.* But so it goes.

"This way, Mrs. Worthington," called Worthy, giving Anne a tender look. Their progress up the gangway was treacherous in the gale, but they reached the safety of the foredeck, which swarmed with passengers shouting directions to their servants and men of business. Worthy had already been on board the East Indiaman, when it lay anchored in the Thames off the old Brunswick Dock; he had confirmed the delivery of furniture and bedding suitable for a small space.

Have I lost my mind? Anne wondered, her heart leaping in her chest. This is to be my home for three months. The vessel that soared overhead from the safety of the quay looked short and squat and unsteady from the vantage of the deck.

Mr. Worthington escorted them down a steep flight of stairs to the first class compartment. On first glimpsing the tiny cabin, Anne blurted, "Why, I have seen closets bigger than this." At Worthy's surprise she was quick to add: "Pray excuse me. I was startled, for I had no idea what to expect."

Worthy grinned, saying with mock seriousness, "It is a rude discovery, to be sure, but we shall enjoy each other's company, even here." His twitching eyebrows made her laugh.

"Of course. You are perfectly right. Where will Emily sleep?"

"On the deck below. Wait here, love," said Worthy. "I shall return for you."

When their luggage had been stowed, they climbed the steep stairs to the deck to watch the vessel being readied for departure. There were whistles, a cacophony of cries, and a bewildering mass of men thronging the deck like restless ants. Eventually the ropes were cast off and the vessel creaked and moaned. Anne stood next to Worthy at the rail, the wind whipping her bonnet strings. His excitement was infectious. She squeezed his hand as the vessel lumbered past the tidal marshes near Tilbury East, which river reaches she had never seen.

Her goodbyes had been tendered with tears. She and Tilly laughed and cried for the better part of an afternoon and Mr. Sparke's eyes grew misty. While Patrick slept, little Marianne found the fuss exciting and saw no cause for tears. Kisses and well wishes were bestowed by the Collinses and many neighbors and villagers. Dr. Bailey's cheek was wet with tears. Knowing what he was thinking, she said, "I shall write you often and whenever I hear of any poisons that might interest you." Shaw was visibly distressed, for she was losing a sister and a mistress. Mrs. Beath, still upset over her son's devilment, prepared a special ointment for her rheumatic pains.

The western Kent tenants had all been visited and reassured of Arnot's steady guidance while she was abroad. The steward himself, his face coloring with emotion, had told her of his betrothal to Mrs. Faber, which news made her happy for them both. "I have other news to make you smile. I received a letter from Mr. Helden," he said. "Roger Tench started his job as an apprentice maltster and seems right happy. Who would have thought it possible? Well, enough chatter. I have been charged to tell you this: we all bless Mr. Worthington for bringing a shine to your face. You shall be happy, and while you are adventuring, don't worry about Rosings. We shall take good care of her and do all that lies within our power to make her ladyship comfortable, how ever so much she tests our nerves." On seeing his laughing eyes, Anne blinked quickly, lest she begin to cry.

Only Lady Catherine, true to form, remained stoic and defiant, unmoved by tears.

Anne turned her back against the gale and gazed across the prow, where purple-tinged clouds hugged the horizon. Worthy pulled her arm through his. She touched the brooch at her throat—a gift presented on their wedding night: a faithful rendering of his eye, painted by his own hand and mounted in silver, a token of his affection and promise. Her eyes brimmed with tears as she leaned into him and heard his laugh snatched on the wind.

We go to greet the world. May God go with us.

—ɯ—

Group discussion questions can be
found on pp. 313-314

Acknowledgements

This book could not have been written without the help and support of numerous people. First, for invaluable assistance with the thorny aspects of inheritance laws during Jane Austen's time, I would like to thank Eileen Spring, author of *Law, Land & Family: Aristocratic Inheritance in England, 1300 to 1800*. She answered numerous questions about my scheme for Anne de Bourgh's inheritance and wondered, as I did, why Anne's mother, Lady Catherine, still resided at Rosings after the death of her husband. For help sorting the changing terminology related to a woman's confinement during pregnancy, I would like to thank Elena Greene, whose website (www.elenagreene.com/childbirth.html) hosts a succinct, referenced discussion of pregnancy and childbirth practices during the 18th century and the Late Georgian and Regency periods, among other eras.

I have been privileged to work with the Knoxville Writers' Group, especially the members of its newest critique croup. Thanks to you all for fellowship and feedback.

Finally, I want to thank my dear friends—you know who you are—for never doubting that I would finish this book. A special thank you goes to my husband, Peter, for supporting my ideas and ventures, buying the best chocolates, and making me laugh.

Quotations

Many of the quotations cited in this work were obtained from books or periodicals downloaded from Google Books (books.google.com). In these cases the Google book PDF page number is included in parentheses below to help you locate the quoted material.

Volume I

Page

2   "the unexpected spark, the brightest blaze of joy": Adapted from Johnson, The *Idler*, No. 58, May 26, 1759, p. 323.

12 "I know that my redeemer liveth": Anon., *The Book of Common Prayer: The Order for the Burial of the Dead* (PDF p. 325).

19 "A midwife ought to be": Smellie, p. 431 (PDF p. 454).

25 "Your father's estate is entailed . . . a slave to your education": Austen, p. 144 (PDF p. 159).

26 "Has your governess . . . your education" and "those who chose . . . given me a treasure": Austen, pp. 144-145 (PDF pp. 159-160).

32 "They also serve": Milton (online).

41 "Are you prepared to take a pain": Denman, p. 152 (PDF p. 191).

45 "An idle brain is the devil's workhouse": Bohn, p. 311 (PDF p. 338).

49 "It is a maxim commonly received": Johnson, The *Rambler*, No. 29, June 26, 1750, p. 70.

50 "An idle and thoughtless": Johnson, The *Rambler*, No. 29, June 26, 1750, p. 70.

209 "Unto the woman he said": Anon., *King James Bible*, Genesis, verse 3:16, p. 2 (PDF p. 23).

214 "God moves in a mysterious way": Cowper (online).

220 "The sleeping Thames": Farmer, p. 144 (PDF p. 173).

228 "Too much courtesy": Bohn, p. 545 (PDF p. 572).

250 "The truest wealth": Bohn, p. 517 (PDF p. 544).

255 "Appearances often deceive": Adapted from Penn, p. 108 (PDF p. 111), No. 258 and 259.

259 "With the death of each day's life": Adapted from Shakespeare, *Macbeth*, Act II, Scene 2.

268 "marriage is an indissoluble contract": Adapted from Perkin, p. 22.

273 "at five o'clock in the afternoon": J. H. S., p. 161 (PDF p. 182).

285 "Cold weather and knaves": Bohn, p. 338 (PDF p. 365).

290 "Too much consulting": Bohn, p. 545 (PDF p. 572).

299 "It will be all the same": Bohn, p. 435 (PDF p. 462).

Bibliography

Anon. *The Book of Common Prayer, and Administration of the Sacraments, and Other Rites and Ceremonies of the Church, According to the Use of The Church of England: Together with the Psalter or Psalms of David.* Cambridge: John Baskerville, 1761.

Anon. *The King James Version of the Holy Bible* [PDF version], 2001/2004. Available at DaVince. Retrieved January 24, 2016, from http://www.davince.com/download/kjvbible.pdf

Austen, Jane. *Pride and Prejudice.* London: RD Bentley, 1853.

Bohn, Henry G. *A Hand-Book of Proverbs.* London: H. G. Bohn, 1855.

Burns, Robert. "To a Mouse." Available at Project Gutenberg. Retrieved January 24, 2016, from www.gutenberg.org/files/1279/1279-h/1279-h.htm#link2H_4_0085

Coleridge, Samuel Taylor. "The Rime of the Ancient Mariner." Available at Project Gutenberg. Retrieved January 24, 2016, from http://www.gutenberg.org/ebooks/151

Cowper, William. "Olney Hymns: Light Shining out of Darkness." Available at Christian Classics Ethereal Library. Retrieved January 24, 2016, from www.ccel.org/ccel/newton/olneyhymns.Book3.conflict.h3_15.html

Denman, Thomas. *An Introduction to the Practice of Midwifery.* Brattleborough: William Fessenden, 1807.

Farmer, John S. *Merry Songs and Ballads Prior to the Year A.D. 1800*, Vol. III. [Privately Printed for Subscribers Only], 1897.

Goldsmith, Oliver. Adapted from *The Vicar of Wakefield* [Kindle edition].

J. H. S. "Account of the late Earthquake at the Caraccas." In: Tilloch, Alexander. *The Philosophical Magazine*, Vol. 41 (Jan-Jun). London: Richard Taylor and Co., 1813.

Johnson, Samuel. *Selected Essays from the* Rambler, Adventurer, *and* Idler. W. J. Bate, ed. New Haven and London: Yale University Press, 1968.

———. "All travel has its advantages . . ." Available at BrainyQuote. Retrieved January 24, 2016, from http://www.brainyquote.com/quotes/quotes/s/samuel-john133863.html

Milton, John. Sonnet titled "On His Blindness," available at Sonnet Central: John Milton (1608-1674). Retrieved January 24, 2016, from http://www.sonnets.org/milton.htm

Penn, William. *Some Fruits of Solitude*. New York/Boston: H. M. Caldwell Co., 1682/c. 1903.

Perkin, Joan. *Women and Marriage in Nineteenth-Century England.* Chicago: Lyceum Books, 1989.

Pope, Alexander. "An Essay on Criticism." In: Allison, Alexander W., et al., eds. *The Norton Anthology of Poetry Revised*. New York: W. W. Norton & Company, Inc., 1970/1975.

Prothero, Rowland E. *English Farming: Past and Present*. London: Longmans, Green and Co., 1917.

Richardson, Samuel. *Pamela*. London: Penquin Classics, 1740/1985.

Shakespeare, William. Available at The Complete Works of William Shakespeare [online]:

———. Adapted from *Cymbeline*. Retrieved January 24, 2016, from http://shakespeare.mit.edu/cymbeline/cymbeline.4.2.html

———. *A Midsummer Night's Dream*. Retrieved January 24, 2016, from http://shakespeare.mit.edu/midsummer/midsummer.3.1.html

———. Adapted from *Macbeth*. Retrieved January 24, 2016, from http://shakespeare.mit.edu/macbeth/macbeth.2.2.html

———. *Hamlet*. Retrieved January 24, 2016, from http://shakespeare.mit.edu/hamlet/hamlet.3.1.html

Smellie, William. *Smellie's Treatise on the Theory and Practice of Midwifery*. McClintock, A.H., ed. London: The New Sydenham Society, Vol. 68, 1876 (originally published in 1788).

Steele, Richard. The Spectator, in *The British Essayists*, Vol. XIII. New York: Sargeant and Ward, 1810.

The Gentleman's Magazine. "Hallucination of Gilb. Wakefield," letter submitted by A Westminster Scholar, November, 1813.

Rosings Park: Discussion Questions

1. In Jane Austen's day—and, indeed, for centuries before that—it was common for a pregnant woman to invite her mother, sisters, and female friends and neighbors to sit with her during the infant's delivery and provide comfort and support. This activity was called "gossiping." The historical record is not clear on whether a woman must be married to sit as a gossip—there is an absence of evidence either way. Anne is unmarried but chooses to sit with her dearest friend, Tilly, even though doing so might invite censure. Would an unmarried Jane Austen sit with her pregnant sister Cassandra (assuming, of course, that Cassandra had married)? Do you believe an unmarried Elizabeth Bennet would sit with her expecting sister, Jane? Would you be willing to do the same for a friend in Tilly's situation? (For background, read the author's blog on this topic: "Anne de Bourgh Sits as a Gossip: Is Society Shocked?" posted June 11, 2015 — available at http://bit.ly/1L3AHpO)

2. Two popular medical therapies during the Regency era were leeching and bloodletting. Both are in use today, although bloodletting is generally used only in certain narrowly-defined circumstances. Does this surprise you? (Read the author's blog: "There's a Leech for That!" posted July 28, 2014 — available at http://bit.ly/1R8uSuc)

3. Is *Rosings Park* a "coming of age" story?

4. Lady Catherine is irascible, meddling, self-centered, and opinionated. Why is she so discontented? Is there anything Anne can do to improve her mother's disposition?

5. Depending on the source of data related to the Regency era, men usually married between the ages of 25 and 30, while women married between the ages of 20 and 26. Darcy is "eight and twenty" at the end of *Pride and Prejudice* (Chapter 58); Anne is perhaps 25 or 26. Both are pushing against the upper boundary of the typical age for marriage when Austen's novel opens. Darcy, as we know, falls

in love with and marries Elizabeth Bennet, which begs the question: Why have Darcy and Anne not married by the time he meets Lizzie?

6. Does Anne hold one notion of duty when applying expectations to herself while employing a more stringent notion of duty to her servants? Is she typical in this regard?

7. Anne is criticized for visiting unchaperoned her estate's tenant farms with her new steward, Arnot. Would she suffer such criticism if old Tench, her recently deceased steward, were still living? (Tench had worked at Rosings for more than two decades and was widely known in the district.) Did it matter that Anne had reached her majority? (That is, at age 21 she was considered an adult.)

8. Lady Catherine doesn't have much affection for her daughter. What factors might account for this? How do her actions affect Anne?

9. What is the one "unspeakable" thing Anne most desires in life?

10. What qualities does Anne value most in Mr. Worthington?

11. Which is the most important theme in Anne's story and why?

About the Author

For many years Diane H. Morris worked as a teacher, researcher, and technical writer in the field of nutrition. After retiring, she settled down to write about Anne de Bourgh—a *Pride and Prejudice* character who had been pestering her for more than twenty years. She discovered along the way a true interest in the Regency era and blogs regularly about Jane Austen, Mr. Darcy, medicine, and women's lives in that time. She lives with her charming husband—a true Brit who loves eating Branston Pickle and sometimes says "Oy!"—near the Great Smoky Mountains National Park. He studies Japanese and hikes the 900 miles of park trails (he's on his fourth map) while she reads and writes about England and marriage in the 18th and early 19th centuries. They love London and visit the Great Metropolis whenever possible.